HUNGER FOR LOVE

"A man does indeed have his uses, querida," *Rafe whispered against her cheek.*

She lifted her hands and placed them on his chest, intending to push him away. Beneath her fingers was the erratic beat of his heart. The tempo quickened her breath. She stared at the red scarf at his neck, at the firm chin and mouth, and at last on up to his eyes, smouldering with desire.

Then his lips were on hers and a heat coursed through her that had nothing to do with the sun at her back.

She arched, offering herself more easily to him; his body tightened and she knew she pleased him. With deft, sure movements he pulled her down to the blanket.

His touch was agony. A hot, hungry passion curled within her . . .

D1523827

GIVE YOUR HEART
TO ZEBRA'S HEARTFIRE!

COMANCHE CARESS (2268, $3.75)
by Cheryl Black
With her father missing, her train held up by bandits and her money stolen, Ciara Davenport wondered what else could possibly go wrong. Until a powerful savage rescued her from a band of ruffians in the Rocky Mountains and Ciara realized the very worst had come to pass: she had fallen desperately in love with a wild, handsome half-breed she could never hope to tame!

IVORY ROSE (2269, $3.75)
by Kathleen McCall
Standing in for her long-lost twin sister, innocent Sabrina Buchanan was tricked into marrying the virile estate owner Garrison McBride. Furious with her sibling, Sabrina was even angrier with herself — for she could not deny her intense yearning to become a woman at the masterful hands of the handsome stranger!

STARLIT SURRENDER (2270, $3.75)
by Judy Cuevas
From the moment she first set eyes on the handsome swashbuckler Adrien Hunt, lovely Christina Bower was determined to fend off the practiced advances of the rich, hot-blooded womanizer. But even as her sweet lips protested each caress, her womanly curves eagerly welcomed his arousing embrace!

RECKLESS DESIRE (2271, $3.75)
by Thea Devine
Kalida Ryland had always despised her neighbor Deuce Cavender, so she was shocked by his brazen proposal of marriage. The arrogant lady's man would never get his hands on her ranch! And even if Kalida had occasionally wondered how those same rough, powerful hands would feel caressing her skin, she'd die before she let him know it!

Available wherever paperbacks are sold, or order direct from the Publisher. Send cover price plus 50¢ per copy for mailing and handling to Zebra Books, Dept. 2291, 475 Park Avenue South, New York, N.Y. 10016. Residents of New York, New Jersey and Pennsylvania must include sales tax. DO NOT SEND CASH.

DESIRE'S FURY
KELLER GRAVES

ZEBRA BOOKS
KENSINGTON PUBLISHING CORP.

ZEBRA BOOKS

are published by

Kensington Publishing Corp.
475 Park Avenue South
New York, NY 10016

First printing: February, 1988

Printed in the United States of America

To Dinah, Larry,
Laura, and Scott

Chapter One

Gabrielle Deschamps settled back in her chair in San Antonio's crowded Hidden Nugget Saloon and ran one finger through a recalcitrant curl of hair. A feeling of excitement bubbled within her. After four years in an exclusive girls' school in Virginia, she thought, it was great to be back in Texas. At age twenty she had returned to the city of her birth alone — without family or even a guardian to greet her — but she had something else that gave her purpose and strength. She had a dream.

She'd only been in town a few hours, but she had no doubt that she was doing the right thing. Her claim was just and modest. All she wanted was a home.

Outside, a beautiful September afternoon awaited her on her return to the hotel; beside her was Erin Barrett, the saloon's beautiful young owner and her friend from years ago, who was filling her in on events during Gabrielle's absence. Only one thing was unsettling her concentration — the man who had minutes ago sauntered up to the bar.

Her gaze slipped past Erin and focused on him. Tall and lean, he stood half turned in her direction, one booted and spurred foot propped against the brass rail. He looked . . . efficient was the word that came to mind. Nothing about him was excessive, nothing that is save the effect he was having on her.

Her eyes traveled down the tanned column of his neck, to the open vee of his shirt, which gave a tantalizing hint of the muscled strength of his chest, and on down the closely fitted trousers covering his spare hips and long legs. His pants and shirt were the color of his flesh and for an instant she was beset by the thought of what he would look like without them.

Such a thought was too audacious even for Gabrielle. She might have had a rather lonely and unorthodox upbringing, but that shouldn't render her vulnerable to the attractions of some stranger in a saloon, no matter how handsome he was. Besides, the last thing she needed to think about was a man.

She jerked her eyes upward and looked directly into the warmest brown eyes she had ever seen. The impact left her breathless. A shock of dark hair lay across his forehead. His skin was burnished bronze. High cheekbones and a twisted smile gave him an almost feral look as he stared at her across the smoke-filled room.

He winked slowly, and his smile broadened, lightening the dark contours of his face. The warmth of that smile traveled through her, and she was infuriated at her blush. Relief washed over her when the contact with the man was broken by the arrival of a raven-haired woman in a tight-fitting gown who moved between them and draped herself on his arm. Gabrielle brushed aside as childish the wave of irritation she felt. The man obviously was used to the attentions of bar girls and couldn't be taken seriously.

Still, she continued to look in his direction and even leaned sideways trying to see his profile behind the new arrival.

"I'm thinking of taking a lover," Erin said.

The words came through with a shock, and Gabrielle turned widened eyes on her friend. She'd always thought Erin had the perfect marriage — if there was any such thing.

"What are you talking about?" Gabrielle asked.

Erin drummed her fingers on the table. "Anything and everything to get your attention. Thus far I've mentioned strangling the bartender and swimming naked in the San Antonio River, but I've still been no competition for Rafe Jericho."

"Rafe Jericho? Who is he?"

"The man you've been undressing for the past few minutes."

"I have—" The denial died on Gabrielle's lips. She was not one to deny the truth. "Maybe I was, but it doesn't hurt to look, does it?"

Erin laughed sharply. "Still as outspoken as ever, I see. I'm glad that girls' school didn't change you, Gabrielle, although" — her voice took on a thoughtful edge — "I still think you talk brashly to cover up a very sensitive soul. You're as susceptible to an attractive man as the rest of womanhood."

"Of course I am," she said lightly. "The difference is that all I want to do is look."

"With Rafe that could be dangerous. There aren't

9

many women who can resist him. He drops by every few months when he's in town, and every time he's got a flock of birds flapping their wings at him." Erin smiled. "Well, flapping something at least. I'm sure you get the picture."

Gabrielle allowed herself a quick look past Erin. The dark-haired stranger was laughing down at the woman, who had managed to get even closer to him.

"I get the picture all right. He'll be covered in feathers before the night is done," she said dryly. "I wouldn't think a man like that sleeps alone very often. Even if he has a wife waiting for him back home. Along with six children."

"Not Rafe. Running a saloon, you get to be a pretty good judge of character. I'll bet once he picks his woman, she'll be his for life. And he won't be tomcatting around, either."

Gabrielle looked at her friend disbelievingly. "You seem to know a lot about him."

"Don't forget my father was a gambler. Judging a man sometimes meant the difference between eating and going hungry. I can read the signs. Rafe gambles a little, although he never goes for high stakes. He ought to. He usually wins. And when he does lose, there's no blame laid on the house or his luck. I like the way he carries himself."

"He sounds like a veritable saint," said Gabrielle.

Erin laughed. "Now that's one thing he most definitely is not, although he *is* a special man. There's usually one woman who manages to get his attention. Seldom, I might add, the same one. It's my guess he hasn't found what he's looking for yet."

Gabrielle took one last look at him. Erin seemed to

think he was looking for the right woman; the thought was curiously intriguing. She shook it off.

"I'm surprised he doesn't carry the girls off two at a time," she said bluntly, "one on each shoulder. He looks as though he could manage such a feat."

"He would certainly know what to do with them when he got to his room," Erin said, then added quickly, "Sorry. We old married women talk a little too bluntly sometimes."

Again Gabrielle felt a blush coming on. Not at all the thing for a determined young miss to do, she decided, dismissing Rafe Jericho with a shrug. A lively discussion with Erin about men and life in general was far more appropriate than concentrating on one particular man.

She'd met Erin at San Antonio's Ursuline Academy, a Catholic school and convent where Gabrielle had been placed after her mother's death. Erin had come there after her marriage to learn how to read, and the two had become immediate and fast friends. Through the years of Gabrielle's eastern schooling they had corresponded. Even with the extended absence, their friendship had strengthened.

"You're scarcely five years older than I am, Erin," Gabrielle said. "I'm not supposed to know about the things that go on between a man and a woman? Remember the way I was raised."

Erin settled unnerving eyes on her. "Does it bother you?"

"Not in the least."

Erin reached out and touched her hand. "I said you were the same Gabrielle who left here, but that isn't strictly true. You've changed. I noticed it as soon as you walked in today. There's something—I don't know—a kind of controlled excitement about you, as though you knew exactly where your life was heading and couldn't be happier about it. Until I met Cole, I didn't have the vaguest idea what I was about. He showed me soon enough."

"I don't need a husband to give me purpose, Erin, although I'm not saying I'll never marry. What I want out of a marriage is security. Not a reason for being. Cole gives you both. And," she said, glancing around the saloon, "lets you live your own life at the same time."

"You mean this place?" Erin's hand waved around at the Hidden Nugget. She'd bought it years ago and turned it into San Antonio's most respectable and popular gambling saloon. "Cole lets me run it while he's taking care of his business interests. Which I may say, if you'll allow a wife to brag, are increasing daily."

"So the Nugget is your pastime. Another woman might choose something else. A man, for instance."

Erin slapped her hand against the table. "Are you really saying a married woman should take a lover? The nuns never taught you that."

"Not a married woman. Vows should not be given lightly." Gabrielle, filled with her own sense of independence and purpose, warmed to the topic. "I'm talking about those who are on their own."

"Your mother was on her own, wasn't she? Is that what you're remembering?"

"Colette is never far from my thoughts. It was hard for me when my father died. She was carrying me and didn't have two pennies to rub together. She did what she had to do."

"It's funny the way you often refer to your parents as Colette and Roberto."

Gabrielle shrugged. "Colette was almost my sole companion. We were more like friends than mother and daughter. And since I never knew my father, I referred to him the way she did."

"You still have some unusual ideas about men and women. At least you say you do."

"It's 1885, Erin, not the Dark Ages. A woman shouldn't be embarrassed to admit that men have their uses," she said, her voice rising with the justness of her words.

"You keep talking loud that way and you'll have plenty of offers, Gabrielle. Half the men in here are probably ready to head this way right now."

A faint blush tinged Gabrielle's cheeks. A bad habit, she decided, and one she would have to work on. "Little good it will do them," she said bravely, but her voice was lowered to little more than a whisper. "I'm talking about women in general. Not me."

"I knew your talk was just a cover," Erin said. "One would think you had known hundreds of men and slept with at least dozens. What a fraud you are!"

"What I am, Erin, is a woman ready to begin her life. Everything up to now has been a preparation. The early years with Mama. The convent. Virginia. I know what I want. And I know what I need. A secure home. And roots. Nothing is more important, and one doesn't need one man for that."

"Tell me something," Erin said in a conspiratorial whisper. "Have you ever been kissed?"

Gabrielle thought of the fuzzy-faced young men who had called at Miss Martha Emmett's School for

Young Ladies. They'd come hoping for a kiss beneath the thick-leafed oak trees. Once or twice she had complied, although never with much enthusiasm.

"Of course I have."

"And did you enjoy it?"

"Well . . . I didn't *not* enjoy it."

"Then," said Erin, "I'd say you haven't been kissed."

Gabrielle looked past Erin and found herself gazing once more into the warm brown eyes of Rafe Jericho. This time he was the one to let his eyes drift appreciatively downward to her lips and throat and on down to her blue silk gown.

Turning her attention abruptly back to Erin, Gabrielle threw her hands up in surrender. "Enough! I didn't come back to Texas to get a man, and you know it. If I enjoy the scenery around here, it doesn't mean I've forgotten what I'm really after—my rightful portion of that land down on the border that once belonged to my father's family. Settling there was my mother's dream and now it's mine. Only dreams won't satisfy me."

"Were you able to get in touch with Oscar Cantu, that lawyer I wrote you about?"

"I stopped by his office on the way to the Nugget but he was in court. I'm supposed to meet with him sometime tomorrow. Several months ago I wrote him the bare facts about the land, and his clerk assured me Cantu had been working to find out more. As to exactly what, he couldn't say."

"I sure hope you'll get what you want, Gabrielle."

"I must." Gabrielle's strong words came from her heart. She had to gain some of the ranch that had been stolen from the Cordero family. Roberto Cor-

14

dero had convinced his young bride the land should be theirs.

Unfortunately, after his sudden death at the hands of a Union soldier, her mother had not possessed the physical strength or money to fight for it. That fight she had entrusted to her daughter. In the meantime, Colette had earned her keep in the only way she saw open to her, at the same time lavishing upon Gabrielle stories of what should have been hers.

In doing so, Colette had shown her love for her daughter, little realizing that another need of Gabrielle's remained unfulfilled. She had never felt she belonged anywhere. The Cordero land would give her a link with the past, would provide her with roots.

The few financial investments Colette was able to make had, after her death, grown beyond anything she might have imagined, and one of her dreams had already come true—her daughter's schooling in the East.

Backed by the remainder of that money and papers to prove her identity, Gabrielle was in Texas ready to negotiate for the home of her dreams. Tomorrow she would surely hear from the lawyer Cantu that legally at least some of the land should be hers.

If only the owner, an old fellow by the name of Benito Hidalgo, would be willing to bow graciously to the justice of her cause.

"I've lost you again," Erin said.

Gabrielle's eyes focused on Erin, determination flashing in their blue depths. "Yes, but this time not to something so unimportant as a man. Land is forever, Erin, as much as anything in this life can be. I want something that will last. Mama must have regretted not being able to fight for what was hers as a Cordero."

"Are you planning on calling yourself Cordero now?"

"Mama kept her own name to be a teacher of French. Mama sacrificed for me after Roberto Cordero died and left her penniless. For Mama, I'll stay a Deschamps."

"You never told me much about your father, Gabrielle. Just that he died fighting in the Civil War before you were born."

"There's not much to tell. Roberto Cordero was a Confederate soldier serving near his Laredo home. He came up here for a shipment of rifles and met Mama." Gabrielle grinned. "A hot-blooded Spaniard and a seventeen-year-old French orphan. They were wed in a week."

"That's some heritage! No wonder you talk so boldly of men."

"The only passion I'm harboring right now is for a home of my own. When my father died, he left Mama with two things—a daughter he never knew and stories of his land." Gabrielle's eyes darkened. "And no money. I don't intend to let anything like that happen to me."

"Too bad the Cordero family didn't help her."

"There was only Roberto's mother, Maria, and she returned to her family in Madrid. She never accepted Colette Deschamps as her son's widow."

"Do you look like your mother?"

"She was fair like me, but she said my features were those of my father."

"If he looked anything like his daughter, he must

16

have been an attractive man." Erin's eyes fell to Gabrielle's graceful hand wrapped around a brandy snifter, then moved up to her delicate face. "The last thing you look like is a rancher, Gabrielle. You can't even ride a horse."

"I'll learn what's necessary. On the outside I may not be very tough, but that's not where toughness counts."

"Another lesson learned from Colette?"

"Exactly," Gabrielle said.

The bartender caught Erin's eye. "Excuse me a moment, Gabrielle. I've some business to take care of."

"In truth, I'd like to be getting back to the hotel. To rest up for my meeting with Cantu tomorrow. I know you'll be busy here tonight."

"You're welcome to stay here with me in my apartment upstairs."

"I've imposed on your hospitality long enough," said Gabrielle.

"At least let me give you the loan of my carriage and driver," Erin said, signaling one of her workers to fetch the carriage. "And you will let me know how your meeting goes tomorrow, won't you?"

"Good news or bad, I will. And it had better be good. I've waited too long for this moment to quit because a lawyer advises me I should."

The two made their good-byes and Gabrielle watched as Erin followed the bartender into the room at the rear of the saloon. Tomorrow. It had a ring of promise to it. Colette Deschamps had been taken from her too soon, felled in an epidemic of influenza that swept through San Antonio. But somewhere,

17

Gabrielle knew, her Mama was watching and smiling encouragement.

Clutching the small purse that had been resting in her lap, she stood and headed toward the door. As if by some unspoken command, her gaze turned toward the bar. She expected to see a smiling Rafe Jericho enraptured by the voluptuous dark-haired woman who had pressed herself against him. Neither Jericho nor the woman was in sight.

Gabrielle brushed aside her annoyance as too naive for the woman she knew herself to be. She might be innocent, but she certainly wasn't ignorant. Of course the two were gone.

Besides, Rafe Jericho's whereabouts were no concern of hers. Holding the skirt of her blue silk gown to her, she walked out into the warm September afternoon.

Rafe Jericho sat alone at a corner table far away from the bar and watched the swinging doors through which the young beauty had departed. There wasn't much he hadn't noticed about her since he'd felt her gaze on him and turned to look into her incredibly blue eyes. And bold eyes they were, too. For a moment they made him forget the worries on his mind, so much so that if Carmen hadn't appeared, he might have pursued the matter further.

Even with her frank stare, there had been something young and innocent about her. Maybe it was the way her fingers wound themselves in her hair. Or the faint tinges of pink in her cheeks when their eyes locked. Or the way she couldn't hold that look, instead looking down as if afraid he might read her mind.

And then had come her words drifting across the suddenly quiet air. *Men have their uses.* She hadn't seemed to care the way her silvered voice carried in the stillness.

So men had their uses, did they? As she watched him, she must have been thinking of a few. And any she missed, he would be more than happy to point out.

She had paused in the doorway, giving him ample time to study her tall, slender figure. Slender and yet rounded in the right places. Particulars etched themselves in his mind—the smooth curve of her jawline, the way she held her head as though she were poised to take flight, the full lips at odds with the fine features of her face, the sign of a passionate woman.

The late afternoon sun streaming through the portal had lighted her golden hair, like a jeweled corona embracing the top of her head. A queen with a crown. Or a princess. And yet, despite the set of her shoulders and her straight back, there was something young and vulnerable about her as she had prepared to go out into the world.

Whoa, boy. This was the woman who had sat in a saloon and talked about men in the way men referred to women. *They have their uses.* He had at times said much the same thing about women. No matter who she was, this woman was no more a queen than he was a king. And with the troubles he'd been having lately down at the ranch, he felt far from ready to claim any sort of crown.

For a while back there at the bar, when Carmen

had none too subtly offered him her charms, he'd been tempted to use her to forget his unpleasant mission tomorrow at the bank. But then he'd looked into the summer-blue eyes of his mystery woman again and had lost interest. Tonight he would settle for a few drinks.

He emptied his glass. The Arroyo Seco, his grandfather's fifty-thousand-acre ranch, was enough to occupy his mind without adding the worry of a tempting woman. It was just as well the young woman was gone, yet he was surprised at his disappointment.

He signaled for another whiskey and was about to send it the way of his other drinks when he heard a commotion on the street outside—a man's voice and the angry words of the woman who had just left the Hidden Nugget. Only this time her voice wasn't silvered. Flinging a coin on the table, he grabbed his hat and hurried outside.

A flash of blue to his left caught his eye and he turned to see her standing at the edge of the uneven walkway, hands on hips. Standing close in front of her—too damned close—was Luke Sneed.

Rafe knew Luke Sneed well and liked him none the better for it. He was one of the thugs who worked on the spread next to the Seco, a place dubbed the Rancho Perro by its owner Earl Hunter. Hunter was smooth and mean; Sneed was just mean. What was he doing up here in San Antonio? He could cause enough trouble down on the border.

A sweat-stained hat was pushed back on Sneed's head and even in the shadows of late afternoon Rafe could make out his small green eyes stabbing at the girl.

"Only one reason a purty thing like you is hangin' around. No man in sight. Must be waitin' for one." A leathered hand reached out and gripped her shoulder. "I'm all the man you'll be wantin'."

She jerked free. "Get away from me," she said. "One scream and help will come running."

"Don't be makin' too hasty a decision." He leaned closer and whispered something into her ear—too softly for Rafe to hear. Not that he needed to. Luke Sneed had all the subtlety of a Texas twister. His words would be crude and to the point.

Rafe stepped closer. "Do what the lady asks, Luke. Back off."

Narrowed eyes darted up at him. "Jericho, is it?" Surprise turned to warning. "Stay out of this. Doesn't concern you."

"And what if it does?" He nodded to Gabrielle and took another step closer. "Could be I was the man she was waiting for. One thing's for sure. You're not the one."

Rafe's hands rested against his thighs. Too bad his gun wasn't strapped where he could reach it, but he hadn't left his room looking for this kind of trouble.

Gabrielle moved from between the two men, her eyes going to the black revolver inches from Luke's right hand. "There's no reason to do anything foolish," she said, edging closer to Rafe. "I'll go back inside and we can just forget—"

"No need to do that, little lady," Luke said. His thumb rested on the gun. "Mr. Jericho here'll be movin' on."

Rafe judged the distance about right. "You know me better than that, Luke." He extended his body.

21

Without warning his arm whipped out and he hit Sneed square on the jaw. Sneed reeled backward and sat down hard on the sharp stones of the walkway, his hat landing in a puddle of mud. Rafe kicked the gun out of Sneed's hand and into the street.

Rafe ignored the startled cry behind him. "Leave it be, Luke," he warned. "Get on back to your boss. Tell him he'll have to send more than just you to take me down."

Sneed scrambled to his feet, calloused fingers rubbing at his jaw. He reached down for his hat and then hit it hard against his buckskin trousers. Eyes that had been green were now dark with anger and with something that a man like Sneed would consider hard to swallow — humiliation because he'd been bested in front of a woman.

Sneed glanced at Gabrielle and then back to Rafe. "I'm not forgettin' this, Jericho. And neither will Hunter. He's here in town. He won't like you pushin' around his men."

"And I don't like his men dogging my path. That is what you were up to, wasn't it? Before you got a few ideas you weren't able to carry through on. He set you on my trail. And maybe came along to see you did it right?"

Sneed slapped the muddied hat on his head. "I ain't talkin'."

"You don't have to. Except to tell your boss that if he expects to know what I'm up to, he'll have to do his own nosing around. Like those hounds he keeps."

As Rafe talked, Sneed's eyes shifted to the street.

"Don't even think about that gun," said Rafe. "I'll leave it with the bartender and you can pick it up the next time you come slithering around here."

The rattle of an approaching horse and carriage, harness jingling and wheels grating on the brick street, interrupted Sneed's response, and with a muttered curse he disappeared around the corner of the saloon.

The ugliness of the encounter was partially erased by the sight of the smart black buggy, its top rolled back and in its traces a gleaming bay. The buggy halted before Gabrielle and Rafe, and a young man scrambled to the sidewalk. "Miss Deschamps? Mrs. Barrett sent me to take you down to the Menger."

Gabrielle nodded, then smiled at Rafe. "Help seems to come in pairs around here," she said. "Please let me thank you. That man came up so suddenly—"

"No thanks needed," Rafe said, his voice low and warm like a caress. "Are you all right?"

"I'm fine," Gabrielle said, aware of dark eyes resting on her in a disturbingly intense way. "That was just some fool trying to cause trouble."

"And doing a damned good job of it." Rafe settled his hat lower on his forehead. "I'd never dispute a lady's word, but it seems to me you're looking a little paler than you did inside." But not any less beautiful with her wan smile, he thought. The sudden violence had startled her more than she seemed willing to admit. The vulnerability he had detected as she stood in the doorway seemed more evident out here in the lengthening shadows of early evening.

Gabrielle's blue eyes flashed their disagreement. "I think I was handling the situation all right. Surely that Mr. Sneed wouldn't have done anything out here on the street."

Rafe shook his head in disbelief. Gabrielle Des-champs might be brave, but in thinking she could handle someone like Luke Sneed, she was also being foolish. If she continued to feel that way, she was liable someday to do something decidedly rash.

"He may have been only talking out here today, but if Luke Sneed got the chance, he'd do what he had a mind to—and what he was able to do—in a pile of horse manure. Don't ever take a man like him too lightly."

Gabrielle smiled grimly. "I get the picture, thank you, Mr. Jericho. Now, if you will excuse me, I must be getting back to the hotel."

Rafe grinned. "And where might that be?"

"The Menger," Gabrielle heard herself say. "I'm staying there while I'm in town. It's a business trip." Silently she cursed herself for talking too much. What difference did it make to him why she was there?

"Sure thing," said Rafe. He stepped past the driver and, putting his hands around Gabrielle's waist, lifted her into the carriage. "I'll be driving the lady to her hotel," he said to the young man. "Tell Mrs. Barrett I'll bring the carriage back to the stables and pick up my horse."

Giving Gabrielle no time to argue, Rafe scooped up Luke Sneed's gun and tossed it onto the floor of the carriage. He swung into the narrow seat, his rangy body seeming to fill the small space. His thigh, heated from the recent violence of his confrontation with Sneed, rested snugly against Gabrielle's knee. He clucked the horse into motion. Once the carriage had turned the corner and passed over the bridge at San Pedro Creek, he leaned back.

"You sure you're all right?" he asked.

Gabrielle nodded, almost breathless from the masterful way Rafe Jericho had taken over since he came on the scene. "It's just that he came up on me so suddenly," she managed.

"Snakes do that."

She shivered. "I wasn't watching where I was going. The sun was just at the top of the building across the way from the Nugget and I guess I was thinking more of the colors it cast than where I was going. And there he was in front of me. He must have misunderstood why I was there."

"Standing on a street corner on the west side of town was not a smart move. Especially looking the way you do. You're lucky someone was around besides Luke Sneed."

Again her blue eyes studied him in a way that left him unnerved. "I'm lucky *you* were around," she said.

"Maybe not. I'm probably the reason he was there in the first place."

Gabrielle remembered the words that had flown between the two men. "You said something about his boss."

"That's right. Another snake, only a much more dangerous one."

She shuddered. "Do you think he might —"

"There's no telling what he might do. But I can take care of him."

Gabrielle smiled. "I have a feeling you can."

Rafe let out his breath slowly. The young beauty had a smile that would melt the Seco's hardest rocks. "Allow me to introduce myself. Rafael Jericho, at your service." A gleam lit the depths of his brown

25

eyes. "Whatever you decide that might be."

Gabrielle sat straight in the narrow seat and pulled herself away from the thigh that had been burning against hers. "Mr. Jericho—"

"Rafe. After all we've been through, there's no need for formality."

"Rafe, then." Gabrielle stirred nervously. "I'm Gabrielle Deschamps."

"Ah, French," he said. "I should have known. French ladies are always so . . . charming."

"And what is that supposed to mean?"

"No offense, Gabby. It was meant as a compliment."

Gabrielle started at the informal shortening of her name. Colette had called her Gabby, and she discovered she liked very much the way the name sounded coming from Rafe.

"Something wrong with my calling you Gabby?"

"No. It's just that my mother called me by that name. I haven't heard it since she died."

Rafe's gaze was sympathetic. "Do you have any other family here?"

"No family anywhere, not for a long time." Gabrielle's chin tilted upward. "I've learned to take care of myself. Usually. But that doesn't mean I'm not grateful for your help. I wish there were some way I could thank you properly."

Rafe studied her for a moment. This temptress sitting beside him was a mixture of innocence and seduction. Which was the real Gabrielle Deschamps?

Curls as soft as angels' hair fell about her delicate face. Her wide-set blue eyes were darkly lashed, and there was a hint of pink on her cheeks and sensual lips. It was doubtful she realized how expressive her lovely face could be. He read there an interest in him that she could not cover up.

The feeling was mutual. He couldn't remember a woman's mere presence affecting him so strongly. Whatever way she wanted to thank him, proper or otherwise, he certainly didn't plan to turn it down. *A man has his uses*. He most certainly does.

He expertly turned the carriage onto a narrow, shadowed side street and halted. Resting his arm casually on the back of the seat behind her shoulders, he shifted his weight to face her. Padded leather squeaked under him, the sound invading the silence that had fallen around them. In the pause, their eyes locked.

"So you want a way to thank me?" Rafe said quietly. "I didn't face down Luke Sneed with that in mind, but"—one finger snared a curl—"I might be persuaded to take something. Depends on what's offered."

Even in the cool, fresh air Gabby felt as though she were suffocating, and she pulled free from his touch. "Don't misunderstand me," she said with a firmness she was far from feeling.

"Then tell me what you mean." He paused a moment. "Or better yet, show me."

Too late she lowered her lashes. Rafe had already read in the depths of her sapphire eyes the same emotions that were racing through him now. He pulled her against his chest. The touch of her body was as delightful as he'd known it would be. Her fingers pushed against him, but not hard enough to offer any discouragement—not nearly hard enough.

His head bent close and his lips brushed hers. Soft and sweet she was, and her kiss held the promise of

27

untouched riches.

She pulled back and breathed a barely whispered "Oh!"

Rafe heard wonderment in the word and again he kissed her, this time more deeply, his tongue tracing a light, electric pattern along the inside of her upper lip and then dipping briefly inside to the dark moistness awaiting him. He felt her tremble beneath his touch, her hands pushing ineffectually against him.

Rafe pulled away. "Gabrielle Deschamps," he said, his eyes burning into hers, "you do know how to thank a man."

Even in the shadowed light he could see her blue eyes darken. When he tried to hold her close once more, she again pushed him back, this time with more authority behind fisted hands. "I'm afraid you have the wrong idea about me."

He grinned at her. He'd felt her response too sharply to listen to her words. Leaning forward until his face was only inches from hers, he ran his thumb along her lower lip. "I wonder if you realize exactly how you feel. Or the effect you are having on me. Pulling back the way you did is liable to cause a little discomfort. A man can't turn his urges on and off the way a woman can."

Again her blue eyes flared in opposition to his words. "And what do you know about my—" She stopped, the natural blush of her cheeks deepening.

He leaned back in the seat. "Perhaps you'd like to tell me."

Gabby sat ramrod straight and stared past the horse and on down the deserted street. The physical shock of his kiss had not yet abated. Rafe Jericho was affecting her far more than she was willing to admit — and in ways she didn't understand.

Erin had been right. Until today she had never received a real kiss. If a complete loss of willpower went with it, she would be better off stopping with one.

"It's getting late, Rafe. Please take me to the hotel."

Rafe was reluctant to leave off with any shadow of ill feeling between them. Hell, he was reluctant to leave off at all but supposed he must. They were still on a public street.

"Okay. But consider one more request." He put up his hands to protest the sharp look she threw him. "You said you were in San Antonio on business. Are you going to be here long?"

"My plans are uncertain, but I'll be here for at least a few more days."

"Then how about lunch tomorrow? Give me a chance to prove I can behave myself. Unless there's some man around who might object." Not that it mattered a damn whether he did or not.

She met his questioning look straight on. "There's no one like that. I told you I take care of myself."

Brave words, Rafe thought, for a girl who looked as though she needed protecting. At least to him she did.

"The weather is holding fine," he said, "and we could find us a place to eat outdoors. Maybe somewhere along the river. Daylight. Lots of people around. Just in case you still don't trust me."

Gabby sat quietly for a moment, thoughts tumbling about in her head. The feel of his hand in her hair was still on her, as was the touch of his lips. Tentative young men in Virginia had been easy to hold off.

29

Rafe Jericho was another matter.

Everything told her to say no to him.

"That sounds nice," she heard herself say, felt her lips curl into a smile of pleasure, wondered at the quickening of her heart.

"I have some business of my own to take care of at the bank tomorrow sometime before noon. I don't know how long it will take."

Guiltily, Gabby remembered her own plans. "As a matter of fact," she said, "I need to go there myself. My attorney has his office in the bank building, and I can see him in the morning as easily as later."

"Then I can come by for you about eleven o'clock?"

There was only one answer Gabby could give, and she nodded. In minutes she was being whisked toward the heart of San Antonio, the Alamo and the nearby Menger Hotel. Rafe was very much the gentleman as he helped her from the carriage and into the lobby.

She started up the stairs, then glanced back at Rafe, an image of Luke Sneed flashing across her mind. "You will be careful, won't you?"

Rafe's lips twisted into a smile. "Nothing is going to get in the way of tomorrow." He took his leave with a tilt of his hat and was soon on his way to the stables.

Now why, boy, are you feeling so good, he asked himself as the carriage headed into the late afternoon sun. You've got a no-good rancher named Earl Hunter threatening you or offering riches for your land, a banker breathing down your neck, and several chancy ventures that just might save your skin — if they don't break you.

A slender, blue-eyed beauty was the answer. He had a score of worries that she'd made him forget for a while, something a half dozen women like Carmen back at the Nugget hadn't been able to do.

Rafe was affected by Gabby in a way he hadn't felt before. Sitting in that carriage in the middle of a city street, he had wanted to talk to her, to tell her about himself and flood her with questions about her own life. And when the talk was done, he would have kissed her until she panted for his lovemaking. He'd had women in some unusual ways, but with this one he wanted to make love slow and special. And not just one time. With Gabby he sensed that once would not be nearly enough.

Well, Ben Hidalgo, he said to the still air, maybe your grandson just might bring home something more than good news from the bank. As rough and unyielding as they both were, the ranch and Ben meant everything to him, but that didn't mean there might not be enough room in his life for someone else.

Sure he was moving quickly, if only in his mind, but then he made most important decisions that way — and he rarely had to change directions. Instinct for survival, he told himself. And instinct told him Gabrielle Deschamps was to play a very important part in his life.

Chapter Two

Late the next morning Gabby descended the hotel stairs in time to watch Rafe Jericho, his long, lean figure dressed in close-fitting brown shirt and trousers, striding toward her across the lobby. He shifted his strong legs in the rolling gait of someone used to being on horseback. It was a walk she hadn't seen in the East, the walk of a cowboy.

From his tanned skin and work-rough hands she'd already figured out he spent little time in saloons. Other than that, she knew only what Erin had told her. He was from out of town — and women liked him. The latter she'd realized as soon as he walked through the Nugget's swinging doors.

And there was one more thing, she thought as she remembered the way they'd met. Someone — that obnoxious Luke Sneed's boss — was out to get him. A man as strong-willed as Rafe Jericho would most likely make enemies, and she breathed a sigh of relief that he had returned to the Menger unharmed.

She pulled herself up short. Silly girl. Rafe Jericho

could take care of himself.

Her eyes dropped in an involuntary inventory of him from his calf-tight black boots, to the red scarf knotted at his throat, to the dark hair that lay across his forehead. He more than matched the image that had haunted her since he left her at the hotel door. No wonder she'd spent a restless night.

Gabby issued a silent warning to herself to be careful. She would enjoy the day and the time spent with, admittedly, the most attractive man she'd ever seen. And that was all. Whatever reactions she had to him could be attributed to the inexperience that Erin had teased her about, and nothing more. After a few hours in Rafe Jericho's company, she would bid him good-bye and, with her energies turned toward her quest, most likely never see him again.

Despite her misgivings, she was inordinately glad she had chosen her favorite gown, a pink cotton day dress that accented her slim waist and gave a soft glow to her complexion. It was a man's world she was attempting to enter, but that didn't mean she couldn't enjoy for a while the pleasures of being a woman.

With smooth courtliness Rafe extended his arm. "I was afraid you would change your mind about coming along with me today," he said. "I'm glad you didn't."

Gabby surveyed him with open skepticism. "I don't believe you for a minute. When's the last time a woman turned you down?"

Rafe's eyes settled on her lips. "It's happened. Believe me. But when's the last time I cared?"

The man had style. More to the point, his presence caused a peculiar feeling in her—a tightening in the chest, a warmth when he smiled. She found herself grinning at him, encouraging a return of that smile. As she accepted his arm and allowed him to guide her to his hired carriage, she decided that on this bright September day nothing could go wrong.

When they arrived at the building that housed both the bank and the offices of attorney Oscar Cantu, Rafe grew more solemn. "I may be awhile," he said as he escorted her inside.

"Please don't rush your business. I told you I needed to see my attorney. I may be some time myself."

"Nothing wrong, I hope," Rafe said.

Gabby smiled confidently. "Most certainly not. I'll meet you here as quickly as I can."

Rafe agreed and disappeared through an inner door that led to the bank. Within minutes Gabby was at the other end of the building, settling back in the chair fronting Oscar Cantu's desk, pushing thoughts of Rafe from her mind. Right now she had more immediate concerns, concerns she'd waited most of her short life to settle.

"Miss Deschamps," Cantu said as he leaned back into his chair, "from what I have learned in your letters and from investigations, I think you have a good case."

The worry lines that had been on Gabby's face since she'd entered softened. In his gray broadcloth suit with matching waistcoat, shelves of law books at his back, and her file in front of him, Oscar Cantu was the way she had pictured him from his brief correspondence, everything she could have wanted — mature, professional, and well aware of the details of her case. She read in his dark Spanish eyes an intelligent concern for the business at hand.

More important, he was encouraging.

"Is my case good enough to convince this Benito Hidalgo to negotiate with me?"

"Ah, Miss Deschamps, that is another matter. From what I understand, Senor Hidalgo is a proud and . . . difficult man. And one who will most certainly not feel pleasure at the arrival of a young woman asking for a portion of his land."

"I've always known there would be trouble, but surely there's a way that some of it could be avoided. It is only justice that I seek."

"There is nothing, senorita, of value that comes without a struggle. The question you must ask is are you willing to do what is necessary to achieve your goal?"

"Mr. Cantu, I've spent most of my life either listening to my mother talk about the dream of Roberto Cordero or planning ways I could see that the dream was realized. I cannot back down now. I will not."

"Strong words, senorita. It may be necessary to go to court. Such cases can be long. The wheels of justice do not always turn as quickly as we would like."

"I had hoped to avoid such an action," she said, realizing how naive she must sound to the attorney. "We must get the negotiations under way."

"Then let me tell you what I learned. The Corderos received the land in a grant from the king of Spain in the early part of this century, when Texas still belonged to that country."

"Aren't these Spanish land grants honored by the state of Texas?"

"In most cases, yes. But the proceedings that took the land from your father's people were legal according to evidence presented at the time. There was much feeling against Mexico after Texas became a republic, and Hidalgo swore your grandfather Carlos Cordero had sided with the Mexican cause. In that year"—he consulted his notes for a minute—"1840, it was reason enough to strip him of the title."

Gabrielle's heart sank. "So what is different now? If the transfer was legal then, it is legal now."

"Perhaps not. The evidence against Cordero was scant. Only Hidalgo testified against him." Settling back in his chair, Cantu warmed to the subject. "You must think of the time. Feelings against supporters of Santa Anna were running high. Your grandfather challenged Hidalgo to bring forth further witnesses but he could not do so. The judge ruled that the single testimony was enough."

"So Hidalgo lied to get the land. How much was involved?"

"With the acquisition of the Rancho Cordero, Senor Hidalgo more than doubled the size of his own spread. Twenty thousand acres before the settlement, fifty thousand afterwards. It was a fortunate thing for him the courts were quick to believe his story. He paid little for the land."

"And received much," she said in wonder. Thirty thousand acres sounded like more land than anyone could ever want.

"I sense from what little I've been able to find that there was bad blood between the men, senorita. Even before the trial."

"Something like a feud you mean."

36

Cantu nodded solemnly. "It is perhaps not too strong a word."

"Mr. Cantu, I am aware that by the time my father came to San Antonio and married my mother, his father was dead and it wasn't long before his mother returned to Spain. Roberto Cordero felt he had the right to a large holding along the Rio Grande. He convinced Colette of that right. I know little about this feud."

"What exactly did your mother say?"

"Before the war, Roberto had already started investigating the possibility of regaining his land. My grandfather had been killed in some kind of confrontation with Ben Hidalgo, although no charges were ever brought. The investigation of Grandfather Carlos's death revealed nothing conclusive. No one knew what their feud, if you can call it that, was about."

"The history of Texas is a bloody one, senorita, and shows little signs of changing. *Tejanos*, the Mexicans who live in the state, still struggle against the *gringo*. At that time they would have closed ranks around their own and settled things as they saw justice."

Cantu's voice became thoughtful. "Many still believe Texas belongs to Mexico and that Mexicans have the right to settle their own differences, even that Texas will revert to its rightful owner, Mexico. Added to that have been cattlemen against sheepmen, free range cattlemen against farmers and barbed wire. That at least is changing. Barbed wire is bringing an end to the open range, and those on the land will become more entrenched and hard to remove."

"Meaning Ben Hidalgo," Gabby said. "He is both

Mexican and a cattleman. And difficult, you said. Well, I am Spanish, too, as well as French and Texan." For the first time since the interview began, Gabby smiled. "I can be difficult, too, senor. I also intend to become a rancher, at least in a small way."

Over steepled fingers Cantu studied Gabby. "And as I told you earlier, you stand a good chance of meeting with success. If you are patient. There have been similar cases which have been won."

"I want only a portion of original Rancho Cordero. Enough, with the money my mother left, to live on. Enough to build a home."

Cantu's lips twitched. "It is my opinion you ask for too little, although even in this modest request Senor Hidalgo may not be grateful."

"I am not after his gratitude," said Gabby, her head lifted in determination. "It is his understanding that I hope for."

"In this, you ask for much," said Cantu. "And at the same time not enough. Only a portion of the land, you say. I advise you to claim the thirty thousand acres that was the original Rancho Cordero."

Gabby shook her head. "The Hidalgos worked that land for forty years. For that they should receive compensation, their fair share. It is this that should be negotiated, not whether I claim everything. Besides," she said, her determined look softening, "what would I do with all that land? My mother referred to it as our *refuge primitif*. That is all I am after—a refuge, a place to call my own. And at the same time a link with my father's family."

Gabby opened her purse. "I brought these papers along. Perhaps they can help."

Carefully she set a large, wrinkled envelope on the desk in front of Cantu. "You will find the certificate of my parents' marriage, the church registry of my birth, and a letter from my father's commanding officer, Santos Benavides, declaring he died with valor while scouting the Union troops that were moving along the Rio Grande."

"*Muy bien*," he said, fingering the documents. "Benavides is now representing Laredo in the legislature and might at least be a character witness, if, in the likely event our negotiations with Senor Hidalgo fail, we must go to court. But again I must stress that with all of the evidence on our side and even if we file suit in Austin tomorrow, we are in for a long struggle that might take years."

"Years! Surely you're mistaken. I was thinking more like months."

"You are very young, senorita. Similar titles have been tied up in the courts for almost as long as you have been alive."

Gabby sat back in the chair. To wait years was as bad as defeat. She fought off a feeling of disheartenment.

"Then I'll go see this Hidalgo myself. Perhaps I can convince him of my cause."

"That is unwise, senorita. Some things should be left in the hands of attorneys. And you will be facing not only an old man. There is also a grandson who lives on the ranch. The last of the Hidalgo's family. It is he that the old man hopes will carry on with the ranch."

"The Arroyo Seco, I believe you wrote."

"Yes. When the ranches were combined, Hidalgo

39

named it for the usually dry creek that had separated them."

"This grandson will have to settle for less than he planned." She looked the lawyer squarely in the eye. "And I'll tell him so as soon as I can see him."

"You are a determined young woman. Most of your age think only of *amor*. Of love."

Gabrielle brushed aside his words, along with a momentary vision of Rafe. The important consideration here was the dream she'd had all her life.

"As your client, Mr. Cantu, I'd like you to do something for me," she said. "Hold off filing that suit, at least until I pay a visit to the ranch. I promise," she added with a sigh, "that if it looks as though I have no chance of convincing the old man or his grandson, then we'll go ahead in court."

Cantu looked at her for a long moment, and she could see resignation settling on his face.

"At least," he said, closing the folder on his desk, "let me put you in the hands of another attorney whose office is in Laredo. I have already told him something of your case. He will be nearby in the event you should need him. His name is Franklin Bernard and he should be in San Antonio in a day or two. Perhaps he can accompany you down on the train. If"—his solemn face broke into a smile—"you can wait that long."

Gabby grinned in return. "That's about as long as I can wait. I'll be happy to let Mr. Bernard advise me— if I don't always have to listen."

She made arrangements for Cantu to let her know when the Laredo attorney arrived in town. Her business concluded, she'd made her departure to wait for

Rafe near the front door of the office building and think about what Cantu had said. Even under the threat of a long wait, she would not allow herself to be poor spirited.

So Hidalgo had a grandson, did he? Probably just as difficult as the old man, but she must not let the thought discourage her. The memory of Colette Deschamps was too dear, and she made too many promises to that memory.

Others might think Colette had sacrificed her honor in living the kind of life she had, but Gabby knew otherwise. There had never been a more honorable woman. Or a more gentle and cultured one, with her knowledge of music and painting and her skills with needle and thread. Such accoutrements of learning she had passed on to her daughter, along with her inner strength. And one more thing, Gabby thought—a definitely unromantic and distrusting view of men.

So it was strange how her pulse quickened when she thought about the man who was about to join her. It was a purely physical reaction, she decided, though it had a somewhat greater urgency than she'd expected—just as Erin had hinted.

As she saw the subject of her contemplations walking toward her with his graceful gait, she warned herself once again to guard herself against his rakish charms.

With such assurances settling her mind, she smoothed the pink cotton skirt across her hips and lifted her lashes to look into Rafe's dark eyes. She was surprised to find a look of displeasure in their depths.

"Is something wrong?"

"Bankers!" Rafe said in disgust. "They should all spend a week of hard labor on a spread that hasn't seen a good rain in a year. Perhaps then they'd understand the problems we face."

"We?"

"Ranchers. We're at the mercy of both nature and the marketplace. And each other." Just as quickly as his anger had overtaken him, it was gone and he grinned at her. "Not all of us are upright and honorable. Or even lucky. It's something for you to remember, Gabby."

"Then," she said, a trifle breathless, "I suggest you take me for that food you offered and fill me in on the details. I hope to do some ranching myself. You could provide me a valuable service."

"No doubt I could," he said softly as they passed outside.

As he helped her into the carriage, Rafe indicated a cloth-covered basket behind the seat. "Cold chicken and wine provided by the restaurant at the Menger. I hope it meets with your approval."

Gabby's eye fell on a dark object beside the basket. "And the gun?"

"I don't intend to be caught empty-handed the way I was yesterday." He reached for the gun and holster and strapped them on. The revolver looked right at home against his thigh.

Climbing in beside her, he bent his head close to hers. "And now to find the crowds I promised you."

Gabby looked at Rafe from the corner of her eye. The idea of being surrounded by strangers didn't seem very important right now. Probably, she told herself, it was the bright light from the September sun overhead that made a secluded site seem safe.

"Crowds aren't really necessary. Not if we're going to . . . talk. After all, you promised to tell me about the hazards of your profession."

Again came the tightening in her chest and the flush of warmth as he gazed at her with penetrating brown eyes.

"Whatever you say, Gabby. I know of just the place." Again came the warm, unsettling smile. "Came highly recommended by an *hombre* at the bank."

He grabbed up the reins and soon had them weaving in and out of the city traffic at a rate of speed that left her dizzy. The warm wind caught in her hair and freed tendrils of golden curls that she had pinned up with such care that morning. She knew her cheeks were flushed from the exhilaration of the ride and from the nearness of Rafe Jericho. She must look an absolute mess but she didn't care a whit. For a while she would forget her cares. Her laugh of pure joy filled the air.

Rafe grinned appreciatively at her. "Feeling good, Gabby?" He put one arm around her and stroked the sleeve of her dress. "Don't answer. I'd say you feel very good."

She pulled free of his touch and attempted a prim smile. "I'm also very hungry."

"I'll need to do something about that."

"I'm sure you can. Of course I don't know everything that's in your basket."

His eyes held a wicked sparkle. "There's enough, Gabby. I'll see that you get your fill."

For once she had no reply and was relieved to see him turn his attention again to the road. Within minutes they were out of town and moving down a winding road that paralleled the wandering river. Scattered trees and brush lined the waterway, only occasionally blocking the view, and Gabby was able to see the canals that had been dredged from the river to the homes along their route.

The traffic gradually thinned, as did the number of houses, and the growth along the river thickened. Still Rafe did not slow down. By the time he turned off the road onto a rutted path and guided the horse toward a grove of trees near the water, the sun was already past its zenith. Civilization seemed far behind, and Gabby had the curious feeling they had traveled to the ends of the earth.

Without waiting for his assistance, she scrambled down from the carriage and made her way to the water's edge to wait while Rafe tethered the horse and strapped a feed bag under the mare's nose. The grass-covered bank was curtained by heavy brush and one thick-leaved cottonwood tree that cast dappled shade onto the site. The San Antonio River was small by eastern standards, not much more than a creek, and yet there was effervescent beauty in its clear water moving rapidly over the pebbled bed.

At the sound of Rafe's footstep behind her, she turned to face him. "What a charming spot," she said.

His eyes lingered on her for an eternity before he spoke. Her pink gown was high necked and enticing in the innocent way it rested against her body, and he found himself entranced by the loose curls of hair that framed her face.

"Did anyone ever tell you your hair is the color of sunlight?"

"Hundreds of men, as a matter of fact," she said, surprised she could sound so flippant when she longed to hear more of his sweet words. "I thought we came out here to talk about you."

"And to satisfy our hunger. I've never been much for talk."

Gabby focused on a low-hanging branch of the cottonwood. She forced herself to look back at him. "You don't like to talk? Not even about ranching?" she said. "You were going to tell me about the hazards of your work."

Again she saw the look of displeasure in his eyes that she'd noticed back at the bank.

"Surprisingly enough," he said, "I might enjoy that. As long as you're close by to listen."

Setting the basket on the ground, he spread out a blanket on the soft grass and produced two crystal goblets and a bottle of wine, which he proceeded to uncork.

His movements were practiced as he poured the clear liquid and handed her a glass. Gabby sat beside Rafe on the blanket and sipped at the cool wine, watching him down his drink quickly and pour another.

"Just trying to get the taste of banker out of my mouth," he explained. "I had to do a lot of talking to get him on my side. You'd think a man in his line of work would know a good thing when he sees it. I plan to make money, Gabby, and lots of it. But not in the next few months. Not until I can get the first sheep to market in the spring."

Gabby accepted his offer of more wine, but she let the drink sit untouched as she watched him. Gone was the rake who had cast his spell so effectively upon her; in his place was a man intent on his cause, determined to overcome the obstacles in his path. He was none the less attractive for the change.

"I assumed you were a cattleman."

"I am. Does it sound unusual that I can run both cattle and sheep? You'll find more and more of us around. The two herds can graze together as long as you don't overstock. Right now I've got mine separated by fencing."

"Fencing?" Gabby thought of Cantu's talk about the barbed wire that was being used on the range. "What kind?"

"Any kind takes a great deal of *dinero*. That's part of the reason I'm in debt. But I figure you have to spend money to make money. And if I'm right, I'll be rich, considering all I'm investing in right now. Breed cattle. Barbed wire. Sheep. A spur line to tie in with the railroad and ship the cattle directly to market in San Antonio and Corpus Christi. From Corpus I can ship them to Cuba. There's quite a market for our beef on that island."

Rafe had a dream, too, one that wasn't very different from her own.

She sipped her wine, studying him over the edge of the goblet. "There's one thing I just can't figure out. If you talked this way back at the bank, why weren't you given the keys to the safe? You've certainly convinced me you'll get what you want."

Rafe smiled. "And you'd better not forget it either."

More than ever Gabby was aware of his magnetism. "I'll remember that warning," she said, "but I was speaking about your ranch. Weren't you after a loan?"

"I got that last year, with the ranch as security. The problem is my banker wants more of his money back. And he's not all that happy about waiting until spring—even with the payment I was able to bring him today. He kept muttering something about stock-holders and foreclosures."

"Not very bright, is he? You sound like a good investment risk to me."

"That's because I've only told you the good part. There's also the drought, a rough winter five years ago we're just beginning to overcome, trouble with some of the breeding stock, and a neighbor as mean a sidewinder as you'll find this side of hell who's trying his damnedest to run me off."

"Luke Sneed's boss?" Rafe's grimace told her she was right. "Is he . . . dangerous?"

"Earl Hunter? He'd like me to think so. Hunter likes to do pesky little things like that to shake me up. What he doesn't understand is I'm as mean as he is. And a damned sight more stubborn."

The frown on Rafe's face was enough to drive away the sun, and she had an inordinate desire to see him smile again.

Gabby lowered her lashes. "You promised lunch, remember?"

"And I'm a man of my word. If it's food you want right now, it's food you'll be getting."

Gabby watched as he unloaded the basket. Soon a feast of cold sliced chicken, a loaf of bread, and red apples was on the cloth between them. How pleasant it was to look at him, at his lean, rugged face and powerful body. As her gaze dropped, she focused on the gun strapped to his leg.

"Expecting bears, perhaps?" she asked.

"I'm not expecting anything," he said, not answering her smile. "I wasn't expecting Luke Sneed yesterday. That's the last time I'll be caught with my pants down." A gleam lightened his dark eyes. "That's just a figure of speech, you understand."

"I understand," Gabby said, reaching for the bread.

Rafe spread the napkin in front of her and served up the chicken and fruit. Again he poured the wine and raised his glass.

"To good times, Gabrielle Deschamps."

They ate in silence for a while, savoring the taste of the food and drink, enjoying the nearness of each other. At last Rafe set down his glass and turned unswerving attention to her.

"You know," he said, "I've done all the talking. And I know very little about you, except that you have no family."

"There's not much to tell. My father died before I was born and my mother died almost ten years ago."

"It's hard to believe you don't have some man taking care of you, begging you to marry him."

"I'm not after a man." Her blue eyes flashed with pride. "I can take care of myself."

Rafe grinned. "It seems a terrible waste. What's this plan you mentioned about going into ranching?"

"It's more than a plan. It's what I'm going to do. My father was raised on a ranch in South Texas and I want to follow in his footsteps, at least in a small way."

"Then we might be neighbors. That brings lots of possibilities to mind."

Rafe's eyes drifted down the close-fitting pink gown,

to the slender hands resting in her lap, and back up to the fine features of her face. "I'm hoping you get what you want," he said.

"I plan to."

"You also plan on having a man around to run the place?"

"I won't be the first woman to own a ranch. I'll hire whatever help I need."

"In other words, taking advantage of whatever services a man can provide."

Gabby looked at him suspiciously. Had he heard her yesterday in the saloon?

"Whoever I hire," she said, "will be adequately compensated."

"I'm sure he will." He grinned at the pride in her eyes. "Just being around a boss as beautiful as you would be compensation enough. Although, I must warn you, Gabby. There are lots of men who won't want to take orders from a woman."

"I'm fully aware of that, Rafe. I understand a great deal about men."

There it was again, Rafe thought, that flash of seductive worldliness that underscored the delicate gentility of her look and manner. It was a bewitching mixture.

"I thought I did about women," he said. "But you've got me wondering, *querida*."

"I'm not your darling." She smiled at the surprise on his face. "My mother taught me to speak the language. After all, I am half Spanish, Rafe."

"No wonder you seemed *simpatico*. So am I. And *querida* has several meanings—lover and mistress among them."

Rafe didn't wait for her response. With slow deliberation he moved aside the food that lay between them, stood, and pulled her to her feet, pleased that she offered no protest. His hands rested on her shoulders, then drew her close to him. She was taller than her delicate build indicated. Rafe topped six feet by two inches and yet if he leaned nearer, his lips would brush against her forehead.

Again he was struck by the sense of rightness in having her near. She was as fair as he was dark, her skin as silken as his was weathered, her body soft and finely sculpted where his was hard. And yet they fit.

"A man does indeed have his uses, *querida*," he whispered against her cheek. "One is to love a woman. Another is to show her that love."

She looked at him in alarm. "You *did* hear me yesterday!"

"*Si*, I heard. You said only what other women think."

"Not all."

"*Es verdad*. Some don't care for a man's touch. Or only pretend to. That's not the case with you, Gabby." Her eyes told him he was right.

Rafe's lips hovered near hers until Gabby wondered if he would ever kiss her. Conflicts tore at her—to push him away and to hold him tight. Above all else, she needed to stay in control.

Would the touch of his lips be as electric as it had been the day before? The question was absurd. Of course it would.

She lifted her hands and placed them on his chest. Beneath her fingers was the erratic beat of his heart. The tempo quickened her breath. She stared at the red scarf at his neck, at his firm chin and partly open lips, and at last on up to his eyes. She drowned in his gaze and when he bent his head to kiss her, she inched her hands up to his shoulders.

Persuasive lips touched hers and a warmth coursed through her that had nothing to do with the sun at her back. With her fingers entwined in the thick hair that met the collar of his shirt, she responded to his kiss, hesitantly at first, but then gradually her lips moved against his and she gave in to the wondrous urges that flowed through her.

Her lips parted to welcome the thrust of his tongue, and she fell deeper under his spell, welcoming his sweet invasion. Gabby held him tightly to her, marveling at the strength of him, trembling in wonderment. The mysteries of sensual pleasure that she had long ago accepted as fact but not yet felt were unfolding beneath Rafe's kiss; the reality of that pleasure, mixed as it was with the beginnings of a deeper emotion, was far more powerful than her imaginings had ever been.

Insistently he stroked her back as his kiss deepened. She thrilled at his touch, and when one hand moved around to caress her breast she was unable to push it away. Her back arched as she offered herself more easily to him; his body tightened and she knew she pleased him—as much as he did her.

With deft, sure movements Rafe pulled her down to the blanket and she found herself lying beside him. He propped himself on one elbow and leaned over to stroke her hair, her face, her throat down to the edge of her lace collar.

His touch was agony. A hot, hungry passion curled

within her. Why was he teasing her with such expert movements? And why didn't he do more? She freed her hands from their imprisonment against his chest and wrapped her arms around his neck, drawing him closer until her lips burned against his.

He cradled her tightly, the full length of his body against hers. She felt the pressure of his gun against her thigh and then in the valley between her legs something else, firm and hard. Desire obliterated thought. With no experience to guide her, she did what seemed natural and pulled herself deeper into his embrace. His response was a low moan. His mouth was rough against hers. She melted in his arms.

As suddenly as he had embraced her, he stopped all movement, his lips pulled away, his body rigid and still, no longer inflaming her with hot demands.

His eyes were riveted beyond her toward the water's edge. She heard a rustling in the grass. Puzzled, Gabby dropped her arms reluctantly from around his neck and concentrated on the grim set to his lips. Amazed, she watched as those lips settled into what looked suspiciously like a smile.

"It was nothing," he said and relaxed beside her.

"Nothing?"

Rafe grinned down at her. "Did you hear the grass rustle just then?"

"Yes, I guess I did. It didn't seem important."

"You're a woman after my heart, Gabby. Unfortunately snakes tend to break my concentration."

"Snakes?" Gabby's voice was a squeal and a cry. Like a shot she was out of his arms and on her feet. Terror was in her rounded eyes. Lifting the hem of her gown off the ground as if she expected at any moment something to slither up her legs, she ran toward the buggy.

Rafe followed and swept her into his arms, cradling her against his chest. Free of the ground and the dangers it held, she trembled against him.

"It was just a harmless water snake. Although I couldn't be sure at first. Bound to be some cottonmouths around here."

She buried her head in the crook of his shoulder. "Ugh!" she muttered indelicately.

"That snake is halfway to town, Gabby. Now," he said, bending his head to hers, "where were we?"

One hand curled into a fist and struck him in the back. "We were leaving," she said. She raised her head and stared fearfully around the clearing.

"It's okay," he whispered into her ear. "The snake really is gone. And he really was harmless."

She pulled back and looked skeptically at him, her hands clutching his shoulders for support. A mocking gleam was in his eyes. "There's no such thing as a harmless snake," she said.

"Whatever you say, rancher."

His gently teasing words killed her fear more quickly than any lecture could have done, and she felt like a dimwit. Some rancher she would make. She wasn't nearly as tough as she'd thought, not nearly tough enough for her chosen course. At least not yet.

Suddenly she became aware of his breath on her cheek, of the intimate way he held her in his arms. "You can put me down, Rafe."

"What I'm going to do," he said, heading in the direction of the buggy, "is take you back to town."

Unreasonable disappointment washed through her. In her reaction to that snake, she had obviously made herself look foolish in his eyes.

She shook off the thought. The best thing that had happened to her today was that snake. Otherwise, aroused as she had been by Rafe's kisses, there was no telling what she would have done—against all her resolve and dreams. Given time to take care of her own plans, she might eventually accept marriage, and with it security. But Rafe had hardly offered her that.

Embarrassed by the images in her mind, she struggled against him. Still he held her to his chest, his arms binding her to him, one under her knees, the other around her body, his hand tantalizingly near her breast.

"Pay attention to me, Rafe."

He stopped walking, but her struggles only caused him to grip her more tightly.

"That I am doing, *querida*. And trying to provide a service."

"You're not going to let me forget that, are you? What I said in the bar yesterday wasn't meant for you to hear." She concentrated on the red scarf at his neck. "I may have been . . . talking about something I didn't understand. Sometimes I do that. And I wasn't talking about myself."

"But you weren't necessarily wrong, Gabby. If you think I'm going to take you back to the sanctity of your hotel and bid you good-bye, you don't know me very well." A grin brightened his dark face. "Which of course you don't. A fact I intend to alter."

"Put me down," she said, then added, "please." He did as she asked and she took a cautious step away through the thick grass.

"I guess I should have pushed you away back at the river. Or slapped your face. Or"— she studied the dark lines of his face carefully— "never agreed to come out alone with you in the first place."

Rafe made no move to draw her near. "If we hadn't come out here today, *querida*, we would have seen each other again sometime. Our destinies are entwined." Despite his words, his tone was light.

But as they set off back to town, Gabby wondered why she felt there was truth in his statement.

Chapter Three

Gabby stood on the rough pavement outside a Commerce Street mart and fingered the crucifix that hung around her neck. The sign above the door behind her read ALAMO JEWELERS, PURVEYORS OF FINE METALS, GUNS FOR SALE.

Her eyes were on the man at her side. "I'm not sure I can accept this, Rafe."

"The last time, *querida,* I bought a gift for a woman I was ten years old. The woman was my mother and the gift was a *rebozo,* a scarf of fine wool. I figure if I wait twenty years between gifts, the woman can at least accept my humble offering."

Gabby laughed. "There's nothing humble about you or your gift. It's gold and much too expensive for someone with the troubles you claim."

"The time to be extravagant is when you can't afford it. Otherwise, the gift has little value."

Rafe had a way of surprising her, of keeping her on edge. And of pleasing her very much. The cross, tiny and delicately etched, hung from a thin golden chain.

56

He had insisted on selecting it himself.

Rafe stood close, his breath on her cheek, his velvet brown eyes caressing her. Without another word he helped her into the carriage. She watched his strong hands on the reins as they moved along the crowded street. He turned to pass in front of the Alamo, a short block from the Menger Hotel. What she would do when they got there seemed out of her hands. This feeling of dependence was new and unsettling, but she couldn't call it unwelcome. If a man had his uses, was one of them to help a woman make up her mind?

Her senses were sent reeling by the deafening sound of a gunshot. The horse that had been pulling them so tranquilly reared back, then in his fright plunged ahead without warning.

Instinctively Gabby reached for Rafe to keep from being thrown from the carriage, then looked to the danger that lay ahead. The terrified animal was hurtling them directly into the path of an oncoming trolley car.

Cries of caution and alarm came from the startled onlookers who scurried out of harm's way. It took all of Rafe's strength to avoid disaster as he fought the reins. Gabby stifled a scream and held onto the side of the buggy.

Just when it seemed there was no avoiding a collision, the frightened horse responded to the cut of the bit in his mouth and veered. Miraculously a path opened up in front of them on the crowded street, and Rafe pulled the animal to a halt not ten feet from the door of Gabby's hotel.

"Are you all right?" he asked.

Gabby nodded. "It happened so suddenly."

"But not without plan." Rafe's body was rigid, coiled and ready to spring into action. "Not much bad that's happened to me lately has been an accident. If I could figure how he did it, I'd say Hunter even arranged the drought."

Rafe's eyes settled on the corner of the hotel, and he loosened the gun in his holster. "Just as I figured. Somebody was curious as to whether we'd be hurt or not. And I'd guess disappointed when we weren't."

"You saw who fired the shot?"

"Yes."

He jumped down and secured the horse to a post at the edge of the walk. "Get inside the hotel, Gabby. I've got some unfinished business to attend to. Business I should have taken care of yesterday." His voice was a mixture of anger and resignation, and something far more deadly.

He walked through the parting crowds toward the shadows cast by the hotel. Stunned, Gabby sat in the buggy, her eyes pinned to the tall, lean figure moving away from her. She looked around for a weapon with which to help him and spied only the buggy whip. It wasn't much to protect a man against a bullet, certainly not wielded by someone as inexpert as she.

Frustrated by her impotence, she looked around for help. The crowds that had moments ago responded with cries at their impending peril now turned away. Nothing, after all, had happened but a runaway horse frightened by what sounded like a gunshot. It was much too fine a day, they seemed to be saying, for anything to be wrong.

But Gabby knew different, and from her vantage point in the carriage she scanned the faces around her for the sight of a lawman. She had decided to hurry into the hotel and ask for help when another gunshot rent the air. Without thinking, Gabby dropped to the ground and hurried toward the side of the hotel to find out its source.

The sight that greeted her struck terror in her heart. Rafe stood in the shadowed side street beside the hotel, his attention directed to the swaying figure of a man twenty feet away. Immediately she recognized the man who'd approached her yesterday outside the saloon. Like Rafe, he stood in the middle of the deserted street; like Rafe, he held a gun.

Mesmerized, Gabby stared from one man to the other.

"Luke," Rafe said, "put the gun down. Next time I'll be aiming lower."

"Don' reckon to," Sneed slurred. "I ain't done nothin' wrong." His voice cackled out. "You shore had a hard time gettin' that nag under control."

"Shooting like that was stupid. If you've got a quarrel with me, then face me down."

"I was jus' havin' a little fun."

Fun! If that's all this was about, a drunken fool trying to have a good time, Gabby would soon tell him what she thought of the whole ridiculous matter. Imagine frightening her this way!

She moved forward. The rustling sound of her dress caught Rafe's attention. He didn't have to turn around to know who it was. The hair on the back of his neck bristled.

59

"Yep," Sneed said. "A little fun." His voice turned ugly. "Like you and the woman there. Too bad she picked the wrong man yestiddy."

Gabby stopped. Something in the set of Rafe's body, in the mean look of Sneed and the cruelty of his voice, told her this was not a game.

"Gabby," Rafe said over his shoulder, his eyes still on Sneed, "get back out of here."

"Let 'er stay. You push me too far, Jericho, I'll have to gun you down. Then she'll know who's the real man here." Sneed's revolver waved in the air.

Rafe was careful to hold his own gun steady. There was no reason to rile the fool, not until he made sure Gabby wouldn't be hurt. He had to draw the fire away from her.

He allowed himself a quick look back. Gabby was standing on the sidewalk, her eyes frozen on Sneed. Slowly Rafe moved to his right, away from her. Sneed was most likely a good shot—Hunter wouldn't have hired him otherwise—but he was also drunk.

All the while Rafe talked. "What I can't figure, Luke, is how you knew I'd be coming this way."

Sneed grinned. "I knew the woman was staying here. Figured you'd be sniffing her out. Just like an old hound."

Gabby smothered an indignant cry.

"It's a wonder all the women don't take to you, Sneed," Rafe drawled, "with the sweet way you have of talking."

"Don't do much jawin' with women. Not what they're for."

Gabby was unable to hold her tongue any longer,

and her angry voice spit out at Sneed. "And where would you find a woman who would listen to you?"

Anger flared in Sneed's eyes. "No woman talks to me that way," he snarled.

Rafe turned to warn Gabby away from taunting the drunken gunman, to get her out of the way, but he was too late. The explosion of a gunshot blasted the air. A bullet hit the wall above Gabby's head, showering her with fragments of stone.

"Get down," he yelled, wheeled back to Sneed, and when he saw the gunman's weapon raised to fire once more, pulled the trigger of his own pistol. The bullet slammed into Sneed's chest and he fell, hitting the ground loosely like a sack of feed.

"Damn!" The word echoed in the ringing silence. Rafe watched the fallen body for movement, then slowly closed the distance to kneel in the dusty street. Probing fingers at Sneed's throat told him what he already knew. The man was dead.

"Damn," he said again, this time more in resignation than in anger at what he'd been forced to do.

He pulled himself to his feet and turned to see Gabby standing rigid and white-lipped against the wall. She was about to break, he figured. Any sympathy from him and she would.

He dropped his gun into its holster. "We need a lawman," he said brusquely. "Think you can round one up?"

"Not necessary."

Rafe looked past Gabby to a broad figure behind her leaning against the wall of the hotel. A flat-brimmed hat was pulled low over a craggy face, and the man's thumbs were looped inside his belt. A holster was strapped low on his hips; a pearl-handled Colt rested against each muscled thigh.

Rafe shook his head. "Jeff McGowan. Might have known you'd show up right after all the action is over."

"You're wrong about that. Happens I saw the whole thing. For which you should be glad. Always handy to have a Texas Ranger as a backup when another man draws on you. And I'll be a good witness, too, that you had to shoot him down to save someone else's life, not just your own hide." He glanced at Gabby, and his eyes warmed in appreciation.

Behind McGowan Rafe saw a crowd of curious onlookers round the side of the building and begin to draw near. A uniformed member of the city's armed patrol pushed his way through the crowd. His eyes flashed from McGowan to Rafe, then settled on the body in the street.

"Heard the shooting two blocks away," he said. "Got here as quick as I could. Is he dead?"

McGowan nodded to the officer. "I'll be working with you on this one," he said in a commanding voice. "Clear case of self-defense." One hand tugged briefly at his vest to reveal the badge pinned underneath.

The officer studied McGowan for a minute. "Sure thing, Captain," he said at last, then directed his attention toward the crowd. "Everybody back now. Excitement's over."

He glanced back at McGowan. "I'll be going for help to get that body out of here." He pulled at the jacket of his uniform and turned to make his way through the bunched onlookers. "You keep an eye on

62

it 'til I get back."

As the lawmen talked, Rafe moved closer to Gabby, saw color return to her cheeks, saw the look of horror dim from her blue eyes. Relieved, he turned to McGowan. The Ranger had removed his hat, revealing steady dark eyes above a crooked nose and a large mustache.

"What the hell brings you to San Antonio?" Rafe asked. "I thought you were working out of Dallas now."

"New orders." McGowan's voice was deep and friendly. "I'll be near your place. Remember that in case you need some help."

"I will, *amigo*, I will."

McGowan stepped closer. His attention turned to Gabby with a look that Rafe thought much too appreciative. The lawman had a way with the ladies. Might as well set the rules down now.

"Back off, Ranger," he said softly. "The territory's been staked."

Gabby stared in amazement at the two men. Muttering an exclamation of disgust, she gestured toward the hotel. "Would you two gentlemen like to discuss all this over a cup of tea?"

Her voice was biting and, Rafe was glad to note, under control. Only someone who had heard her speak before would detect a faint tremor of distress.

"You will introduce me, won't you, Jericho?" asked McGowan smoothly.

Gabby shook her head. "I guess four years is too long to have been gone from Texas. I've lost touch with reality. There's a body on the ground, and you two act like it's a social occasion."

Rafe's voice turned low and grim. "Some might say with that particular body it is. That doesn't mean I'm glad I'm the one that did it."

"First time, right?" McGowan asked.

Rafe nodded. "You ever get used to it?"

"Nope. Just don't spread it around. Folks like to think a Ranger is tough."

Gabby reached out to touch Rafe's arm. "You did it," she said, "because I was stupid enough to come running when I heard that shot. I guess I'm in your debt again."

Rafe grinned. "You sure are—in my debt, I mean. You're not stupid. Want to tell me why you came running around that corner?"

"I . . . wanted to be sure you were all right." Her words brought a grin to Rafe's face.

McGowan coughed. "Still haven't got that introduction."

Rafe shrugged. "Can't get out of it, I guess. Gabby, this is an old friend, Captain Jeff McGowan, Texas Ranger. McGowan, Gabrielle Deschamps."

"Pleased to make your acquaintance, Miss Deschamps."

"Captain McGowan, it's my pleasure." She held out her hand to meet his brief clasp. "I guess standing here passing the time of day makes me as crazy as you two."

"Sometimes it's like that after a shooting. The shock comes later." McGowan shifted his broad body and stared down at Gabby, a look of admiration on his seamed face. "I'd like to compliment you, ma'am, for not falling down in a swoon or giving in to a fit of hysterics."

Gabby thought of the body lying a few feet away. "Don't speak too soon," she said, a wan smile on her lips.

Rafe's arm moved around her waist to give her support. Satisfaction was his when she leaned against him. "Not as tough as you thought you were?" he asked. Without waiting for an answer, he turned to McGowan. "I'm taking her to her room. Unless I'll be needed here."

"I'll wait and vouch for you, but come by police headquarters later so they can get a statement." He gestured toward the body. "You happen to know who he is? They might want to notify the next of kin."

"He's Luke Sneed, one of Earl Hunter's thugs. He's been tailing me for the last couple of days."

"I've heard stories about Hunter," said McGowan.

"If the stories are bad, they're most likely true. Now if you have no objection, I'll be getting Miss Deschamps to her room."

The Ranger looked knowingly from Rafe to Gabby. "You take your time getting Miss Deschamps settled."

Rafe's dark eyes flickered with irritation. "Thanks, *amigo*. I'll do that."

"Ah," McGowan said slowly, a smile splitting his craggy face, "so that's the way it is."

Gabby cut off Rafe's reply. "Do you two always carry on this way?"

"For a woman about to give in to the vapors," Rafe said, guiding her toward the side entrance of the Menger, "you have a lot of spirit."

Inside the hotel he ordered a bottle of whiskey sent up to Gabby's room, asked for the key, and within minutes had her in the confines of her suite.

He whistled in appreciation at the large room with its broad feather bed on one side and parlor area on the other.

"You live well," he said, closing the door behind them. "My room at the Southern's not half so fine."

"I treated myself," said Gabby, grateful for the small talk. "I've been quartered in a girls' school for four years."

Rafe stood close beside her. "And you've come back home," he said in a low voice.

Her eyes locked with his. "I've come back to find my home."

His breath was warm on her cheek. "Do you have any objections to my being up here with you?"

"I'm not afraid, if that's what you mean," she said, telling herself she spoke the truth.

"It's your reputation I was thinking of. We drew quite a crowd down there. And in the lobby, too. San Antonio's not such a big city. By morning people around here are going to know who you are. And they're going to know you had a man in your room."

Gabby hid her disappointment behind a shrug. "Are you saying you're going to leave?"

"No," he said softly, his eyes raking her face and lips, "I just want you to understand what my staying might mean."

"It's all right, Rafe," she said softly, her eyes lowered, "if you stay awhile."

A sharp knock at the door broke the spell.

"That'll be the whiskey," said Rafe. "I imagine we both could use a drink."

Gabby sank onto a settee at the far side of the room, grateful for its support. Behind her, the late afternoon sun played at the edges of the partially open curtain.

When Rafe returned to her side, he opened the sealed bottle and poured generous servings of amber liquid into two glasses.

"Here," he said, "drink this."

She stared without speaking at the glass he held out, and he placed it in her hands.

For a brief moment Rafe imagined the room filled with the smell of gunpowder. A sharp image of flashing gunfire and a falling body seared his mind, then was gone. He raised his glass. Disgusted at the unsteadiness of his hand, he downed the whiskey quickly. "Your turn."

Imitating his movements, she sputtered as the sharp whiskey burned her throat.

He sat beside her on the settee and leaned back. "Any of that work its way down to do you some good?"

"A little," she managed to say and set the glass beside his on the table. "At least I can think a little better. That dreadful man said yesterday he wouldn't forget what you did and neither would his boss."

Rafe could see the way her mind was working. "Forget Sneed. He's not a problem any longer."

"And his boss?" Gabby asked, barely giving voice to the fear that had settled in her heart. "Will he send somebody else after you?"

"I don't imagine Earl Hunter sent Sneed to gun me down."

"And I also don't think he planned on Sneed's getting killed."

"Anybody ever tell you that you think too much?"

"Don't change the subject," Gabby said. "What might he do?"

"You'd have to ask Earl Hunter that question. Hunter wants my land. I'm just not sure how far he'll go to get it."

Rafe poured another drink and downed it. This time the glass held steady and he let the liquid warmth settle the taut muscles of his body. Until he relaxed, he hadn't realized how tightly strung he'd been.

Gabby's eyes followed each movement. She couldn't have looked away for the world. "You saved my life down there, Rafe. For someone who has led a very sedate life the past few years, I've gotten myself into a lot of trouble lately." She reached out and touched his hand. "And you've been around to rescue me. Every time."

"Sneed was after me, not you, Gabby. Don't blame yourself for what happened down on the street. I'm the one who should be apologizing to you." He cradled her cheek with one hand, his fingers playing in the tendrils of hair that covered her ear.

His steady gaze bore into her. The killing had shaken Rafe more than she would have thought, considering the easy way he wore his gun. He wasn't a gunman and he wasn't a killer, but he did what had to be done. That didn't mean he liked doing it.

Regardless of his denial, she knew he had saved her from harm. But who would save her from Rafe? Gabby tried to summon the firmness of purpose that might protect her from her own desires, tried in vain to remember just why she'd distrusted men.

He leaned close. Gabby's dark brown lashes curled up thickly from a pair of sapphire eyes. Spun gold hair rested against her face. Everything about her was right. Especially the fires of passion that he knew were stoked within her waiting to burst into flame.

He took the pendant in his fingers, touching only it. "My pledge to you that you will come to no harm," he said, dropping the gold piece back onto her bosom and lightly brushing his fingers downward until he held her by the waist. His touch was light as fairy dust but drew her to him with the strength of iron chains. She moved closer to him on the settee, her thigh pressed to his.

"Ah, *querida*. The word also means lover." He pulled her into his arms. "Someone who will do this." He brushed a light kiss against the corner of her mouth. "And this." His lips trailed to her cheeks and eyes, then back to her lips. The kiss deepened.

A warm longing curled through Gabby, displacing her fears, and she pressed herself tightly against the muscled wall of his chest. After a long, sweet moment Rafe pulled away, and she was startled by the depth of desire she saw in his eyes.

Gabby's fingers traced the angular lines of his face and rested against his lips. She knew she ought to push him away but she couldn't. "Don't stop, Rafe." Her voice was little more than a whisper.

Rafe pulled her back into his arms and covered her face and throat with hungry, relentless kisses. When their lips met at last, the world went away. Gabby was powerless to resist, even if she had wanted to. The warmth she'd felt at his first light kiss became a fire. Whatever reasons she'd given herself for surrender to his will were lost in its flames. Under the spell of his hot kisses, she wanted him in a primal way that had nothing to do with thought.

Her hands rubbed against his shirt, felt the muscles tense, felt the tremor that shook him so deeply it was almost a sound. Instinct guided her, age-old knowledge spurred on by the force of his response.

He pulled away but only to stand and pick her up in his arms. With her head nestled against his shoulder, he carried her to the bed. She expected to be laid down, expected to feel the length of his body on hers. Instead he stood her on her feet and cradled her face in his hands.

"Mi corazon," he whispered, his eyes roving over her face as his lips had done. "My heart. I want to look at you."

Pulling the pins from her hair, he watched the long, honeyed curls tumble about her shoulders. His hands moved down to the collar of her dress. One by one he undid the long row of tiny buttons; deftly he released the tie at her waist. Gabby gave only a passing thought to the skill and smoothness with which he worked, marveled little that he knew so easily the mechanics of a woman's gown.

He slipped the dress from her shoulders and let it fall to the carpet. All the while his eyes burned into

70

hers, dropping only when the gown had been pushed aside.

He gazed at the white shoulders and creamy breasts half exposed above the top of her chemise. His eyes caressed her like velvet.

"You wear a lot of clothes, *corazon*," he said, then proceeded to remove the rest of them, his fingers moving unerringly to the hooks and buttons that secured her undergarments. Only the cross was left in place nestled between her breasts.

When she stood naked before him, a shyness that Gabby hadn't expected overcame her and she tried to cover herself with her arms and hands. Rafe pulled them aside.

"Don't be ashamed." His eyes left her face and moved to the fullness of her high-tipped young breasts, to the gentle curve of her hips, to the fine, pale down between her thighs. His gaze lingered, then trailed the length of her slender legs before moving slowly back to her face. Gabby was indeed a woman — one who would welcome his love.

"Beautiful," he whispered, then drew her into his embrace, his hands stroking where his eyes had been. He held her for a long moment. His breath quickened and his lips pressed against her hair. Whatever Gabby had expected, it wasn't this gentle loving, this slow, inexorable movement into the mists of passion.

She felt like a treasure in his arms, but somehow she knew the next step was hers. She tried to follow the example he had so smoothly set. By the time her nervous fingers had managed to unfasten the scarf at his neck, he was grinning down at her.

"At this rate, Gabrielle," he said, his hands resting lightly on her shoulders, "I'll be an old man when you're through. And not much use to you then."

She opened her mouth to protest but found it covered by his own. He seemed to draw her within him and again she let him take control. Her bare skin against the roughness of his clothing had an electrifying effect on her.

His arms encircled her and his fingers dug lightly into her spine, seeming to count each vertebra on their journey down. They paused, then made little circles in the hollows above the flare of her buttocks, then moved lower to cup her firmly against him. Rafe's muscled strength, she discovered, extended the full length of him and included places that pressed against her in incredibly erotic ways.

By the time he lifted her into his arms and laid her on the bed, she was burning from the sweet torture of his touch. Through passion-drugged eyes she watched him disrobe. His movements were quick and graceful, and when he stood before her in his unleashed magnificence she was reminded of the idealized versions of manhood in statues and paintings.

Only Rafe wasn't painted on canvas or sculpted from marble. He was made of hot, demanding flesh, and beneath a fine layer of dark hair, the skin on his arms and legs was tight and smooth. He knelt, one knee on the bed beside her, his hand on her white breast a startling brown.

He bent to take her breast into his mouth, and the banked fires of Gabby's desire flamed anew. As his fingers moved slowly down her body, gently massaging the path down to her parting thighs, she felt her body moist and warm and waiting. Everything was happening without her will. Everything that was happening was right.

And good. So very good, she thought as she felt his hand move to her inner thigh. Then slowly upward. When at last he caressed her with gentle, gradually quickening thoroughness, a passion of unimagined urgency coursed through her; with hands clutching at the taut sinews of his arms, she writhed beneath his touch.

"Rafe," she pleaded, little realizing what she begged for, knowing only that she wanted more.

"It is time," he whispered into her open mouth.

His hand parted her legs wider and he laid his body on top of hers, pressing her down into the soft bed with the weight of his flesh.

He covered her mouth with his own as their bodies joined. He swallowed her cry of pain. A pleasure born of that pain obliterated everything but the desire to follow his guidance and return the slow, even movements of his hips and thighs. The tingling sensations that she had felt from his hand multiplied with the increasing tempo of their rhythmic thrusts and at last, with her hands raking his back, exploded into ecstasy.

"Rafe!" Her cry mingled with his. Deep shudders rent his powerful body, matching her own shattering tremors, and she followed him into the dark ethereal void of passion fulfilled. Her arms tightly enfolded him, as though to let go would cast her adrift forever. She reveled in the feel of his sweat-slick strength, in the musky smell of him, in the sound of her name whispered fervently into her ear.

How easy it was to give herself up to him, to let him hold her in the aftermath of their lovemaking, to return slowly to the world, still clinging to him, drawing strength as her own was spent. Her first wild demands satisfied, she discovered another, unexpected need—the need for a comfort of her own. The need for his love.

An unspoken bond held them as he cradled her in his arms. His breathing slowed. How sweet it was to lie in his arms. How safe. What harm would be done if she trusted herself to him? With the way he made her feel, forever wouldn't be too long. Whatever barriers she'd erected around her heart had fallen in the onslaught of his passion and, more importantly, of his caring. With dusk settling on the world outside her room, she fell asleep.

Consciousness returned slowly, interrupting her dream of a dark-haired man carrying her through a mist of unseen danger. It was the first romantic dream she'd experienced in her life.

The room was dark and she was alone in the bed. She'd never before fallen asleep with a man's arms around her, and she'd expected him to be there when she awoke.

She sat up in the bed and clutched the covers to her naked body. Her heart pounded. Had Rafe Jericho taken what he wanted and then left without saying good-bye? Even as she lectured herself against disappointment, her spirit soared when she heard movement on the other side of the room.

"Ah, *querida*." His soft voice caressed her. "I've been

waiting for you."

Relief flooded her. He sounded—she searched for the word—possessive. The thought delighted her. She wanted him there with her, she wanted to tell him how changed she felt, how much she wanted him again. And yet with that growing desire to call him to her bed again came a rising panic that she should have such thoughts. Would he turn out after all to be like the men her mother had told her about?

In the dark, a match burst into flame and she could see the shadowed planes of Rafe's face. She let her eyes linger, watched as he lit the lamp in front of the window, followed his movements as he walked across the room toward the bed. She felt a sharp disappointment that he was dressed.

Clad in the same shirt and trousers he'd had on earlier, he looked somehow different. After a moment she realized why. She knew what lay beneath those tight-fitting clothes, had touched his muscled strength, had felt his flesh against hers. A loss of innocence, it was called. For the first time she understood the phrase.

He sat beside her and took her hands in his. "Are you all right?"

She smiled in happiness. "All right? I'm certainly that. And I hope a little more."

"Then the first time was not a disappointment." His fingers touched her lips. "There's no need to answer that, Gabby. You've already told me in other ways."

"And for you?" she asked softly, embarrassed that she wanted to hear him give voice to what she read in his eyes.

"Ah, *querida*, I have much to tell you." He shook his head in disgust. "It is unfortunate that I must leave."

The memory of the shooting intruded into the dark room. Rafe had to give the police and McGowan an account of what had happened.

"Do you want me to come with you?" she asked.

"If the police need you, they can talk to you later. Just stay in bed and think about tomorrow. I know I'll think of little else."

His good-bye kiss was lingering and held a warm promise of more to come. She took pleasure in watching his long-legged, graceful movements as he walked away from her.

He paused in the doorway, then moved quickly back to the bed and pulled her into his arms. This time his kiss was hard and hot and left her breathless. His lips burned against her throat and inched slowly down to press against the cross between her breasts.

Then he was gone.

Chapter Four

Earl Hunter hated Rafael Jericho. More than he coveted Jericho's land, more than he wanted power, more than he cared for Sarah, the rancher's daughter he'd married three years ago, he longed to bring about the bastard's ruin.

Jericho had two things Hunter wanted most in life — the Arroyo Seco and the affection of his wife. And for once he saw a chance to do something about getting them for his own. The financially troubled Seco was within his grasp — he could almost taste the victory — and Sarah was enough of a realist to stay with him when Rafe was brought to ruin.

Hunter had fallen privy to some very interesting information concerning the ownership of the Arroyo Seco — a source that would shock a few citizens of Laredo. After that, he kept watch until Rafe left for San Antonio. Hunter, too, had business in the city and, taking along a couple of his men, he had followed.

He may have lost one of those men, but the loss

had been worth what he'd gained, worth the long wait at the corner table in the Menger Hotel restaurant while his enemy was with the woman upstairs.

Hunter was good at knowing a man's weaknesses. Until today he'd found only two of Jericho's—his grandfather and his land. Now there was a third, a woman. He'd known she was in town and what she was after, but he hadn't known what she looked like. Her fair beauty had indeed been a pleasant surprise.

For the past three years he'd been studying Rafe carefully. There had been women before, but Rafe always kept them at the edge of his life. But not this one. Hunter had known it as soon as he saw the two together yesterday when they arrived at the hotel. He'd been in the lobby when Rafe escorted her inside, and the looks that passed between them had been unmistakable.

They'd been inseparable all day today—another first for Jericho. He'd even gone so far as to buy her a gift, an intimate one. Jewelry. It was enough to warm Hunter's heart—especially since he knew what the woman was up to. He admired her style.

As soon as he'd learned of Gabrielle Deschamps' existence, he had a feeling she was the weapon he was looking for. And he'd been right. At the least she would prove a valuable distraction, even if she didn't get what she was after. And if she did, that was all right, too. He'd a damned sight rather deal with a woman than a man like Rafe.

Hunter's thin lips twisted into a smile. He liked the irony that a woman could be Jericho's undoing, considering the soft look in Sarah's eyes every time his name cropped up. Hunter would take a great deal of pleasure in seeing Jericho hurt.

He fingered the broad-brimmed white hat that he always wore, then dropped it on the chair beside him. At age forty Hunter looked like a man of property. His suit was of fine broadcloth, tailored to fit his thickening body. His silk vest covered a white shirt and at his neck was a black string tie.

Appearances mattered to Hunter—almost as much as getting his way. He'd been born to the ruling class, a Southern plantation family wiped out by the Civil War. Like others of his generation, he had been left with no land, no home, no roots to hold him.

But for Hunter the war hadn't been a total loss. A wild young man, he'd learned skills as he fought his way across Georgia that no planter's son should know. He'd learned to kill. He'd learned to survive. Most of all he'd learned that it didn't matter how you got what you wanted—as long as you won.

If Sherman and his troops hadn't burned their way across his land, he would most likely be mired in cotton farming, married to a Southern belle and siring offspring among the servants. That was a soft life, meant to be lived in a land that no longer existed. Hunter intended to recreate at least part of it in arid South Texas, no matter what he had to do.

During the war and its destructive aftermath, he'd grown mean, mean enough to get by in a tough place during tough times. Along with the others without a home, he'd drifted west, skirted the law, toughened as the years passed. The meanness that was in him grew, and so did the bitterness. But he'd also grown smart. By the time he had arrived in Laredo three years ago, he was ready to settle.

He'd done all right in marrying Sarah Miller, the lusty, well-fleshed daughter of a border rancher. He had even come to care for her. Her father's ranch was big and well stocked — a tempting plum as ripe as Sarah herself. Hunter wanted it for his own. Nathaniel Miller had had to die.

But since Miller's death Hunter had discovered he wasn't cut out to be a rancher. He had lost money through bad management and the drought that had hurt the other landowners too. He lacked the funds to buy up Rafe's loan, but if a man was smart enough there were other ways to make money, ways like smuggling stolen horses and cattle across the Mexican border. For that he needed access to the river and men to do the work.

He felt pleased, remembering the consternation among his neighbors when he'd fired most of the vaqueros that Miller had employed and brought in gunmen to pose as cowhands. Some were thugs like Sneed and he paid them little. Others were smart and tough, particularly Dallas Pryor, who had traveled with him to San Antonio along with the foolhardy Sneed.

He'd first seen Pryor in a saloon brawl and liked the way he handled himself. The man Pryor had beaten, a popular figure around Laredo, claimed the drifter had been cheating at cards. He changed his tune when Pryor was through with him, but Hunter had found it necessary to spread a little folding money around to get Pryor out of trouble. The money had been well spent. Pryor had come to be his best hand.

To match the hardened men, he got himself a pack of dogs that owed allegiance to him and him alone.

Nobody called his spread the Miller Ranch anymore. It was known as Rancho Perro. Dog Ranch. The name had a mean, tough sound that Hunter liked.

The setup was fine. The only thing he lacked was a direct route from the United States into Mexico. For that he needed Jericho's land, which stretched along the river separating the two countries.

He'd tried to scare Jericho and his grandfather off, tried to break them with acts of vandalism. Nothing had worked—not the rustling of the Seco herd nor the poisoning of its breeding stock.

For his efforts Hunter had received a bitter reward—the stretch of barbed wire that now blocked his path to the Rio Grande. Every time he cut the wire, Jericho or one of his men was there to repair the damage.

And now a herd of potentially valuable sheep was grazing on the north end of the Seco. Instead of weakening under the obstacles Hunter was throwing his way, Rafe Jericho was expanding his operations. Jericho was proving a hard man to bring down.

But most of all there was Sarah, who had taken to looking at him with scorn, especially when he was cursing Rafe. She hadn't said anything about his firing the vaqueros, but he sometimes wondered if she were suspicious about old Nathaniel's death. If she was, she never let on. With Sarah he could never be sure.

What she did let her husband know was that she still wanted Rafe Jericho, even though years ago he'd turned his back on a plan, hatched by Ben Hidalgo and Nathaniel Miller, for the two of them to marry and the ranches to merge.

81

She never said it directly, but he'd seen the way she looked at Rafe when they passed him in town. Once, in the midst of their lovemaking, she'd cried out his name. Earl Hunter had reason to hate.

Hunter directed his attention to the doorway that led to the Menger lobby. Standing just inside the restaurant was Dallas Pryor, his black pig eyes trained on the winding staircase that led to the second floor. Pryor would let him know when Rafe walked through the lobby.

Hunter trusted Pryor, even while he viewed him with distaste. The gunman's hard-lined face was stubbled with a two-day's growth of beard. The scarf knotted loosely around his neck was sweat-stained, and the sleeves of his cotton shirt were rolled halfway up to reveal powerful, hairy arms that reminded Hunter of an ape. Pryor might be the best hand he had, but he would never be taken for a gentleman.

Suddenly he saw Pryor's body stiffen, then after a moment relax. Pryor turned and headed for Hunter's table, which was well out of the path of traffic. He dropped his swarthy body into a chair and reached for his glass of whiskey. "Jericho's gone. Sure you don't want me to follow him?"

"I know where he's going, Dallas. To the city marshal to give a statement about the shooting. You overheard McGowan say so to the lawman after Jericho left the scene."

Pryor scowled. "If I'd been there a few minutes earlier he couldn't have been in any condition to leave."

"Don't make the mistake of underestimating Rafe Jericho the way that fool Luke did. He's not a gunman, but he's tough."

"And I'm not Luke Sneed, either. You let me follow him now and I'll take care of him."

"He's mine," Hunter said. "When the time is right."

"At least we'd know where he was for sure. I don't like leaving anything to chance."

"I'm not. We've known where Rafe Jericho has been every minute since he got to town." Hunter's voice hardened. "He'll go down and give his statement and then likely be given a medal for killing Luke."

Pryor signaled the waiter for another drink, then turned to Hunter. "Since when do you give a damn about Luke Sneed?"

Hunter viewed Pryor's empty glass with disdain. "This isn't a saloon, Dallas," he said.

"I don't know what the hell we're doing hanging around here anyway," Pryor said.

"We were waiting for Jericho to leave. Let's give him a few minutes more and then join him at the station. See what story he tells."

Pryor studied Hunter. "You're up to something. I've got so I can smell it. Ever since he started hanging around that woman, you've been tighter'n a tick."

"I'm always up to something, Dallas." He patted the envelope tucked inside his coat pocket. "And sometimes things just fall into my lap. What did our friend Mr. Jericho look like to you just now? Any signs of remorse that he'd killed a man?"

"Had a satisfied look to him. Like he'd been humping a woman."

"Crudely put but I'm sure accurate." Hunter's pale eyes narrowed in speculation. "The fair Miss Gabrielle Deschamps. When I first found out what she was up to, I wasn't sure she might not just get in the way. That's why we came up here, to find out. But I sure as hell liked the way she managed to meet Jericho without arousing his suspicion. It begins to look as though she might help our cause."

"How you figure that? She ain't the first woman spent some time in bed with Jericho."

"Read the signs, Dallas. Learn. When did you ever know Rafe to put himself out for a woman? They usually come to him. But with Miss Deschamps he escorts her for a picnic and then makes a stop to buy her a gift. Before he takes her to bed. He even takes her to her meeting with the lawyer."

Hunter laughed out loud. "I'd bet the family farm he doesn't know what she was there for. Even if she doesn't win her case—and I'd rather deal with her than Rafe and that fool of a grandfather—she'll keep him tied up in court so long he won't have time or money to fight us."

Pryor's black eyes peered at Hunter in satisfaction. "Damned if I know how you find out these things, Earl."

"My sources of information, Dallas, are none of your concern. A little luck—like seeing him stop by a jewelry store—but mostly careful planning. And a few well-placed dollars in the right hands never hurts."

Hunter signaled the waiter for another drink. "Now I'd say we wait a little longer and then head out for that city marshal's office and start spreading a little of our information around."

Outside the Menger Hotel a hint of autumn hung

on the September night. The cool air brought a briskness to Rafe's stride as he returned the rented carriage and caught a street car to the Bat Cave, the decrepit building on Military Plaza halfway across town where the city marshal's headquarters were housed.

Inside the musty offices he found Jeff McGowan had smoothed the path for him with the town authorities, and his business was quickly taken care of. He nodded to the Ranger, who was sprawled in a chair beside him.

"Thanks for your help, Jeff."

"Figured you hadn't done anything like this before," McGowan said. "The marshal ought to give you a medal for taking Luke Sneed out."

"You got time for a drink?" Rafe asked.

McGowan grinned. "You're not headed back for the hotel?"

"Tomorrow. Give the woman some time to think. Not that I plan to let her make any decision other than the one I want."

McGowan's face grew solemn. "Sounds serious."

Rafe thought about Gabby and the way things had been between them in the hotel. He'd never been more serious about anything in his life. Serious enough to tell a friend like Jeff McGowan, but not here in the city marshal's office.

"How about that drink?" he asked.

"Sorry. I'll be tied up here for a while longer. Probably won't catch you again 'til I get down your way on the border."

Rafe nodded and headed for the door. Maybe it was best to be alone for a while and make some plans.

A great deal had happened to him during the past day and a half. He'd managed to buy a little time at the bank. He'd killed a man and he'd found his woman.

His woman. Could it really be the truth? He knew damned little about Gabby—except the way she fit in his arms and the way they got along. Yet with Gabby it was more than just sex, although he'd never had it better, never been moved as deeply as he had been with her.

She was *simpatico,* the way a mate ought to be. Concerned about his troubles, interested in what interested him. She wasn't at all like most women he'd met.

Rafe wasn't used to being—he struggled for the word—*comforted.* His mother, Consuelo, Ben's only child, had been like a bright flame, warming and shedding light, but a fire didn't hold a child or caress him. Rafe had gotten more steady attention from his father Sam Jericho, the ranch foreman she'd fallen in love with and married.

Consuelo taught him to enjoy life. Sam gave him a need for constancy, a love of ranching, a desire for something to belong to and to nurture. The two had been killed years ago when a carriage Consuelo was driving too fast overturned, but the young boy they left behind had learned his lessons well.

For a long time the companionship of Ben had been enough, but lately Rafe had grown restless. He was thirty years old, and it was time he took a wife.

With her passionate nature that matched his own and the way she had of leaning on him even as she gave him support, Gabby was the one for him. And, by damn, he thought, grinning, after very little practice she had learned to kiss better than any woman he had ever held in his arms. She cared for him as much as he cared for her. Some things in his life were just meant to be.

His stride lengthened as he headed down the hall-way toward the outer door. He pulled up short when he recognized the figure walking toward him. Earl Hunter.

Hunter was two inches shorter than Rafe and twenty pounds heavier. He might dress like a gentle-man, Rafe thought, but it would take more than clothes to cover the hard-bitten look about him or the shifty movements of his watery gray eyes set deep under husky eyebrows.

Hunter was a thug. He'd proven that to Rafe by firing his vaqueros and replacing them with a passel of men no better than Luke Sneed—and some much worse. For a while old Ben had let Hunter cross the Seco to the river. But there had been too many instances of trouble between Hunter's men and Ben's. When Rafe decided to mortgage the ranch, he made sure there was enough cash to put up the fence.

Whatever Hunter was up to on his spread, Rafe didn't like him. There was a grasping edge to the man, as though he were always looking for an angle to play. Rafe had known gamblers with that same look, ones who tried to deal from the bottom of the deck.

Hunter paused beside him in the narrow hallway. "Just the man I expected to see, although I was hoping they would throw you behind bars for the killing today."

Rafe tried to pass but stopped when Hunter's arm

shot up to block the way.

"He fired first," Rafe said. "You should have trained him better. Or hired someone smarter to trail me." His dark eyes burned steadily at Hunter, then moved to the figure standing in the doorway to the street. Dallas Pryor, Hunter's shadow. The air in the hallway became close and stale.

Rafe looked again at Hunter. "If you've got anyone smarter than Sneed. He may have been the best you have."

Pryor growled in anger, but Hunter silenced him with a glance.

"Sneed was a fool," Hunter said. "He wasn't supposed to be hanging around the hotel."

"At least you're not denying you had me followed."

"I'm interested in everything you do, Jericho. Your grandfather is a stubborn old fool. I figure I can get the Seco through you."

"You're figuring wrong, senor." Again Rafe started to pass.

"Hold up." Hunter looked at Rafe with malevolent eyes. "We've got a score to settle up. Fool or not, Sneed was still my man. You can't get away with killing him."

Rafe dropped both arms to his sides, elbows bent, a thumb casually hooked over the front of his gun belt. It was a deceptively casual pose.

"If you're willing enough to try something with a Texas Ranger in the next room," he said, "then I'm game. I say we go outside and settle this now."

"Hot tempered, aren't you? I'm not even packing a gun."

"I don't suppose you are. Not as long as you can

hire men to do it for you." Rafe settled into a relaxed stance, suddenly enjoying the confrontation. "Hunter, I don't think you're very bright, letting your ranch go the way you are. Sarah was a fool to marry you and her father an even bigger one for letting her. Well, he paid the price. I never could figure out how he managed to get himself trampled to death."

Hunter's eye twitched. "Careful what you say, Jericho. There was nothing suspicious about the way Nathaniel Miller died."

"Nothing except he'd been working cattle all his life. And you got everything that had been his."

"If you're trying to goad me into a fight, it won't work. Although you might have a tougher time taking me down than you think." Hunter's hardened face broke into a humorless grin. "Talk is all I want. Talk about that little filly you have back at the hotel."

Rafe's hands curled into fists. His eyes narrowed dangerously. "What the hell are you getting at, Hunter?"

"Just the truth about Gabrielle Deschamps. Something I doubt she's told you. You know she plans to file suit against your grandfather for title to his land?"

Hunter's smile grew genuine, and Rafe fought the urge to smash his face. "Earl," he said with deadly calm, "have you been hitting the bottle today?"

"I'm as sober as you are. And a hell of a lot more clearheaded. Wait until you hear it all, Jericho. A slick little operator, Miss Deschamps. I guess she's a little like her mother, Colette."

Hunter paused, and Rafe waited with him. There was no way he would give Hunter the satisfaction of asking what his point was.

"Quite a woman, Colette Deschamps. At least that's what I heard. She died about ten years ago, but there are men around San Antonio who still remember her. That's quite a tribute for a whore. A high-priced one, for sure, but still a whore."

Hunter waited for a reaction, got none, and shrugged. "A courtesan, I think she preferred to be called. Sounded better to the rich Germans who hired her. At least that's what I hear."

"What's all this got to do with a suit against the Seco? You're full of bullshit, Earl."

"Keep listening, Jericho. I noticed you haven't left yet. You may even thank me for the investigating I've been doing."

He ignored the scornful look that shadowed Rafe's face. "Colette married the son of Carlos Cordero just before he got killed in the Civil War. Now I know you've heard of the Corderos. They used to own most of your spread."

Hunter pushed back his white Stetson and used his middle finger to smooth the red crease left on his forehead.

"You're lying, Hunter," Rafe said, eyeing his opponent's nervous gesture.

"Easy to check. Miss Deschamps went to see her lawyer this morning about filing that suit. I believe you took her, as a matter of fact. You mean in all the time you've been spending together she didn't say what that meeting was about?"

Doubt about Gabby was slow coming. Rafe had been so sure of her. He may have allowed himself to make plans without even considering what had brought her back to San Antonio, but he wasn't going

90

to change directions at the word of a man like Earl Hunter.

"I'll bet she and that lawyer had a good laugh about you over there in the bank negotiating over some land that you'll never inherit," Hunter said. "I've never met the lady or her lawyer, but I have to admit I like the way she works."

Rafe tried to picture the scene Hunter was describing—Gabby's eyes alight with an avaricious gleam, the laughter she shared with Oscar Cantu. He couldn't do it.

"I still say you're lying."

Hunter reached inside his jacket and Rafe's hand moved toward his gun. In the background Dallas Pryor shifted his position, both hands tense, inches away from the guns he was wearing.

"Careful, Rafe," Hunter said. "I told you I wasn't armed. Only wanted to give you this." He pulled out a folded envelope. "It's a copy of a letter she sent to the lawyer while she was still back east."

Rafe hesitated to take it and Hunter thrust it into his hand. "Read it later. You'll find it interesting, I'm sure."

"Where did you get this, Hunter? Assuming it contains the information you say it does."

"My source must remain my business and mine alone. Needless to say, Miss Deschamps knows nothing about that copy. She'll be as surprised as you."

"You're not getting the Seco, Hunter," Rafe said, his voice steady. "Whether or not you're lying about Miss Deschamps."

"You're a fool." Hunter settled his hat back in its place, all nervousness gone. His mouth twitched in anger. "I offered you a good price."

"There's nothing you own, Hunter, that would make me change my mind. Besides, the ranch is Ben's land. That scrub brush has worked its way into his blood. And mine."

His voice rasping with anger grown to fury, Hunter said, "Listen here, you better start protecting that blood before some of it's spilled."

"Need any help?" Jeff McGowan's voice was quiet behind them.

Rafe turned to face him. "A lot of vermin in here," he said. "I'm just trying to get around a rat."

"Captain," Hunter said, his voice once more under control, "they letting this man go? He's a killer."

McGowan shook his head. "That's not the way I see it. It happens I witnessed the shooting. I'd be more likely to go after the man that hired this Luke Sneed and set him on Mr. Jericho."

Hunter's pale eyes shifted from McGowan to Rafe and back to the Ranger. "You two a team or something?"

"It was a clear case of self-defense," McGowan said. "But if you don't mind stepping in the back, the marshal might want to ask a few questions about the dead man. Just to clear up some loose ends."

"Not at all, Captain," Hunter said smoothly, then turned to Rafe. "Don't forget what I was telling you, Jericho. And you might take a look at that letter. It should make for interesting reading." Following the Ranger's gesture, he headed for the door at the end of the hall.

McGowan followed, pausing in the doorway to study Rafe. "You sure everything is all right? You don't look like the same man who was talking to me a while ago."

"Hunter." Rafe hoped the answer would satisfy. He had a lot of thinking to do and he was glad McGowan hadn't taken him up on his offer for a drink. He needed some time alone to work things out.

"Well," McGowan said, doubt still in his voice, "give Miss Deschamps my regards."

Rafe gestured a quick good-bye and headed for the Hole-in-the-Wall Saloon across the street. He ordered a bottle of whiskey and made his way to a back table where he wouldn't be disturbed, the envelope that Hunter had forced on him burning in his hand.

For several moments he held it unopened, debating whether to destroy it unread. It was probably just more vicious innuendoes about Gabby's past.

Two drinks later he was staring at the open pages on the table, stunned into a momentary acceptance of what he read. Maybe Hunter hadn't been lying after all, at least not if the letter was genuine. It was all laid out before him—the story of her parents' quick marriage and of her father's dreams about regaining what he claimed was his inheritance. She'd instructed the lawyer Cantu to proceed with his investigations of her case.

He wasn't sure whether she wanted only what had once belonged to the Corderos or the entire spread, but it was all the same to him. Gabby was after his land.

She'd told him she was going into ranching. She'd even asked him to tell her about the problems he was facing. Just probing to find his weaknesses was all and hoping, no doubt, to be added to the list of them.

You arrogant bastard, Rafe told himself. He'd been so sure she wanted to sacrifice her virginity because of him. What she'd really been after was something she obviously considered far more valuable. The Seco.

As if he would let a woman come between him and the ranch. She thought he'd become so damned smitten with her he'd do whatever she asked. Even get old Ben to sign whatever papers she waved his way.

Rafe had never experienced thoughts like the ones that now whipped at him with such pain, at their center an image of golden-haired Gabrielle Deschamps with her look of an angel and her full, sensual lips that begged to be kissed. He might have known she was too good to be true. No wonder she had been eager to give up her innocence. It was merely something she'd held in reserve to trade — an asset to be used as her mother had done before her.

At least he found out the truth before he'd made a bigger fool of himself, he thought. And then he felt a niggling doubt playing at the back of his mind. He'd found out, all right — maybe too neatly and from the one man he knew to be his enemy — and he pulled away from the anger that threatened to erupt. How in hell had Hunter got hold of the letter? Maybe spread a little money around? He might even have created it himself, just to cause trouble. Rafe wouldn't put anything past him.

There were a lot of *mights* and *maybes* here, too many for Rafe to accept without question.

He crushed the letter and balled it between the palms of his hands, then squeezed it, seeing not paper but Earl Hunter's neck. What Rafe needed to do was see Gabby and get her explanation before going off half-cocked.

He didn't bother with transportation but settled on a long walk back to the Menger. He needed the air to clear his mind. Would Gabby still be lying in bed naked beneath the covers the way he'd left her? Would the cross be nestled between her breasts?

His body tightened at the remembrance and the way she had responded to him. There were some things Gabby hadn't been faking. Rafe knew women. She'd enjoyed their lovemaking as much as he. Despite his doubts, despite the heavy heart he carried within him, he felt a stirring inside at the memory.

He walked through the hotel's double doors and came to a halt. Standing at the desk was the familiar figure of Franklin Bernard, a Laredo lawyer prominent in Webb County politics. Rafe had never had legal dealings with him, but Laredo wasn't so large a place that their paths didn't occasionally cross.

". . . 201," he heard the clerk say. "I believe Miss Deschamps is in. Would you like me to send a message that you're here, Mister Bernard?"

"Just let her know that I'm in town and will drop by the hotel in the morning. I won't disturb her tonight."

When Bernard turned to leave, Rafe moved away from the door, out of the lawyer's line of vision. He stared grim-faced at the man. Here at least was tangible proof that Hunter had been right. In Rafe's mind at last was the picture he'd been unable to imagine earlier—of Gabby smiling in triumph over her deception. She'd hired a Laredo lawyer; only a fool would believe she wanted his help in obtaining just any land.

Rafe didn't know the full story about how the

Cordero ranch had been combined into the Seco, only that Ben had bought it cheap after Carlos Cordero had been judged a traitor in the Texas revolution. Ben didn't like to talk much about it; all Rafe knew was there had been bad blood between the two men. Gabby could possibly have a case.

Or—more likely—she hoped to get what she wanted through the owner's grandson. Was she willing to marry him for it, or just weave a spell to bring him to her side? Rafe was damned tired of speculating. There was only one person who could give him any answers, and he headed for the stairs to give her the chance.

Gabby was half asleep when she heard the pounding on the door and an insistent voice saying, "I need to see you." She stirred beneath the warm sheet, then stretched slim arms above her head, feeling a delicious sense of fulfillment she wanted to continue to savor.

But the banging on the door brought her reluctantly awake. Again she heard her name, and a tremor ran through her as she recognized the voice. Scrambling from beneath the covers, she called out, "Just a moment."

Hurriedly she slipped into a wrapper of Brunswick blue mull. Perhaps, she thought as she put her arms into the wide sleeves and tied the belt at her waist, the gossamer-like garment wasn't the proper clothing in which to receive a gentleman caller, but under the circumstances this particular gentleman would most certainly understand. With a shiver of joy she considered the years she could spend teaching him what a lady she really was.

She opened the door to a Rafe Jericho far different

from the one who had left her only two hours before. A strong odor of whiskey entered the room with him, and he wasn't smiling in his usual admiring way, taking time to rest his eyes on hers and then on her lips in a gaze as tender as his touch. Instead, he avoided looking directly at her as he strode into the room. When he whirled around, she was startled by the piercing anger directed toward her.

"What's wrong, Rafe?" she asked, concerned only that something terrible must have happened to him. "Did you have trouble about Luke Sneed's death?"

It took Rafe a second to realize what Gabby was referring to. He'd been deeply shaken by the shooting, and here he was a few hours later barely able to recall it. And no wonder, with Gabby standing so close to him, her soft and golden hair falling free around her face, her slender body provocatively visible through the filmy clothes.

But he'd fallen into that particular trap before, and he looked at her with an uncompromising stare. "I'd forgotten all about Sneed. Something else came up."

His words were heavy with insinuations she couldn't begin to understand. Whatever the something was, it must be bad to trouble him so, especially when he'd left her a short while ago in a vastly different mood. Nothing short of a disaster could have brought about such a change.

"Would you like a drink?" she asked, closing the door and turning once again to study him. "I imagine there's plenty left in the bottle you ordered earlier."

"I tried whiskey already, Gabby, and it didn't work. What I need are a few answers. Why are you here in San Antonio? What brought you back?"

Whatever Gabby was expecting, it certainly wasn't an interrogation, and she answered sharply, "I told you. To get a ranch."

"So you did." He measured his words out carefully. "You just didn't tell me which one."

Gabby's instinct was to protect herself against the ill will implied in his words. Her eyes flashed in anger and she tossed her head back proudly, blond curls falling loosely on her shoulders. "You didn't ask."

"That I didn't, Gabby. Score one point for you."

Gabby couldn't believe this was happening. She'd arisen from a half-sleep, still cushioned by her young woman's dreams of a first and forever lover, only to have him barge in and begin an inquisition.

"You act as though I'm playing a game, Rafe," she said, embarrassed that her face was flushed with distress. "I don't know what you're getting at."

"Come on, Gabby. You're smart enough to figure it out. I know the ranch you're after. The Arroyo Seco. Or"—his voice lowered—"can you tell me I'm wrong? God knows I wish you would."

"You're speaking in riddles. I'm not about to deny something that's true."

Without blinking, her eyes held his, and she saw in their brown depths a glimpse of a private, living hell.

The look was quickly gone, so quickly she doubted it ever existed, and an unreadable mask slipped over his features.

"Then you are after the Seco. Are you going to deny you know who I am?" Rafe said.

Rafe stood still only a few feet from her, but she felt the distance growing, felt him slipping away. Who could he be that his identity should be known to her?

He was a Texas rancher, one who had troubles — but then there were thousands of men who fit that description.

Until she'd met him, there was only one such man she hoped to meet, Benito Hidalgo. Rafe hardly fit the description she'd heard of old Ben.

And then she knew.

A sharp intake of breath, then she said in a whisper, "You're Hidalgo's grandson."

"Very good, Gabrielle. You almost sound surprised."

His words were like a slap. "You think I'm lying?" she asked.

Rafe studied her for a long time, fighting the urge to forget what he'd found out and pull her into his arms. He shielded himself against the vulnerable look that had attracted him when he'd first seen her. No doubt it was just a pose.

"I'd move heaven and earth to believe otherwise," he said. "Convince me I'm wrong."

Gabby wanted to strike out at him, to hurt him as much as his words hurt her. However he had found out her purpose in coming back to Texas, he'd been quick to believe the worst about her. It was an experience she'd grown used to as a child, this being condemned without cause, but she hadn't expected it from Rafe. As she stood looking at him in the dim light she felt something inside her die.

"You left here with words of love on your lips, Rafe. What happened while you were gone?"

"Earl Hunter happened. I don't suppose you've met him, have you? He has a way of destroying things. I told you he's been keeping an eye on me. Apparently he's been watching you, too."

The import of his words left her stunned. Earl Hunter had obviously accused her of unspeakable things. And Rafe had listened to the man he'd called enemy rather than to the woman he professed to care for deeply. She would not—she could not—defend herself against such an assault. Not when she had given Rafe everything. He couldn't even give her his trust.

"Believe what you have to, Rafe. I've come to claim a small portion of what is rightfully mine. And I don't intend to lose."

There it was, he thought, the issue settled, but still he couldn't let it go. "Did you really think you could get at Ben through me? My grandfather is much too smart an old man for that scheme to work."

How little he thought of her, how little he knew what she was really like. When she had been pliable, sympathetic, responsive to everything he asked of her, he had wanted her for his own. But the woman he'd made love to wasn't the real Gabrielle Deschamps, just a fool who had forgotten her way for a while.

"I didn't scheme, Rafe, no matter what you think. Get that much straight. But I also have no intention of backing down on my claim. I don't want the entire ranch, just enough of my grandfather's land to give me security."

"Carlos Cordero, the traitor?"

"You seem to throw a lot of accusations around." Gabby heard the tremor in her voice and hated the sound. She would not break down in front of him. She absolutely would not. Oscar Cantu had warned that the pursuit of her land would be difficult. He had no idea just how prophetic he had been.

She held the skirt of her thin wrapper around her and stepped aside to leave him a clear path to the door. "I suggest you go now, Rafe. It would seem we have nothing more to say to one another. I don't intend to defend myself to you any longer. What hurts is that it was ever necessary."

"Let's just say you didn't do a very good job of answering my questions, *querida*. I wish you had." Rafe paused in the doorway. "I almost forgot. There's a message for you at the desk. Another of your attorneys, Franklin Bernard, is in town and will meet with you tomorrow. Plan well, Gabby. I warn you now you are in for a fight."

Chapter Five

Two days later Gabby sat in the waiting room of the International and Great Northern Railroad, her heart and mind wrapped in a thick, protective casing of resignation and renewed vows. If her eyes were a little too wide as she looked around the crowded room, and her smile a little too rigid, there was no one present who knew her well enough to ask what was wrong—except Erin—and Erin had developed a decided myopia as far as Gabby's demeanor was concerned. She simply did not seem to notice that anything was wrong.

The train would be pulling out soon for the day-long trip to Laredo and to the destiny that had awaited Gabby since her birth. Nothing that had happened during her brief stay in town had changed that, nothing that she couldn't eventually forget.

Gabby glanced sideways at her nearby friend. Erin knew Gabby had seen Rafe again, knew about the shooting of Luke Sneed, but Gabby hadn't told her who Rafe Jericho really was. She would save that little bit of news for a letter. Otherwise, the impulsive gambler would most certainly be traveling with her on the train.

As if she could read her thoughts, Erin moved closer to her on the bentwood bench. "Gabrielle," she said over the increasing noise, "I was thinking I needed to get away for a while. Always wanted to see the Rio Grande."

"You have?"

"There are a lot of gambling halls down there. Monte's the big game. Maybe I need to try my luck."

"What? And leave the Hidden Nugget? And Cole?"

Erin shook her head impatiently. "But you might need me."

Gabby felt too close to the edge of confession, and she pulled back. "I can take care of myself."

A frown darkened Erin's face, and Gabby almost laughed. Take care of herself? She'd exhibited little proof of that.

Briefly she took Erin's hand in her own. "Now what possible use could I have for a card-dealing redhead who has been known to act before she thinks?"

Erin grinned. "You never know. I might come in very handy."

"You might at that," said Gabby, her smile fading for a moment. The mask was quickly back in place. She must stay away from even the smallest show of sentiment.

This self-possessed role was one she was getting good at. She hadn't even cried when Rafe left her after that painful scene at the hotel. Instead, she'd put her mind to calculating how much better off she was without him. He had turned too quickly from her,

103

been too quick to believe she had lied. A man like that wouldn't last a lifetime. He wouldn't be there for the security she needed.

Bitterness and anger had dried whatever tears she might have shed. To think he could doubt her so soon after the lovemaking they had shared. And all because of the accusations of the one man Rafe had called his enemy. He had chosen to listen to Earl Hunter rather than to her.

Gabby had found the two long nights since then useful for one thing — figuring out where she had gone wrong. From the moment Rafe had walked into the Hidden Nugget she'd been too dazzled by his presence to remember why she was in town. Like a silly schoolgirl who'd never had much experience with men. And that simply wasn't true. She might have been innocent, but she was far from ignorant. She had only herself to blame.

Most galling was the memory of her thoughts just before his return to her room. With her body still tingling from the wonders of his touch, Gabby had lain naked beneath the covers, breathing in the smell of him that lingered in the bed, stroking the cross between her breasts — and thinking of the marvelous times that lay ahead.

Her thoughts had been the stuff of both practicality and romance, rooted as they were in old dreams and new. She would gain possession of some land and use it to clear him of debt. She would let him teach her the ways of running a ranch. And, if things worked out as they had begun, the two of them would eventually settle down together, maybe even sell her small place so they could always be together.

She blushed to think how hard and fast she'd fallen for his sweet words and his erotic touch.

But then had come the fateful knock on the door. Colette had told her something like it always came — and always to expect the worst. She'd opened the door to the real Rafe Jericho, a judge and jury to her alleged crime.

He had never loved her, at least not in the unbounded way she had thought. She shuddered, remembering the accusing eyes that had killed her joy.

Men had their uses, all right. They taught gullible girls to grow up.

One thought tore at her mind. How had Hunter known why she was in town?

"I do not know of this Senor Hunter," Oscar Cantu had said when she confronted him the next day. "But I have long ago sent inquiries to the courthouse in Laredo about the Cordero land. Perhaps Senor Hunter has friends there."

"Perhaps," Gabby had replied. It would be just her luck for Hunter to have stumbled upon her story. And when he'd set Luke Sneed on Rafe, how pleased he must have been to discover she and Rafe had accidentally met.

Thoughts of Hunter preyed on her mind, and one of the first things she'd asked Franklin Bernard was if he had ever seen him around the courthouse.

His answer had been sharp. "Not the sort of man I associate with," he'd said, then turned the conversation to questions about her plans.

Silently, Gabby added a vow to the growing list she carried in her heart. If she ever did meet the scoundrel Hunter, she would put her questions to him point-blank. Contemplating that meeting had an extra fillip. The more she thought about Earl Hunter, the less she thought about Rafe.

In the meantime she had to get on with her life, and heard herself saying to Erin, almost by rote, "I really will be all right." She glanced at the crowds of travelers swirling around her. "Franklin Bernard should be here any minute with the tickets and will escort me on the train. When I get to Laredo, I promise to check into a respectable hotel."

"And then?"

"I'll get to know the town and its people. After all, it's going to be my home. Then I'll go see Benito Hidalgo and discuss a settlement."

Erin's laugh was sharp. "Of course he'll meet you at the door with deed in hand."

"Of course he won't." Gabby lifted her chin in determination. "But I intend to be reasonable. I'm not asking for as much as Mr. Cantu has advised. It wouldn't surprise me if Hidalgo and I reach an agreement without any outside help."

"Is that what the lawyer told you? To expect a quick victory?"

Gabby smoothed the skirt of her blue linen dress. "Oh, you know how lawyers are," she said, remembering the way Cantu had warned her away from Hidalgo. "A settlement would mean no trial—and a smaller fee for them." And Bernard had supported Cantu's description of the Seco owner, calling him an irascible old man. She hadn't asked him about Rafe.

"I gather they advised you against pursuing the case yourself. Why don't you listen to them?" said Erin.

Gabby looked at her friend in surprise. Such words

106

of caution were out of character.

"Is this the Erin who bought a run-down cantina and turned it into a fashionable gambling salon? Is this the Erin who almost single-handedly is bringing government attention to the plight of the Comanches in Indian Territory? Is this the Erin—"

"Enough! I get your point. I guess"—Erin's voice lowered until Gabby had to strain to hear her—"impending motherhood makes one conservative."

Gabby let out a shriek and gave Erin a brief, tight hug. "You silly goose. And here you are offering to ride down to Laredo with me. You should be sitting somewhere with your feet propped up and Cole nearby to tend to your every need."

"He already did. How do you suppose I got this way?"

Gabby studied her friend carefully. "Aren't you happy?"

A warm glow lit Erin's amber eyes. "As happy as I've ever been."

"Did you know about the baby the other day when I was at the Nugget?"

"I was pretty sure, but I hadn't had a chance to tell Cole yet. He came back to town and we went to the doctor yesterday afternoon. I had the devil of a time convincing him I would be all right coming here in the carriage to see you off."

"I guess fathers-to-be are conservative, too."

"And," Erin said softly, "very loving."

Gabby's reply caught in her throat. A loving man was the last thing she wanted to talk about. And then she felt shame that she should think about her own problems when Erin was so ecstatic over her news.

"Miss Deschamps." Gabby was aware of a deep voice behind her, a cough, and then a louder, "Miss Deschamps."

She looked up at the fair-haired, brown-suited man who had spoken. She stood and extended her hand.

"Good morning, Mister Bernard." She introduced the Laredo attorney to Erin, who kept a disconcertingly steady gaze on him. No doubt, Gabby thought, to determine if he really had her best interests in mind. From the look on Erin's face she couldn't determine if he passed the test or not.

"Miss Deschamps, let me help you with your luggage." Bernard's tone was businesslike. "The train will be leaving shortly and there won't be another one until tomorrow."

Gabby gestured toward the end of the bench to the matched pair of leather cases. As she watched Bernard pick them up, she couldn't see how Erin could find anything wrong with the man. He was clean shaven, neatly dressed, polite, efficient, courteous, and—if she were in the market for such a man—not bad looking. Perhaps a little too pale for her tastes, a little too short and squat. But then she'd had enough of tall, dark men to last a lifetime.

Bernard guided the two women through the throngs of people on the platform to one of the passenger trains.

"I'll get on board and locate us a place to sit. Facing forward, of course. Never could stand riding backward on a train." He nodded a polite good-bye to Erin and disappeared into the car.

Gabby and Erin both burst into laughter.

"Now how could anything happen to me with such

a gentleman taking me in his care?" Gabby said.

Erin's eyes traveled down Gabby's full length, from the black, feathered hat placed at an angle in the midst of her blond curls, on down the fitted linen traveling dress that matched the blue of her eyes, to the black leather slippers on her feet.

She shook her head slowly. "I'd say any number of things could go wrong. Even your gentlemanly Mister Bernard was eyeing you with appreciation before you looked at him. Gabrielle, you're the sorriest excuse for a cowboy I've ever seen. Are you sure you want to be a rancher?"

"I'm sure," she said, her voice steady. "Each of us, it seems, is embarking on a new course in our lives, Erin. Trust me to know what I'm about." A sparkle lit her blue eyes. "And I promise to learn to ride a horse as soon as I can."

Erin's skeptical frown was replaced by a smile. "It seems the least you can do. Just promise you'll be careful. Of everyone, including your gentleman attorney."

Gabby's reply was drowned out by the warning whistle of the train. The air darkened with flying cinders, giving rise to a brief good-bye. It was the best kind, Gabby decided as she boarded the car. She moved quickly down the aisle to slide in front of Franklin Bernard and take her place next to the open window.

As the train pulled out of the station, Gabby forced her mind to exactly where she was heading—to the home of the one man in the world she wanted never to see again. But face him, she most certainly would. And she would not break down, nor succumb to his certain demands that she forget her suit. Roberto Cordero had felt his cause was just. For the sake of justice delayed, Gabby could do no less.

It was a premise she had a long, hot day to impress on her mind as the train chugged its way south over the uneven roadbed. After a while she even managed to supplant Rafe's image with a study of the country-side.

From the gently rolling hills around San Antonio the land stretched out to flatness, providing a harsh view from the train window. For a long while after the train crossed the Nueces River, the scene outside her window offered few trees and only the thick, low-lying brush that Bernard explained was almost impenetrable in places, sharp thorns making travel by horseback a dangerous undertaking for both rider and animal.

There were few towns on the route, and for most of the day's journey they seemed to have left civilization behind. The land had a rugged charm that worked its magic on her the deeper she slipped into its depths. A *refuge primitif*. Gabby smiled. Her mother had been right.

The terrain changed as the train neared the border. They topped a hill, and from her window Gabby could see sharp rises and falls of land, dry creek beds cutting through brown fields, gray foliage interspersed with the rich blue-green of cedar trees and the squat, tenacious mesquite.

The setting sun cast a shadowed light onto the land, giving it a forbidding, otherworldly look. It was an uncompromising country, yet Gabby felt a thrill as she gazed across the miles. Lurking in those shadows might be wildcats, scorpions, snakes. She shuddered.

Rafe Jericho seemed to belong on that list.

But also somewhere out there lay the Arroyo Seco. She vowed anew to make it her home.

As if she willed it, the International and Great Northern train moved unimpeded along the track and hurtled her right into the heart of Laredo before jerking to a stop at the small depot. The passengers who remained aboard would travel across the trestle that spanned the Rio Grande and then head for Monterrey. For Gabby, the journey was done.

When she moved ahead of Bernard toward the city's streets for the first time, she felt as though she were stepping into another country. Even in the shadows of evening she felt surrounded by the Spanish influence of its residents, even more so than in San Antonio. Mexican and American flags hung side by side and on the street corners across from the station she saw fruit and food stands and vendors with colorful baskets of flowers. With its bicultural charm, the town drew her in and she was soon able to quit seeing Rafe behind every post.

For a woman who'd spent much of her life in a French convent and then in an eastern school for girls, she felt very much at home. She attributed it to the heritage of her father, and she let the town give her succor. Spanish blood flowed in her veins as much as did French, and she thanked her mother for insisting she learn to speak his language.

Of course she would be a little slow at first, but all she needed was practice. And from the looks of the gaily clad people around her with their dark good looks, she would get a great deal of that.

Bernard, her luggage in hand, directed her toward

a carriage for hire a block from the depot.

"I'll get you to the hotel and out of this barbarity as soon as possible," he said. "The Commercial Hotel is the best. Unfortunately, it's also across the street from the plaza. You'll have to put up with a little celebrating through tomorrow night."

Gabby kept her smile to herself. She could hardly see explaining to Franklin Bernard that she rather enjoyed the noise and light-hearted mood of the town.

"Is Laredo like this all the time?" she asked.

"Thank the Lord no. It's the celebration of *Dieciseis*. The sixteenth of September. Mexican Independence Day. Some border towns have tried to outlaw it but without success. You can be grateful it ends tomorrow."

Gabby felt a fleeting disappointment that every day on the border was not so festive but, certain Bernard wouldn't agree, she kept her feelings to herself. It was one thing to get advice from her dearest friend Erin, but quite another to be lectured by a man, even one as solicitous as Bernard.

As they rode toward the hotel, Gabby noticed the streets were narrow and dusty, and there were no sidewalks in front of the houses of business that lined them, but the lack of traveling amenities didn't detract from the town's festive air. Dozens of brightly colored booths and carts lined the way.

And there seemed an inordinate number of gambling and drinking houses for a place so small. She'd expected to come down to a small, sleepy border town; instead she'd found a fiesta.

Assuring the attorney she would be all right, she went quickly to the room he had reserved for her by a telegram sent yesterday from San Antonio. At first she thought herself capable of splashing a little water on her face, perhaps changing into another, more festive, dress and heading out for the brightly lit plaza across the street. She certainly wouldn't worry about running into somebody she didn't want to meet. The odds against that would be high, and besides, she didn't plan to live her life avoiding him. She'd go anywhere any time that she chose, including a fiesta her first night in town.

But that was before she closed the door of her room behind her and got a good look at the bed. She'd not slept much in two days, and the ten hours spent today on the train had done little to give her rest.

Using the bedpost for support, she was barely able to remove her soot-soiled dress and her hat and slippers before collapsing atop the covers and giving herself up to the sweet oblivion of sleep.

Bright sunlight was streaming in the window when she awoke. Sometime during the night she had managed to slip beneath the blanket, and she lay huddled in its thin protection trying to figure out where she was.

She peered at the floor beside her and saw a tangle of blue linen. At the end of the bed was her once jaunty hat, its lone feather bent at an unnatural angle. The walls surrounding her were covered in primrose-patterned paper. On the table close to her head were a pitcher and basin.

She stretched—and immediately regretted the action. Every muscle cried out in protest, and she realized why. Yesterday's bouncing train ride, of course. She was in Laredo. Pulling herself out of bed, she stared into a mottled mirror. After a disgusted look at the smudges on her face and her tangled mop of blond curls, she got to work. Using the water in the almost full pitcher, she cleaned off most of the dirt from yesterday's travel, pulled out the least wrinkled dress in her tightly packed suitcases, and when she was satisfied that she made a proper appearance, headed down for the biggest breakfast she could find.

The street vendors were still plying their trade, or had begun once more after a respite—she didn't know which. But instead of the *dulces*, the sweets and the flame-cooked meats they offered, she settled on more traditional fare at a nearby restaurant.

A quick stop by Franklin Bernard's office brought her only admonitions for caution.

"Pardon my saying so, Miss Deschamps," he said, not waiting for her to respond, "but *Dieciseis* is not a proper time for a young woman to be out walking the streets."

"Why ever not? It's a beautiful day and everyone has been most friendly."

Bernard sniffed. "That's just what I mean. These people get too friendly."

Gabby's eyes turned a frosty blue. "By these people I assume you mean those whose heritage lies in Mexico and Spain."

"Don't misunderstand me, Miss Deschamps. Some of my clients are from Mexico. I even number several among my friends, but on the whole they're just too hot-blooded for my tastes."

"May I remind you my father's people were named Cordero? You might find me a little hot-blooded, too, especially"—her smile was deceptively sweet—"if I were to empty that inkpot in your lap."

The lawyer couldn't hide a startled look but quickly got himself under control.

"I see you have a sense of humor, Miss Deschamps," he said, "but please don't get me wrong. I only have your best interests at heart. You ought to let me escort you around town and introduce you to some of the citizens."

Gabby rose to leave, embarrassed that she'd spoken so rudely. The lawyer was only trying to be helpful; thanks to Rafe, she read hidden meanings into everyone's words. "I appreciate the offer, Mister Bernard, but I really would like to do a little exploring on my own."

Bernard frowned. "I'm afraid you haven't been listening. You may be a Cordero, but, if you'll pardon my saying so, you don't look it. You will be a curiosity if you try to take part in the celebration."

Gabby was quickly catching on to the ways of the legal profession — stay quick on your feet and always have an answer.

"I've been a curiosity most of my life, Mister Bernard, so that won't be a problem for me."

Surely he could figure that one out, she thought as she bid him good day. Oscar Cantu knew her mother's background and there was no reason to think he hadn't passed on the information to his Laredo associate. It didn't matter one way or the other to Gabby.

Before leaving, she did make one promise to Bernard — not to go out to the Arroyo Seco before conferring with him. It was a safe promise. Her resolve might be stronger than ever, but that didn't mean she would rush into facing Rafe so soon.

Once more on the street she was delighted to find the air still cool and, forgetting Bernard's cautious words, headed out for a walk along the dusty streets. Her perambulations brought her to A. M. Bruni and Brother, one of the largest of the town's general stores, and she went inside to see what it had to offer.

She was fingering the various weights and colors of yarn, wondering if she shouldn't begin knitting a shawl for the cool months ahead, when a woman's voice interrupted her thoughts.

"Buy the blue. It will go with your eyes."

Gabby looked up into a pair of warm gray eyes studying her with a gentle curiosity she found comforting.

"Most everything I have is blue," she said.

"Then," the woman said, shrugging her matronly shoulders, "go for red. Something different."

Gabby grinned. "Something different." She thought about her new life. "That's not a bad idea."

"I haven't seen you around here before. Emma Talbert's the name. My husband owns Talbert's Dry Goods across the street."

"And you're patronizing the opposition?"

"When they have something we don't, I sure do. Just don't tell Alexander, Miss—"

"Deschamps." Gabby extended her hand. "Gabrielle Deschamps." She hesitated a moment, then added, "Cordero. That's really my last name. I guess it's time I started using it."

"Well, Miss Gabrielle Whoever, what brings you down here to the border? Lots of people moving in here now. Germans. Bohemians. Used to be you only had to know one or two languages to get along. Place is turning into a real boom town. Everyone wants to be a rancher and have a chance at burning his tail. If you'll pardon the language. Should have said losing his money. Alexander keeps correcting me about things like that."

Gabby felt she had tumbled into a whirlwind, but one that blew balmy air.

"I'll bet correcting you doesn't do Alexander much good," she said.

"Sure doesn't. We've lived in the town for almost twenty years. Came here right after the war from outside Nacogdoches over in East Texas. Learned to talk plain over there. Now then, Gabby—you don't mind if I call you that, do you? Seems it fits me better than it does you, but then things don't always turn out the way you'd think they would. Emma. Now that's a good, solid name for a woman. Something I have to live up to." She shifted her matronly frame. "Don't know how *good* I am, but I'm for sure *solid.*"

"I don't mind," Gabby said softly.

"Mind what? That I'm built solid?"

"No," Gabby said, laughing. "I don't mind if you shorten my name."

Emma Talbert studied Gabby for a moment. "Seems to me you're not telling me the truth. Noticed you flinched when I said your name. Think I'll stick with Gabrielle. Something worrying you, my dear? You never did tell me what brought you to town."

"How *could* I have been so rude?"

Emma threw her head back and laughed. "Gabrielle, you give as good as you get. That's the nicest setdown I ever got. You have time for a cup of tea?"

Just as Gabby expected, Emma gave her no time

117

for a response, but directed her toward the door. "You want that yarn, come back for it. But we got just as good across the street and just as good a price. I may shop here once in a while but that don't mean I want everyone to."

Within minutes Gabby found herself at a corner table of a tea shop two blocks from the stores.

"English couple moved in and opened this up. Never thought it would go in Laredo, but it sure did. Now then," she said as their order of tea and scones was delivered, "I plan to say not another word until you tell me if you're here permanent. Sure hope you say yes."

Gabby stirred a teaspoon of sugar into her tea and buttered a scone, each movement slow and deliberate.

"I'm here permanent. I've taken a room in the Commercial Hotel until I can get another place, maybe a boarding house, but eventually I plan on going into ranching. And I don't" — her lips broke into a wry smile — "plan on burning my tail."

"Nobody plans on it. 'Pears to me maybe you already have. Something's troubling you, Gabrielle. Saw it as soon as I spied you playing with that yarn. Something in the way you were holding yourself. I don't know. But when you looked up at me, I could read it in your eyes plain as if the words were writ there. Pardon an old fool of a woman for speaking up, but there's only one thing generally puts that kind of look into a beautiful girl's eyes. A man."

Gabby pulled back from the woman's scrutiny. Some things were too private to discuss. "Tell me about Laredo," she said lightly. "If it's going to be my home, I'd like to know all about it."

Emma looked at her for a long, thoughtful moment. "You'll tell me when you're ready, I reckon, and not a moment before." She proceeded to give Gabby a brief history of the border town with its mingling of cultures, political fighting, and promise of a strong economy.

"Business has been down a long time, but what with the sheep ranching that's been started and the railroads shipping the stock out, we figure it's time things were turning around."

"And I plan to be a part of it, Emma. I'm part French and part Spanish. I ought to fit into the town just fine. Even the celebration that's going on now, although my lawyer Franklin Bernard seems to think I should take no part in it."

Emma took up the new thread of conversation, putting Gabby at ease. "Franklin Bernard is a good enough lawyer, I suppose, but he's a pantywaist. Not that he might not be right in this case. Most folks get along down here, no matter what their background. Money is what divides, not who your grandpa was. But not at *Dieciseis*. It's strictly a Mexican celebration. You sure don't look as though you'd belong."

"I'm half Spanish, remember? I'll tell you frankly, Emma, after the past few days, I've found a decided stubborn streak in myself. The more you tell me no, the more I think yes."

Emma grinned. "You're sounding more and more like me, Gabby. Welcome to Laredo."

She leaned across the table. "Now, if you're really interested in what's going on around here — and I can't say as how I blame you — go to the fandango tonight. The dance. It'll be held on the plaza across from your

119

hotel. A wild thing. It'll go on all night. Lots of food and a little drinking. Watch out for the clear-looking stuff they bring up from across the river. Tequila, it's called. Your fan will be dangoed for sure if you have more than a sip of that."

"You sound as though you know from experience."

"Alexander brought some home once. Sure did make him loving. Me, too, for that matter." The lines around Emma's eyes softened. "Come to think it, I might take home a bottle for tonight. Have our own little celebration in the privacy of our home. Don't need a crowd to have a good time."

"I think I need a crowd, Emma."

"Mood you're in, I suspect you're right. If you want to do it right, get one of those blouses the women wear, maybe some dangly earrings, let your hair down. Then watch yourself. Keep a clear shot at the hotel door. I'm betting you'll be running there for safety before the night's out."

"I'll be careful, Emma. You have any children of your own?"

"None. One of life's disappointments, Gabby. So if I tend to lecture you a little, just let me be. Seems like every woman has a little motherly advice tucked away inside her waiting to get out."

"My mother certainly did. And she would have told me much the same as you. I'll be careful. I just want to take in some of the sights."

"Gabby," Emma said with a laugh, "I'd say you're going to *be* one of them. Especially if you dress up the way I said. I think we might have just what you're looking for over at a little place called Talbert's Dry Goods. Never hurts to round up a little business for

Alexander. It makes him feel frisky and ready for that tequila I'll be bringing home tonight."

Gabby took Emma's advice and made several purchases, including a half dozen skeins of scarlet yarn. In the privacy of her hotel room she studied the results of her day's shopping. The white blouse she'd bought featured a wide ruffle that draped low across her arms and breasts, revealing her shoulders. The cotton skirt, woven with multicolored threads, brushed against her ankles, and around her waist she wore a wide green sash.

Her hair was brushed until it shone and lay in soft curls against her skin. A wide loop of gold hung from each ear. The only other piece of jewelry she wore was the cross. Her blue eyes and blond hair might disguise the fact, but she very much felt under the influence of her Spanish forebears as she made her way downstairs and across the street to the plaza.

Night had already fallen and overhead a myriad of stars shone like diamonds against a bed of black velvet. The strains of guitars seemed to surround her, and then she heard the sharper sounds of a brass horn adding a rhythmic contrast. The tempo quickened and, even while she reminded herself she had come only to watch, she couldn't bury the hope that someone might ask her to dance.

Benches sat nestled in trees and flowering shrubs along the sides of the plaza. Here was where the girls waited for the strolling men to approach them.

Tapping her foot in time to the music, Gabby stood to one side and observed. Back and forth the men walked with studied ease, but if she looked carefully she could tell the girl each one was eyeing. Once the man had chosen his partner, he came slowly to a halt in front of her and asked her to dance. Gabby never saw a girl refuse.

The dance was different from any she had witnessed before, the man's hands resting at his partner's waist, the girl's arms held loosely at her sides. Some couples dipped and swirled, some barely moved; the only thing they had in common was that their eyes never strayed from one another. Their bodies never touched, and yet Gabby thought it one of the most sensual sights she had ever seen.

Perhaps it was best that no one approached her, and she purposefully kept away from the well-lighted benches. As it was she felt curious stares directed her way. She wanted to speak to some of the women, but she got the idea that might be considered too forward. Everyone seemed to know everyone else and she was beginning to see why Franklin Bernard had warned her she wouldn't fit in.

"*Buenos tardes, senorita.*" The low-pitched voice of a tall, handsome man startled her. His eyes were dark and much too frankly approving as they rested on the rise of her breasts above the low-cut blouse. Gray hairs flecked his temples and moustache, and Gabby could see harsh lines around his mouth that gave him the look of a perpetual sneer.

But the look in those eyes was far from disdainful, and Gabby shifted away from him.

"*Buenos tardes, senor,*" she said.

"*Habla espanol?*"

"*Un pequeno.*"

"Only a little? Then let us speak in English, my dear. I would not want to be misunderstood by so lovely a young woman." He swayed in her direction. "Would you care to dance?"

Whatever thoughts Gabby had entertained about joining the other dancers fled under the frank stare of the stranger.

"No, thank you. I've come only to observe."

"Do you find our celebration amusing?" His voice took on a harsh note.

"I find it charming."

The man drew nearer. "Not as charming as you, *cielo*. Allow me to introduce myself. I am Don Alfredo Felipe Marcos Almeida y Juarez. And to whom have I the pleasure of speaking?"

"To an observer, senor. Someone who wishes to stand only at the side."

Almeida's eyes narrowed. "It would be a waste of a beautiful evening if we both only observed." His long fingers grasped her wrist, and for the first time Gabby realized the man was drunk.

She tried to free herself but failed. His fingers were like iron bands around her arm as he stepped deeper into the shadowy bushes at the edge of the plaza and pulled her after him. Leafy branches blocked out the crowds and light. How embarrassing, she thought, to have to call for help. But there was no point worrying about that. Over the increasingly loud music that only moments ago she had found so entrancing, she would never be heard. She would just have to take care of this Don Juan herself.

"Senor," she said, "I agree the night is too lovely to waste. But here in the shrubs with so many people

123

around? Surely you are more romantic than that."

"Ah, I understand what you mean. Of course." The grip on her wrist remained firm and he pulled her against his chest. His breath reeked of stale whiskey.

"If you could just let me go, I'd be glad to accompany you. A man as handsome as yourself is hard to resist." A bit strong, she thought, but then the man had been drinking. And he was after all only a man.

She felt the pressure of his hand relax and she jerked free. Pushing through the confined shrubbery, she burst into the open air and hurried toward the lighted part of the plaza, her eyes trained on the route that would take her across to the sanctuary of her hotel. Almeida was close on her heels, and she quickened her step, her only thought to get away from him.

A dark-suited figure moved into her path and she was forced to halt.

"I had in mind rescuing you from an unwanted suitor, Gabrielle," a familiar voice whipped at her, "but as usual you seem to be taking care of yourself."

The light was behind him, casting his face in shadows, but there was no mistaking the identity of the man. Long before she was prepared to face him, Rafe Jericho had appeared.

Chapter Six

Gabby's first instinct was to welcome Rafe with a touch of her hand, but the instinct quickly died. As he stepped from the shadows, she was struck by the harsh visage he presented. Quick to misjudge the situation, he seemed even angrier than she'd last seen him. Dark eyes that had a lifetime ago been warmed by a too-brief affection stared coldly at her, and his lean face was taut and unsmiling.

Stunned by his unexpected presence — and the onslaught of his gaze — she dropped her eyes to the black shirt open deep at his throat, revealing the strong neck and sinewed muscles of his chest. The trousers, too, were black and skintight, his nightlike appearance relieved only by a silver buckle at his narrow waist.

Like a devil, he'd come out of the night to tempt her, and she fought against his power. Fighting the impulse to slap him, she flashed a brilliant smile.

"Why, Rafe Jericho," she said, the tinkling laughter she attempted sounding brittle and false to her ears, "I didn't expect to see you so soon."

Her laughter cut into him like shards of broken glass. "Didn't you?"

"Of course not." How dare he think she would seek him out.

Almeida stepped closer and gripped her arm. "Senor Jericho, the lady and I were just leaving."

She looked back at Almeida. "You know Rafe, too?"

"*Si.* Senor Jericho is a very popular man in Laredo. Especially with the ladies." Almeida's arm snaked around her waist, and he frowned at Rafe.

So he was popular with the ladies, was he? That was one thing in this whole painful situation she could believe.

Rafe fought the urge to snap in two the arm that touched Gabby. If she didn't push Almeida away, why should he? "I wouldn't want to keep you and the *lady* from wherever you were going," he said. "I know how eager she can be at times."

Gabby's cheeks flushed. Rafe was the one man in the world who had aroused that eagerness in her, and now he made it sound like something that should bring her shame. To speak in such a common way of what they had shared, no matter what he believed had been her purpose, he must have no conscience at all.

Pulling free of Almeida's hold on her, she slipped from between the two men and into the bright light of a row of lanterns draped in the overhead branches of a tree. Looking back at Rafe, she was unable to keep up her cheerful facade.

"You're wrong about what you witnessed, Rafe. But

126

of course it's not your first mistake." Before he could reply, she hurried on. "How nice that you know Senor Almeida. I'm sure you'll have much to talk about." Her voice almost broke.

Stop, she told herself. *Don't let him see how much you hurt.* Slipping back into her carefree role, she saw definite advantages to the Emma Talbert approach. Overwhelm them with words.

"My, but it's warm this evening since the breeze has died down," she said, fanning herself with one hand. "What I want right now more than anything in the world"—she ignored Rafe's derisive laugh—"is something to drink."

She twirled away from them and headed toward one of the booths that ringed the plaza. Behind her she could hear a loud protest from her drunken suitor and Rafe telling him he should find another woman.

Wending her way through the crowd, she stopped at the first booth she came to, pulled a coin from the pocket of her skirt, and, speaking Spanish, ordered a glass of whatever the vendor was serving. Peering out with curiosity from under a silver-and-gold sombrero, he handed her a small cup of clear liquid, a slice of lime floating on the surface.

She took a sip of the drink and found it almost tasteless—and amazingly sharp as it went down. She took a bite of the lime and then another sip. The sharpness had mellowed. With the third swallow she decided whatever the liquor was, she liked it very much.

"I didn't realize you had a taste for tequila."

She whirled around to face Rafe. Her head seemed

to spin as much as the hem of her skirt.

"Tequila?" A warning bell sounded in her mind. Emma had said something about the effects of the Mexican drink.

But then Colette had warned her about men, and it hadn't done her much good, either. Maybe, Gabby decided, she was meant to learn about things first-hand.

She finished off the drink and ordered another.

Rafe flipped a coin to the vendor and took the drink from her hands. He downed it in one gulp.

"Too much of a good thing, Gabby, and one finds only disappointment." His voice was silken and yet sharply edged. She looked away, and he moved closer until she could feel his breath hot on her neck. "Don Almeida would have no doubt learned that to his regret."

There was such scorn in his voice, scorn meant to hurt her. Rafe Jericho was obviously one of those men who drew special pleasure from inflicting pain.

"I had no intention of remaining with that man," she said, uncaring whether or not he believed her. "Now please excuse me, Rafe. The air is very close on this side of the plaza and I'd like to watch the dancers for a while."

Her head held high, she walked past him toward the benches that lined the center of the square and sat on the first one she came to, glad for its steadfast support.

The strains of guitar music swelled, filling the night with a melodic harmony that was at odds with the turmoil she felt inside. Through the haze brought on by her introduction to tequila, she tried to accept what was happening. She'd seen Rafe again, as she knew she would. What she hadn't counted on was that he would affect her in ways he always had. She might have presented a cool apperance to him, but much of what she'd said and done had been a lie.

When their eyes had locked, she'd hardly been able to breathe. With an intensity that stunned her she had wanted him to touch her again. No matter what he thought of her, all she'd been able to think about was the way his black hair fell casually across his forehead, the way the muscles in his neck corded when he was tense, and a thousand other trivial details about him that shut out the rest of the world.

That she was capable of such thoughts and in such circumstances left her shaken. At age twenty, Gabby was discovering things about herself that she didn't like at all.

Without realizing it, Gabby reached for the cross, her thumb tracing its beveled edges, her eyes trained on the flagstone at her feet. As soon as her head quit seeming to whirl on her shoulders, she would slip away. The chances were too great Rafe would reappear among the swirling revelers thronging the square.

Even as she resolved to leave, a pair of black boots stopped beside her. Slowly her eyes trailed a long, well-muscled path to brown eyes as unreadable as the night.

Rafe stared down at her for a long moment—at the fire in her eyes, at the proud set of her lips, at the golden cross resting in her delicate hand. "You surprise me, *querida*," he said at last, "that you still wear it."

As though the cross seared her fingers, she dropped it. How dare he use that term of affection and in such a scornful tone of voice! His mockery gave her courage and she met his bold gaze without blinking.

"It seemed to go with the blouse, and today I saw so many of the women wearing crosses. Don't forget I share an ancestry in common with them."

"I have forgotten nothing about you, Gabrielle Deschamps."

Gabby blushed to think of the many intimate things he had to remember. She tried to think clearly, to seek out a path of retreat, but Rafe was too quick for her. He reached down to grip her arms and pull her to her feet.

"The music should not be wasted," he said, drawing her with him into the midst of the dancers.

His hands spanned her waist, forcing her to sway with him in time to the rhythms swirling around them. Their bodies were inches apart, their breath intermingling, and Gabby could feel the heat of him penetrating her skin. His fingers cut into her body as he tightened his hold, and, without wondering why she should have such a reaction, Gabby felt a tremor of fear.

He pulled her closer until her breasts brushed against his shirt and he was able to whisper into her ear.

"You are a beautiful woman, Gabrielle. Many men here are jealous that I hold you in my arms."

"I don't seek the admiration of many men," she

hissed, trying valiantly to hold herself with dignity away from him. "It's not why I came here tonight."

"And why did you come?"

"To—" She paused. How could she tell him the simple truth, that she wanted to understand the ancestry of her father, that she wanted only to belong?

"You wouldn't understand," she said curtly.

"And perhaps the problem is that I would."

He gave her no chance to respond, instead spinning her around the center of the plaza until she had to hold on tightly to his arms in order to maintain her balance. The music grew more frantic, the strums of the guitars more insistent, as faster and faster they twirled past the other dancers, the surrounding trees and shrubs a blur around them.

The music stopped and Gabby fell against Rafe, her breathing forced, her heart pounding so hard he must surely feel its beat through the thin clothing that separated them. Beneath her clinging fingers his arms felt powerful and somehow reassuring.

He stepped away and the spell was broken.

"As in so many other things, *querida*, you are a charming dancer."

What insinuating words they were. She tossed her head back, long blond curls flying free in the night breeze. Coming to the fandango tonight had been a terrible risk, she realized. Rafe obviously thought she was offering herself to another man, as though she were. . . . She couldn't thrust the word *whore* from her mind. And Almeida seemed to think close to the same thing.

All she had wanted was to fit in. Gabby had

integrity, no matter what Rafe Jericho thought. As though she would give herself to just any man!

Pulling away from him, she realized completely how much she had learned—and how late. She'd told herself a woman could use a man and walk away if she wanted. But some women weren't made like that. They were not at all like men, especially men like Rafe.

She sensed Rafe's eyes on her. Why didn't he just retreat and find someone else to debauch? She turned and hurried away from him, instinctively heading for a crowd of revelers. Perhaps she could lose herself in their midst. Booted footsteps behind her hastened her on, but she was pulled up short at the edge of the plaza by a firm hand on her arm.

"You're making a spectacle of yourself," he said angrily as he spun her around. "I know you are half Spanish, but to the others you are a *gringa* hanging around to mock their celebration."

"I came to learn about the people of Laredo. All of the people, not just the *gringos*." Gabby ignored the warning look in his eyes. "And to have a good time. I was doing just that when you appeared."

Her words lashed him like a whip. "When I appeared, you were leading that idiot Almeida somewhere away from the plaza. For some sort of assignation, I suppose."

"I was not leading him anywhere, but I doubt if you would ever believe me. And what if you are right? It should make no difference to you." Throwing caution to the night air, she pulled the key to her hotel room from her pocket and waved it in the air. "I might even have been taking him to my hotel room across the street. I find hotel rooms so useful for certain things."

"And what did you hope to gain from him, *querida?* His land?"

"You—"

Rafe jerked the key from her hand and pulled her hard against him, crushing into silence the words she would have uttered.

"Do you want a man? Now that you have tasted of passion, will you not be satisfied until you have more?" His lips came down hard on hers, demanding she submit to his will, brooking no dissent.

She struggled in his grasp, trying to twist her body away from his, and succeeded only in strengthening his hold on her. The more she fought, the more insistent became his demands, his hands stroking her back, holding her tight against the length of him until there was no mistaking the need he had for her, a need that would not be denied.

In the midst of her anger and fear came another, more commanding feeling. Desire. She wasn't sure just when her struggles turned to a fiery embrace, but suddenly she found herself answering his assault with her lips, with her arms, with her body, as she pressed herself hard against him, held him tightly, and opened her mouth to welcome the invasion of his tongue.

The night exploded around her as she clung to him. When he thrust her away, she felt lost.

"Rafe—" she began, unaware of time and place, knowing only that she was no longer in his arms.

He wrapped an arm around her and pulled her through the shadows toward the street that ran along-

133

side the plaza. Whatever happened tomorrow, he needed her tonight, and he guided her toward the one place he knew would provide them privacy.

Rafe's strength, his will, and Gabby's own private needs that only he had ever aroused left her powerless to resist.

Until she realized he was taking her toward the hotel. A feeling of déjà vu washed over her. Once more he was ready to claim his conquest over her. Once more he planned to take her to bed. And in her own hotel room again. This time she knew he would not stroke her with words of love. But this time she would not give in so readily.

"No, Rafe," she said, pulling away, but he seemed prepared for her dissent and his hold on her tightened. His stride lengthened, and she felt herself borne along beside him, her feet scarcely touching the ground.

Inside, with their pace slowed, only the hotel clerk gave them a passing glance, and Gabby found herself unable to appeal to that pinched-lipped man for assistance. What could she tell him, anyway — that Rafe had inflamed her with his kiss and she wasn't sure what more she wanted him to do? All she could manage was to walk beside Rafe with as much dignity as she could muster and to plan how she would handle him — and herself — upstairs.

By the time she walked into the narrow room and heard the door close behind her, the key turning in the lock like a precursor of doom, she realized she could no longer behave as though he had meant nothing to her back in San Antonio. After their confrontation in the hotel, she had felt the life crushed out of her. Only with the greatest will had she convinced herself to put memories of him aside.

It had been easy enough to laugh up at him without a show of care on the brightly lit plaza surrounded by crowds. But in the privacy of her room, its lone lamp turned down low, she was not capable of such subterfuge. Here he was again, about to claim her as his own. For a little while. The thought tore at her mind.

When he turned to face her, his long, lithe body close to hers, she tried to speak. "Rafe, I don't want this."

"I know exactly what you want, Gabby. It is the same for me." His fingers worked at the silver buckle at his waist. "I'll see that in one way we are both satisfied."

He worked at the fastenings of his trousers, then pulled his shirt free, unbuttoned it, and dropped it to the floor. She watched, mesmerized by his movements, her breathing shallow, her heart pounding in her ears.

No matter what protestations she might make, he saw desire in her eyes. With her parted lips still swollen from his kiss, her breasts visibly erect beneath her blouse, she drove him mad.

"You want a man's body, *querida? A su servicio.* I am at your service."

His trousers, half opened, rested low on his lean hips, and she could see the thickening abdominal hair and through his clothes the hard fullness that told her of his desire. Her own body answered with a gathering warmth, a pulsing need, a moist, welcoming throb. And he had yet to touch her.

"No!" Her cry was an anguished plea for him to desist — and for herself to push him away.

"*Yes.*" He grabbed her arms and pulled her against him.

Her fingers touched his chest, felt the heat of his body, the tautness of his muscles, the coarseness of his black body hair — and recoiled into fists. She pounded against him, striking out to cover the growing need to throw herself into his arms. She could not. She must not submit to his will.

Her protests were as feathers in a storm, brushed aside as though they had never been. Rough hands pulled at her blouse, jerking it down to her waist. Hungry eyes devoured the sight of her swollen breasts; his hungry mouth swallowed her half-uttered cry. He ground his body against hers, pushing her back against the door. Caught in the fury of his demands, Gabby flailed against him, at first in protest and then, as her breasts rubbed against his hot skin, as his tongue plundered the recesses of her mouth, in an answering explosion of need that obliterated everything but their mutual desire.

The sweetness of their first lovemaking was forgotten. Rafe needed her more than he ever had, and her wild responses drove him deeper under her spell. He tore the clothes from her, his hands and lips making tracks of passion on her body. Her eager fingers stripped his lean hips of their trousers, and they were soon lying naked in bed, their arms and legs wrapped around one another, each caught in the maelstrom of their separate desires and yet each compelled into a deeper frenzy by the responses their lovemaking aroused.

There was nothing Gabby could deny him now, nothing he demanded of her that she didn't give in wild excitement. His lips burned against her throat and breasts, his hands stroked her buttocks, his fingers parted the moist, intimate folds between her thighs and relentlessly caressed her until she was at the brink of ecstasy.

And then he stopped. She heard herself whimper against him a soft, incredulous "No."

He'd meant to be cruel, to taunt her and make her beg for the release he could give her, but when he looked into her pleading eyes he knew for a bitter second how much she meant to him. Tonight at least she would know a wondrous rapture in his arms. He would give her nothing to regret.

Under Rafe's hot gaze, Gabby cried out again. What was he doing to her? What special torment had he devised that she could so completely debase herself to everything that he wanted her to do? Her body was on fire for him; it little mattered that he was deliberately fanning the flames.

And then there was no time for thought as Rafe answered her cry and parted her legs, his body coming down on hers, his penetration of her flesh at once both a torment and a release. Faster and faster came his unsparing thrust, and she answered him with an equal frenzy, her body arched to meet his. They were of one mind, one desire. Their joining was more than just body to body. As their passions brought them together again and again until violent tremors of fulfillment shook them simultaneously, Gabby felt they were joined heart to heart.

Even as the long, slow, downward spiral to reality began, she clung to him, hoping with a foolish hope that she could postpone forever the words that must eventually pass between them. Even through the haze of satiety, she knew they would not be words of love.

Rafe held her tightly, and then with a gentleness that belied the turmoil of his thoughts. He brushed those thoughts aside. Whatever bond held her to him in such sweet contentment, he knew it was too fragile for examination.

They lay silent in each other's arms for a long while, only the sound of their measured breath breaking the stillness of the room. Outside Gabby could hear the echoes of a sonorous guitar, of laughter, of the world. It all seemed a million miles away.

Rafe pulled away first, and she lifted love-drugged, heavy lids to look up at him, expecting to see satisfaction, even triumph in his eyes. Well, let him enjoy his victory. She had certainly proven that he had been right. She wanted him. No matter how he had treated her, no matter what vows she had made. All that had been necessary for him to do was to reach out, and she had been his.

She was not prepared for his searing look of pain. The contempt which quickly followed it was more to her expectations. Even as she recoiled from the power of that stare, she thought that it was directed not so much at her as at two of them. As though he shared her weakness, and reviled himself for it as much as he

138

did her. Twisting away from him, she used the blanket they had been lying on to cover her nakedness.

"I hadn't meant for that to happen," he said, more to himself than to her, his eyes directed to a dark corner of the room.

She felt chilled and slipped further under the blanket. "Somehow," she said, her voice curt, "I thought otherwise. Especially considering the way you dragged me up to the room."

Rafe's lips twisted into a sardonic smile. "You misunderstand me. From the moment I saw you with Almeida, I knew we would end up this way. And so did you." His eyes hardened. "I was talking about something else. When I left you in San Antonio, I told myself that one time with you was enough."

Gabby fought against the hurt that settled in her heart. "You're right, I don't understand. I may not have much experience, Rafe, but I would have sworn you received your share of pleasure from what just happened. This time maybe more than before."

"I'm not talking about pleasure, Gabby. That you certainly give. I just keep forgetting what you want in return." He moved from the bed and reached for his clothes, pulling them on in graceful, sure movements.

How often must he have played this scene before, she wondered, dressing in front of a woman after a moment of passion. Perhaps this was the way love-making often ended. If so, she wanted no part of it ever again. No matter how glorious it could seem for a while, passion wasn't worth the pain.

"Then tell me, Rafe. Just what do you remember?"

He closed the silver buckle of his belt with a snap.

"Don't be coy with me, Gabby. I know what you really want from me."

"So we're back to that, are we?" she murmured. "You seem intent on believing the worst."

Her lovely vulnerability reached out to him, but he steeled himself against its power. "Your mother was a whore, wasn't she? Were you trying to follow in her path back in San Antonio? Maybe trade your considerable charms—and your virginity—for my cooperation? I'm sorry I disappointed you, *querida*. Nobody's that good in bed."

Without knowing what she was doing, she came out from under the blanket, her arms raised, and flung herself at him. Her nails scratched deep furrows in his face. He threw her back onto the bed, but she rejoiced to see a thin line of blood stain his cheek.

"You bastard!"

"Now that I'm not. Can you prove the same? Did Roberto Cordero bother to call in a preacher before he enjoyed what your mother had to offer?"

Tears glittered in her eyes, but her voice was unwavering. "Don't mention my mother again, Rafe. Ever. I'll kill you if you do. Whatever you believe about me, she is no part of what's happening now."

Rafe stared at her for a long time. "All right," he said at last. "For that and that alone I apologize. We'll both be better off if I don't see you again. Stay away from the Seco, and from Ben. If you're smart, you'll get out of town and forget whatever it is you're planning. You'll regret it if you don't."

"Is that a threat?"

"It's a promise."

140

The whole scene had taken on the aspects of a nightmare from which Gabby thought she would never awake.

"Get out!" Breaking the gold chain that hung suspended from her neck, she threw the cross at his feet. "And take this with you. If you think I'm so vile, I can't imagine why you ever bought it in the first place."

He stared down contemptuously at the jewelry, then turned to leave. Unlocking the door, he paused to look back at her.

"If you try to get that land, I'll keep the case tied up in court so long you'll be as old as Ben before it's settled."

The door slammed behind him, and she sat in stunned silence for a moment. From deep within her a violent rage began to build, obliterating whatever tender thoughts she had ever held for him, replacing the hurt that had threatened to crush her.

So Rafe Jericho thought he had already won their battle, did he? What puny threats he had flung at her, as though they were strong enough to destroy her dream.

If anything, she ought to be grateful to him. She'd thrilled to the pleasures of his lovemaking and for a time let dreams of him blur what she always considered her destiny. And all for the way she felt in his arms.

But no more. She'd been burned twice by passion. There was no way between heaven and hell she would ever submit to him again.

It was almost midnight by the time Rafe spurred his horse through the gate of the Arroyo Seco. He'd ridden hard away from town and from the woman who had so quickly destroyed what was left of his peace of mind. He'd been a great deal better off when all he'd had to fight were natural disasters and Earl Hunter. Now he had to struggle with himself.

After San Antonio, he'd been so sure he would forget his passion for Gabby. When he saw her again, the only thing he had planned was inflicting a little of the pain she'd brought to him.

But that was before he came upon her accidentally with that fool Almeida, saw the way she flirted and tossed that lovely, scheming head of hers. Maybe she had been trying to get away from him, but that didn't mean she wouldn't have picked out someone else. If she was so hot for a man, he'd made damned sure she sought relief with nobody but him.

He was glad he'd pulled himself back from that delectable trap that she so expertly presented to him. Too late and too weakly did she protest her innocence. If she'd confessed her scheme when he'd first confronted her back in San Antonio, perhaps even then he might have forgiven her, fool that he was. But she was too dishonest for that.

She was convincing, all right, with her wide blue eyes and trembling, full lips. He wondered if she'd practiced that look in the mirror since she used it with such expert ease against him. There wasn't much that he wouldn't put past her.

He topped a rise and looked down on the moon-bathed hacienda that was his home. Waiting inside for him was his grandfather, a lonely and bitter man. Rafe knew a woman had been the cause of his unhappiness, but Ben had never revealed the full story. It was his secret to keep. Puzzled that such bitterness could last through the years, Rafe had nevertheless respected his privacy. Now, with the memory of Gabby sharp in his mind and her fragrance still clinging to his skin, he understood the power a woman could have over a man.

Slowly he began his descent to the hacienda. "Don't worry, Ben," he said into the night air. "I know how much this place means to you. Old man, it's all we've got, it and each other. I swear by your daughter's grave that nothing will ever break us apart."

Chapter Seven

"Gabrielle Deschamps, you've been attacking those knitting needles for almost twenty minutes, and I'll have for lunch any row of stitches you haven't pulled out twice."

Gabby lifted her dark lashes and looked across the parlor at Emma Talbert, the simmering distress she was holding just beneath the surface of her calm temporarily dispelled. "Does that hold true for any I might eventually complete?" she asked, smiling. "If that's true, I'll have this shawl finished by noon."

"Humph!" Emma shifted in the large rocking chair. "Never could stand a smart aleck. You know what I'm getting at. If I thought you were troubled when I first set eyes on you, I was wrong. Compared to today, you were singing in the streets."

Gabby couldn't argue with that. When she first met Emma, she hadn't seen Rafe again, hadn't . . .

She tried to shut her mind to thoughts of the fandango and to the memories of how easily she'd submitted to Rafe's fiery touch. Emma called her troubled, but she was a great deal more than that. Throughout the long hours Saturday night listening to the music from the plaza, she had lain in a tangle of covers where she'd answered with passionate abandon Rafe's demands and come close to despair. The feeling was with her still.

The man had a power over her that tore at the shreds of composure she held to her like a shield. Whenever he appeared, she couldn't think clearly, couldn't be true to everything she held dear about herself and her dreams.

Yesterday had been a hard day to get through alone. Rising early, she had roamed Laredo, first attending Mass, then walking around the plaza, alternately feeding the many pigeons and herself, trying to ignore the empty stalls and scattered debris that were all that remained of the fiesta.

Beside her had walked memories of Rafe. Since she couldn't get him out of her mind, she tried to think only of the few happy times they'd had together — Rafe holding her close, Rafe facing the snake in their interrupted idyll by the river, Rafe fastening the cross around her neck.

The last look of him was the image that kept returning. In frustration she had leaped from a bench on the plaza and stridden through a gray sea of pigeons. The image had remained. Only the birds had given way before her wrath.

She needed something ordinary to occupy her mind, like sitting in the sun-filled parlor of the Talbert home and knitting while she and the pleasant woman across the room exchanged innocuous talk of needlework and cooking, of where she might take a room until she found a more permanent place. Emma's invitation delivered to the hotel a few hours ago had been readily accepted.

The Talberts' two-story frame home with its verandas that wrapped around both stories and its gingerbread ornamentation was only a few blocks from the hotel, nestled in a wooded oasis close to the Rio Grande. Gabby had no sooner settled in and taken her knitting in hand than the memories she was fighting stirred restlessly in her mind. Perhaps what she did need was to share them — at least some of them — but there were personal details she could never put into words.

Turning once more to her knitting, she observed with disgust the mess she was making with the tangle of red yarn in her lap and tossed it aside on the floor.

"I've not done a thing right since I arrived on the train, Emma."

"I'm guessin'," Emma said, her eyes on her needlework, "that fandango didn't turn out the way you were hoping."

"You're guessing right."

"Now, Gabrielle, you don't have to tell me what's troubling you, but to my way of thinking a person with a heavy load of worry like yours ought to share the burden. I've got broad shoulders and big ears. And contrary to what you may think, I can keep a confidence."

Gabby took a deep breath and plunged into her story of why she had come to town, including the way she had met Rafe Jericho outside a San Antonio saloon. She didn't go into the details of everything that had passed between them — or the reasons they had parted—but the look on Emma's face told Gabby the woman understood much of what had been withheld.

"I saw Rafe again Saturday night," Gabby said bluntly. "He accused me of some pretty ugly things."

She looked out the window at a scattering of post oak and mesquite that dotted an expanse of green lawn. She thought for a long time of what had brought her this heaviness of heart, of the accusations Rafe had hurled at her about her past. His apology had come too late for her to even try to tell him the truth. But she wanted someone to understand, and when she looked back at Emma her mind was made up.

"I'd like to tell you a few things about myself," she said. "About the way I was raised."

Emma continued to rock, her hands moving smoothly at her needlework, her eyes resting on Gabby.

"My mother was a courtesan," Gabby said, holding Emma's gaze. "Some people called her a whore. Some still do."

Emma's expression remained unchanged. "And what did you call her?"

"She was Mama to me, and sometimes Colette. She was so young when I was born, and she used to talk to me like another grown-up. Advising me on how to live my life. And the ways of men. I should have listened and believed more about that, but sometimes I just wished for someone my own age to talk to."

"Sounds to me like there was a lot of love between you two."

"There was. She was all I had." Gabby's voice broke

and she paused for a moment. "She was only seventeen when my father rode into town in his Confederate uniform. She said the uniform may have been tattered and dirty, but when she looked up at him on that stallion he was the handsomest thing she had ever seen. Mama's family had been killed by Apaches soon after they came over from France and she was working at a restaurant near the Alamo. My father was in town to get a shipment of guns his unit was waiting on back in Laredo."

"And it was love at first sight," Emma said.

Gabby laughed sharply. "Yes, if there is such a thing. I don't know what would have happened if Roberto Cordero had lived. As it was he was in town only long enough to marry Mama. He left her with a lot of stories about his land down here. And of course with me."

" 'Pears to me he left a great deal."

"What he left was a young bride who couldn't work much longer doing the tasks she'd done before. She saved what little she could and the Laredo commander, Santos Benavides, did send a little money after my father's death. He wrote her it was all that was left of what had once been a fortune before the Corderos lost their land. After I was born, Mama outfitted herself and started looking for a job as a nanny. She knew music and poetry and languages. And she could sew as well as the finest seamstress."

"Was there much demand in San Antonio for nannies?"

"Not a lot. Except on King William Street, where the wealthy Germans lived. Some of them had been counts or barons back in Germany. At least they claimed they had. She found one who set us up in a little house in the back of his estate, and for little more than her upkeep he had her try to teach his three sons the ways of the Old World."

"Did she succeed?"

"In a manner of speaking, yes. I don't think the boys ever learned much. I was never allowed to play with them so I can't be sure. But it wasn't long before Papa Fritz—that's what he said to call him—fell in love with her, he said. I didn't know it until years later, but he started visiting her at night. All I knew was we were moved to a bigger place away from his home. Mama says she learned to care for him. Claimed he couldn't get a divorce because of his religion and because of his boys. Men do learn to use women, don't they?"

"Did your Mama ever think about leaving?"

"I guess if she'd been stronger she might have. But she had me to worry about. And she never was very healthy. She taught me at home—protecting me, I suppose, from what the other children said at school. I never really had much of a childhood, but with Mama so close I didn't miss it. We were happy. The problems began when Papa Fritz died."

The soft look on Gabby's face hardened. "She had taken Fritz's regard and continued support for granted. Everything he gave was soon spent, and his sudden death left her nearly destitute. She couldn't really blame him for dying early, but she could for what happened next. It seems he had done a little bragging to his friends, and he was no sooner in the ground when one of them came around. Colette wasn't so trusting after that, and she had a series of gentleman callers. Never more than one at a time, but they each lasted only a few months. She never again gave her heart away."

Gabby looked defiantly at Emma. "Have I shocked you by what I've said?"

"My dear, it would take a lot more than that to shock Emma Talbert. Seems to me you got someone to be proud of."

"Thank you for that. Colette never took to the streets, no matter what anyone else might say." Rafe's ugly words of Saturday night rang in her mind. "She did what she had to do to get by, and for that she should never be harshly judged. No one would think of condemning the men who came to call."

"There are some things in this world, Gabrielle, that will just never change."

Gabby laughed sharply. "You want to know the funny thing about all of this? I'm financially well off. Not rich, but I'm not worried about my next meal, either. Mama managed it by being frugal the way she wasn't when Fritz was alive. If she got any jewelry, she sold it, and whatever "gifts of money" as she called them were bestowed she invested. Some of the gentlemen were shrewd businessmen and gave her financial advice. The investments didn't really begin to grow in value until after her death. That was how I was able to go back east to school. And how I'm able to have the money to negotiate with Ben Hidalgo now."

Gabby lifted her head proudly. "That's one thing Rafe may not realize about me. I've got money in the bank."

"You reckon there's enough to fix up a place of your own? When you get the land, that is."

"It will be enough," Gabby said. "And to take care of me until I get what I came for."

"You sound mighty determined, Gabrielle. When I met you the other day, I figured you'd be heading back pretty soon to San Antonio. Looks like I figured wrong."

"Looks like you did. I'm not going back. I've come to make a home for myself. It's only just that I settle on at least a corner of my father's land."

"You sure you're after only a home?"

"I was until yesterday. Now," Gabby said, her hands curled into fists, "I'm after Rafe Jericho's hide."

"Sounds like more than just a squabble over land. You willing to take a little advice from a busybody? You want your own place, don't you? Don't let anything Rafe may have said or done steer you away from what you're after."

"Maybe I can get them both, Emma." Gabby thought of the bitter disappointment of Rafe's tenuous affection, of the hopes he had raised for their loving union, and of his doubts that had so quickly dashed those hopes. "I've enough determination in me right now to get it all. A few acres of the Cordero land and Rafe's head laid out on a stretch of cowhide. Talking with you has done me a lot of good. Instead of sitting around feeling sorry for myself and stewing in a pointless anger, I'm ready to take up the battle again."

"You got a plan in mind?"

"The one I had when I first decided to come down here. I'm going to pay a little visit to the Arroyo Seco and find out if Benito Hidalgo is any more honorable than Rafe."

"He's just as stubborn. And a mean old codger, to

151

boot. Folks around here don't have much to do with him. You sure that's the thing for you to do?"

"Emma, now you sound like Franklin Bernard."

"Bite your tongue, Gabrielle. I'm just thinking of you. Seems to me you don't need to ask for any more problems than you've already got."

"I can handle them." Gabby's eyes flashed blue fire. "And there's somebody else I'd like to meet. Ever hear of a man named Earl Hunter?"

Emma's face registered surprise. "What do you have to do with that man? He's as mean and crooked as they come."

"He's also the man Rafe listened to back in San Antonio. Hunter told him some lies about me, and Rafe believed him."

"That don't sound like Rafe to me. Not a better liked man in the county. Nor a more respected one."

"I'm telling you the truth. Hunter set one of his men onto Rafe. The man was killed. I guess telling lies about me was a kind of revenge. Rafe and I had . . . become friends."

"Figured as much," Emma said. "Gabrielle, Earl Hunter has been after that ranch land, too. Rumor is he'd do most anything to get it. Only been around these parts for a few years, but he's not exactly ingratiated himself to folks. Especially old Ben and Rafe."

Nor has he made a friend of me, Gabby thought.

Perhaps if Rafe had learned another way, if they'd learned at the same time who the other was, much heartache—and hatred—could have been avoided. Perhaps. But Rafe had been too quick to condemn her. He'd demanded she justify herself. And he wanted her to give up her dream. Rafe Jericho didn't know her at all.

Emma's voice penetrated her thoughts. "Earl Hunter is a powerful enemy, Gabrielle. Stay away from him."

"I'll be careful, Emma. All I want to do is talk to the man. The same as with Ben."

Emma shook her head. "Old Ben loves that grandson of his even more than he loves the ranch. Only two things he cares about in the whole world. If Rafe's against you, you don't stand a snowball's chance in hell of convincing the old man to listen."

"I've got to try. Is the ranch far from town?"

"About an hour's ride by wagon. The trail is easy to make out. I hear when Consuelo and her husband were still alive, lots of traffic rode out that way. Parties and such. You thinking about going soon?"

"I'm thinking about going today."

"You want some company?"

"All I need is some information about where I can get a horse and wagon."

Emma shook her head. "Now that I can let you borrow. That and a man to ride escort." She held up a hand. "Don't tell me you don't need one. Unless you're a sharpshooter with a rifle, and I'm guessing you're not. Let me get a little lunch down you and a little more advice. You've got to take them both before I'll have the wagon readied and send you on your way."

Gabby took at least a part of Emma's advice. She dressed in the most conservative traveling suit she owned, pulled her hair back in a sedate twist at the nape of her neck, and didn't argue anymore about the escort guiding the rig. Ephraim Bartz, a purse-lipped little man Emma had borrowed from her husband's dry goods store, said little on the journey out to the ranch, but she noticed he kept his eye warily on the surrounding countryside. An old carbine lay at his feet. Perhaps he was a more competent guard than he looked.

"Are there many bandits in the area?" she asked when they were out of town.

"Not many. Just can't be too cautious, I always say." He patted the bulge in his shirt pocket. "Got plenty bullets," he said. Hastily he clamped both hands back on the reins and gripped them tightly, allowing the horse to maintain the plodding walk more typical of a plowhorse than one providing transportation.

Gabby was irritated at their slow pace but declined to initiate any more conversation. Now that the meeting she had been determined to have was at hand, she had too much on her mind to hurry into it. Did Ben Hidalgo even know she existed? Or had Rafe thought her quest so trivial that he hadn't bothered to mention her when he returned to the ranch?

She spent a few minutes thinking that with any luck Rafe would be out on the range somewhere this time of day, but her experience on ranches was limited. He could be anywhere, even around the next bend or behind the nearest rock.

She found herself sitting ramrod straight, every muscle tense as she stared anxiously down the rutted path in front of the creaking wagon. Disgusted at her lack of self-control, she relaxed. If she had to face

Rafe and his grandfather together, so be it. In truth, she'd rather face the two of them than Rafe alone.

True to her promise to Franklin Bernard, she'd stopped by his office to tell him where she'd be. She was relieved to find he was at the courthouse, and she settled for a hastily scribbled message. Maybe she should have waited until the attorney could come with her, but when she tried to picture Franklin Bernard serving as a barricade between her and Rafe, she had failed.

Bartz finally spoke. "The house is over that rise," he said, nodding toward the south, and once again Gabby sat in rigid expectation.

When the wagon topped the hill, she looked down on the house and smiled. The main hacienda of the ranch, a rambling, white stucco structure with a red tile roof, was nestled in a valley not far off the main trail. The sun beamed on the brightly colored flowers that grew in neat rows along the front, a cheerful contrast to the surrounding brown land sharply ridged and dotted with cactus and low-lying brush.

Her stomach tightened as the wagon headed down the narrow trail leading to the house. The afternoon air was hot and the steady hum of invisible cicadas filled the air. Any minute she expected to see a tall, lean figure appear at the door, a cynical look sharpening his face, his brown eyes daring her to come closer. Her hands gripped the side of the wagon, her back straight, unblinking eyes held steady on her destination.

A sharp sound as loud as a gunshot came from the side of the hacienda. The startled Bartz flung the reins away and reached for the gun at his feet. The horse, relieved of the bit's pull against his mouth, set out at a quickened pace. Jounced from her rigid position, Gabby grabbed up the reins just before they drifted out of reach and by the time the wagon neared the bottom of the slope had the horse again under control.

Bartz, oblivious to her efforts, was still attempting to force a shell into the breech of the rifle.

Gabby pulled the horse to a halt. "All your bullets were in your pocket?" she asked, unable to hide her incredulity. Even a green girl who'd been years in the East knew the folly of that.

"Unsafe to ride with a loaded gun. Knew a man once who shot off his foot."

If Gabby hadn't seen Ephraim Bartz walking without any sign of a limp, she might have guessed he was that man.

"There is such a thing as being too cautious," she said. "Could you hit anything even if that thing was loaded?"

"I don't know for sure. It's been a while since I tried." Bartz shifted nervously in the seat. "Besides, Miz Talbert didn't send me along to ride shotgun. A wheel might come off or something, she said, and you shouldn't be alone."

Wait until Emma hears about this, Gabby thought, then changed her mind. Emma shouldn't be told anything. If Gabby talked too much, the well-meaning woman would send out the cavalry from Fort McIntosh as escort the next time she left town.

Drawing her eyes away from Bartz, Gabby looked once more toward the house. The sharp sound hadn't repeated itself. If it did, she would have to defend herself, although she very much doubted Rafe would be after her with a gun. He had a much more devastating way of getting to her.

She relaxed. "No problem anyway," she said, nodding toward the house. "We weren't under attack after all."

A young vaquero she estimated to be no more than sixteen years old had strolled into view and was staring at them. In one hand was the handle of a leather bullwhip, its long tail trailing like a serpent in the grass at his feet. The whip had most certainly been the source of the startling sound.

Gabby, waving in greeting, was glad to see a hesitant wave in return. She was even happier to note that Rafe was nowhere in sight. *"Buenos dias,"* she said. "Is Senor Hidalgo at home?"

"Si." The young man continued to stare up at her.

"Do you speak English?"

"Si."

"Would you tell the senor he has a visitor and then help Mister Bartz here take care of the horse?" Gabby smiled at him. "And please don't say just *si.*"

A grin split his dark face. "No."

Gabby could recognize a teaser when she met one, and she was facing one now. Climbing down from the wagon, she walked over to the vaquero. "That's not much of an improvement. Would you mind telling me your name?"

The young man pulled his body erect. "Francisco de la Guerra. *A su servicio.* Please call me Cisco, senorita."

"Cisco, I'm Gabrielle Deschamps." She waited for the hostility that would show Rafe had ordered her

157

thrown off the ranch if she was daring enough to come calling. Cisco continued to smile warmly at her.

"Would it be possible for me to meet with Senor Hidalgo?" she asked.

"It is possible, senorita," Cisco said, "but—"

His reply was interrupted by the closing of the hacienda's front door.

"Cisco, *por favor*—" The rhythmic Spanish words stopped, and the young girl who had emerged into the sunlight looked toward the Seco's visitors with widened dark eyes. When she saw Gabby, her alarm seemed to pass.

At most a year older than Cisco, the girl was beautiful. Gabby could think of no other way to describe her. A mass of black hair fell loosely to her shoulders, her tawny skin was flawless, and her lips full and red, yet there was a childlike innocence about her gentle features that Gabby found charming. Her cotton dress, belted tightly around her narrow waist by an apron, revealed a woman's body at variance with the youthful look of her face. When she looked into the girl's eyes, Gabby was reminded of a frightened doe she'd seen once in the woods, a hunted look that didn't go away despite the smile of greeting on her face.

"*Buenos días,*" the girl said, then slipped into a soft, sibilant English. "Welcome to the Arroyo Seco. Forgive Cisco if he has been rude to you. Sometimes he likes to play like a *niño.*" She looked sternly at the boy. "Senor Jericho might flay all the skin from your body if you don't get to him soon with the wagon," she said, waving to the buckboard loaded with red spools of wire.

158

Cisco grinned and flicked the whip at the ground near the girl's feet. "Senor Rafael also tells me to practice," he said. "It is with pride I do well all the jobs the senor gives me to do."

The girl smiled. "Always the bragging," she said. "Be gone with you. *Mañana* comes!"

"He wasn't rude at all," Gabby said, interrupting the exchange and extending her hand. "Good afternoon. My name is Gabrielle Deschamps." Again her name was met with nothing more than a pleasant smile tinged with curiosity. "Please forgive my coming unannounced, but I need to see the owner of the ranch. I have some business I'd like to discuss with him."

"I am sorry, but Senor Jericho is not at home. He is on the range with the foreman Antonio. They should be gone most of the day where the lazy Cisco must go."

Gabby couldn't miss the softness in the girl's eyes when she mentioned the foreman. At the same time she felt a fleeting pang of regret that Rafe wasn't lurking around somewhere ready to pounce. As though she had wanted to see him again. She really *was* a foolish girl to miss such unpleasantness.

"You misunderstood me," said Gabby. "I said the owner, Ben Hidalgo."

"Forgive me, senorita, but Rafael has for so long acted as the senor."

"What is your name, senorita?" Gabby asked.

"Lupita," the girl said, her eyes lowered.

"Lupita, could you please ask Senor Hidalgo if he could see me? I've come a long way and waited a long time for this visit."

159

"Por supuesto." Lupita stood aside and gestured a slender hand to the door. Gabby noticed a puckered scar that nearly encircled her wrist, jagged like a wound caused by a wild animal.

Bartz and Cisco disappeared around the house and Gabby followed Lupita inside. The house, she found, was built around a large tiled area that was open to the sky. Plants and flowers in earthen pots decorated it, and there were scattered chairs beneath a single tall oak tree in one corner. A walkway bordered the patio, and it was along this path that she followed the girl.

They entered a large kitchen. One wall was taken with a huge fireplace and iron stove; along another was a bank of open windows that allowed the fresh air to cool the room. Blue and white tile adorned the walls and cabinets, and through the windows Gabby could see a vegetable garden and in the background a rising expanse of gray-green hills.

From the kitchen Gabby followed Lupita through a large dining room, also with colored tiles around the wall, then into a larger salon with heavy oak furniture relieved only by two comfortable-looking leather wing chairs. On a sideboard were two clay pitchers and an array of bottles and glasses.

Lupita waved toward one of the chairs. "If you will wait here, senorita, I will bring you refreshment and announce you to Senor Benito." She poured water from one of the pitchers and handed it to Gabby. "It is cool," she said. "Senor Rafael insists we keep much water in the house. Next year he has promised a pump in *la cocina.*" She smiled proudly and disappeared through another door beside the dormant fireplace.

Sipping gratefully from the cool glass, Gabby decided the place was clean and homelike. If Rafe dictated that the place be kept comfortable and convenient, that must mean he spent a lot of time here. She pushed the thought aside. It was her father who had brought her here, and she should be concentrating on the coming meeting with Ben Hidalgo.

Lupita returned almost immediately, looking downcast. "Senor Benito is awake and will see you, but I fear he is not *simpatico* this afternoon."

The girl seemed genuinely disturbed about Hidalgo, and Gabby wondered what the old man had done to upset her. Everyone had told her what a difficult person he was, and, her heartbeat quickening, she decided everyone was no doubt right.

Gabby took a deep breath and prayed Rafe hadn't told his grandfather about her. She would rather approach the man with what she knew were reasonable requests, without his having already been swayed by Rafe's harsh interpretations.

She drank, using the edge of the glass to hide any expression that might reveal her thoughts. When she lowered it, Lupita seemed in no hurry to announce her, and Gabby decided a little conversation was in order.

"Is Senor Hidalgo well?"

"The senor grows tired in the afternoons, yet I have heard him and Rafael talk far into the night. They argue. They discuss the *rancho*."

"Have you been at the Seco long?" Gabby asked.

"A year. I came here with my parents after . . . some trouble." Lupita rubbed at the scar on her wrist. "Senor Rafael saved my life by letting me remain."

The girl grew silent with what Gabby could see were uncomfortable memories.

From somewhere in the house came the sound of an insistent bell.

"Senor Benito is ready to see you now," said Lupita. "I will take you to him."

Gabby smoothed her skirts and followed the young housekeeper. When she entered the large room, darkened by curtains drawn against the afternoon sun, she was able to make out Ben Hidalgo sitting facing her behind a large desk.

Even in the dim light she could see how much he resembled Rafe. Despite the wrinkles and narrowed eyes, she could make out the same high cheekbones, straight nose, and determined mouth. His hair, thick and worn to his collar's edge, was as white as his grandson's was dark.

He was erect over a ledger open before him. In his hand was a pen; when she drew nearer, she could see the ink had long since dried on its nib.

He closed the book and shoved it back on the desk, then dropped the pen into the drawer, leaving the cleared desk top to reflect the dim light from a brass oil lamp burning despite the daylight outside. The Arroyo Seco's owners were not ones to pinch pennies by saving oil. Rising slightly from his chair, Hidalgo gestured toward another, then sank back and clasped his mottled hands on the desk.

As Gabby sat and arranged her skirts, she was grateful for the dimness that would help obscure the reluctance she felt. Ben Hidalgo did indeed look perpetually angry, as Lupita had said. She'd expected a man bowed by the troubles that were besetting his land. Instead, he sat like an eagle casting a proud eye over a domain that was his. Implacable, unyielding, she thought as she studied his hard eyes and mouth. Already she could taste the defeat the interview was sure to bring.

But, she reminded herself, this was the man who had lied under oath to get what he wanted. She sat up straighter and waited for him to speak, watching his belligerent expression settle into one of calculation.

"We get few visitors to the *rancho*, only those who would bring trouble," he said in excellent English. "Are you one of these, Senorita Deschamps?"

The old man was like his grandson in more than just looks, Gabby thought. He said exactly what was on his mind. And without any of Rafe's undisputed charm. So far, Ben had done no more than offer her a chair, something he would have done for a cowhand, and he didn't yet know why she had come to see him, had no reason to be rude. For all he knew, she had come from the bank with a million dollars.

She swallowed an angry retort and reminded herself of the reasonable arguments she'd come to present. Now was not the time for her usual and unadorned candor. "No, I'm not here to make trouble," she said. "At least I hope you won't see it that way."

He peered at her through the dust motes caught in a shaft of light from the window. "Why are you here, senorita?"

"I am here," Gabby said, well aware of the tremor in her voice, "about my Grandfather Cordero."

"Carlos!" The name was at once a whisper and a curse on the old man's lips.

"I am the only child of his son, Roberto," she

continued. There was no way to soften her words. "I have returned to his home."

Hidalgo sat stiff in his chair, his only reaction a malevolent gleam in his eyes. "There is nothing here that is Cordero, nor ever will be again." He spoke with finality.

Gabby forced herself to hold the man's stare. "Senor Hidalgo, my mother died a long time ago, but she left me with a dream, a desire for a home on the land that is my patrimony." She kept her tone carefully controlled. "I ask that you listen to what I have to say. Surely we can find a settlement that will be fair to both of us."

"There can never be fairness between a Cordero and a Hidalgo. Your family does not know the word."

The old man's rancor was rubbing off on Gabby. He hadn't heard so much as a syllable of her proposition, and already he was dismissing her with hurtful words.

"Senor," she said, undisguised impatience in her voice, "I have heard of the court proceedings by which the Corderos lost their property. I seek only redress for the wrongs that were committed then."

"Speak bluntly, senorita. What is it you want?"

"A fair share of what should have been Cordero land."

If the man was shaken by her words, he didn't show it by so much as a blink of an eye. "I have worked this land for forty years. My sweat and blood have watered its dryness. There is nothing that would be your fair share."

"My attorney tells me differently. Although I want only enough to serve as my home, he says I should demand the entire Cordero ranch, the original Spanish land grant. All thirty thousand acres. It was your testimony, and yours alone, that went against my grandfather and led to the taking of his land. Testimony that was never substantiated."

Hidalgo's tight lips curled in disgust. "Carlos got only what was coming to him, a part of what was his due."

"Why do you say that? I can prove otherwise. Don't force me to bring suit against you when we could settle this now."

Hidalgo pushed back from the desk, and the chair legs against the tile underfoot seemed to shriek in harmony with his renewed anger. He rose to tower over the desk.

"Do not mention the name Cordero in my presence," he hissed. "Is it not enough that we have to fight a greedy neighbor on one side and the bank on the other? That the bankers have gone back on their word to extend our loan? Must we be tortured by ghosts from the past as well?"

"I am no ghost, Senor Hidalgo. And I will not go away."

Here it was, Gabby thought, the confrontation everyone had warned her to avoid. Somehow she must convince the enraged Hidalgo of her strength of purpose. She stood and moved closer to the light so that he could see her face.

"Don't dismiss me so quickly," she said, leaning forward against the desk and looking directly into his dark eyes. "I don't want to fight you. But I will not back down."

She paused, waiting for his response, but he remained strangely still, his eyes now empty of anger as he stared at her face in the light.

"*Madre de Dios,*" he whispered. "You've come back."

Gabby stared back at him, wondering if the old man were quite sane. His rages came and went with bewildering speed. "Is something wrong, Senor Hidalgo? Perhaps," she said, trying to soften her approach, "you need time to think over what I have said. Surely you will decide—"

His fist came down hard on the desk, interrupting her plea.

"Never will you get my land! Never!" he screamed.

Gabby backed up until her legs were against the chair. "Senor Hidalgo—"

Hidalgo gave her no chance to talk. "You are but a woman," he said in a staccato voice. "You will not have what you seek. This land is mine, and it will be my grandson's. But never yours. Never a Cordero's. You are not worth the dirt beneath your feet. Never will the land be yours. Never."

Eyes wide, Gabby listened to his ranting, felt the words hit her like the sting of a whip. But she held her ground. For some reason that she did not know, the old man viewed her as a personal enemy. Whatever that reason, it went far beyond her attempts to bargain for a corner of his land.

"You question my worth?" she asked. "I can see where your grandson gets his arrogance."

"So you know Rafe, do you?" he said, suddenly quiet as his eyes moved down her body. His gaze made her feel unclean. "He is quite good with such as you." Hidalgo leaned over the desk and in an obscenely confidential tone, asked, "Did you try very

166

hard to get the land from him first?'

Gabby forced herself not to shrink before his insinuating question.

"I'm surprised he didn't fill you with lies about our meeting," she said.

"A Hidalgo does not lie. Only the Corderos lie."

"When did a Cordero lie to you? It seems that my family received only injustice at your hands. My grandfather died, just how I will never know, and his land was lost." And, she thought bitterly, she too had been the victim of injustice at the hands of the old man's grandson, but she could never tell him that. She could imagine what names would be thrown in her face.

"Carlos once took what was mine. No one will do so again—not you, not the banks, not Hunter—"

"You did not answer my question, Senor Hidalgo. When and how did a Cordero lie to you? And now you say he took something that was yours. Was it as valuable as a stolen ranch?"

His face shuttered all emotion. "It is of no matter," he said. "We will forget I ever spoke of it." Thin, trembling hands raked through a shock of white hair, the only sign of his continued agitation.

Again Hidalgo was acting crazy, Gabby thought, and gave up trying to find out what he had been talking about with his accusations of Cordero lies. It was enough that the battle lines between them had been drawn. She stood tall, sure she was in her right, proud that she had the courage to face the fury of his opposition.

"You cannot forget me, Senor. I am real and I am going to fight you in the courts. Can you afford such a fight?"

Hidalgo drew himself up and laughed harshly. "What's money? Bah! As you can see, you are merely one gnat among a cloud of other troubles. But the Hidalgos never back down."

Impulsively Gabby reached out for his hand. "This time you will lose, indomitable old man. This time you will."

He flung off her touch. "Do not try to sway me, senorita. With your woman's touch or your woman's lies. The *rancho* is mine. You have no place here. Now get out."

"You insinuate ugly things about me, senor," she said, her head held high as his. "It is a trait that runs in your family. And you also make the mistake of assuming that because I am a woman, I am weak. I can assure you, Senor Hidalgo, that assumption is your biggest mistake of all."

She turned and, summoning her dignity, walked rapidly from the room and down the walkway that stretched toward a door she assumed opened to the outside. Once more in the sunlight, she motioned to Ephraim Bartz to bring the wagon. Lupita did not appear and the wagon loaded with barbed wire was gone.

As they rode up the long incline that led from the hacienda, she picked up the now loaded rifle and stood it beside her knee. "Let's go," she said. Bartz took one look at her set face and sent the wagon forward at a fast clip.

She allowed herself a last glance at the hacienda and wondered if it were the childhood home of the father she had never known. In her mind's eye she could picture standing in the door of the hacienda the young Roberto Cordero that her mother had often described. Slowly the vision of her father faded; in its place appeared the ghost of another man. Tall and dark, Rafe seemed to be waving a good-bye. She blinked. The vision was gone, but the sharp pain it had brought lingered in her heart.

How false appearances could be! Rafe had seemed warmly caring on that brief, wonderful day when he took her for a ride along the river back in San Antonio. Beneath the rakish, handsome face she'd caught glimpses of a man of worth, one that she could depend upon. But she'd been wrong.

The hacienda was just as deceiving. The place looked as pleasant under the lowering sun as it had when she had first arrived. But now she knew how superficial that pleasantness was, for inside lived two men who could brook neither disagreement or opposition.

She settled back in the wagon and watched the rump of the trotting horse, but her thoughts were on the visit. Dignified dress and manner had done her little good in facing the old man; he'd treated her with no more respect than Rafe had shown. When she'd moved into the light to plead her cause and he'd gotten a better look at her, the shouting and scorn had died, replaced by an eerie stillness, as though he were seeing her for the first time. No, it had been more than that. It had been as though he were seeing someone else.

You've come back. She wondered who that someone was.

Even with his extraordinary behavior, Hidalgo had

169

revealed perhaps more than he realized. The bank had failed to extend Rafe's loan. Although she had enough money to buy the land from the bank, to her surprise she took no triumph in the thought. She didn't want all of it, had *never* done so. But she could not sit idly by and let unknown men — bankers — hold title to the Seco for even a short while. Well, strangers had been owning it, she told herself, then shrugged off the irritating thought. Direct action was essential. The reason was of little import.

Gabby stared out at the jagged land. How naive she had been to think she could come to such a country and find easy justice, for that was exactly what she had thought, no matter how much she assured Oscar Cantu she would fight for as long as it took. Rafe and his grandfather would hold her off forever. And if somehow she managed to convince them of her cause, there would most likely be the villainous Earl Hunter, with his own avaricious eye on the land, to see that events didn't progress her way.

Too many men were figuring in her life in ways she had never planned. They were keeping her from her dream.

Leaning back, she began to plan her next move, hardly noticing the heat and dust of the trip. By the time they neared the plaza, she knew what she wanted to do.

She sat up straighter and turned to the silent Bartz. "Please take me to Franklin Bernard's office instead of the hotel," she said. "Perhaps he is keeping late hours today."

Seeing a light in the window, she was grateful that for once luck was on her side. She thanked Bartz for his time and entered Bernard's office without bothering to knock.

Seated at his desk, a stack of papers in his hands, the lawyer looked up at Gabby in surprise.

"Why, Miss Deschamps, what an unexpected pleasure."

Gabby nodded briefly. "If you can do what I want, Mister Bernard, the pleasure will be all mine."

Bernard's high forehead furrowed. "And what is that, Miss Deschamps? I was most distressed when I read your note that you were going out, rather precipitately I'm afraid, to see Senor Hidalgo."

"You were no more distressed than I was after I had seen him. But the visit wasn't entirely wasted. Not at all. I learned several things while I was there. One was that Hidalgo has no intention of negotiating with me. And I have no intention of giving up the fight."

Bernard smiled knowingly. "I could have saved you the trip and told you that."

"I'm not through. There's one more thing—the most important of all. I learned the bank is demanding payment on the loan Rafe took out. The loan for which collateral was the entire Arroyo Seco."

Bernard looked surprised at the news. "Now this I did not know," he said, "nor do I think—" He stopped, then added, "How is this important news, Miss Deschamps? Do you think it will affect your case?"

"What I hope is that I can do something to forestall it. I want you to send a telegram to Oscar Cantu first thing in the morning instructing him to negotiate with the bank officials concerning the purchase of the note they hold against the Seco. I have money in an account there. I trust there will be no problem."

Bernard shook his head nervously. "What exactly is it that you seek?"

"I want to bring the arrogant Rafael Jericho and his grandfather to a position where they will be forced to bargain with me. They think they will postpone a settlement until I am too tired to fight them any further. But they think wrong." Her lips curled into a determined smile. "I have a sudden urge to make a little investment, Mister Bernard. Instruct Canto to buy up the loan."

Under his astonished stare, she held her head high. "Surely you know what I am after. I want the bearer of the note to be changed. After tomorrow it is to be in my name."

Chapter Eight

Rafe planted his boots in the rocky soil and gripped the crowbar in his leather-gloved hands. Lifting the crowbar high, he plunged it downward into dirt as hard and dry as granite; the force jarred his arms and strained the already sore muscles of his back and shoulders.

Rafe paid no mind to the pain, hardly even felt it, preferring to think of the pleasure he would get from burying more than a post in each hole he laboriously dug. He'd gladly dig even deeper and wider if in the hole he could inter all the bankers of the world.

Jabbing viciously at the hole, he saw only Ralph Gentry's face, the very face that had promised his loan would be extended until he could get his spur line built and open up markets in Cuba for his stock. At least, he had taken Gentry's words as a promise, hadn't even known the loan officer could be outvoted on such a thing.

Gentry's letter had been simple enough. The rest of the bank bigwigs feared a glut on the market and the loss of their money. Unless Rafe could come up with payment in full soon, they had no option but to foreclose. The news had hit Ben hard.

And then had come Gabby's visit. Even considering her demands, Ben had reacted strangely to her—talking about someone named Maria, slipping off into the past as he'd been doing lately, then returning to the present to curse the Cordero name.

Rafe had told Ben only that he had met Gabby in San Antonio and found out about her claim against the Seco. No need to tell him the details of her plan to soften Rafe up for the land. His grandfather was upset enough as it was.

It wasn't the old man's irascibility that got to Rafe—he was used to that—but rather the quiet moments when he stared off into space. Once or twice Rafe had thought Ben was going to tell him a story from his past, but he hadn't done so.

There was only one thing Rafe could do now—return to San Antonio and present his case to the bankers again, talk to all of them the way he'd presented his arguments to Gentry. He would take the train north at the end of the week; in the meantime, he'd get this fence strung and make himself too tired to think.

But it was damned hard. When he wasn't planning what he would say in San Antonio or trapped by visions of a blue-eyed blonde, he thought about a problem closer at hand. His neighbor Earl Hunter. Rafe would be less frustrated if his troubles with Hunter would break into open warfare. So far there had been no overt battles—even Sneed hadn't been sent by Hunter to do more than spy—just a kind of frustrating harassment that kept Rafe spending money he would rather invest elsewhere. Downed wires, occasional breed stock missing or poisoned. And, of course, their meeting in San Antonio. Hunter had been at his slimy worst when he'd handed over a copy of the letter Gabby had written to Oscar Cantu.

Rafe plunged the crowbar into the hole again and again. About eighteen feet down the way his foreman Antonio worked industriously at deepening his own posthole. A good man, Antonio, stubborn and quick-tempered, but maybe now ready to settle down. At dawn that day when they'd crawled out of their bedrolls, Antonio had told him of his plans to marry the housekeeper Lupita.

"I have found the one, Rafael," the foreman had said, a grin creating new lines on his face. "She has had a life that was *muy difícil* before coming to your *rancho*. She makes me happy. I want to do the same for her."

Rafe had swallowed a cynical comment about women and their power over men. It had sprung unbidden to mind along with an image of Gabrielle Deschamps. Unlike Gabby, Lupita did indeed seem like a good woman. In the months since she and her parents had fled from Hunter's ranch and sought refuge on the Seco, she'd brought warmth and a kind of gentleness to the hacienda. The only one who hadn't welcomed her was Ben, but Antonio seemed to have made up for that. It could be that the foreman was a lucky man.

Rafe lifted his stiff-brimmed Stetson, wiped the damp hair and sweat from his forehead, and clamped the hat back in place. Behind him he heard Cisco cracking the bullwhip that seldom left his hands. Cisco, at sixteen already tall and well-muscled, would, like Antonio, be a good man.

"Hey, Antonio," called Rafe, "don't you envy Cisco a little? He's not giving up his freedom, just enjoying today. A little work, a little play."

"A lot of play," said Antonio as the whip cracked again, "but he is young and will get over it. I, myself, once saw little use in working."

"Should be that way," said Rafe, punctuating each word with powerful jabs of the crowbar. "The young should play as long as they can and let the men work."

"And worry about tomorrow," added Antonio, his eyes turned thoughtfully on Rafe.

"I'm doing that for sure," said Rafe and grimaced. "Too bad I can't worry in a clean office the way bankers do."

He paused a moment to stretch, his sweat-stained shirt pulling across the tight muscles of his back. For two days he'd been out on the range, mostly laying fence, but he'd taken time to check on the herd, talk to his men, learn a little more about the sheep that he hoped would thrive on the Seco and multiply. He knew cattle but he knew damned little about the Merinos he'd invested borrowed money in. He depended on an old Mexican sheepherder called Padre to teach him what he needed to know.

The days had been hot, hard, and long, but at least, wrapped in a bedroll and stretched out under the stars last night, he'd been able to sleep. That was more than he'd managed back at the hacienda. It wasn't the bankers that kept him awake, nor even Hunter, but visions of Gabrielle Deschamps. She was a hard woman to forget.

Even out on the range Rafe thought about her at the damnedest times. The rays of the sun beamed down and he was reminded of her honey-gold hair. He stopped for a drink from his canteen and remembered the way she tried to toss down the whiskey he'd handed her at the Menger. A mockingbird sang from somewhere overhead and her laughter filled the air.

And worst of all, when he was tired and sore and still hours away from a good night's sleep, he thought of the times he'd spent in bed with her. Gabby filled a need he hadn't realized existed—a need for one woman to call his own. Not the quick relief for a man's wants he'd had before, but something more permanent. Something shared.

Sometimes he wondered if he'd been too hard. Maybe he'd misjudged her. Hell, he'd gone over the scene in the Menger until it burned in his mind. He had told her what he heard, faced her with it straight out. All she'd done was raise that fine chin of hers and refuse to deny anything he said.

He'd wanted to pull the thin wrapper from around her sweet body and mold her to him again. He'd wanted to ignore the defiance—or was it triumph—in her sapphire eyes, but it had been impossible. He had seen no tenderness, no compassion, just the stubbornness of a woman who had tried to play him for a fool. There was no other conclusion he could draw.

177

Cut your losses, his father had told him a long time ago. Sam Jericho had been talking about an ill-fated attempt by Ben to plant cotton in the sun-baked Seco soil. But the same could hold true for a conniving woman. That's what Rafe had been doing—cutting his losses—when he walked away from Gabby back in San Antonio.

In spite of the defiance he'd seen, he hadn't really expected her to persist in claiming his land, but she'd come after him, or at least after what was his. He'd lost control, the way he always did around her, but he had no regrets. She'd wanted him as much as he wanted her. The memory of her passion—and more—ate at him, wouldn't leave his mind. Mixed with sharing bodily pleasure, he'd sensed a true caring and sweetness of spirit he'd shared with no one else.

He grinned sardonically at the thought that the pleasure-seeking loner Rafe Jericho was, like Antonio, ready to settle down—and was dumb enough to fall for Gabby Deschamps Cordero, one of the few women he hadn't been able to charm.

Again and again he struck at the stubborn caliche and rock. Sparks flew as the crowbar slowly forced its way into the ground. Kneeling, Rafe scooped out the dirt and bits of stone, tossed them aside, and eyed the depth of the hole. Deep enough to hold a fence post, he decided. He might not be able to keep the woman he wanted, but he could protect his expensive cross-breed cattle from the likes of Earl Hunter.

Ever since the hard winter of '80 when most of his stock had died in a rare snowstorm, he'd been strengthening the herd that was left. Herefords were

178

meaty and sold well at the markets in the North, but they were too prone to disease.

He'd been crossing the Herefords with Longhorn cattle, a hardy breed known for its resistance to disease. He liked the results thus far. No way was he going to risk letting those crossbreeds wander onto the Rancho Perro and get mixed in with Hunter's ill-kept maverick stock, especially since his vaqueros kept telling him another bad winter was coming up, one worse than ever, when he'd have to know where to find his herd to feed it.

The crack of a bullwhip split the air, interrupting his thoughts.

"Cisco, leave the lizards alone and get your carcass over here," Rafe said, knocking dust from his worn denim pants with a gloved hand. "And bring one of the cedar posts with you."

"*Sí*, Senor Rafael," Cisco said, his black button eyes flashing a smile. Carefully he curled the long tail of the whip around his waist, leaving the handle to hang at his side.

He treats that thing gentler than most men do a woman, Rafe thought, and then pulled back. There he went again.

Grabbing the crowbar, he motioned to Cisco and marched down the fence line past Antonio and to the next stake. Behind him stretched a long row of fence posts set like rigid sentinels against the Hunter spread. Soon those posts would hold four strands of heavy wire, each studded with sharp, twisted barbs. A simple device, really, Rafe thought, simple and inexpensive considering what it was able to do — fence in

179

what a man valued and fence out everything else.

As Rafe approached Antonio, he stopped. Three riders were coming toward them, coming up the row of flag-topped stakes. Shading his eyes with one hand, he watched warily as the men approached. At last he grunted and frowned. Dallas Pryor was in the lead.

Rafe curled his fingers tighter around the crowbar and looked around. His gun was back at the wagon. Antonio, too, had no weapon. There should have been a gun handy for killing snakes if for no other reason, but a gun got in a man's way when he was laying fence.

"Bastardo!" Antonio muttered, his body crouched like a panther at Rafe's side.

"Hold your temper," Rafe said. "I'll handle 'em." He damned well better if he were going to keep his foreman from doing something foolish.

The trouble involved Lupita. She'd told both Rafe and Antonio about the way Pryor had tried to catch her alone when her family worked on the Perro. She was afraid of him. She'd claimed he never actually hurt her, but not because he hadn't tried. She'd just always managed to get away.

But Rafe and Antonio figured different. The ugly scar on her wrist was most likely the result of a tangle with Hunter's dogs. Pryor was mean enough to have set them on her.

Lupita was Antonio's woman now. Rafe knew he carried a load of hate directed against Hunter's man.

Rafe's fingers itched for the feel of his gun back at the wagon. A crowbar wasn't likely to impress a pack of gunmen, especially one with Pryor in the lead. He threw a quick look over his shoulder to Cisco, slapped his thigh where a gun should have ridden, and nodded in the direction of the wagon. The kid seemed to get the message and, clutching the bullwhip handle close to his leg, slunk off in the brush as though he were afraid.

Pryor reined in his horse just short of the fence line and leaned his heavyset body back in the saddle, his cold eyes watching Cisco retreat. A wide-brimmed Stetson, looking newly bought with its smooth crease and shiny snakeskin band, was pulled low on his face.

"Sendin' for help, Jericho?"

Rafe rested easy. "Why would I be needing any help?" he asked, his eyes shifting to each of the riders before returning to Pryor. The other men held back, apparently content to let Pryor do the talking.

Pryor looked down the long row of fence posts and back in the other direction at the red-flagged stakes where other holes were to be dug.

"Lot of work here for nothin'. Wasn't some of your wire cut the other night 'bout a mile from here?"

"It's been repaired. And the work's not wasted. A fence can keep out a lot of vermin."

Slowly Antonio rose to his feet, the crowbar gripped in his hand.

Pryor's jaw tightened. "You best be careful the names you call a man, Jericho. Hunter might let you get away with it, but not me."

"If you've got something to say, say it, Pryor. Otherwise ride on out of here. We've got work to do."

"I'm just tellin' you some facts. You lay this fence today, you might find yourself laying the same fence

181

tomorrow. And the day after that, too."

Rafe stood tall, his eyes never leaving Pryor's leathered face. "You tell Hunter I consider your visit here a threat. If this fence is damaged, I'm calling in the law. And I'll be coming to see him myself."

"You know a lawman around here with the nerve to come onto Hunter's land and drag him off to jail?"

"I might," Rafe said, remembering the tall, thickset Texas Ranger he called friend. Jeff McGowan wasn't afraid to tackle a mountain lion in his den.

Pryor shifted in his saddle. "You know," he said, his narrow eyes sparked by a thought, "I been wonderin' if I shouldn't pay a visit over your way. Call on a lady friend."

A deep, animal sound came from beside Rafe. Pryor's eyes shifted from Rafe to Antonio. "Now don't tell me that sweet little Lupita has found herself another man while she's waiting for me. Guess she got to thinking about what she gave up when she left. Guess she got to wantin' it—"

Uttering a low grunt, Antonio dropped his crowbar and hurtled through the air, his only weapon angry hands that clutched at Pryor's shirt. Pryor was ready. He raised his quirt and slashed Antonio across the face. He drew back to strike again, but this time Antonio was the quick one. He grabbed the quirt and pulled Pryor sprawling to the ground.

Pryor's legs snaked out, tripping Antonio; the two grappled in the dirt. The gunman outweighed Antonio by fifty pounds and was quick for a big man. He was the first to break free and rise to his knees. He jabbed at Antonio's jaw and scrambled to his feet.

182

Antonio rose and Pryor punched him lower in the stomach, raising his other fist in a blow to the jaw. Antonio stumbled backward.

Rafe raised the crowbar to protect his man and heard the ominous click of a gun.

One of Pryor's men rode closer, a six-shooter pointed at Rafe's head. Rafe lowered his weapon and helplessly looked on as Antonio, weakened by the punches, staggered forward and thrashed out at Pryor, only to be struck again. This time he went down, and a cut on his cheek opened up, dripping blood onto the hard-packed earth.

Cold calculation filled Rafe. It was no time for unthinking rage. Suddenly swerving to the left, placing the fighters between himself and the drawn pistol, he crashed his fist into Pryor's jaw. Pryor sprawled backward onto the ground and Rafe was astride him, his punches landing with precision on Pryor's jaw, nose, eye.

The other two riders dropped to the ground and moved in. A bullet hit the dirt beside Rafe, but he ignored it. Another one zinged past his head, closer than the first, and he lowered his fist. A cocked pistol moved in on a line with his chest.

Slowly he shifted his weight off of Pryor and stood, his hands hanging loosely at his side, his breath heavy. Pryor staggered to his feet, one thick hand rubbing at his jaw, the other clawing for his gun. He looked at Rafe with murderous eyes, one already half-swollen from Rafe's assault.

Without warning, a gunshot split the stillness behind Pryor, the unerring bullet knocking the gun from

183

the hands of Pryor's backer. Rafe whirled in time to see Cisco's whip lash out for Pryor's drawn gun pointed at Rafe's chest; at the same time Cisco tossed Rafe his pistol still hot from the shot he had fired.

Rafe caught the gun and blazed a bullet at the third gunman, hitting him in the shoulder. The man yipped in pain and his pistol hit the dirt.

Motioning with his gun, Rafe eyed Pryor carefully. "Now then," he said coolly, "You're on my land. Get off."

Pryor reached down. Rafe cocked the pistol.

"Just gettin' my hat," Pryor said, picking up a now battered Stetson and slapping it on his head. The three gunmen mounted, and Pryor sneered down at Rafe. "I'll be back to see you, Jericho."

"I'll be waiting," Rafe said, then watched as the gunmen headed back up the hill and dropped from sight.

"*Yo tambien,*" Antonio said softly. He wiped at the dried blood on his face. "I, too, will be waiting."

"Are you all right?" asked Rafe.

"It will take more than a *bastardo* like that one to stop me."

"He's mean and he's big, Antonio. Be careful of him."

"*Si*, Rafael. I will be very careful."

Rafe leaned down and picked up the crowbar that he'd been using in his labors. He turned to Cisco. "That was a hell of an entry you made, kid. Seems to me you're a man now."

Cisco's brown face broke into a grin. "I think the same thing, Senor Rafael."

184

"Good. Then you can do a man's work with Antonio." He tossed the crowbar at Cisco and gestured at the red flags. "The other men will be along soon stringing the wire. You see how much you can get done."

Cisco's face fell, but he picked up the bar and started poking at the ground.

Rafe turned his gaze out to the wide land that was the Rancho Perro. "I'll be leaving you two alone for just a while. Our neighbors came calling on us. It might seem rude if I didn't do the same. Besides," he said, his voice grim, "it's time I cleared up a few points with Earl Hunter. His man as much as admitted he's behind the fence cuttings. This visit is a damned sight overdue."

Earl Hunter moistened the thin Mexican cheroot, struck a match on one sole of the tooled leather boots he'd received only that morning, and leaned back in his chair. He peered through puffs of white smoke at his visitor, a grin on his face.

"You've got me convinced, Senor Ramirez. Mexico has a great deal to offer in trade. Under the right circumstances."

Juan Ramirez sat with his back straight, his raisin eyes trained on Hunter. The suit-clad Ramirez was a dapper man with pencil-thin moustache and short-cropped hair, a string tie caught by an intricately carved silver holder at his neck. His nails were clean and clipped, and on his left hand he wore a large turquoise ring.

"Please tell me, Senor Hunter, the nature of these . . . circumstances."

Hunter puffed at the cigar before speaking. "Things are different this side of the border. Down in Mexico smugglers are heroes. You take stolen cattle or horses into any village and no one asks for a bill of sale. You take enough of 'em, you're liable to be elected mayor."

Ramirez's moustache twitched. "What you say is true. I myself have been honored as an *alcalde*."

"In Texas you would have been introduced to the curved end of a rope. And for doing the same thing."

"What is your point, senor?"

Hunter leaned forward and punctuated his words with the fiery end of the cigar. "Just this. I have to be a damned sight more careful than you do. I don't aim to end up at a necktie party."

"Of course not, Senor. Such an event would not be profitable for either of us."

"You have a practical way of looking at things, Ramirez. I like the way you talk. When I was in San Antonio I met a few businessmen who might be interested in your goods." He crossed one leg and fingered the tooling on his boot. "This is quality leather. From Monterrey, you say?"

"There are expert craftsmen in my country," Ramirez said. "In both leather and silver. I could provide you the best. But it is *Tejas* cattle and horses I am most interested in."

"Me, too," Hunter said, his eyes narrowing. "That's where the money is. My problem is access to the river. I had it for a while, but that damned Rafe Jericho is busy fencing it off. I can cut the wires all right, but there's no guarantee he won't string them right back up. And he's got men everywhere on that ranch. Damned bunch of vaqueros I ran off when I took over here plus his own."

"Can these men not be bought?"

"They didn't leave here under the best of conditions."

"I have found, senor, that it is sometimes best not to make enemies."

Hunter smiled, but his eyes held steady. "And I've found little use for friends." The sound of barking dogs drifted in through the window. "They're my friends, Ramirez. They're more loyal than any two-legged kind you'll find."

"You will pardon my saying so, senor, but they do not sound like friends."

"They're my friends only. And they'll tolerate Dallas Pryor. I keep 'em pinned up usually and sometimes give 'em the run of the front. Like today. Tends to keep down visitors." The barking turned to growls and a shot rang out. "Sounds like we have somebody stubborn out front."

Hunter headed for the door. "Wait here. There's no sense in letting anyone see you."

Ramirez nodded, waited until Hunter had left the room, then followed him out. He positioned himself near a window that opened onto the front porch of the Rancho Perro main house. Ramirez liked to be cautious, liked to gather whatever information he could. The habit had saved his life more than once.

Hunter stood in the shadows of the front hall and checked the gun he had strapped to his waist beneath his suit coat. When he stepped out into the late afternoon sun, he stared at the scene in front of him. Rafe Jericho sat astride a chestnut stallion, his pistol pointed at the pack of hounds snarling and growling around the horse's front legs.

The skittish stallion reared back, his hoofs coming dangerously close to the dogs, and Rafe let go with another shot. The dogs backed off, settling on a loud chorus of barks. With a whistle Hunter quieted them, and Rafe brought his mount under control.

"Welcome to the Rancho Perro," came a soft voice behind Hunter. "It's been a long time since we've seen you around here."

Rafe looked past Hunter to his wife Sarah. He'd seen her in town only a few weeks ago, but every time they met he was surprised at the change in her since her marriage. Her face was thinner—unattractively so—and she wore a tight red dress that scooped down over her full bosom. Once a gentle and modest young woman, she now looked like one of the women who walked the streets of San Antonio.

What was worse, there was a hard look to her eyes and her mouth that he'd never noticed when her father was alive. Taking Earl Hunter into her bed hadn't seemed to do her much good. Rafe was sure it hadn't made her happy.

The thought angered him. He'd always liked Sarah, just not enough to marry her the way Ben and Nathaniel had planned. She deserved a lot better than what she'd got.

"Hello, Sarah," he said. "It's good to see you again."

"Have you come calling on my wife," Hunter said

sharply, "or is your business with me?"

Rafe looked down at Hunter calmly, allowing none of his anger to show. The last time he'd seen the man was in police headquarters in San Antonio. He hadn't had a peaceful moment since.

"I came to warn you off my land, Hunter. You send your men to threaten me again and you'll find you've made a big mistake."

"What the hell are you talking about?"

"Ask Dallas Pryor what I'm talking about. Have you seen him lately? He's probably off somewhere licking his wounds."

"You say he threatened you? What about?"

"He's got a dirty mind. And he doesn't care too much for barbed wire."

"No real cattleman does," Hunter said.

"I didn't realize that's what he was," Rafe said. "Or you either."

Hunter scowled. "Mind your mouth, Jericho. I've more sense than to send Dallas on a fool's errand like that. You're not about to take a little advice from him or me."

"It wasn't advice. I said it was a threat and that's what it was."

From deeper on the porch came Sarah's voice. "If that's what Rafe said it was—"

Hunter turned on her. "Get back inside, Sarah," he said sharply. "I'll handle Rafe Jericho."

Sarah matched his sharpness. "That'll be the day."

Husband and wife stood staring at each other for a long moment. At last Sarah shrugged, gave a quick look at Rafe, and disappeared through the front door.

When Hunter turned back to Rafe, his face was flushed with anger. "You've got no business coming over here," he said. "I don't want you coming back."

"That's the only thing we agree on, Earl," Rafe said softly. "I stay on my land and you stay on yours. I'll shoot the first trespasser I see. Consider your men warned. Any of my men harmed and somebody will pay."

Rafe gave Hunter no time to respond. He turned his chestnut around and rode away without a backward glance, heading out down the long, hot trail that led back to the Seco. On either side were patches of yucca and agave mixed in with the taller brush, all of it dry and in places virtually impenetrable. As much as he needed to get rid of Earl Hunter, his land needed rain.

Rafe was sure his warning would do no good — whatever Hunter was up to, he wouldn't be stopped by words — but he felt good because he'd delivered it. The only thing he couldn't shake from his mind was the hard look in Sarah's eyes, but he was damned if he knew what he could do about it. Probably a hard, combative front worked better against a man like Hunter than cowed submissiveness.

A red-faced Ben Hidalgo met him at the front of the hacienda.

"She has done it again," he shouted at Rafe before he had a chance to dismount. "She has done it again."

Rafe had no trouble figuring out who the "she" was. His breath caught. "You mean Gabby's been around?"

"No, Rafe, she hasn't dared to face me again. Follow me and I will show you the treachery of her new attack. She vowed she would sue, but what she has done is much worse."

Rafe dropped to the ground and signaled to one of his men to take the horse. He knew there was no use asking Ben what had upset him. If he wanted Rafe to know, he would tell him in his own good time and in his own way.

In the large, dark office, Ben walked behind the desk and picked up a piece of paper. He thrust it at Rafe. "The letter was addressed to me as owner of the Seco, but it concerns the money that was borrowed."

Damn! Another letter from the bank, this one somehow concerning Gabby. Rafe was getting tired of nothing but bad news about the woman he'd almost— He stopped. Hell, he'd done more than almost fall for her.

There was nothing for it but to read whatever had enraged Ben. The letter was another from Ralph Gentry. As Rafe scanned its contents, his face hardened, his eyes narrowed. He finished and read it again.

Rafe needn't, it said, worry about the bank mortgage. The bank no longer held the loan. Gabby did. Gentry even went so far as to say he figured it was good news for Rafe. Gentry thought Gabby was a friend.

Rafe crushed the letter. Cold rage settled in his heart and he stood rigidly, twisting the paper but seeing Gabby's white throat between his fingers. It was time he fought back against her constant intrusions with something more than impotent rage.

"Are you all right, Rafe?" Ben asked.

"Finally," he said softly. "I'm finally all right. You remember that invitation Emma Talbert sent asking me to a barbecue Sunday afternoon? I said no way was I going to ride into town and risk seeing Gabby again. But I've changed my mind. That's just what I'm going to do."

Ben grinned. "I think you did not tell everything about meeting the senorita in San Antonio, but I could guess what she might have done to win you to her side. At last you have the old look back in your eye. It's not been there since you got back from your journey."

Rafe tossed the crumpled letter onto the desk. "Don't worry about that letter, Ben. I promise you, one way or the other, Senorita Deschamps will find out she's made a terrible mistake."

Chapter Nine

Gabby paced the length of her small hotel room, pivoted sharply by the window, and began the return journey toward the door. An impatient nod of her head loosened a lock of blond hair, and she tucked it into place among the cascade of ringlets adorning her head.

The intricate style was rather too much, she thought, for a Sunday afternoon barbecue along the Rio Grande. Maybe she should remove the sapphire blue ribbon that was intertwined in the curls. Maybe she should brush out the whole design and wear her hair in a bun at the nape of her neck. Or maybe she should just go back to bed and forget about leaving the hotel.

The last thought might be her best one yet since she'd started preparing for Emma Talbert's party two hours ago. Any minute now Franklin Bernard would come calling to escort her the few short blocks to the Talbert home, but she could certainly plead a headache and send him on his way. As a matter of fact—if she concentrated hard enough—she could feel the beginning tentacles of pain.

But feigning illness would be the act of a coward. She knew Rafe would most likely be there. She'd been telling herself she was glad. It was time they faced one another again.

Since she had instructed Franklin Bernard to buy up the Seco loan, there had been plenty of time for Rafe to confront her on the issue, but he hadn't done so. If he hadn't heard from the bank about the transfer of the note, she would simply have to tell him. Let him rage as he no doubt would. Gabby knew in her heart she was right.

She hadn't bought his note to laugh in his face—or even to foreclose. That was something she doubted she could ever do. The reasons were more complex. Rafe had implied terrible things about her, and his grandfather had behaved no better. She'd been angry, angrier than she had ever been in her life. In that anger she'd found solace and strength.

How naive she had been to think *anyone*, let alone two men as strong-willed as Rafe and his grandfather, would willingly negotiate away a portion of what they considered family land. Just because she was willing to ask for so little. Just because, with her head filled more with dreams than common sense, she'd felt justified in her pursuits.

She cringed remembering how she'd paraded her ignorance about men and women before Erin. She had been ignorant about a lot of things, so much so that she realized her education had only really begun after she'd left her eastern school.

But in his own way, Rafe was ignorant, too. He was older and had traveled far more roads than she had. He should have realized the power of his presence on her, should have seen how quickly she fell under his spell. If he was half the man the townspeople thought he was, he would sooner or later try to be fair. By now whatever tender but temporary emotions she'd aroused in him were beyond recall—she didn't dwell too long on the painful thought—but with the passing of those feelings should come the realization on his part that she was asking for no more than she deserved.

Six days had gone by since she'd been to the Seco. She spent most of that time learning about the town, the old cathedral, the plazas, the shops. Proprietors along the narrow streets had been curious about her presence, and she'd told them she was looking into her heritage.

Thus far she'd been able to find no one who had known her father, but when she mentioned that the Corderos had once owned a large part of the Arroyo Seco, their attitude had changed.

"Ben Hidalgo's place?" was a typical rejoinder. "Don't see much of the old man anymore. Got so cranky folks could hardly stand to see him coming to town. But that grandson of his is a different breed. Not a better man than Jericho in these parts."

Gabby figured that with the way her luck was running lately, it was inevitable she would have run afoul of one of the most popular men along the border. The trouble was that she couldn't disagree with the speaker. In some ways there probably wasn't a better man around. Twice he'd stood between her and trouble back in San Antonio. She could still see him standing in the shadows beside the Menger Hotel, gun in hand, shielding her with his own body against the attack from a drunken gunman.

And later in the hotel room. . . . She'd quickly blacked out the thought and the memories it evoked.

Over tea one day, after listening to Gabby's description of the trip to the Seco and her actions afterward, Emma had looked beyond the words of determination that Gabby had uttered to the meaning underneath.

"Sounds like you may be right about old Ben lying in court," she'd said, "but I'm not sure you'd ever be able to prove it. At least not to Rafe. He's a tough man, Gabby. I already told you he's close to his mean old cuss of a grandfather and to that ranch. Rafe stands up for what's his. You sure you want to face him Sunday? I'm thinking he just might show up."

Gabby had met her probing stare head on. "I'm not at all sure it's the right thing, Emma, but I'll be there. I may not be the smartest woman who ever rode that train south, but I know it would be wrong to cower in my room."

"I'm thinking you're quick to get riled up where Rafe is concerned." Emma paused. "You're either having second thoughts about what you've done. Or you love him."

"A woman doesn't love a man like Rafe."

Emma's eyes had gleamed. "Now there I might argue with you."

"Love involves a great deal more than"—Gabby had

196

hesitated, remembering the way her breath caught, the way her body tightened and warmed when Rafe was near—"than wanting a man."

"That may be," Emma had said, her voice skeptical, "but wanting a man is part of it, Gabby. A big part."

"It's not everything. Respect and trust figure in, too. Rafe looks on me as his enemy. From his viewpoint I guess I am. Since that's the role I've been cast in, I'd better be a strong one."

"Seems to me Rafe's got enemies enough with that Earl Hunter after his land. Remember, Gabrielle, most of the people around here think a lot of Rafe. They might not be so quick to welcome you if you do get what you're after."

The thought had been sobering. Gabby was after roots and a home as much as she wanted justice. In the back of her mind was born the fear that the lonely little girl who'd been an outcast in San Antonio might possibly in her chosen home become a grown-up version of that child.

Again she began pacing the floor of her hotel room. She hadn't told Emma all the truth about her relationship with Rafe. Even now, when she pictured a pair of glinting brown eyes smiling at her, she was sharply aware of a need simply to be near him. Those feelings had been born that first time she looked at him. No matter what had passed between them, she hadn't been able to set them aside.

She'd proven that the night of the fandango. Somehow she would have to face Rafe today with reasoned calm. And it wouldn't hurt that she would be surrounded by dozens of other guests. Unlike that fiery night, this afternoon all aspects of Laredo life would be represented. Emma had said men outnumbered women in Laredo by a large margin; the odds were on her side she could keep busy dancing the entire afternoon and create a wall of admirers Rafe couldn't get through — until she decided it was time for them to talk.

A soft knock at the door announced the arrival of her escort. Good, dependable Franklin Bernard. He was the one person in town who didn't rush to praise Rafe. Too bad he couldn't tell her more about Earl Hunter and the problems he was causing Rafe. She'd asked Bernard for his opinion, but he'd cut her off short, saying he didn't have any knowledge of what a man like Hunter would do.

Again came a soft knock. Grabbing up a small purse, she opened the door and stood smoothing the blue muslin of her skirt. "It's a perfect day for a walk," she said brightly, "and the Talbert home isn't far."

"The buggy is much more proper," he said. Gabby immediately acquiesced. The lawyer had also told her not to go to the fandango, and considering her reception there she had since decided that in matters of propriety Franklin Bernard had by far the wiser head.

The guests of Emma and Alexander Talbert had spilled out onto the shaded lawn of their home. Unable to keep from casting anxious eyes around, Gabby saw no tall, ruggedly lean man with brown eyes that penetrated through her strongest resolve. She allowed Bernard to help her down from the buggy and within minutes was swept up in Emma's arms.

"Thought you'd never get here," Emma said, giving

her a firm hug. "And you can quit looking around. Haven't seen hide nor hair of him—yet."

"Let me know when you do, Emma. I've decided to look forward to seeing him again."

Emma cast her a dubious look before bustling off to see about her other guests. Bernard seated Gabby on a bench under a nearby tree and, after a fussy assurance that he would be right back, went off to fetch them both punch. She studied the crowd milling about the broad lawn that stretched down to the river to the point where a huge willow tree dipped its branches near the water's edge. A scattering of ash trees provided the guests shade.

The people were as diverse as she had imagined they would be—ranchers, farmers, merchants, bankers, railroad men, and even a few politicians she recognized from the election posters that were distributed around town. She even picked out members from Laredo's two warring political parties Alexander Talbert had told her about—one known as *botas*, boots, and the other *huaraches*, sandals. Most were sipping at punch or ale as they conversed and joked. Only Emma could pull off the feat of getting such a volatile mixture together at one party.

Gabby folded her hands in her lap and leaned back against the bench, contented for the moment to observe. The men and women looked relaxed and comfortable within their groups, even the rival politicians. Would Gabby ever feel as though she belonged?

She heard a scuffling foot on the nearby ground. "Good afternoon. It's Miss Deschamps, isn't it?"

She lifted a hand. "Captain McGowan," she said to

199

the broad-shouldered Texas Ranger hovering over her, "what a pleasant surprise." She meant it.

Jeff McGowan tipped his hat. "The pleasure's mine. Haven't been in town long and one of the first faces I see is a friendly one."

Gabby matched his smile. "I imagine most people would hesitate to show you anything but friendship."

"To my face, ma'am, that's probably true, although I've pulled in a few thieves and murderers that didn't mind if I took offense at what they thought about me. And about my ancestry. They've had some mighty sharp comments to make that wouldn't be proper repeated to a lady."

"Please drop that *ma'am* business. I consider us old friends. Especially after that messy business in San Antonio." She gestured for McGowan to join her on the bench. "I'd like to thank you for your help. The police never did come around asking questions. I'm sure you're to thank for that."

McGowan settled his huge frame beside her. "Rafe as much as me. There weren't many questions left to ask when he got through telling his story." He looked around the crowd. "Where is that rascal anyway? Figured he'd be hovering nearby ready to protect his claim."

Gabby waved one hand airily, her thoughts buried deep behind the flash of a bright smile. "You figured wrong. Rafe and I have no claim on one another."

"You saying you're not down this way because of him?"

"That's what I'm saying. I'm in town on business. And I plan to make this my home. Rafe Jericho has nothing whatsoever to do with that decision. I made it long before we ever met."

McGowan's eyes made a quick survey of Gabby in her soft flowing blue gown. "Can't believe Rafe let you get away."

"I'm not exactly game to be hunted, Captain."

"Game, huh?" McGowan threw back his head and laughed. "Guess that is the way I was talking. I've not been in the company of ladies too much lately. You'll have to pardon me if I come across as a little blunt."

Gabby didn't mind pardoning him at all. Jeff McGowan called her a lady and in his own rough frontier way treated her as such.

"There's nothing to forgive," she said, then added, "Jeff. Let's drop the formality."

A familiar voice cut between the two. "I've brought Miss Deschamps her refreshment," Franklin Bernard said, thrusting a crystal cup in Gabby's direction and introducing himself to the Ranger.

"An attorney, aren't you?" Jeff asked and looked curiously at Gabby.

"That's right. I'm both friend and attorney to Miss Deschamps. May I ask how you came to make her acquaintance?"

Gabby found herself irritated by Bernard's interference. Accepting the cup of punch, she smiled innocently up at him. "How else would two people meet in Texas?" she said. "We met at a shooting near the Alamo."

Bernard's lips pursed. "I heard about that shooting," he said. "You really ought to be more careful."

The lawyer's words took Gabby by surprise. She'd

never mentioned the killing of Luke Sneed to him — after all, it had nothing whatsoever to do with the case he was handling for her. But shootings weren't so common. There must have been talk about all aspects of it, and Bernard had been in town. It was strange he had not mentioned it before.

"If you've got some kind of problem you need a lawyer for, Gabrielle," Jeff said, casting a sharp glance at Bernard, "you might want to check with me. Especially, as I'm thinking, it has something to do with Rafe."

"I told you I'm not here because of him," Gabby said shortly. "The situation involves his grandfather."

"Sorry," said Jeff. "None of my business. Lawmen are as pushy sometimes as lawyers. Seems to come with the job."

The clattering sound of a fast-driven wagon drowned out Gabby's reply. The wagon pulled to a halt close by. When Gabby looked past Jeff McGowan to see who had arrived, she found she was staring directly into Rafe's dark eyes. He was sitting in the wagon, one hand gripping the reins of the single horse, the other raised to greet the threesome. Beside him was a gray-haired gentleman Gabby recognized from one of the posters she'd seen in town. He was the district judge, John Russell.

Here she was at the gathering with her lawyer; it seemed appropriate, as well as ironic, that Rafe had brought along a judge. Unwillingly her eyes returned to Rafe. Even knowing he would probably appear, she hadn't been prepared for the first sight of his darkly handsome face staring down at her. Vivid in her mind was the spark that had passed between them when he'd driven up. It had been like a flash of summer lightning, sudden and unmistakable in its brilliance, and just as quickly gone.

Jeff raised his hand in answer to Rafe's salute, then looked pointedly at Gabby's knuckles gripping the crystal cup of punch and white with the effort. "Speak of the devil," he said.

Gabby cast a side glance at the Ranger. "I'm beginning to think all men are devils." When she glanced back at the wagon, Rafe's eyes were boring into her.

Hot anger she could have dealt with, even inflamed desire, but neither showed in his expression. Eyes that once burned her with golden warmth now glittered with icy shards of bitter disdain. A shiver ran through her. There was only one thing that could put such glacial fury in his eyes. Rafe had heard from the bank.

She watched as he dropped gracefully from the wagon, conferred with the judge for a minute, then turned his dark eyes back to her. Gabby had to hold on to her courage. Each time she saw him he looked different. More handsome, more coolly superior. Today he was dressed in a black suit, a gentleman among gentlemen, a far cry from the hot-blooded man who had kidnapped her away from the fandango, the wild Spanish lover who had forged her rebellious fury into a passion that matched his own.

Her quickening heartbeat drowned out the sounds of music and laughter, which had been drifting from the side of the house. Everything that Gabby had prepared herself for — from her earliest childhood until the painful present — was wrapped up in what she would do now.

Gabby was only vaguely aware of Jeff as he excused himself and took Franklin Bernard with him. Judge Russell, too, disappeared from view. Her eyes were for Rafe only as he strode to her side.

The closer he got, the more clearly she could see the sharp, shadowed lines of his face, the tousled black hair that would not stay in place, the set mouth and strong chin that she had once stroked and kissed with such tender affection. He looked almost cast in bronze, so still he was and unsmiling. If he hoped to intimidate her with his unwavering manly stare, he would soon know he was wrong.

Even through his fury, Rafe watched in a kind of fascinated awe as he approached Gabby. As much as he wanted to get his hands around that lovely throat, he admired the way she stood her ground, her magnificent head held high, her sapphire eyes bright and clear as the sky overhead.

Honeyed hair fell in ringlets around her finely sculpted face, and the soft fabric of her blue muslin dress fell enticingly against her slender body. To someone who didn't know her, who didn't see the firmness of her delicately curved jaw, who couldn't see into the depths of her eyes, she might be a beautiful young woman waiting for an innocent flirtation. Almost, just almost, he regretted the disappointment he was going to hand her.

But, he reminded himself, there was nothing innocent about Gabrielle Deschamps, nor anything weak.

She was a worthy opponent, he'd found out to his regret. He searched in vain for a sign of the vulnerability that had once attracted him to her.

He stopped before her skirt brushed against the trousers of his suit. "It's time we talked," he said. "And that's all I plan to do, Gabby. There will be no repeat of Saturday night."

The memory of the fandango burned in Gabby's mind. "You dare to mention that? I thought even you would have more character."

"I mention it only to apologize for what happened. In case you're worried about what I might do now."

Apologize for making love to her? That's the least he could do, she thought, ignoring the sharp, hurtful edge of regret that brushed against her heart. Her brows raised over eyes lit with proud disapprobation. "Do I look worried?"

"You look —" He paused for a moment. There were many things he could tell her about the way she looked, but none that he would allow himself. Not again. "No, you don't look worried," he said, conceding the point with a nod of his head. "There's a gazebo nearby not many people know about. We can talk privately."

He extended his arm in the general direction of the thickening trees, but she ignored his gesture and he spoke in a flare of anger. "Gabby, we can have this out here and now in front of everybody if you like, but you're the one who will be embarrassed, not I. I've said my last apology. The rest you're not going to like hearing."

Gabby's eyes flashed fire. "That's certainly nothing

new," she said harshly. A nearby rustle of clothing and half-heard whispers told her they were being overheard, and she held back a further retort.

Rafe extended his arm in what must appear to onlookers as a gesture of courtesy. Gabby knew otherwise, but she also saw the wisdom of the seclusion he had proposed. Resting her hand on the sleeve of his coat lightly as possible, she could still feel the heat of his body. Remembrances of him in gentler times flooded her mind, and she forced them aside.

"Do lead on," she said in her best Miss Martha Emmett voice. "I have a few things I want to say myself."

The trees and brush thickened the farther they removed themselves from the crowd. Some twenty yards away they emerged into a clearing, at the center of which was an octagonal gazebo with a turreted roof, a curious structure, Gabby thought, one more likely to be found in the Black Forest of Germany than tucked away here in the woods by the Rio Grande.

"Emma has a sense of humor," Rafe said, stepping aside to let Gabby walk up the steps to the gazebo's interior.

"No," she said softly as she passed him, "she has a romantic streak. I haven't seen it before, but she told me her husband Alexander had built it for her."

Gabby passed close to Rafe to climb the steps into the small house. He caught the elusive fragrance of frangipani, and his lips twisted cynically.

Rafe waited for Gabby to step into the protection of the gazebo and turn to face him. Gabby had dealt herself some losing cards, and for a while he might enjoy watching her try to play them. She would have no idea he'd consulted with Judge Russell and found he held the winning hand.

"I received a letter from San Antonio this week," he said.

"If you're expecting me to play coy, Rafe, I won't. I know what the letter must have said." Gabby held his eyes as she talked, determined not to look away, not to let him know how fragile was her self-control.

"I don't want you to play at anything, Gabby. Just tell me why you bought the loan."

"I don't intend to defend myself to you, Rafe. I don't want to take everything away from you. I never have."

"For someone who plans us no harm, you're going about your business in a strange way, Gabby."

"The only thing I'm planning is to continue the fight, Rafe, for at least part of what should have been my father's and my mother's. And I'll get what I'm after. Even though I've not gotten much I wanted since I came back to seek a home."

Rafe ignored the bitterness in her voice. "I'd call that a lie. I know of a couple of times myself I gave you just what you wanted."

She lashed out in self-defense. "What you did was come along at the right time. Don't let your arrogance lead you to believe you were special."

Rafe moved close until his breath was hot on her cheek. Gabby stepped away from him, her back to one of the gazebo's posts, her body only inches from his as he followed.

His velvet eyes caressed her face, her throat, the ivory softness of her breasts above the low curve of her gown. The man was more devil than human to torment her so, and she fought the compelling sensations he aroused within her.

"I was ready to offer you everything I owned, Gabby. For a few hours your scheme almost worked."

Gabby twisted away from him and put distance between them. Blinking away unshed tears, she turned to him.

"Listen to me carefully, Rafe. I didn't try to trap you. And I don't want to use the loan to gain what is rightfully mine. But if I have to," she said, forcing her voice to a certainty she no longer felt, "I will. I can't see how I can do otherwise."

Her eyes were bright with daring pride. Before he could reply, Jeff's deep voice rang out through the woods.

"Rafe! Gabrielle! Where are you? It's important."

Rafe turned his head toward the sound. "Over here. In the gazebo, Jeff."

McGowan bounded up the stairs. "You got trouble Rafe. Out at the Seco."

"Is it Ben? Has something happened to him?"

"No. That kid Cisco came riding in. It's a fire on the north edge of the range. He said it looks bad."

Before McGowan had finished, Rafe was pushing past him and heading for the Talbert home.

Gabby rushed past McGowan and hurried after Rafe. Fire. In the middle of a drought! She should have been thinking of the ranch but the fear that clutched at her heart was for Rafe. He would do anything to stop the spread of the fire, throw himself into any danger. She flew down the winding path, determined to catch up with him.

She emerged onto the lawn of the Talbert home in time to see Cisco, his face streaked with dirt and sweat, drinking water from an upturned dipper. Rafe took the dipper and handed it to Emma, then gripped Cisco's shoulder. "Just take it easy," he said, "and tell it straight. What's the damage so far?"

"Antonio and some of the others have moved the sheep and breed stock to the river," Cisco said, his stance rigid from the importance of his mission. "Antonio says the grass is burning bad over a large front and the wind is from the north. He needs you, Senor Rafael, and as much help as you can bring."

Alexander Talbert stepped beside Rafe. "Sounds like the blamed thing is moving south. With luck it'll burn itself out at the river, but depending on how close it is, the hacienda might go. As soon as Cisco got here with the news, some of the men left to check it out."

"The women'll be out there, too," Emma said. "You'll be needing some takin' care of if this thing goes on for a while."

Gabby listened to the talk, heard the people scurrying around in response to Rafe's need. Instead of joining Emma and the women who would round up food and drink to sustain the men, she ran past them all to the hitching rail at the front of the house. When she was out of sight, she bundled her full skirts around her and climbed into Rafe's wagon. As she settled herself on the seat, she saw Jeff McGowan riding hard toward the river ferry and wondered where he was going. He seemed headed in the wrong way.

Rafe rounded the corner of the house followed by three other men and pulled up short.

"You're not going with me, Gabby. Get down. A tenderfoot like you will just get in the way."

"My place is out there, Rafe. Don't tell me any different."

The other men leaped into another wagon and sped off. One shouted to Rafe, "Let's go. She can stay back somewhere later."

Gabby grabbed up the reins and whip, flicking the horse on his shoulder, and Rafe had to scramble to catch up to the fast-moving buckboard and pull himself up beside Gabby.

"Damn you, Gabby," he muttered as he jerked the reins from her hands.

It was the last thing he said to her on the long, wild ride out to the Seco, her hands gripping the side of the wagon in a desperate attempt to keep her seat, her feet and legs straining against the floor. She'd made the trip in an hour riding beside Ephraim Bartz. Rafe, who easily passed the other wagons headed out to the ranch, made it in a third of that time.

As they neared the ranch, she heard behind them the pounding hoofs of another horse and took a daring look over her shoulder. Cisco was close to the rear of the wagon. When they came to the rise leading down to the main house, Rafe pulled the wagon to a halt. In the distance they could see a black, ominous cloud on the horizon.

"It looks bad," Gabby said. "Do you think you can stop it?"

"I have no choice," Rafe said flatly and sent the buckboard hurtling down the long incline to pull up with a jolt near the barn.

He threw the reins at Gabby. "This is as far as you go." He turned to Cisco. "The other men will be along soon," he said. "Get the horses rubbed down and ready to haul out some shovels and picks. I'm riding on out alone."

In fluid movements, he jumped to the ground and, pulling off his coat and string tie, ran toward the corral. Cisco jumped to follow orders, grabbing up a tow sack off the fence and rubbing down his mount. Frustrated, Gabby could only follow suit as she got another sack and began to soothe the trembling cart horse and unhitch him.

Within minutes Rafe, keeping a tight rein on a great black stallion eager to be gone, came out of the barn. "All the vaqueros are already out," he said crisply. "Cisco, rest that mount, then come along. Gabby, don't allow that horse too much water. Tie him up and get yourself into the hacienda."

Hooves digging into the dirt behind him, Rafe was gone, leaving only a cloud of dust behind him.

Gabby whirled to face Cisco. "How far out to the fire?"

"Maybe two miles, senorita."

"Can this wagon get there?"

Cisco's eyes widened. "The way is too rough. Anyway, you heard Senor Rafael. The horse is needed later."

Gabby looked toward the hacienda but saw no sign of anyone there. She looked around and saw not even a dogcart.

"Cisco, I'm going out there, one way or the other."

He glanced at her full-skirted dress and slippered feet. "There are no other horses, senorita, and I do not think you could get very far on foot."

Gabby brushed carelessly at the fallen curls framing her face. "Maybe I should have come out with the other ladies, but I didn't. It's up to you to get me out to Rafe."

"Senor Rafael will flay the skin from my body if we do not do as he says."

Gabby took a threatening step toward the boy. "Someone will skin you later either way. You go on if you have to, but I'm getting to that fire somehow. I don't intend to stay back here brewing tea."

Leading his piebald mare to the watering trough, Cisco allowed the beast a few slurps of water, then tugged her away. Gabby backed out of the path, trying not to look at the animal's wide eyes bent down toward her.

"Then we will ride double, senorita," said Cisco. "The skirts will not get in the way if you do as I say."

"Anything, Cisco," she said, her eyes studying the distance from the horse's back to the ground. "You're the expert."

He mounted, gathered up his reins carefully, and took his left foot from the stirrup, extending his hand toward Gabby. With Cisco's help she was quickly seated sideways on the mare's rump, her skirts spread out around her and her hands grasping the young

212

man's gunbelt for support.

As they headed slowly toward the distant rising clouds of black, Cisco muttered, "Senor Rafael, he will kill me."

Gabby didn't answer. She was too busy trying to balance herself and regretting she hadn't insisted on hiking her skirt to ride astride the mare. They could have made better time if her perch were less precarious.

As they left the hacienda behind them, her thoughts turned to their destination and, as it had back in town, fear clutched at her heart. Somewhere ahead of her a very stubborn man was riding all out to throw himself into danger.

All her foolish prating had been a futile denial of what she knew was the truth. Rafe meant more to her than any parcel of land on the face of the earth. She would do anything to keep him from harm.

Chapter Ten

Long before Rafe arrived on the scene, he heard the roar of the fire, carried on hot, cinder-filled air across the Seco's jagged terrain. With the sound came an acrid smell that overpowered the naturally perfumed fragrance of the brush.

The stallion, too, smelled the danger ahead and instinctively shied, his proud head rearing, his gait slowing erratically, but under Rafe's strong hand he responded to command and thundered forward once more through the thick scrub.

Horse and rider topped a rise, and Rafe pulled to a halt. Thick black smoke boiled slowly toward him, borne along by a wind he found himself praying would remain a gentle breeze. The smoke issued from a wall of bright flames two hundred yards wide licking its way through the cedar brush and mesquite. The Seco's vaqueros scrambled in front of the fire valiantly trying to stall its progress with blankets and shovels and whatever else was at hand. It was like trying to beat back hell.

A rustle of movement in the underbrush caught Rafe's attention, and he glanced down to see a rabbit doe and her young scurrying across a clearing, bold in their desperation to flee. Silently he cursed whatever had caused the fire. Cisco had said the stock was safe, but flame-ravaged land could be a long time regaining the wildlife and precious grass that had been lost. And this particular conflagration was headed straight for his home. With vengeful determination he spurred the stallion down the hill.

"Rafael!" His grandfather's anxious voice came to him through the sparks and cinders that were carried aloft in the hot air. "Over here."

Rafe followed the sound and saw Ben astride his bay stallion at the foot of the hill. In the flickering light the old man sat tall and straight. Fifty yards away orange flames ate their way toward him.

"Ben!" Rafe reined his horse in his direction. Rafe had been too intent on getting out to the fire to look for him back at the hacienda. The ranch was his grandfather's only passion. He should have known Ben would be there.

Up close, Rafe could see near panic in Ben's eyes. "It's getting worse, Rafe," he shouted across the steady roar. "We'll lose it all."

Rafe glanced back down at the scene. The fire was contained on either side by sharply rising cliffs that formed a wide tunnel—contained for sure from spreading wider, but at the same time directed southward with increasing force. An image flashed in Rafe's mind, of flames working their way across the

215

hills and shallow gullies, consuming everything in their path, roaring through the hacienda, dying only when the river had been reached.

Only one thing stood in their way—a deep, tree-lined ravine that lay between here and the main house. Without hindrance the fire would swoop down across the dry bed and continue on its way unimpeded.

Filled with pride for his grandfather's courage and anger that he should place himself in such danger, Rafe rode to Ben's side. "Get back to the house, Ben, and let me fight it. Help is coming. Some of the men from town are already here."

"I'm needed," Ben said stubbornly. "To direct the men. I can't hide back at the house like one of the women."

Rafe shook his head in exasperation. "Everyone knows what you'd do for the Seco." He saw the set of the old man's jaw. "At least stay here until I find Antonio."

"He's down there to the left," Ben said. "Not doing more than slowing the damned thing down. Not stopping it."

Jumping to the ground, Rafe ran through the gathering heat. He stopped when he spied the foreman valiantly trying to shovel dirt onto the burning grass at the forward edge of the blaze.

"Give it up," Rafe yelled as he came to a halt. "We can't meet it head on. Have to try another way."

The two men pulled back from the wall of crackling heat. Flying cinders filled the air. One landed on

Rafe's sleeve, ate into the cotton. He slapped at the widening hole, then cut his eyes through the thick smoke and took in the angle of the sun on its trail halfway toward the horizon. Two hours to dusk, he figured. He gestured to the southeast. "How far you estimate that ravine is?"

"A mile," Antonio yelled. "Maybe more."

Rafe's mind worked quickly. This time of year and after a long dry spell there wasn't much moisture in the vegetation. Everything would go fast.

"Pull the men back to the ravine. We've got maybe a couple of hours before the fire reaches there — unless a gully-washer comes along, and that's not likely to happen. We'll give it the mile, but by God that's all it will get."

Antonio shook his head. "Rafael, that ravine's not wide enough to kill the flames."

"Not by itself it's not. That's why we'll build a fire line there. A wide one that'll give the ravine a little help."

Antonio nodded in agreement and ran toward the vaqueros and the men who'd made it out from town, waving them back from the fire's edge, directing them toward the ravine.

Some gathered in the horses that had been tethered away from the fire. They rode double. Some scrambled through the brush on foot. Rafe rode among them, at one point stretching his arm toward a young vaquero and pulling him onto the stallion's rump. Behind him was Ben's thundering bay.

They arrived at the edge of the steep-sided ravine,

and Rafe barked his orders in Spanish: Start at the edge and move back toward the fire. Clear away anything that might burn. Use the horses to root up trees and bigger brush; clear out everything else with whatever tools are available — shovels, picks, bare hands.

Knowing the more ground he gave up the larger the conflagration would grow, Rafe hoped he was giving the fire enough room to burn while they stripped a wide swath of the land.

He turned to Ben. "I'll be depending on you to ride on down the way and get the men started. There'll be more coming out. Tell 'em what we're up to."

Ben nodded crisply and spurred his horse away.

Dismounting, Rafe turned at the sound of an approaching horse crashing up the steep path that cut through the ravine. Could be Jeff, he thought. The horse came into view. A flash of blue muslin struck him as hard as the scene of the fire. He ran toward the sight, swearing.

Cisco pulled his mare to a halt a half dozen yards away and dropped to the ground, helping Gabby after him. She gripped the young man's arm for a moment to catch her balance, then pulled herself erect.

"Senor Rafael," the young man said, not meeting Rafe's glare, "I go help the others now." He scrambled back on the mare.

"You damned well better keep away from me," Rafe said to Cisco's retreating back, then stared at Gabby. The swift ride across the Seco had sent her hair tumbling wildly about her shoulders, and she lifted her chin in proud defiance. Rage rose within him until he could taste it. It had the taste of soot.

"You've gone against my orders," he said icily, "and now you'll only get in the way."

Lashed by his scorn, Gabby fought to hold her ground. "Tell me that when the fire's out. Until then, we've got work to do."

"I'll tell you a lot of things later. If there was any way I could spare one of the men, I'd have you headed back toward the house."

She squared her shoulders. "You don't always get your way, Rafe." She whirled away from him.

"At least," he called after her, "stay out of the men's way. And get the hell away if the fire should move in before we've crossed the ravine. We've got enough to do without worrying about your clothing catching on fire. Although it's no more than you deserve."

Her only answer was to tug her flowing skirt free of the thorny shrubs. Making her way to a couple of townsmen she'd seen at the Talbert party, she took her place beside them to begin pulling at the tall grass.

"Miss Deschamps!" one of them exclaimed.

A defiant glare dared him to say more, and, shrugging, he tossed her a short-handled pick. She began thrashing at the roots, imagining Rafe's cold eyes on her as she worked.

She soon realized the inappropriateness of a muslin gown out in the brush. Each bush and blade of grass caught in its folds, and she repeatedly had to rip the snagged cloth free. After a few minutes of struggling, she glanced up and forgot about her skirt. In the

219

distance was the boiling black smoke and orange horizon that reminded her exactly why all of them were here. A fire threatened her land. Frustrations with her inadequacies and with Rafe turned to vengeance. The flames bearing down on them would not win.

More and more townspeople joined them, and once again she was struck by the friendship and loyalty they showed toward Rafe. Sometime during the first half hour of work she saw Jeff McGowan ride up with a contingent of two dozen men.

"Railroad workers," one of the townsmen said, and Gabby remembered how Jeff had ridden away from them after Cisco had arrived at the Talbert home. It was a tough-looking crew that accompanied him, hard workers who set about felling the trees with the axes they'd brought along.

When Jeff spied her down the way, he stared in open amazement, then grinned and tipped his hat in acknowledgment of her presence. It was almost a courtly gesture, and Gabby nodded in return before plunging back to her work.

The time sped by but her progress was slow. Still she kept on. For the first time she had her hands in the dirt; through her own sweat and strain she felt a genuine bond with the land. Far from the city and its trappings of civilization, she felt an exhilaration in working side by side with people who shared a common goal.

Her hands blistered, the blisters broke, but she ignored the pain. She soon realized that if she concentrated on small patches of ground, she could ignore the stretch of land in front of her. Each cleared patch was a victory. Occasionally she rewarded herself with a quick glance around. And occasionally she saw the man she was seeking.

Rafe seemed to be everywhere at once, directing the men, adding his strength to their efforts, encouraging them on. A curious pride filled her heart at the sight.

Once he strode by and paused for a second, his eyes examining her before settling on her hands. With a frown of concern, he pulled off his leather gloves and dropped them at her feet. Then he was gone.

She looked at the gloves, then slowly bent and picked them up. She held them close to her face. They smelled of sweat and smoke and dirt. And of Rafe. Brushing aside the thought, she slipped her hands inside them. They were too big and made her work cumbersome, but she kept them on, grateful for their protection.

Sometimes Gabby pulled at the small shrubs and grass, sometimes she helped clear the land by dragging the uprooted brush back toward the ravine and shoving it over the edge. If once or twice she stumbled over the tattered remains of her skirt, no one seemed to notice. In the distance beneath sky-darkening clouds of black smoke, an orange glow grew brighter. They all knew the fire would soon be in sight.

In minutes a blanket of fast-moving smoke and flames came into view, obliterating the sky. The long line of weary workers stopped and stared. Rafe looked at the staggered row of men—and somewhere among them one woman—that stretched out to either side of him. Behind them were fifty yards of cleared land. Was it enough? For more than two hours they'd been working without pausing.

And no matter what else he thought of Gabby, he knew she had done her share. She would never know the number of times he had looked for her, watched her slender figure bent over a stubborn shrub, caught the triumph in the set of her shoulders when she managed to dislodge it and the frustration when she failed.

As much as the smoke had turned day into night when he'd first arrived, Rafe saw that the fire turned twilight into day and he motioned everyone back. They would watch from the far side of the ravine.

Retrieving his horse, which had been tethered to a boulder at the edge of the clearing, he mounted and studied the barren stretch of land between him and the inferno. Another rider came up beside him, and he glanced at the leathered face of Jeff McGowan.

"Should be quite a spectacle watching the fire die," Jeff said.

"That's what I'm hoping."

"And if it doesn't?"

"Then we bought a little time to come up with something else."

Both men kept their eyes on the fast-moving flames. "Got any idea what that something else might be?" Jeff asked.

"No."

Jeff shrugged. "I best be seeing everyone gets across the ravine okay. You all right, Rafe?"

Rafe nodded, shifting his eyes toward the Ranger. "Thanks for bringing those railroad men out. We must have upwards of two hundred men out here today. Everyone was needed."

"You got a lot of friends in these parts. That's got to make you feel good." Without waiting for a response, Jeff pulled at the reins and rode away.

Rafe found himself grinning at his departing friend. By damn, he *did* feel good. Among the sweat-streaked faces around him there were storekeepers and ranchers alike. Some of those townsmen weren't used to hard physical labor. He owed them a special thanks—and a long drink of whiskey for those who indulged in the habit. They'd feel like hell tomorrow. Might as well enjoy what was left of the night.

Most of the neighboring ranchers had brought the men they could spare and worked alongside them. Only one he hadn't seen. Earl Hunter. For a moment Rafe speculated about what might have caused the fire. He had a hunch it hadn't been spontaneous.

As the workers began to pull back down the angled wall of the ravine, he found himself looking for one of them in particular. In the dim light he spied her trudging across the clearing. No longer was her gown the color of a noon sky; no longer did its skirt flow around her body in graceful folds. Blending into the dusty ground where she trod, the muslin hung limp and tattered. One sleeve was torn halfway off, and her hair fell in a tangled mass about her shoulders. On her hands she still wore his outsized gloves.

Without thinking, he turned the stallion and pulled to a halt beside her. "Ride in front of me," he said, extending his hand.

She ignored it. "I'll walk with the others."

"You're barely able to put one foot in front of the other. And you think you'll make it up the far side of the ravine?"

"I'll make it." Straightening her shoulders, she quickened her pace, her eyes pinned on the pockmarked land stretching in front of her. The truth was she didn't want to be on that horse leaning against him. He might find out exactly how close to exhaustion she was, how much her hands pained her, how loud her muscles screamed in protest to her every move.

More than once during the past hours when she'd viewed her small contribution to the task, she thought he'd been right after all. She could have done more good preparing food and drink back at the hacienda. But she would swallow coal oil before she'd let him know it.

Rafe whirled the horse away and directed his efforts to seeing that Ben and the rest of the workers made their way to safety before the oncoming flames brought their wall of heat and danger any closer. Still, his eyes returned again and again to make sure that Gabby was among them.

The scramble into the dry bed that lay at the base of the gorge was made difficult by the debris that had been tossed into its depths. Movement was slow.

The sound of popping mesquite grew louder. With the air thickened by cinders and flying ash, the workers hastened to the safety of the ravine's far side. There Emma Talbert and the other women greeted them with ladles of cool water and baskets of food. They waited their turn patiently for the drink. A few ate. More collapsed into the grass beside the wagons and stared back at the oncoming fire.

The housekeeper Lupita, her young eyes round with worry, pushed through the crowd to find Rafe. "Is Antonio—"

"Antonio is fine," Rafe interrupted. "He's down by the far wagon." She hurried away.

After the flurry of the men's arrival, a strange quiet settled over the men and women, their faces turned in the direction of the raging fire. Between them and the fire lay the ravine and fifty yards of barren land; at their back came the first stirring of a southerly evening breeze which would push against the flames.

The end was as quick and undramatic as the work had been frenzied. Hungry flames licked at the clearing's edge, then turned back on themselves. Rendered impotent, they soon settled into smoldering coals. As the smoke drifted aloft on the wind, a full moon came into view, casting ghostly light on the scene. Occasionally a spit of flame would arise from the hellish landscape, only to burn briefly and then die.

Just as Rafe was about to signal for everyone to withdraw, the unpredictable border wind swirled across the clearing, fanning a shower of sparks, raining that shower onto the debris in the ravine. Small, scattered fires, nuisances that must be nevertheless extinguished, flared up in several places. Joined by a hundred others, some trying to replace boots on swollen feet, Rafe grabbed a blanket from the nearest wagon and headed back into the ravine. Halfway down the slope he stopped to slap at a burning bush and realized that nearby Gabby was doing the same.

"Get on back up," he growled. "I'll take care of this."

Her retort never came. A snake, slithering its way to safety, crossed the path at her feet, and with a scream she whirled to get away. The movement sent her skirt flying into the low flames consuming the bush. The cloth burned quickly. Rafe jumped to smother it in his blanket, tearing at the material of her skirt, pulling it away from her legs.

He was too late to save her from injury. A narrow burn extended from halfway up her outer thigh down past her knee. He tore the rest of the skirt from the waist of her dress. Only a tattered petticoat remained. Lifting her into his arms, he carried her back up the hill and laid her onto the grass. In the moonlight he could see the burn was already blistering. It must be hurting like the devil but Gabby said not a word, only kept her wide eyes turned on him. She refused to look down at the burn.

Rafe kept his face straight. "Need to get that taken care of," he said. "I guess you'll have to ride with me after all. A wagon would be too slow."

A shadow fell across them. "Can I help?" Jeff McGowan asked.

Rafe nodded brusquely. "Stay here with Antonio

226

and Ben. See that everything is all right. Get everyone back as soon as you can. There'll be food and whiskey waiting, and the horse trough for bathing. Pass the word." He paused. "And thanks again, Jeff."

"*De nada.*" Jeff turned his gaze to Gabby. "I'd trust this man over most sawbones I've seen, Gabby. He'll fix you up just fine."

Behind him Emma Talbert moved closer. "You need me, Rafe?" she asked.

"Just ride on back in the first wagon. Gabby might find she prefers a female nurse."

"I'm not an invalid," Gabby said crossly, attempting to rise, but Rafe would have none of it. Standing, he lifted her into his arms.

"And you're not exactly in top shape either." He carried her to his horse and settled her sideways in the saddle, careful not to touch her burn, then pulled himself up behind the cantle. She leaned gratefully against him.

He started out. Soon they were out of sight of the others.

Rafe stared at the gloved hands in her lap. "Think you could part with those gloves now?"

She started to pull at them, winced, then in a quick motion pulled them from her hands. She pushed them at Rafe. Thrusting them in his belt, he reached for her hands and turned them over. Deep, open blisters cut into her palms, and even in the moonlight he could see they were beginning to fester. He swore, pulled her tighter against him, and urged the stallion into a faster clip. Still, it was a slow journey, and only

227

when the stallion headed down toward the barn did Rafe let himself begin to relax.

Dismounting, he took great care in cradling her in his arms. He entered the house through the back door and surprised a half dozen women busy in the kitchen preparing food for the returning men. The smell of fried pork and boiled beans filled the air.

The women turned surprised faces to him. "Think a couple of you could bring me some buckets of hot water?"

One of the women recognized Gabby. "Why, it's that Miss Deschamps. Is she hurt?"

Gabby started to answer, but Rafe spoke up first.

"Nothing that can't be cured," he said, moving toward the door. "My room's on the other side of the courtyard. You'll see the light. Get the water over as soon as you can." He paused in the doorway. "My housekeeper has a room at the back. One of you might see if you can find something Miss Deschamps could change into."

One woman sprang into action, directing two others toward the pump and heading for the back room. "We'll be over directly to help out."

Halfway across the moon-bathed courtyard, Gabby struggled against him. "I'm not helpless, you know. I can walk."

"I was wondering when you were going to start fighting me."

"I'm not fighting you. It's just that I can take care of myself."

Rafe shook his head in disbelief. "You're exhausted

and you're carrying some injuries that would slow a big man. For once put yourself in my hands."

Gabby had a retort for that but she held it back. Her hands and leg hurt more than she would ever admit.

His room was large and comfortable, and its furnishings showed his Spanish heritage—dark, massive furniture, brightly colored woven rugs and bedspread. When he laid her down on the high bed, she settled her weary bones into its softness and, with a sigh, decided she could stay there forever.

After a sharp knock at the door, the woman who'd spoken up in the kitchen entered. "The water will be along directly. It's heating now." She waved a white cotton gown in the air. "I think this will do for now. Looks like it ought to fit."

"Thank you, Mrs. Dean," Rafe said, reluctant to leave but knowing the formidable woman standing in the doorway would brook nothing less. From outside his room, he watched as the other women carried in towels and buckets of hot water, then reluctantly went to the shadows behind the house and, using cold water from the pump, kept busy washing the soot and dirt from his own body.

After pulling on a stiff pair of pants and a shirt that Lupita had hung out earlier to dry, he at last gathered the medicines he planned to use. Gabby would not be happy, but at least she would be cured.

When he was allowed to reenter his room, he caught her struggling to sit up in bed. Light from a wall lantern fell across the room. She was clad in a

229

demure cotton gown that buttoned to her throat. Gone were the smudges of ash that had covered her face and arms. Her hair was brushed smooth and fell in soft, loose curls down her back. Once he'd thought of that hair as sunlight. In the dim light he was reminded more of the moon.

The skirt of Gabby's nightgown was pulled high to avoid irritating the burn, and she watched Rafe as he rested his gaze on her exposed legs. She felt foolish that she had allowed such a stupid injury to happen, after she had been sure she would cause no trouble. And she'd been so vocal about it. Rafe had every right to mock her. She was relieved to see only clinical concern in his eyes.

He deposited the few items he'd brought with him on the table beside the bed and bent over to study the burn, which ran like a narrow stripe down the outside of her leg. His expression betrayed nothing. To her the injury looked shallow and inconsequential, but if that were true, then why did it hurt so much?

To her surprise Rafe reached for the long, finger-shaped leaf spine of a plant she'd seen growing at the front of the house. "Aloe vera," he said to her unasked question, snapping the stalk in half. A thick, milky substance oozed from the break, and in gentle, sure strokes he smoothed it onto her leg.

"The *curanderos* use the plant for burns," Rafe said. "I've never seen a doctor come up with anything better."

At first his touch was painful, but as the pain subsided she found the lotion was soothing away the

230

pain. She smiled up at him. Rafe's eyes met hers. Gabby's body tightened. Forgetting her injured hands, she reached up to brush aside the unruly shock of hair that fell across his forehead. She winced in pain.

"Gabby," he said softly. "I'm not quite done."

Gabby watched as he reached for a jar on the table and removed the lid. An unpleasant odor assailed her. He scooped a wooden spatula into the jar and came up with a thick substance which he lathered across her palms. The stench was close to unbearable.

"Coal oil and sugar," Rafe said simply. "For the infection."

Gabby wrinkled her nose. "Have the *curanderos* struck again?"

"My father this time. Sam Jericho had a cure for almost everything."

Gabby was reminded anew that, like her, Rafe was the product of two cultures. With him it was Spanish and Texas cowboy, a combination that had played havoc with her heart.

When he had covered the open blisters with the obnoxious substance, he wrapped her hands in clean rags. Gabby looked down in dismay. "How am I supposed to take care of myself?" she said.

"You're not." Rafe leaned down until his breath warmed her cheek. "We'll work something out."

In that moment Gabby felt her will slipping into his. She could just as easily have walked the floor on her hands as doubt his word or his good will. He'd offered her care and comfort; whatever discomfort she was suffering lessened under the balm of his assur-

231

ance.

Rafe pulled away. How easy it would be to take advantage of Gabby, to pull her into his arms and kiss her as thoroughly as he wanted to.

"You didn't have any business out there today," he said more harshly than he'd intended. "If you'd done as I asked, you wouldn't be hurt."

Bewilderment flashed in her eyes, followed by a spark of resentment. As quickly as the rare moment of gentleness had settled over them, it was gone. "The burn's not so bad as I thought," she said, at last managing to sit up on the smothering mattress. "And as I recall, you didn't ask. You ordered."

He glanced at her bandaged hands. "What I should have done was set you out on the side of the road a few miles from the ranch. Except that Cisco would have come to your rescue. Next time don't rope him in for one of your schemes."

"I didn't get in the way, Rafe. At least not until the end. You just don't want me anywhere on the ranch."

Pride and defiance were in her eyes and in the lift of her chin. Rafe stared at her without speaking. Not want her on the ranch? He'd had a few sleepless nights imagining how her presence might grace his lonely home. But that was before she'd bought up the loan.

What a futile effort that had been, although she little knew it. With a few words he could crush the spirit from her, but they were words he'd already decided not to say, even before she'd labored bravely out on the range.

"We'll see about that," he said, backing toward the door. "I'll have Lupita check on you later to see if you need anything."

He turned and exited into the moonlit courtyard. Across the way he could hear the sounds that came with the arrival of the men and women from the range. The fires must all be out. Now he was free to consider how to manage the headstrong Gabby in view of the latest turn of events.

She was so sure she had him with that mortgage — that she could foreclose and take over everything that he and Ben had worked for. How wrong she was. He'd sought out Judge Russell that morning to see just what power she held and found it was very little.

The judge had read over the papers from the bank carefully, then smiled. "I'll issue a summary judgment against her," Russell had told him. "As long as you can pay the annual interest on the note, she won't be able to foreclose. You're almost kin, Rafe. I'll make sure you can make that payment."

Rafe had been close to telling Gabby back at the gazebo about what he learned, but Cisco's arrival had interrupted him. If he told her the way things were, she'd only try something else, maybe even head for the courthouse to file her suit. In that pursuit, her only ally would be that fool she had for a lawyer. She didn't stand a chance.

Just the way she didn't stand a chance trying to run a ranch. Gabby had spirit and nerve, but she didn't belong out on the land. He'd seen it as he watched her trying to clear the brush. And it was a damned fool thing she'd done shying away from a harmless coach-whip and into the real danger of the fire. She was a city girl, born and bred. That was where she belonged.

He strode onto the patio and was immediately engulfed by a half dozen celebrants who insisted on congratulating him and themselves for a job well done. The whiskey he'd promised was strong on their breath. At last he made his way to the Judge's side. Russell sat at the edge of the courtyard looking as weary as Rafe felt.

"You'll stay the night, of course, Judge. Provided you do me another small favor."

"For a bed, I'd promise anything."

"Don't tell Ben about the judgment possible against Miss Deschamps. It's important. You know your old friend. Much as we respect him, Ben can fly off the handle and cause problems. I'd like to tell both of them in my own way. You understand?"

"Of course, my boy. Now where's that bed?"

Rafe spotted Lupita and put the Judge into her keeping, then stepped wearily into the hall to think. It seemed at least a year since he'd left home that very morning to see Judge Russell before going to the barbecue. In all the excitement of the long day there had been no opportunity to tell Ben what the judge had said and promised.

Now it seemed a good thing he hadn't told anyone. Once the old man heard the news, he would be so pleased he wouldn't stop to listen to reason. He was far more likely to seize the opportunity to send Gabby

234

packing — and leave them both wondering what she would try next. Rafe almost smiled at the thought of her tenacity.

Rafe knew he would have to handle Ben carefully. Sometime during the past few years the mantle of management had shifted from the old man to his grandson but had never been verbally recognized, and Ben was able to rationalize his lack of real authority. A man's pride was a fragile thing. Once broken, it was hard to repair.

Rafe found Ben in his office pouring himself a glass of brandy.

"Are you all right?" Rafe asked.

Ben stood tall. "I haven't felt this good in years, Rafael. I should get out more often."

"You're going to be sore as hell tomorrow."

"Perhaps. Let me enjoy tonight, though. Lots of those wonderful friends have collapsed, but me, I am not tired in the least." He poured another drink and held it out to Rafe. "We beat that fire, didn't we?"

"We sure did," Rafe said, lifting his drink in a toast before tossing it down his throat. After another two drinks, he thought Ben might be just drunk enough to listen to reason.

"You know we've still got another problem, Ben," he said, settling down into the chair opposite his grandfather's desk. "Gabrielle Deschamps. She might be filing suit pretty soon." That was no lie, Rafe thought. Fruitless though it might be, she was stubborn enough to fight any odds.

"*Madre de Dios*, Rafael. She is no match for such as

we."

"But she can be a real bother. And court is expensive—at a time we need to spend our capital on improvements to the ranch."

Ben settled back in his chair and twirled the brandy in his glass. "*Si*, I understand what you say. But what can we do? The senorita has a strong will."

"You and I know she doesn't belong. We need her to realize it, too."

"What do you propose?"

"That we let her stay out here for a while. Now, now, calm down. With the injuries to her hands, she needs to be taken care of for a time. We already owe her that. And while she's here we'll let her see how rough the life is. Especially for the owner. Maybe she pictures herself lounging behind that desk of yours and issuing orders to some man. We both know that's not the way a ranch is run. The owner has to get his hands dirty, too. Raise a few calluses. And not just in an emergency. I'm talking about day after day."

He could see the agreement in Ben's eyes, could see in the nod of his grandfather's head that he had been convinced. "Gabby is simply too soft. She could never make this her home," Rafe said. As he finished the statement, he felt a moment of intense regret that she would soon be gone.

On the walkway outside the room, Gabby stood in the shadows. It was a good thing she'd grown hungry and had ventured out of her room, or else she'd never have stumbled onto the two men talking. Mindless of her bandaged hands, she pulled tightly around her body the large robe she'd found hanging in Rafe's wardrobe. When she put the robe on to seek out Lupita, she had felt for a moment that his arms were around her and she'd been thrilled.

Now she wanted to pitch the robe in the dirt.

Too bad she'd come along at the end of what must have been a cozy chat. So Rafe thought she was soft, did he? That she didn't belong. The Arroyo Seco was as much hers as it was his. Physical strength wasn't all it took to run a ranch. It also took stamina and heart and desire, and she had those in plenty. She had been storing them up through the years.

So Rafe thought he would win, did he? She'd almost thought so, too, when she'd seen the way the townspeople rallied to his side. But she had also made a few friends today. Several had praised her for her work out on the range, and she'd seen acceptance in the eyes of others, enough that she had begun to feel this was where she belonged.

Let the Hidalgos plan to beat her back with—with what? Hard work? They'd soon find out they were wrong.

She whirled around to return to Rafe's room, reveling in the fact that she had taken over his bed. And without having to share it with him. If he fooled around with her much longer, she would simply call in the loan and do the same with the entire ranch.

Chapter Eleven

When Gabby looked at her unwrapped hands the next morning, she had to admit Rafe knew what he was about.

"The redness is gone," she said, looking up at him as he stood beside her bed.

"Those blisters can still fester," he said, "if you try to do too much. And the burn will take awhile to heal completely."

"Do you really think so?" she asked innocently. "It hardly hurts at all."

"I think so. You'll need looking after. I take it you're still in that hotel."

Gabby didn't bat an eye. "Yes, I am."

A glint lit Rafe's dark eyes. "No one to help you there."

Gabby dropped her eyes as she remembered Rafe's lone visit to her room. "No one," she said.

"Then why not stay here? I imagine Lupita would like the company. The Seco must be a lonely place for a woman."

Gabby bit back a retort. He'd already started on his campaign to show her she wouldn't like the ranch. She shrugged. "You're the doctor."

And so it was done, she thought as he left the room with a promise to send the housekeeper to help her get dressed. Within minutes came a soft knock on the door and Lupita entered, a skirt and blouse on her arm. Gabby had to rely on the girl for assistance as she donned the clothes. From its tight waist the skirt hung loosely against her bare legs, allowing the long burn to heal under its coating of sap from the aloe vera plant.

How different the clothing was from the smartly tailored clothes she'd brought with her from the East, more comfortable and practical for working around the hacienda. And it was far more than that. With its brightly woven threads and simple style, it was a reminder of her Spanish heritage.

When she emerged from Rafe's room, she found he'd gone to inspect the damage left by the fire. The pattern was set for the next few days. Sometimes she would see him early in the morning, then he would disappear to his work, leaving Gabby to spend most of the daylight hours walking as far as she could around the ranch, asking questions of Lupita and the occasionally present Cisco, letting the sun do its healing work on her hands. Clasped awkwardly at her side was a stout stick—in case she came across another snake.

A warm camaraderie developed between the two women as they worked, and Gabby learned much about the labor involved in caring for the house. One fact stayed in Gabby's mind more strongly than all the others. The hacienda was less than twenty years old, having been built after the original Cordero home burned to the ground. No member of Gabby's family before her had trod its tiled floors and yet, as foolish as it seemed, she felt she had come home.

Reason told her she should be seeing Ben Hidalgo, but then reason didn't seem to figure into her relationship with the man. Up early, before she arose, he rode his stately stallion in an inspection of the ranch—Lupita said he was warily looking for signs of another fire. And when he was at home Gabby supposed he spent most of the remaining daylight hours reading in his study. Since Rafe was seldom at home, Ben took his meals alone and retired early. To Gabby it seemed a lonely life, but it was one he had chosen for himself.

At her request, she was moved to the back of the house into an unused room whose lone window opened onto a broad sweep of the Seco. The room was a long way from Rafe's.

Along with her clothing, she tucked away the gold cross. The chain, broken the night she'd torn it from her neck and thrown it at Rafe, had long since been repaired, but she had not put it on. She doubted she ever would and was only waiting for the appropriate time to return it.

That time had not yet come. Free to roam, she took advantage of her solitude and spent most of her time outdoors. As she walked by the neat rows of Lupita's vegetable garden and across the rolling meadow behind the main house, she felt a gradual strengthening of her bond with the land.

Her naturally tawny skin took on a golden tinge

240

and her hair lightened. The youthful Cisco, catching her unawares one morning when she was on a winding path behind the Seco corral, told her she was becoming more beautiful.

"Like a senorita forged from Mayan gold," he said, unsettling her for a moment. The look that flashed in his dark eyes was more that of a man than a youth of sixteen.

She figured it was just his natural, romantic nature that made him speak so grandly, and she replied with a laugh. "Gold is a soft metal, Cisco," she said. "Easily bent. That's not me at all."

At the end of a week Gabby's hands had healed enough to assure her she was ready for the strenuous work Rafe had waiting for her. The palms seemed tougher then they'd been before the fire. As she stood in the morning sunlight behind the hacienda, she viewed the sight of her hands with mixed emotions. At last she could start showing Rafe she could take to ranch life. Unfortunately, that included her learning to ride a horse.

As she looked out onto the rugged, gray-purple hills that stretched toward the Rio Grande and Mexico, she knew she'd been right. This was the home she'd dreamed it would be. No matter how long it took, she would somehow make at least a portion of it hers.

Deciding it was time for her morning walk, she reached for the stick that she used for protection, only to be startled by movement behind her.

"Cisco! How long have you been standing there?"

"Only a few *momentos*. Senor Rafael has sent me back to load another wagon with the wire. For tomorrow's work. I think, senorita, that wood you hold in your hand is a poor weapon." He began to unwind the whip that had been tucked at his waist, a grin splitting his brown face. "Would you like to learn something that would serve you better?"

Gabby looked down the length of the stick, then back to the whip. "I'd have to be awfully close to a snake to hit him with this," she said, dropping her weapon. "If you've got the time, I'd like to give that whip a try."

Cisco pulled his short body to its full height. "*A su servicio,*" he said with a courtly bow. "First, I show you what can be done."

Moving away from Gabby, the young man gripped the bullwhip in one hand and whirled its twenty feet of tail over his head, ending with a sharp snap of his wrist. A loud crack filled the air. He moved down a trail that led away from the hacienda, whirling the whip in the grasses from side to side, severing tall stalks of weed as he walked.

Coming to a halt, he motioned silently for Gabby to join him. He pointed to the trail ahead, and she was able to make out the bloated body of a horned lizard. The lizard seemed to sense danger and held himself still, blending into the dusty ground of the trail.

The disguise wasn't good enough for the hunter Cisco, and in a flash he sent the whip after his prey. Almost too quick for Gabby's eye to follow, the tip lashed around the lizard's body and flipped the reptile into the air. He landed somewhere in the tall grass beside the trail.

Gabby felt unexpectedly squeamish. "I thought those lizards were of use, Cisco. Don't they eat insects?"

Cisco shrugged. "Snakes also dine on the bugs," he said.

"That's different," she replied, brushing aside the illogic of her reply.

"Do you still wish to learn, senorita?"

Gabby thought about the ineffectual stick lying back at the hacienda. "Yes."

Cisco selected a nearby grassy slope for the lesson, but progress was slow. Either Gabby held the whip too far from her body, in which case she got no strength in the flick of her wrist, or the tail of the whip became entangled with her skirt.

"What I need is a pair of trousers," she said in disgust.

Cisco grinned. "If the senorita is telling the truth, I have the new pair which I would gladly give. A man can only wear one at a time."

Gabby studied the young man's slim hips. He wasn't any taller than she. The trousers might possibly fit. Minutes later alone in her room she decided she'd been only too right. It was a good thing her burn had healed until it was only a faint red mark, because the denim pants fit her like a second skin. Decidedly indecent, she thought, at least for a city girl. And most likely for a country girl, too. Why, if Rafe saw her, he would be—

She thought for a moment. He would be positively disapproving. It was that thought that decided her. Tying the tail of her blouse at her waist, she slapped on her head a broad-brimmed straw hat that had also been lent by Cisco. All she needed was a pair of boots to complete the ranch-hand picture, but she had to rely on the *huaraches*, the sandals, borrowed earlier in the week from Lupita.

Gingerly she headed for the door. If the pants didn't stretch through wear, a sudden movement and she might do herself injury.

Outside she was greeted by a low whistle from Cisco and a gasp from Lupita, who was drawing water from the pump near the back door.

"Senorita Gabrielle," the girl said in surprise, then stopped, obviously unwilling to criticize her.

"Too much, isn't it?" Gabby said, then grinned. "But very practical. At least no one else will see me. Cisco, you ready for that lesson?" Without waiting for a reply, she headed for the trail, her stride gradually lengthening, and she was glad to find that the pants did, indeed, stretch with her movements. Maybe men weren't so crazy after all to wear them.

Freed as she was from the confining skirt, her inhibitions with the whip seemed to vanish. If, after an hour, she couldn't get the same sharp crack that Cisco did, nor flick the top of a distant weed, she could at least give a creditable showing for her efforts.

"It is time for the final test," Cisco said at last and, leaving her wondering, headed for the house. He returned shortly and proceeded to line up a half dozen empty tin cans on a flat boulder beside the trail. "Step back, Senorita Gabrielle, and take them down one at a time."

Which is exactly what she did. True, one of the cans actually bounced against another and knocked it down, but she figured the ricochet counted. Really, it ought to count double since she saved herself effort, but she decided not to complain.

Measured applause from the direction of the house caught her attention, and she turned to see Rafe, his long legs covered by dusty leather chaps, his shirt stained with sweat. At his throat was knotted a red bandana. His Stetson was pulled low on his forehead; dark eyes stared from under the brim. He was no more then twenty feet up the trail from her, and she could read disapproval in the grim set of his face.

Defensive hackles immediately rose. "Don't sneak up on me like that," she snapped. "How long have you been standing there, anyway?"

Rafe strolled down the trail toward her. "More to the point, Gabby, how long have you been keeping Cisco from his work?" His eyes flicked to the young vaquero. "I assume you haven't finished what you were sent to do."

Cisco took the whip from Gabby's outstretched hand and backed away. "It will be done before the sun is down, Senor Rafael," he said. Turning, he beat a hasty retreat for the barn.

Rafe turned the full force of his gaze on Gabby. "I suggest you stay away from Cisco, Gabby," he said, his voice deceptively soft. "He's only a kid."

Gabby's eyes flashed angrily. "And what is that supposed to mean?"

"Twice you've got him in trouble. First he took you out to the fire, and now today. I'd never let him know it, but don't think I'm blaming him. I know how you can twist a man."

Gabby was enraged. She fought the impulse to strike back. Words didn't seem to faze Rafe. If only she had that whip back in her hands. Damn the man, anyway. When would he realize she held the upper hand?

And why did he have to look so good? The past days on the range had left him lean, hard, and bristled. Somehow he seemed more — more *Rafe* than he ever had. And she seemed just as weak where he was concerned.

Gabby pushed past him, allowing her hands to touch his arm for only a second. "I'll go help him if I can," she said over her shoulder. "Maybe that will make you happy. My injuries seem to be healed."

"That won't make me happy at all. I said stay away from him and I meant it."

Gabby stopped in her tracks. "Why?" she said, turning to face him. "You couldn't be jealous of a kid, could you?"

Their eyes locked, and for an instant Gabby read something that made her think her hastily spoken words might contain a grain of truth. The moment passed, and she saw only scorn.

"If you're healed, I suggest you spend some time on horseback, Gabby," he said. "Instead of playing games."

"Anytime you say," she lied, "is fine with me. How about right now?"

"I've got a horse I need to ride myself. A wild bronc I found wandering on the Seco. Must have come through the latest hole Earl Hunter's men cut in the fence. No brand on him. As far as I'm concerned, he's mine."

A picture of Rafe astride a bucking horse flashed through Gabby's mind. "Do you mind if I watch?"

Rafe's lips twisted into a half smile. "You might find it interesting, *querida,* to see the way a man can

246

tame a wild thing. When it suits his purpose."

"But then horses aren't very bright, are they?" she retorted. "All they require is brute strength."

She whirled away to avoid whatever answer she figured was coming—getting in the last word with Rafe was usually a matter of leaving the scene first—and hurried up the path away from him.

Rafe watched her go, saw every movement of her body revealed by the tight-fitting pants. Damn it, he *had* been jealous. And of a kid. Ever since he'd met Emma on the trail the day after the fire he'd had mixed emotions about Gabby. Wanting to teach her a lesson about where she belonged and where she didn't. And wanting to teach her a great deal more, about men.

"Rafe!"

He looked up the hill to see Antonio waving to him, and he forced thoughts of Gabby aside. He had a wild bronc waiting for him. He'd tame one thing at a time. By the time he got to the corral, a half dozen vaqueros were leaning against the fence waiting for the show. Included in their number was Cisco, who should have been loading wire. Remembering the foolish jealousy he'd felt when he spied the youth with Gabby, Rafe smiled at him. Maybe he was too lenient on the boy, but he would let him stay.

As he disappeared into the barn, Gabby moved from the shadows cast by the hacienda and took her place beside Antonio. His surprise at her attire was quickly hidden and he nodded hello.

"Where is this brute—" Gabby started and then stopped. The "brute" was standing in the middle of the corral, a rope tied loosely around his neck, then looped around a fence post on the far side of the enclosure. He rolled wild eyes in her direction and tossed his head back proudly. To her mind he snorted fire, and she stepped back from the fence. She didn't need to know much about horses to realize this one was mean.

Ben, astride his bay, rode up at the far end of the corral, and Gabby, nervously awaiting Rafe's appearance, started to wave. Ben didn't look her way, and she pulled her hand back. He didn't want a greeting from her any more than she wanted one from him.

Down the opposite way Rafe, a bridle in one hand, slipped through the fence and circled the corral slowly, his eyes never leaving the horse. He moved quietly, the only sound the jingle of his spurs. By the time he faced the bronco head-on, the bridle was raised and Gabby could hear Rafe's soft, soothing words to the horse. For a moment the animal seemed mesmerized, and he was able to slip on the bridle. Around the edge of the corral all was silence.

Holding the reins firmly, Rafe unfastened the rope and let it fall to the dirt. In one fluid motion he swung himself onto the horse's back and pulled a quirt from the band at his waist. All hell broke loose.

No longer silent, the men yelled encouragement in two languages as the horse bucked and pitched, plunging and rearing in a wild attempt to unseat the rider. Rafe held firm, flogging the animal between the ears when he tried to rear over backwards.

Gabby found herself gripping Antonio's arm. "Why doesn't he have a saddle?" she yelled over the noise of the men.

"That is the *gringo* way," Antonio replied in a voice

much calmer than hers. "Rafael is a *jinete*. What you call a bronco buster. He stays on until the horse knows who is the boss. Do not worry, senorita. No one is better than the senor."

The horse proved stubborn. It seemed an hour — but could have been no more than a quarter of that time — before he learned his lesson and stopped the frenzied performance, a time in which Gabby was near panic that Rafe might be hurt. A vision of his twisted body crashing to the ground beneath the thrashing hoofs seared itself into her mind, and she couldn't shake it, not even when the horse began to tire. If anything happened to Rafe, she could never forgive herself that their last words hadn't been more tender.

At last the horse slowed enough for Rafe to drop to the ground. It gave Gabby no pleasure to see that for a second Rafe's legs were wobbly. For the first time since he'd mounted the beast, she drew a deep breath and her heart dropped from her throat. She even noted with pride that he hadn't lost his hat.

One of the vaqueros jumped into the corral, and Rafe handed him the reins. "See that he's brushed down and watered. One of the men can have another go at him tomorrow." Waving to Ben, he walked over to Gabby.

"He's not broken yet?" she asked.

"It'll take another time or two. Then he'll make a fine mount."

"That was very" — she searched for the word — "exciting. Do you have to do that often?"

His dirt-streaked face broke into a grin. "Not often. Usually the vaqueros handle it. They have a feel for horses. But this one was especially tough. And I thought you ought to see what a rancher is sometimes called on to do." He leaned against the fence and, pulling off the Stetson, wiped sweat from his forehead with his sleeve. "Are you about ready for your first lesson?"

Gabby glanced toward the barn, reminded herself of Rafe's real purpose in having her stay, and met his gaze. "Whenever you say. If you think you're up to it."

"Oh, I'm up to it all right. Just give me time for a little grub and coffee. I've got two horses in mind. A mare I should have disposed of long ago, Bessie by name. And a new one we call Tempest." His dark eyes challenged her. "Which shall it be?"

What was Rafe up to? Calling her bluff about being a rancher? From the moment they met, he'd challenged her. If it wasn't a kiss, it was an angry word. *Stay with me forever. Get the hell out of town.* He'd thrown down so many gauntlets that she was beginning to trip over them. This one she wasn't so sure she wanted to pick up. But she had no choice.

"Tempest, of course. No sense in learning to ride a horse that'll soon be in a glue factory."

Rafe merely nodded and turned to Antonio. "Have Cisco saddle up the roan. Gabby, you come on in to visit with Lupita for a while."

Gabby hadn't eaten since an early breakfast and it was long past noon. Still she couldn't bear the thought of food and spent the next few minutes telling herself she would be able to handle the horse Rafe had mentioned. For all their differences, she knew he wouldn't challenge her with anything that would actually cause her harm. She just didn't want to make a fool of herself so soon after his splendid performance on the back of a horse.

He'd referred to the horse she would ride as a roan, but Gabby didn't have the vaguest idea what that meant. It had an ominous ring to it. But then everything about horseback riding did.

There was little she could do to prepare for the ordeal besides slipping inside to get her gloves. Again she regretted the absence of boots, but she settled for a pair of heavy socks worn with her sandals. Deciding the fashion would never catch on in the city, she headed for the barn.

Gabby kept her head high when Cisco walked out of the barn, Rafe's black stallion and the beast Tempest in tow. Her horse was a brownish color spattered with white. She also had a look in her eye that said she would brook no nonsense from a human.

"Well, Gabby," came a voice behind her, "what do you think of the roan?"

She turned to face a solemn-faced Rafe. Her ignorance frustrated her, but there was only one way to erase it. "What exactly does roan mean?"

Rafe was all business. "Refers to her coloring. Picked her up at an auction not two months ago. She's spirited but there's not a mean streak in her. She'll be a fine mount for whoever can handle her."

And that, Gabby thought, would be her. Provided she made it through the next hour or two. She watched as Rafe dismissed Cisco and led the horses to a grassy area out of view of the house. Without a word, he spanned Gabby's waist with his hands and lifted her into the saddle.

It was too late to think of propriety, and she swung

one leg over the horse. Easing herself into the saddle, she gripped the knotted reins in one hand and the pommel in the other.

"Bad form," Rafe said.

It took her a minute to realize what he meant. The pommel. It seemed her one link to the ground, like a safety line, and reluctantly she let it go. Bad form she didn't want.

The horse snorted and shuffled sideways. "Don't hold the reins so tight," Rafe said. "Pat her neck and talk to her. She'll stand quietly enough."

That was a lot to do at once, she thought, and felt foolish patting and calling the mare "good girl" when that was the last thing she thought the horse was.

Rafe watched a minute from the ground, then mounted. "Now nudge her in the sides and lean forward. To go left, pull the rein left, the opposite to go right. Don't jerk, but don't pull too easy, either."

Gabby nudged, but nothing happened.

"A bit harder."

She dug heels into the beast's sides, and the horse shot forward at a rapid clip. A few yards across the field, Gabby's feet came out of the stirrups, and she slipped sideways. Desperately she grabbed with both hands at the forbidden pommel. The resulting jerk on the bit caused Tempest to rear. Gabby felt herself fly through the air and land with an unladylike thud on the ground.

Rafe was beside her in an instant. "Are you hurt?"

"Just my pride." Gabby picked up the straw hat from beside her on the grass and slapped it back on her head. "You ready to go again?"

"Not quite. That was my fault," he said angrily. "I

didn't have the stirrups adjusted right." Rapidly he shortened them and once more lifted Gabby skyward.

Again she settled in the saddle, forgot the pommel, held tightly to the reins. Tempest wouldn't budge. Remembering Rafe's instructions, she nudged her heels into the animal's sides, harder, and found herself once more bouncing across the meadow, but in a direction she didn't want to go—back toward the corral.

Gabby pulled hard left on the reins. Tempest circled completely around and resumed her course. She pulled hard right, and Tempest started to buck. Gabby found herself once more on the ground, this time perilously close to a low-growing cactus plant. Her backside was beginning to hurt, but she didn't wait for Rafe to come to her. She met him at the side of the horse.

Rafe had to fight the urge to carry her back to the hacienda and tend to her injuries once more. Surely she was getting sore. What she needed was a good rubdown. The look in her eyes told him she would tolerate no such suggestion, and he settled on another course.

"Tempest just wants to go home," he said. "You need to exert your will more." He grinned. "Never thought I'd hear myself telling you that."

One look at that handsome, smiling face and Gabby forgot her aches. Gone was the challenge in Rafe's eyes, replaced by encouragement. There was no way she could quit now.

The third time she was thrown came much later, just when she was getting used to the feel of the horse under her, learning to follow Rafe's careful instructions on the use of the reins, realizing the importance of the pressure she could exert with her knees and heels to let the horse know who was boss. The trouble was, confident from a series of small victories, she took off on her own at a pace that outmatched her fledgling skills.

Rafe yelled at her to halt, but she was too busy hanging onto the forbidden pommel to remember about the reins. When Tempest came to a narrow gully that crossed the field, the mare got no order to jump and suddenly stopped.

Gabby's body kept going forward, and this time she landed on her shoulder, which wasn't nearly as padded as her rump. She cried out in pain.

"That's it, Gabby," Rafe said in a stern voice. "You've had enough for one day. We're heading back."

Gabby was grateful Rafe didn't condescend to climb down and help her to her feet. He'd wanted her to find out how hard she would find ranching; she took it as a curious kind of compliment that he was letting her tough it out.

She pushed herself to her knees, stood, and faced the horse. "I want a good ride back, Rafe. Not a walk. I really was beginning to feel comfortable, and it was my fault about that gully. I should have pulled back on the reins."

This time she didn't wait for Rafe to help her mount. How easy it looked when someone else performed the simple task. For her it was close to impossible, but mount unassisted she did, ignoring the twinge in her shoulder. And she rode back toward the barn in a slow, easy gallop. Somewhere back in the meadow was her hat, but she didn't care. The wind caught her hair and felt good. She might learn to enjoy her new skill. Once she got over the pain.

She insisted on helping Rafe rub down the horses, and slipped inside the house to steal a few cubes of sugar as a treat for the animals. She even felt a flash of affection when Tempest, tucked inside a stall, nuzzled her neck in thanks.

Alone in the barn with Rafe, she felt his eyes on her, and she turned to face him. "Did I pass?" she asked, not bothered by how much she wanted his approval.

"You're at the head of the class."

"That's not saying much. Since I was the only one in it."

They fell silent, their eyes locked. Around them was the sound of a few stirring horses.

At last Rafe spoke. "I need to ride out for a while. Are you going to be all right?"

She nodded and watched him saddle up another horse. "You must have calluses on your backside," she said, "to keep from getting sore."

Pulling himself into the saddle, he couldn't resist a sideways grin at her. "Never noticed any. Did you?"

Gabby blushed. She'd asked for that. Thank goodness he didn't hang around for an answer. Limping toward the house, Gabby felt a curious pride at her two new skills. She pictured herself riding pell mell across the meadow, leaping every obstacle with incredible grace, flicking at passing snakes with a twenty-foot bullwhip. Riding in her wake was Rafe.

She laughed to herself in happiness at the vision and went inside to treat herself to a bath and the biggest steak she could find.

* * *

She wasn't laughing when she awoke in the middle of the night and felt every muscle scream in protest to each tiny move. She shifted in the bed, groaned, and tried to settle back into the depression her body had already made in the down mattress. She cursed the pain that had brought her from the soothing balm of sleep.

A sound from behind the house told her it wasn't pain that had interrupted her rest. Someone was splashing around at the pump. No need to wonder who that someone was. Somehow she knew it was Rafe. Even in her sleep she sensed when he was around.

He hadn't been out of her thoughts since the moment he'd ridden away. True, he had challenged her in the way he told Ben he would. But he had also helped her to meet that challenge. If the man was an enigma to her, he had ceased to be her enemy. And she wasn't sure just when.

She lay still for a minute, listening to the sound of splashing water. She pictured it hitting against his body, beads of moisture catching in the dark hair of his head and on his chest. The image was incredibly clear.

The thought struck her that even though it was late September, the room was certainly warm and still; what she needed was a little fresh air. Gingerly she sat up, flinched in pain, and, after a few tentative movements to decide if she would live, padded on bare feet to the window.

She saw him right away. Bare-chested, he stood at

the pump. The moon was on the wane, but she could still make out the familiar tilt of his head and his broad, bare chest. Her breath caught, and she hugged the thin cotton gown close to her body.

Turning his back to her, he stripped off his trousers and tossed them aside. Strong hands pumped another bucket of water and sent it cascading over his head to run in rivulets down his back and buttocks, down his thighs, through the light dusting of hair on his legs.

Mesmerized, she watched each movement, watched the undulating muscles of his back glistening in the moonlight. A cloud passed overhead and for a moment he stood in the dark. She could make out only the outline of his frame. In the shadowy night he looked more phantom than flesh and blood—a ghost come to haunt her.

Tossing the bucket aside, he turned to face her. Even though she stood in the dark, it was almost as though he sensed her presence, heard the pounding of her heart, the roaring of hot blood through her veins. The cloud drifted past, and he stood in glorious manhood. Slowly, each movement taunting her, he reached for his trousers and pulled them on. Her eyes followed his hands, watched them tug the clothes up his long, hard legs, saw his fingers work at the buttons.

Desire enveloped her, a desire made stronger because of an even deeper need. A need to share more than just her body with Rafe. If there were any justice in the world, he ought to be washing up before coming in to her. It might never come to pass, but she belonged at the Seco. With Rafe. The ranch was her birthright as much as it was his. Her roots were here.

Her home was here.

She blinked away unshed tears. The reason she belonged had nothing to do with the Corderos, with any lawsuit or mortgage. It had everything to do with Rafe. She loved him. Arrogant, unbending Rafe who could be tender and brutal in one moment. Loving Rafe who could bring a sense of contentment unlike anything she'd ever felt.

She would never be able to tell him and risk his scorn. He might be kind to her now, but he was convinced she would soon go away. The most she could do was acquit herself well on the ranch and earn his admiration for her strength.

For tonight she didn't want his admiration. She wanted him. Soundlessly she slipped out of her room and went through the deserted kitchen to stand at the edge of the moonlight on the back porch.

Even before he saw her, Rafe knew he was being watched, knew who the midnight watcher was. Still, as he strode toward the house, he was stunned by the effect the sight of Gabby had on him. She stood in a spill of light against a post, her eyes wide and wanting, her hair a wild mass of curls. He came to a stop and looked for a long moment at her full lower lip. The first time he'd seen it he figured it for the mark of a sensual woman. He'd been right.

His eyes dropped to her bare throat, then lower. A thin cotton gown gave enticing evidence of her body underneath. Dark-tipped breasts curved toward him. He remembered the slender waist so easily spanned by his hands, the long legs that could wrap around him and pull him into ecstasy.

A slender hand reached out to him and he took it

in his, turning it over and kissing the palm. In the short time she'd been on the Seco her hand had toughened; she seemed more womanly for it.

His lips touched her wrist and dropped feather-light kisses on an intoxicating trail to her throat. He pulled her against his chest and felt her tremble. Or was it he? They seemed so much a part of each other that he really didn't know.

"Rafe." Gabby's voice was little more than a whisper.

He lifted his head and looked down at her. Her magnificent eyes smoldered up at him.

"Are you telling me to go away?"

She moistened her lips and sighed. But she kept her gaze locked with his. "No. Tonight I want you to stay. Tonight let's pretend yesterday and tomorrow do not exist."

Embracing her, he pressed his mouth hungrily against hers, heard her moan and stiffen. He pulled away. There would be no repeat of that wild, frantic lovemaking at the hotel. He wanted her to be sure of what she wanted.

Silently, Gabby cursed the sore body that was betraying her with pain. With Rafe staring down at her with such gentle concern, dark hair falling across his forehead, his face lean and wonderfully close, she forgot her discomfort.

A little pain was small enough payment for the pleasure she knew awaited her, and she threw caution to the winds. "I'm just a little stiff, Rafe. Carry me to my room. Be gentle with me."

"I will take great care, *mi cielo,*" he whispered as he picked her up and cradled her against his chest. He kissed the corner of her mouth. Then he kissed her eyes, and a soft moan escaped her lips.

She rested her head in the hollow of his shoulder, hands draped around his neck. Her fingers stroked the taut skin of his back. She melted into his arms.

In her room he laid her gently in the bed and knelt beside her. Unthinking, she moved her arms around his neck and entwined her fingers in his thick, damp hair. Gone was the pain that had torn at her muscles. It was replaced by desire.

Gabby pulled him close. Each breath dragged through her like fire. Each part of her burned for his touch, for the melding of their bodies.

"Querida," he whispered, and she was lost in his embrace. Hungry, demanding lips claimed hers. The tip of his tongue grazed hers, then claimed the moist interior of her mouth. Hot hands stroked her shoulders, pushed aside the straps of her gown, and worked down to play at the tips of her breasts.

Gabby began her own eager assault as her hands moved down his strong chest, fingers massaging as they moved, circling in the coarse hair. His response was a mighty shudder. The feel of his rugged strength brought to tremors under her touch was a thrill unlike any she had ever known. His hands on her breasts brought that same tremor rippling through her own body. They seemed to be moving together in their growing passion. It was a harmony that made her feel they were as one.

Rafe pulled away, straightened, and pulled the trousers from his body, unsheathing the powerful manhood that would bring her such ecstasy. Kneeling once again, he pulled the gown from her body. His lips followed his hands, moving slowly up her abdomen to kiss each breast—a long, teasing play of a kiss—then to the pulse point at her throat.

By the time he stretched his full length beside her on the bed, Gabby was mindless with desire. Again her sure hands stroked his chest, moving around to his back, drifting down to taut buttocks and thighs. His body pressed against hers. He was hot and hard and ready.

Her legs parted and she enfolded him within her. Her soft, moist flesh welcomed him. The reality of Gabby, her body joined with his, was far more enrapturing than anything he had imagined during countless sleepless nights. She was soft and yielding, yet demanding at the same time. Her body, moving with incredible sweetness beneath him, claimed a pleasure for its own even while it drove him to the edge of madness.

Their rhythms quickened, their hearts a primal drumbeat to their need. Each existed only for the other, giving and taking in a union that was born of more than just the bright flame of carnal need.

A violent tremor shook them. Still they clung to one another, arms and legs entwined, lips pressed tight, as though if they loosened their hold the other might slip away forever. For a long, sweetly spinning moment their rapture was complete.

The world seemed gradually to settle into place around them and Gabby stirred, unwilling to let Rafe go, terrified that he would want to leave. He showed no such inclination, instead holding her close against him.

He whispered her name in her hair. The sound was

magic, settling at least for a while the fears that he would take his satisfaction and then disappear. With his strength enveloping her, it was easy to tell herself that all was well. Rafe would never leave her alone again. She snuggled against him, afraid to speak, almost afraid to breathe. At last she drifted into sleep.

For Rafe the oblivion of sleep was a long time in coming. Gabby was everything he wanted, and even while he held her in his arms the thought of the differences separating them brought more pain than he could bear. He thrust the pain aside. She felt good and right in his arms, soft and womanly.

Like a fool he'd been puzzling what to do with her, when the answer was clear. No matter what Ben thought about it, Gabby belonged on the Seco. But not by herself. She might not realize it yet, but she needed Rafe—both in and out of bed.

He'd caught the fear in her eyes when he was on the bronc this morning. He wanted to believe it was prompted by love. She had certainly wanted him tonight, in a kind of wildly rapturous way that spoke of repeated nights of love that might await them. He held her gently, fearful of awakening her but refusing to let her go. No matter what happened in the morning, tonight he had made her his.

Chapter Twelve

"Gabby, those are the lines of a real champion," Rafe said, a thumb pushing his hat to the back of his head. "Strong legs, a wide rump with plenty of meat, broad shoulders. A bull to warm a man's heart. And the hearts of as many cows as he can provide service."

Gabby leaned against the fence rail beside Rafe and looked into the breeding pen. To her unpracticed eye the monster looked merely fat. And, if that impressive appendage hanging between his hind legs was any indication, definitely capable of taking on all the females in the Seco's herd—providing he could get those broad shoulders off the ground.

"Just how many cows can look forward to this . . . service?" she said, careful to keep her voice even. The last thing she wanted to appear as was a rancher who blushed.

Rafe followed her gaze. His lips twisted into a smile. "As many as he wants, Gabby—considering how much he cost. He'll be calling the Seco bull heaven before he's through."

Gabby snorted derisively. "Bull heaven! That doesn't sound like a ranching term to me. More like one you save for the greenhorns."

"I knew I couldn't fool you, lady," Rafe said. "You want facts? You'll get 'em." He proceeded to overwhelm her with information about the various aspects of crossbreeding two strains of cattle.

She listened with what she hoped was an attentive expression on her face, but as he enthusiastically quoted facts and figures, she found herself watching the shift of his eyes, the wayward shock of hair that covered his forehead, the high cheekbones that gave his face strength.

And in a way she relished the conversation. This talk of cattle breeding was the closest they had come to a romantic topic lately. It was as though they had reached some kind of truce, a breathing space welcome to them both.

During the past three days he'd taught her a thousand things about the ranch—from roping and branding cows and tying more knots than a sailor would need to more mundane chores like ordering supplies. She'd found ranch life a complicated and fascinating topic, but it was also an impersonal one. She told herself that was the way she preferred things. She had come to learn about ranching and to prove she could stand up to the work. The one night in his arms was all she had asked for, all she had been prepared to handle considering the differences that still separated them.

Rafe had treated her with friendly courtesy ever

since that night, spending hours answering her questions, walking with her in the moonlight every evening after supper. His treatment was more than she had ever expected when she accepted his invitation to stay.

There was only one question that gnawed in her mind. Why wasn't she more grateful? The answer came from her heart. A woman in love didn't always want to be treated like a friend.

Rafe talked as they headed back toward the house to wash up for the noon meal, and she continued to watch him and copy his rolling gait. It wasn't hard, since she'd almost grown used to spending hours perched on Tempest, perilously far from the hard, cactus-covered ground.

She had even begun to understand the superior attitude of the horseman over a man on foot. Anyone who could ride tall in an uncomfortable saddle with no backrest or pillow hour after hour deserved to feel superior. If he walked with a swagger, that was understandable, too.

She may not have found the riding easy, but at least she'd been outfitted for it. The first thing Rafe had done the day after her initial lesson was send in to Alexander Talbert's store for a pair of boots. Emma had thrown in a gabardine divided skirt and jacket to match.

A smile playing at his lips, Rafe had delivered them to her room. "Here," he had said without ceremony, "wear these whenever you're riding or out on the range. The boots will protect you from stirrup rub."

Gabby held up the divided skirt and matching

jacket. They would fit her far more modestly than the attire she'd been wearing.

"You don't like me in Cisco's pants?"

His eyes had warmed. "On the contrary. But I prefer you wear 'em just for me." He'd stepped close, until she could feel the warmth of his breath on her cheek. "The ideas they give me, *querida*, I wouldn't want any other man to have."

It was the one lapse in his gentlemanly treatment of her. He'd not touched her except for a casual brush of his hand, or an arm resting briefly about her waist as he guided her on their evening walks.

Sometimes their eyes met as they shared a joke after a hard day's work or congratulated each other for a task well done. Such moments were incredibly sweet for Gabby, and she stored them in her memory to pull out like faded photographs when Rafe was no longer at her side.

She refused to consider the possibility that his warmly gracious treatment of her was a plan to keep her from filing suit. The whole issue of the Seco and the loan papers she held seemed to have been set aside for a while—to let her learn the ranch and see if she really would be at home there. To give the two of them time to learn more about each other without challenges.

But no matter how kind and patient he was with her, no matter how much he talked about the ranch in ways that said she had a right to know, she still held a part of herself back. Some lessons were too ingrained. What seemed simple could turn complicated. What seemed favorable could twist into a source of pain.

Colette had taught her that. Gabby paused, struck by the memory of her mother. She'd carried that memory well through the years since her mother died, but she'd hardly thought of her since she'd moved to the ranch. She reminded herself she would be a fool to forget her primary goal of recovering her father's land. She would be an even bigger fool to forget the way Rafe had explained his intended invitation to his grandfather.

Rafe had never ranted at her about the Cordero family—he seemed to harbor none of his grandfather's obsession about her past—but then he'd not conceded her right to the land, either. And she was not yet willing to bring up the subject and shatter the closeness that was growing between them.

At the hacienda following the visit to the bull, Gabby took a cold dinner to her room, leaving Rafe to eat with Ben before he headed back out onto the range to help with the fence laying. Rafe was used to her avoidance of Ben and had asked no questions.

She hadn't mentioned to Rafe anything about the old man's peculiar behavior on her first visit. Even now she sometimes caught Ben watching her with a puzzled expression. No doubt at this very moment he was spending the noon hour entertaining his grandson with tales of their visitor's guile—if he remembered who she was.

On the one occasion she had talked to him, the old man had been lividly offensive and had made it amply clear that his feelings hadn't changed. He'd summoned her, and her hopes had been raised that he was trying to make amends or—foolish thought—would compliment her on her riding skills.

Without preamble, Ben had spoken rapidly in Spanish.

"Senorita Deschamps, you may not realize it, but I have seen the way you look at my grandson. And the way Rafael looks at you. Is it marriage that you seek? If so, you will only be disappointed. I would like to think that someday the house will be filled with children, but unfortunately my grandson, although he has all the desires of a man, is not the kind who chooses to marry." His watery eyes had darkened. "Especially a woman who is not pure and who wants only his land."

Anger stirred in her, threatening to erupt, but she held her voice steady. "You assume too much, Senor Hidalgo. I was invited to learn about the ranch. I expect nothing more. As far as I know, Rafe feels the same."

She read surprise in the old man's eyes that she could speak Spanish with such ease. The surprise quickly passed. "I know my grandson as well as he knows me. When he does decide to choose a bride, it will not be a Cordero." His voice came down on the name hard and full of bitterness. "There is too much hatred for the Cordero and Hidalgo families ever to join."

There it was again, that obsession with the Corderos. Ben seemed almost mad on the subject, but before she could try to learn why, he had stomped from the room. She'd contented herself with muttered imprecations against his ancestry that would have shocked the Ursuline nuns back in San Antonio. Her

268

words surprised even her a little. Out on the ranch she was becoming as emphatic in her language as she was in her view of life.

Gabby brushed out the hair that had been pinned beneath her hat. After the riding outfit, the blouse and skirt she donned felt cool against her skin. She would eat quickly and then turn to the chores that Lupita had discussed with her before riding out with Cisco early that morning to visit her parents' *jacale* for the day. Lupita never hesitated to talk with her about the duties that went with caring for the two men. It was as though she knew that Gabby had a permanent interest in the place.

And of course she must know. Everyone within a hundred yards of the hacienda that first day she'd approached Ben Hidalgo must surely have heard him shouting at her. Lupita simply had more consideration than did the old man. Almost everyone did.

As she entered the kitchen, the sound of wagon wheels on gravel drew her attention. Going up the hall to the front of the house, she peered through the screen door and saw standing in the clearing a four-wheeled buggy, highly polished, its hood folded back to the October sun. In its traces was hitched a sleek-looking horse with braided mane and tail. The man and woman riding in it were no less well turned out.

The dark-suited man doffed his white Stetson, then replaced it on his balding head. "I'm just returning your call, Rafe," he said. "Heard about the fire and wondered if there was anything I could do to help."

Rafe, standing at the edge of the house, kept his face without expression. "Now that's neighborly of

269

you, Hunter," he said, "considering the fire was almost two weeks ago."

Gabby paused inside the doorway, her breath caught in her throat. Earl Hunter, was it? The man who had told Rafe who she was on that bitter night that seemed an eternity ago. Gabby had expected some kind of evil maniac, but in his vested suit and with a smile on his lined face, he looked middle-aged and harmless enough — until she looked at his eyes. They never blinked, never wavered in their intense study of Rafe, nor in their concentrated hate, no matter how politely he spoke.

She'd seen eyes like that before. Ben Hildago had looked at her in much the same way.

The woman, clad in an expensively cut green silk traveling dress, put down her matching parasol. "No one was hurt, I hope," she said.

Rafe's face softened. "No, Sarah. Everyone's all right."

"You'll have to pardon my wife," Hunter said. "She thinks she's the only one who's worried about someone getting injured."

"That's not —" Sarah began, but paused when Hunter glanced sideways at her.

It didn't take a written script for Gabby to figure out what was going on in front of her. Rafe had mentioned once that Sarah Hunter had been an old friend, and Lupita had told her there had been talk of joining her ranch to Rafe's, obviously by marriage. If the concern in Sarah's voice was any indication, she would have liked more than a marriage of convenience. And her husband knew it.

270

Behind the carriage a hard-looking man on horse-back caught her eye. He was dressed in the ordinary clothes of a cowboy, but something about the way he held his broad body, one hand never far from the six-shooter strapped to his thigh, made her think of Luke Sneed. Except that he looked a great deal more dangerous.

Gabby stepped out, letting the screen door slam behind her. All eyes turned in her direction.

Rafe started when he saw Gabby standing in the doorway, her simple skirt and blouse resting loosely on her slender body and her hair falling free about her shoulders. Innocent and fragile, he thought, and he was reminded of the first time he'd seen her. She looked at home where she stood, as though she *should* be greeting their guests. Any guest, that is, but Earl Hunter.

He wanted to tell her to go back inside and get away from the poison that seemed to emanate from the man. Instead, he nodded slowly in greeting and shifted his attention casually back to the carriage.

"Miss Deschamps is visiting us," he said and intro-duced the visitors. When he came to the rider, his eyes grew hard and icy. "Dallas Pryor is Hunter's best watchdog," he said.

Pinched eyes peered out from under a snakeskin-banded hat and for a long, ugly moment Pryor glared at Rafe before turning to assess Gabby with insolent thoroughness.

Rafe shifted protectively closer to her. "Glad you mentioned that fire, Hunter," he said. "I've been meaning to drop by and discuss it. My men reported

271

finding some cleared land near where we figure the blaze started. As though some brush had been piled high and set afire. You wouldn't know anything about that, would you?"

Hunter shrugged. "Not a thing, Rafe. But if I hear anything, I'll be sure to let you know."

"And what about you, Pryor?" Rafe said. "You been clearing some of my land? Maybe let a match or two drop?"

Pryor's thick lips twisted into an ugly smile. "Not that I recall. If I was to come on your land, it would be to see my lady friend. She around somewhere? I'd like to get a look at the pretty little thing." His eyes flicked to Gabby. "Don't seem hardly fair you'd have two women to yourself. Unless you like 'em two at a time."

After a long period in which the very air seemed to stand still, Rafe looked at Hunter. "You usually keep Pryor tied up with the dogs?" he said, his voice almost pleasant. "He doesn't seem to know how to talk with ladies present."

"Dallas just took offense at your letting the girl Lupita and her parents move onto your land. They worked for me."

"Lupita's father was a good hand for Nathaniel Miller. He just didn't care to stay on when you took over." He smiled sympathetically at Sarah Hunter. "Lupita's visiting with her parents now. She'll be sorry she missed you."

"Tell her I sent my regards," Sarah said.

Hunter shifted his body in the carriage to look at Gabby. "You've recently moved here from San Antonio, haven't you, Miss Deschamps?" he said. "Am I to understand we might be neighbors?"

Gabby slowly let out her breath. She'd waited a long time to confront Hunter. She would rather not have Rafe's watchful eyes on her, but she could see no alternative. Questions burned in her mind and, unable to keep silent, she hurried ahead.

"I don't have any idea where you get your information about me, Mr. Hunter, and I'd like to know."

"Why, Miss Deschamps," said Hunter unctuously, "you underestimate yourself. A beautiful woman such as yourself comes into town, it's not long before everyone knows why she's here."

Gabby's eyes flashed blue fire. "You've known a long time why I came back to Texas. I'd like to know how."

She could feel Rafe's dark eyes on her. Casting a quick sideways glance at him, she caught the shadow of a frown cross his face.

Too late to stop now, she thought. This time she would listen along with Rafe to the lies that would no doubt fall from Hunter's lips.

"My business is with Mr. Jericho and his grandfather," she said, meeting Hunter's smirk with a level gaze, "and shouldn't concern anyone else."

"In other words," Hunter said, a pleased look settling on his face, "your business isn't taken care of yet. A word of caution, Miss Deschamps. Watch out for a man who likes to throw accusations around. You heard him almost accuse me of setting the fire, and I'm a man with armed help. I can't imagine what he would say to a defenseless woman."

Rafe listened in silence as long as he could. He'd seen the hurtful look on Gabby's face when she glanced at him, but she couldn't be any more disillusioned by him than he was by himself. He'd been a fool to let a rat like Hunter ever cause trouble between them.

His voice cut through the still air. "I'll do more than talk, Hunter, if you're not off my land in five minutes."

Pryor's hand inched toward the holster strapped to his thigh. "You issuin' a threat?"

"Take it anyway you like. As long as you leave."

Gabby could see the two men were at the razor-thin edge of real trouble. She'd been close to one shooting—one that her foolishness had brought on—and she couldn't let her bravado put Rafe's life at risk again.

"Mr. Hunter," she said in a cool voice, "your warning is unnecessary. I'm always very careful with whom I associate. If you'll excuse me, I'm needed inside." She smiled at Sarah. "Mrs. Hunter, I'm glad to make your acquaintance. Perhaps we can visit longer when it's just the two of us."

Gabby turned and quickly entered the house. Poor Sarah, she thought as she stood in the shadows of the walkway. To want Rafe and be faced with Earl Hunter every night. It was a fate she wouldn't wish on anyone.

Within seconds she heard the buggy pull away. She waited a minute, decided Rafe was probably making sure they rode off his land, and headed for the back of the house. Lupita wasn't expected back until nightfall, and for once Gabby was grateful for the solitude awaiting her. She'd turn the energy that boiled within her to a few of the housekeeper's chores.

If she thought enough about rubbing the smug look off of Earl Hunter's fat-jowled face—or the frown off of Rafe's—the tiled floor would take on a shine the likes of which it had never known.

For the first time in days Gabby didn't meet Rafe outside for an evening stroll. In that brief, tense time spent with the Seco's uninvited guests, she had been reminded of the too-real differences between them, and the fragile bond between them had been broken. She kept to her room.

Sometime after midnight Gabby awoke to the sound of voices at the back of the house. For a ranch tucked away in the middle of nowhere, the Arroyo Seco was becoming a very popular place.

She couldn't make out the words, but she recognized the speakers. Rafe and Cisco. Something about the tone of their voices, drifting through her window on the cool night air, told her there was trouble.

By the time she had a wrapper thrown over her nightgown, Rafe knocked and entered without waiting to be asked. "Gabby, throw some clothes on. I need you out at Lupita's place."

She knew in an instant something bad had happened to Lupita. Even as worry filled Gabby's heart, she warmed at the way Rafe had turned to her. He didn't question that she would respond.

"Now, tell me what's wrong," she said two minutes

later on the way to the corral, quickening her step to match Rafe's long stride.

Rafe paused, put his arm around her for an instant in a brief movement that seemed almost protective. "Lupita's been . . . hurt. And so has Antonio. I'll tell you on the way."

Cisco had the mare Tempest saddled and waiting, along with Rafe's horse. His own gray was tied behind a light wagon hitched to one of the dray horses. When she mounted, he handed her a bullwhip. "For you, Senorita Gabrielle," he said. "I have been braiding it, waiting for the time to make the gift to you."

"I—I thank you, Cisco. But why tonight?"

"Tonight is not a night for the senorita to go unarmed."

"Nothing is going to happen to Gabby," Rafe said curtly. "Not if I have anything to say about it. Cisco, I'm depending on you to help me. I've got the rest of the men out working. A couple of them are to stay by the hacienda."

Gabby waited until the three of them were headed out across the range, stars and a crescent moon as their light, before she put the question to Rafe again. "What's wrong, Rafe? What happened to Lupita and Antonio?"

"The girl started riding back too close to dark," he said. "She was attacked. Raped."

Lupita's lovely laughing face flashed in Gabby's mind. The enormity of Rafe's words erased the vision. "Is she"—Gabby paused, cursing. "Do you know if she's badly injured?"

"That's the hell of it. She won't let any of us enter.

276

Her mother stays with her, and her father stands at the door telling us to go away. It's as though she feels ashamed to face us."

"That's the most absurd thing I ever heard of!"

"I agree with you, Gabby. And I'd like to say everyone else will, too. But that's not true for certain."

Gabby knew exactly what he was talking about, absurd as the idea was to her. Ben had talked about the importance of a woman being pure. There were probably a lot of men like Ben hanging around.

"What about Antonio? You said he was injured."

"He got in late. When he found her still not back, he rode out to check on her. She can handle a horse well, but he was worried about the dark coming on. And he also heard about our visitors today. Antonio found her right after it happened. Someone shot him from ambush. Thank God he was hit in the leg. The wound won't kill him, but it'll lay him up for a few days."

"Where is he now?"

"In one of the other *jacales.*"

"Does he need a doctor?"

"I couldn't wait for that. Lupita's young brother came and got me. Took the bullet out myself."

Gabby nodded, remembering the way Jeff McGowan had praised Rafe's medical skills. But he'd be no good with Lupita. No good at all.

"Do you know who did it?" she said.

"I know, all right. That son of a bitch Dallas Pryor."

"Did Lupita recognize him?"

"That's one of the things I want you to find out, Gabby. Talk to her. Find out what she knows. You

277

two seemed to be getting along fine, and I'm guessing she'd like to have you around. From the sounds inside the *jacale*, her mother is close to hysterics, and her father looks as though he would shoot the first man who stepped inside his home."

"You can't blame him."

"Maybe not, but he's not helping matters, either. A *curandero* is with Lupita, but I'd feel better if you were there, too."

"I'll do what I can, Rafe. But you said Dallas Pryor was the—the man."

"I didn't say I had any proof of it. Not yet. I may have to do a little persuading after I find him."

Thoughts tumbled through Gabby's mind. "Rafe, you can't go out looking for him by yourself."

Rafe turned to face her. "Don't worry about me and Cisco, Gabby. We'll be all right. If I see I need help, I'll send Cisco back. Just take care of Lupita."

The land smoothed out as it dropped down toward the gathering of thatched huts where the vaqueros with families lived, and the three riders were able to pick up their pace. When they pulled up at one of the *jacales*, Gabby saw a grim-faced Mexican man standing in the door, a rifle gripped in his hands.

Gabby dropped to the ground and tethered her horse to the lone post at the front of the hut.

"Senor Lopez," she said in Spanish, "I am a friend of Lupita's. She needs a woman now. I have come to help."

Uncomprehending, he looked at her, then returned his stare into the dark void of the night.

"Senor," she repeated, "I have come to help." Still no

response, but she didn't try a third time. She allowed herself one backward glance at Rafe.

A rush of love warmed her and sent her to the edge of panic. In Rafe's hurry to avenge the crime against Lupita, he looked strong and invincible, but she knew he wasn't. "Be careful," was all she said.

His gaze was intense upon her. Then he wheeled his black stallion and disappeared into the night, followed by Cisco on the gray. The young vaquero waved, proud to be Senor Rafael's trusted companion.

She turned back to the hut. "Please, senor, I am needed inside," she said. "Rafael has asked me to come."

The vaquero paused for a moment, stared at the dark that had swallowed Rafe and his young companion, and at last gave way. She entered the dimly lit room. It was the first time she'd been inside one of the huts, although she had seen many of them, both on the ranch and in town.

The few pieces of furniture scattered about the dirt floor—a couple of chairs and a board table—were crude but sturdy in appearance. Some twelve feet square, the room was kitchen and parlor and bedroom.

From a dark corner came the sounds of a woman crying. Gabby moved closer. The crying woman she figured to be Lupita's mother. Beside her was another woman, this one dry-eyed—the *curandero* Rafe had mentioned. The second woman turned a wrinkled face in Gabby's direction. Gabby figured she could be anywhere from eighty to a hundred years of age, so wrinkled was her face. But her eyes were wide and

279

alert. And definitely distrusting.

Gabby moved closer to see a dim shape lying on a crude bed of hay in the corner. "Is Lupita awake?" she whispered. "I'm Gabrielle Deschamps, her friend from the hacienda. I've come to help."

"There is nothing you can do, Senorita Deschamps," the old woman said. "I have done what is necessary for the child's body." She made the signs of the cross. "Now all is in the hands of God."

"I don't understand," Gabby said, her heart in her throat. "I thought she was not badly injured."

"She will live. But she has the great shame."

Gabby had to fight back impatience. What did Lupita have to be ashamed about? A man had taken her body against her will. But he hadn't taken her honor. And he hadn't taken her life.

She knelt beside the straw bed. "Lupita, I've come to take you back to the hacienda," she said, resting her hand on a blanket-covered shoulder. She was met with silence.

"It's perhaps too soon to leave your home here," she said, her hand still touching the young senorita, "but I will be here when you decide it is time."

Still greeted by silence, she shifted to sit down beside the bed. "I have seen much of the ways of men and women, Lupita," she said softly, "more than you could have guessed. You have the love and support of your friends and family. And that is something to treasure. Whoever did this will not go unpunished. Of that you can be sure."

Gabby had no way of knowing if her words brought any comfort to the girl. A chill settled over her as she murmured softly to Lupita and thought of the course Rafe had set for himself. He seemed so confident he would be all right that she almost believed him — and she certainly would have, if his safety didn't matter to her so much. But she could not talk to Lupita about those fears.

The air in the *jacale* was close and still, so heavy she found it hard to breathe. When she heard the sound of distant thunder, she realized why. A storm was on the way, and with it perhaps an end to the drought that had devastated the area. The thought should have brought comfort, but not tonight, not with Rafe roaming the open land.

Again the thunder sounded, this time much closer, and Lupita stirred. Gabby stretched out beside her and took her in her arms. The girl made no move to push her away. She glanced at the *curandero*, who was standing close by. A knowing look passed between the two. Lupita had responded to Gabby's embrace. With enough loving care and attention, she would be all right.

Riding deeper onto the alien land of the Rancho Perro, Rafe watched the dark clouds roll in overhead and decide they were a gift from heaven. They were heavy with rain — and they brought the welcome cover of darkness for him and Cisco.

Their destination had been quickly determined — the bunkhouse, where they hoped to encounter Dallas Pryor. Pryor was mean enough to be bragging about what he'd done, and probably stupid enough, too.

The shadows of the outbuildings that surrounded the main house loomed. Louder than the rolling thunder came the sound Rafe had expected, the barking of Hunter's dogs. The noise grew louder, and he glanced back at Cisco. "Hand me that package I gave you at the hacienda."

Cisco readily complied. "Do you think, Senor Rafael, the meat will stop the dogs?"

"There's enough loco juice in each of those pieces of meat to knock out a grown bear." Gripping the package, Rafe dropped to the ground. "Tie the horses upwind of the bunkhouse. I'll take care of the mutts and be along directly.'"

Rafe walked quietly into the dark in the direction of the barking hounds. For insurance he kept his hand close to his pistol — in case the dogs weren't hungry. He needn't have worried. By the time they came at him snarling and snapping, he already had the chunks of meat unwrapped and flung on the ground.

Rafe grinned as he watched them stop their charge and fall upon the doped food. Hunter didn't have them so well trained after all. Their snarls soon turned to whimpers, and one by one the three dogs stretched out on the ground. He and Cisco would be long gone with their prisoner when the animals awoke.

The sound of a gunshot shattered the night air, and Rafe whirled back toward the bunkhouse. Cisco! The kid didn't have a gun, only that bullwhip, and Rafe was certain it wasn't the crack of a whip he heard. Unsheathing his gun, he hastened toward the sound, cursing himself for leaving the boy alone.

He saw something gleaming white in the dark shadows of a woodpile some twenty yards from the nearest building. It was unmoving, and his heart thudded. Cisco had worn a white shirt.

Slipping soundlessly through the night, he knelt beside the young vaquero, feeling in vain for a pulse, knowing sudden grief, but knowing also that he had been drawn into exposing himself to whoever had ambushed Cisco.

The click of a gun sounded close to his ear and he felt cold metal pressed against his neck.

"One move and you're as dead as the kid. Now toss the gun aside."

Dallas Pryor's voice was as deadly as the rattle of a snake. Rafe obeyed, burning with a rage he would have to keep under control.

"That's right, Jericho," Pryor said to Rafe's unmoving back. "Now get up slowly. There's something I need for you to do. In case some of your men come sneaking around."

"I'm surprised they're not here now," Rafe said.

"Won't work. The way I figured it, you were arrogant enough to think you could take me by yourself." Pryor's laugh was low and ugly. "Guess you figured wrong. Now stand up slowly and pick up the body. Don't seem fitting we should let the kid lie out in the night like that."

Rafe followed instructions, stumbling along the tussocked ground with the body of his young *compadre* clutched in his arms. They paused once for Pryor to get a shovel from a toolshed near the bunkhouse. Rafe stared at the shovel and held the body tighter. Cisco's blood soaked into his shirt.

Pryor stayed close on Rafe's heels, directing him away from the bunkhouse and out into the brush. They walked in silence for a long while, their boots hitting the hard earth in an uneven cadence. Jagged lightning flashed, and Rafe glanced back at his captor. And at the six-shooter that was aimed in the direction of his head.

"How much farther, Pryor? You aiming to walk me to San Antonio?"

"We can stop about here." He tossed the shovel close to Rafe's feet. "Now put the body down and start digging. You be a good boy and I might even let you say a few words of prayer when you're done. Before you join him in the grave."

Each time the shovel bit into the hard-packed dirt, Rafe calculated whether he could swing it around and catch Pryor in the head. But the gunman was too wily for him and kept his distance. Rafe took his time, hoping Pryor would grow impatient and careless.

His strategy worked in part.

"That's taking too damned long," Pryor said as another bolt of lightning lit the night sky. "It's big enough for one now. I've made other plans for you."

Picking up his burden for the last time, Rafe knelt by the shallow grave and gently straightened the slight, limp body into it. A gust of wind ruffled Cisco's hair, the last sign of life from the fun-loving boy.

Rafe used his own hat to cover Cisco's face, wondering where the prized whip had fallen. He would like to bury it with Cisco, but it was no longer looped at his waist. His last thought as he knelt in silent tribute was that the valiant young vaquero would never live to be a man.

Pryor gave him no time for prayer. "That'll do. I'll finish up."

The words were the last Rafe heard for a long while. Pain split the back of his head as he leaned over the open grave and the night closed in on him. When he came to, he seemed down at the bottom of a deep, damp hole—his own grave—and for a moment he panicked. A throbbing pain tore at his head. He ignored it.

Pulling himself shakily upright, he ran frantic hands around the sides of his prison and as far up as he could reach. As he moved, he realized it was just luck he hadn't drowned. He was standing in shallow water, and his clothes clung wetly to his body. The ranches in the area were studded with abandoned wells. No doubt he was imprisoned in one of them.

Faint light reached him from overhead. He had no idea how deep beneath the surface of the ground he was. Probably about twenty feet. He guessed it must be after dawn by now.

The panic that had seized him vanished, and in its place came a cold fury that he could have let himself get into such a predicament. But he wasn't dead. Pryor had probably got a laugh thinking about how Rafe would die a long, slow death down in the well. He wouldn't be laughing long.

With cold deliberation, Rafe tried to gain a foothold in the side of the well, but all around him the walls proved too slick. And the damned thing was too wide for him to work his way out by bracing his back on one wall and his feet on the other. He would have to think of something else.

Even from his position below ground, he could hear the rolls of thunder and the sound of a driving rain. A storm like this, coming at the end of a drought, could last for hours and send brief floods racing across the parched land. It wasn't long before the first trickles of water worked down onto his head. Wearily he leaned against a damp wall and tried to calculate just how long it would take for the water level in the well to begin to rise.

Chapter Thirteen

Two days.

Her thoughts far from her work, Gabby reached into the sack at her elbow for a handful of corn and tossed the kernels into a *metate*. Her eyes were trained in a sightless gaze out the window of the hacienda kitchen. With vicious indifference she wielded a pestle against the sides of the grinding stone.

Two days they've been gone. Can they both be . . . .

She couldn't let herself continue, couldn't even think the word. Her fingers tightened around the pestle as Cisco's laughing young face flashed through her mind. And the long last look she had received from Rafe. It was that picture that haunted her, chilled her heart, drove her dangerously close to despair.

Safe and well fed in the barn were Rafe's stallion, which had returned riderless halfway through the day yesterday, and Cisco's mare. The latter had been found wandering in the driving rain out on the range. Any tracks that might have led the vaqueros to the lost men were washed away in the storm that had been awaited for so long.

She'd sent word in to Jeff McGowan about what had happened but learned he was in Dallas and would not return for more than a week.

"Senorita," the woman beside her said, "I think the corn will be turned into liquid." She spoke in Spanish. "I think the senorita is concerned with other things."

Gabby glanced down at the pulverized mass that was supposed to be meal. "And I think," she answered in Spanish, "that you're right."

Senora Lopez reached out and touched Gabby's arm, then returned to stirring the dough for the noontime tortillas. She'd been helping Gabby with her daughter's chores ever since Lupita was removed from the *jacale* during a break in yesterday's storm and brought back to her room at the hacienda. Riding in the wagon beside her, Tempest tied at the rear, Gabby had arrived in time to see Rafe's stallion appear.

Lupita, resting, still refused to see anyone but her family and Gabby, although she had allowed a Laredo doctor one quick visit.

"Nothing wrong with her physically," Doctor Crites had declared with a shake of his head. "It's her spirit that's ailing."

Antonio, his leg heavily bandaged, had been brought to her that first night at the *jacale,* but he had been refused admittance. Gabby understood Lupita's reluctance, and yet she didn't. Antonio was the man Lupita loved and would one day marry. Gabby knew no such happiness awaited her with Rafe, but she would have given her life to see him walk through the kitchen door.

The sound of approaching horses cut through her thoughts, and, forgetting all else, she dropped her work and ran out into the weak sunshine breaking intermittently through broken cloud cover. Rounding the corner of the house, she looked toward the barn. Three riders approached. Her heart sank. Three riders who had gone out at dawn to continue the search. There was no sign of Cisco or Rafe.

Leading the trio was Antonio, one leg stiff and tied to a lengthened stirrup. Behind him rode the Lozano brothers, Pedro and Miguel, who had once worked for Earl Hunter and knew his ranch well.

"My injury is only of the flesh," Antonio had insisted at dawn that morning. "There is little I can do here but worry. I cannot even pace. But," he had said in a voice that cut like a knife, "I can ride. I can use the eyes. I can fire the gun."

Gabby had understood his need for action. There was little she could do at the hacienda but comfort Lupita and throw herself into the work of keeping the house going. Ben, his strength lessened from the hours of fire fighting, had exploded into anger when told that Rafe had gone riding out with only the young Cisco. Since receiving the news, he had spent long hours in isolation, allowing only Senora Lopez to deliver the food that remained untouched.

Knowing she would only be rebuffed, Gabby never attempted to approach him, never tried to share the burden of not knowing, and an air of impending doom settled over the house, a mood as dark as the clouds drifting across the noonday sun. She envied Antonio his choice of riding out on the search.

She waited until Antonio and the Lozanos had dismounted, then hurried to the foreman's side. There was no need to ask if he had any news that was good. The vacant, tired look in his eyes told her more than words that they had found no trace of the two men.

The horses were led away toward the barn, and Gabby walked beside the stiff-legged foreman to the pump. Fetching him a bucket of water, she watched as he ladled himself a long drink, then washed a layer of Seco mud from his face and hands.

Tossing the bucket aside, he leaned for support against the pump. "There are many dead sheep and cattle on the Seco range, Senorita Gabrielle," he said in a strained voice, "but of the two men there is no sign."

Gabby listened with a heavy heart as Antonio continued.

"It was . . . kind of Senor Hunter to provide an opening in the fence for us to pass through and continue our search," he said sarcastically. "Rafael believes the area is used for smuggling and plans to put watchers there. Easily we passed through and were able to ride far onto the Perro land."

His eyes wandered toward the house. "How does Lupita fare?"

"She is resting. There is no change," said Gabby.

The weight of the world seemed to settle on the foreman's shoulders. "I must report to Senor Benito. About my visit to the Rancho Perro."

"Did you go near the ranchhouse?"

"*Si.* I have talked with Senor Hunter. And with the

bastardo Pryor."

Cold fury gripped Gabby. "So. They both live."

"It is to be wished a temporary state. Senor Hunter denies all knowledge of Rafael and Cisco. As for the *bastardo,* he stands quietly and smiles." His eyes like agate, Antonio stared into the distance. "It is the smile of a coyote. I will take great pleasure in removing it. Only my fear for Rafael has held me back."

Gabby shook off his words with impatience. She had little time for thoughts of revenge.

"And what next? After your talk with Ben," she said.

"Hope is not gone, senorita," he said, turning to look at her. "There is a part of the Perro which we will return to today. It is on the far side of the ranch in a place where a *familia* of nesters once lived. When the Senora Hunter's *padre* was himself alive. The grass is sparse for the cattle. Still, Senor Hunter will not let the nesters stay."

"The place is abandoned?"

"*Si.* I questioned the senor about the site, but always I keep watch on the *bastardo.* As I talk, his eyes changed. He is, I think, a little frightened."

"That's not much to go on, Antonio," she said, briefly giving in to disappointment.

"Nevertheless, I think this is where we go this afternoon."

"Then I'll get you and the other men some food," Gabby said. "Senor Hidalgo is where he has been most of the time since he heard what happened. I don't think he's even been to bed."

Following Antonio inside, she watched as he headed toward the old man's office. Senora Lopez had already

291

begun dishing up the beans that simmered in a cast iron pot, and Gabby nodded gratefully to her. As she had listened to Antonio talk, a course of action settled in her mind. No longer could she stay behind to wonder and to wait.

In her room she pulled off her skirt, exchanging it for the trousers that Cisco had given her — trousers that Rafe had asked her to wear only for him. Her heart quickened. Let him chastize her when she found him. She'd welcome anything he had to say.

Slipping into the boots and gloves that Rafe had supplied her, she headed for the kitchen, then for Ben's office when she learned that Antonio was still there. The old man's loud voice brought her to a stop.

"Forget Lupita!" Even through the heavy oak door Gabby could hear the angry scorn in Ben's voice. She'd once heard it directed at her. "It is my grandson who matters now."

"Senor Benito —"

"The girl is like all of her sex. She is not pure." Ben's voice rose even louder. "Another has had his hands on her. That you can never forget."

Gabby listened in incredulous silence, stunned that even Ben could say such ugly things. Whatever had happened in Ben's past colored his presence in dark and blinding hues. He seemed to take vengeance on all womankind.

The door crashed opened, and a white-lipped Antonio strode out, his stiff leg barely slowing him down. Gabby hurried after him and called out as he prepared to exit through the kitchen door.

She caught him by the arm and he whirled around.

"Pay no attention to him, Antonio," she said. "Lupita needs you more than ever now. Unless you think Ben may be right."

"The girl is *mi vida*," he said in a whisper, his dark eyes turning to Senora Lopez. "My life."

Gabby followed his gaze, saw a look of understanding on the woman's face, and breathed a sigh of relief that she hadn't heard the old man's cruel words about her daughter.

"Then go to her," Gabby said. "Tell her."

Antonio's lips twisted into a frown. "She does not want to hear my words."

"It could be we were wrong in allowing her to keep away from you," said Gabby. "Lupita *needs* to hear your words." Just as Ben Hidalgo needed to hear a few of hers, she decided, but kept the thought to herself.

Guiding Antonio to Lupita's room, she watched from the hallway as he entered the room and closed the door behind him. She heard a cry of surprise followed by silence; then came the sound of Antonio's low voice. The words were indistinguishable, but their meaning of love came through. Gabby smiled. Lupita had not turned him away.

Turning on her heel, she headed for Ben's office, knocked on the door, and, without waiting for an answer, entered the darkened room. She'd not been there since their first meeting, and she expected to see a straight-shouldered Benito Hidalgo staring at her with hostile eyes. Instead of the proud man who had faced her down, she was startled to see Ben, his white hair matted against his head, hunched over his desk. Briefly her heart went out to him. They shared a common pain.

She'd come to defend Lupita, but the words of

recrimination died on her lips. Ben was what he was. Whatever twisted ideas he might have about women and their purity, he was not likely to change now. The thought had a curiously calming effect, as she realized for the first time that he had been able to hurt her only because she had let him. His insults and accusations had been the maunderings of a bitter old man.

She moved closer to the desk. "I've come to tell you I'll be going with Antonio when he rides out again."

Slowly Ben lifted rheumy eyes to stare at her. "You'll only get in the way."

Gabby shook her head. Even in his despair, Ben could defy her. "I've been staying here at the house thinking the same thing, Ben," she said softly. "I've been thinking wrong."

Ben's trembling hands folded into fists and he struck the desk in a feeble gesture of frustration. "It is a damnable thing to be old," he muttered. "I should be the one who rides out for Rafael. Instead . . ."

Gabby reached across the desk and rested her hand on his shoulder. He jerked free as though he had been touched by fire.

"What is it you want this time?" he hissed.

"I want nothing of you, Ben."

"A Cordero always wants something. Last time you demanded my land."

The force of the old man's hate drove her back.

"Who told you we received the money?" he asked in a continuing assault, his voice gaining strength. "You've got my grandson fooled, but not me." He grabbed up a piece of paper she recognized as a check. "How did you know this arrived?"

"I don't know what you're talking about."

294

"Liar! The railroad stock that Rafael insisted we buy has returned our investment. And like a vulture you begin to circle. While he . . . ." The old man's voice broke, and he slumped back in his chair. The paper fell, forgotten, to the desk. He seemed visibly to fold into his own private hell, shuttering away the world and any comfort it might bring.

Stunned, she backed toward the door. "Rafe is my only concern," she said in quiet protest. "He is—" she remembered Antonio's words—"*mi vida*. And he is not dead. I've not been able to say the word until now, and I understand why. Because I feel in my heart he lives. If it were otherwise, I would know."

Ben gave no sign he was listening, and she let herself out, closing the door softly behind her and hurrying toward the kitchen.

She was greeted by the sight of Antonio and Senora Lopez embracing. Antonio smiled at her over the woman's shoulder. "I think, senorita, that my Lupita has returned to me. All is well with us. For the first time in two days she says she will sleep in peace."

Gabby nodded briefly. "Good. Get some food, and we can head out for that nester's place you mentioned."

"Senorita—"

Gabby lifted her head in defiance. "Rafe didn't teach me to ride so I could take myself to Sunday socials, Antonio. And if you're thinking I'll get in the way, just don't say it. If I live to be a hundred, I don't ever want to hear those words again."

Antonio shrugged. "Then of course I will say no such thing. It is only that the way is long and the course uneven."

"You'll not frighten me into changing my mind," she said. "I wasn't raised to be faint of heart."

"I think, senorita, that whoever believes such a thing is a fool."

"I'll remind you of that when we find Rafe. He's liable to be angry at my tagging along. Could be I'll need somebody speaking up for me for a change."

Turning away, she reached for the plate of food that Senora Lopez was handing her. She wasn't hungry, but she would be a fool to pass up what could be her last meal for a while.

She dipped a freshly fried tortilla into the thick bean broth and took a bite. The food caught in her throat, and she forced herself to swallow.

A ragged edge of worry cut through her calm. Somewhere in that wild land outside the Seco's comfortable hacienda was Rafe. In the past few minutes she'd done a lot of talking about how sure she was he was alive, but so far all she had to be thankful for was that the rain had stopped.

A shudder passed through her. Silently she prayed that her instincts were right and that she hadn't, in fact, been saying only what she wanted to be true.

The sun was halfway to the horizon by the time Gabby passed through the cut barbed wire and rode onto Earl Hunter's land. In front of her was Antonio, and to the rear the two vaqueros who had accompanied him on his morning ride. This time they rode in the wagon she had insisted upon. Thus far, except for the muddy ground, the way had been easy, and they had been able to bypass the thick scrub that would have forced them to leave the wagon behind.

The wagon was important. They would need a place to put Rafe and Cisco when they found them. She pictured the two making their way toward them, Rafe weary and sore-footed as he cursed his whip-cracking young companion. It was an image she kept in her mind.

Gabby pulled up to await the wagon, her gloved hand stroking the neck of her mount. She felt at ease riding Tempest. She could now put to work without conscious thought the myriad instructions Rafe had given her to guide the horse. Indeed, she sometimes didn't even nudge the mare to go one way or the other; Tempest seemed to read her mind.

Overhead, dark clouds made their slow way toward the south. The rains were not over. To curse them after the long drought seemed like defying fate, but that's exactly what Gabby did.

Once more under way, she called out to Antonio. "Where are the dogs Rafe told me about? I expected them to attack us." She patted the bullwhip that Cisco had given her. "If they're as mean as he said, I am looking forward to using this on them."

Antonio waited for her to catch up. "The senorita has a taste for a fight."

Gabby settled her straw hat more firmly in place. "The senorita wants only to be left alone for her search."

Antonio's dark eyes, set deep in his craggy face, studied the land around them. One hand rested close to his rifle. "It is to be hoped you get your wish," he said.

Gabby followed his gaze. The land was much like

297

the Arroyo Seco, miles of rolling hills that dropped off into sudden gulches and deeper ravines. For the first time since she'd come to the border, water flowed across the range, but thus far they hadn't come to any streams that couldn't be crossed.

"Do you think we're being watched?"

"Possibly. And not by the dogs. They are usually kept at the house."

"*Sacrebleu,*" she whispered, her fingers stroking the handle of the whip. In answer, the heavens rumbled overhead.

"We must hurry, senorita, if we are to arrive at the nester's place before dark," Antonio said, quickening the pace. "Over the next rise the land is flatter and is therefore more easily traveled. Still, we have a long way to go."

For the next hour she concentrated on doing as he said, always being careful to keep the wagon in sight behind her. Sometimes she cast uneasy eyes at the land to either side, but she saw no sign that anyone even knew they were there.

A rusted tin can was the first sign that they had arrived. Gabby hadn't known what to expect, but it certainly wasn't the godforsaken place that met her eye. The only structure was a lean-to shed, its door hanging by one hinge. Except for the weed-choked remnants of what appeared to be a garden, the muddy ground surrounding it was bare. Her eyes were drawn again to the shed. She'd seen outhouses that were larger and far more grand.

Although she hadn't expected to see Rafe and Cisco sitting around an open fire, she had hoped for some sign that they had been there—a hat, Cisco's whip, anything to give her assurance they were safe—but there was nothing to indicate a human had passed this way during the past year.

Behind her the wagon rumbled onto the scene, a grim reminder that they had not yet found its intended passengers.

Careful not to bend his injured leg, Antonio dropped to the ground beside Gabby, who didn't miss his quick wince of pain.

"What do we do now?" Gabby asked, trying to keep disappointment from her voice.

"We walk out like the spokes of the wheel. We look. And we listen."

Gabby nodded and dismounted. The ride was the longest she'd taken thus far, and she was not surprised at how unsteady she felt—and how sore. Leading the mare away from the bare land surrounding the shed, she ground-tethered her in a sparse patch of grass and turned full attention to her task. She didn't ask Antonio what she was supposed to look and listen for. She wasn't sure she wanted to know.

The sloping ground around the shed was stubbled with low shrubs and cactus. Gabby picked her way carefully. A rustle in the grass to her right brought her to a stop. Turning swiftly on her booted feet, she strode back to Tempest, and grabbed the whip that hung from the saddle. She'd not go whirling about like a frightened fool again, just because of a snake.

The feeling she'd had of being watched as they rode toward their destination returned to her. Her eyes darted about the uneven land. In this part of the range there wasn't much to hide behind, only a scattering of scrawny mesquite and live oak. There wasn't even a single rock large enough to shelter a man.

Gabby shook off the feeling. There were more important considerations to occupy her mind.

Alone, Gabby could bear the desolate scene no longer.

"Rafe!" Her voice echoed over the hillside. "Cisco!"

Only the breeze answered.

Could Antonio have mistaken the look in Dallas Pryor's eyes? It was such a slim circumstance on which to base their hopes.

"Rafe!" She ran through the grass, stopped, and waited for a response. Wildly she looked around. So much land to cover and so few of them. And what were they looking for, anyway? A familiar hat sodden from yesterday's rain? Freshly turned dirt.

She hadn't gone more than a dozen yards when she heard it. The sound was more like the sigh of the wind than a human voice, but something within Gabby responded. Every sense was alerted as she listened for a repeat of the sound.

Silence.

"Rafe! It's me, Gabby. Let me know where you are."

"In the well."

This time his voice was louder. Her eyes cutting to the right and left fell on a circle of rocks marking an old well. A large covering board had been thrown to one side. In her haste to reach the opening, she stumbled, her hands breaking her fall. Sprawled in the mud and grass beside the rocks, she muttered a curse in several languages.

"Down here. Help."

Frantically she tossed her whip aside and pulled

300

herself upright. The sound seemed to come from the center of the earth. But Gabby had no doubt who called her, and she felt a rush of exhilaration. Rafe was alive and able to talk.

Careful not to push any rocks into the hole, she shifted to the edge and looked down into darkness. The sun was at her back, too low on the horizon to cast light beyond the first three feet of the hole. She could not see him.

"Rafe!" she cried. "It's Gabby." Her voice echoed from the murkiness and almost covered the answer.

"Querida," he said.

Gabby jumped to her feet and issued her own cry for help.

"Antonio! Over here. He's alive!" she cried, then softer, "he's alive."

The next few minutes were a blur of answers to her call, of Antonio, his bandaged leg dragging, making his awkward way toward her, of the Lozano brothers hurrying to her side and after a quick assessment of Rafe's predicament fetching a blanket and rope from the wagon. All the while, Gabby kept a stream of encouraging words pouring into the darkness. Rafe answered, but in such a faint voice she told him to save his strength.

Gabby looked at the thick rope looped in Pedro Lozano's hand, then turned to Antonio. "I'm going down."

"No, senorita—"

"Tie the rope around my waist and lower me, Antonio. Rafe is waiting."

Antonio paused. It was Rafe who answered. "Listen to Antonio. You'll only get wet down here."

For the first time in two days Gabby could breathe easily. Even from a watery prison beneath the earth's surface, Rafe liked to be boss. His words were the surest sign yet he was not seriously hurt.

Pedro dropped a loop into the well.

"It's coming," said Gabby, leaning precariously over the edge to watch the end of the rope disappear. Finally came the triumphant shout, "Got it! Now pull."

Slowly the rope slid over the edge, cutting into the dirt and crumbling bits away.

"Careful," said Antonio, "the whole thing could cave in."

"No, it won't," Gabby said. "I'll be the first to see him. And soon."

At last his pale face appeared, an oval suspended in space. Then she could see him slowly rising, allowing all his weight to dangle and warding off the rough sides of the well with muddy hands. He looked upward with haggard, sunken eyes. Wet tendrils of black hair lay against his face.

He came closer into view, water dripping from him, and she could see he was not just damp but thoroughly soaked. At last he could grasp at the top of the well and help pull himself forward onto his chest.

Tears filled Gabby's eyes, and she was grateful for the coming dark that hid them from him.

"What kept you?" he said in a whisper.

"Don't give me any trouble, senor," she said, "or I'm liable to leave." Unable to resist, she touched her lips to his, unmindful of the men snubbing the rope around an oak tree and rushing to help drag Rafe from the treacherous lip of the well.

Antonio limped forward with a blanket. The sun was dipping behind a far hill, and the October breeze was brisk and cool. Gabby held tightly to Rafe and felt his body begin to shake.

She looked up at Antonio. "He's cold. We need to get him out of these wet clothes."

Quickly she unbuttoned Rafe's shirt, but when she tried to remove it, he groaned in protest.

"You didn't object the last time I did this," she whispered into his ear. "Don't start now."

She gentled her touch as much as she could. When her fingers touched the back of his head, Rafe flinched. Traces of dried blood on a deep cut told her he had been hit hard, and she marveled that he had survived his ordeal.

She gave one brief thought to who might have attacked him. Dallas Pryor, most likely, with Earl Hunter urging him on. She looked at Rafe's deep-set eyes and at the lines of fatigue on his face, and she chalked up one more thing the owner of the Perro would have to answer for.

Tossing the shirt aside, she covered Rafe's bare chest with the blanket and, while the wagon was brought closer, removed his wet boots. She used her bandanna to clean his stubbly face.

"Legs feel numb," he said, and she began to massage them until he declared himself able to walk to the wagon. Soon he was stretched out in the back, additional blankets around him and his head cradled in Gabby's lap.

"Would you like some water?"

He answered with a curse, and she was surprised he had the strength to deliver it with such force.

Antonio handed her a small flask. "I think Rafael had all the water he wanted. Whiskey will warm him more."

She gave him a small swallow, then another, and he settled back, handing the flask back to Antonio. "When you feel strong enough, you can tell us what happened," she said, "but first let's go after Cisco."

Rafe stiffened in her arms.

Gabby glanced at the whip that had been placed in the wagon by her feet. Cisco had made the whip for her with his own hands. "Where is he, Rafe?"

Afraid to hear the answer, she forced herself to look into his eyes. Even in the gathering dusk she saw in their brown depths an anguish more eloquent than words. A sob escaped her. She took Rafe's hands in hers and held on tight.

Antonio gripped her shoulder, then lifted the flask to his own lips. He lowered it and wiped his lips. *"El bastardo,"* he said.

Rafe stared toward the hills that lay between him and the main house of the Perro. "I swear vengeance," he said in a voice that only she could hear, but it carried a strength that frightened Gabby.

So, she thought, the ugliness was not yet done. The culprits must be made to pay, but not at the risk of losing Rafe. Nothing was worth that. Silent tears welled in Gabby's eyes and spilled onto her cheeks— for Rafe and for the brave young man with the quick smile and flashing whip.

Slowly the wagon began its uneven journey home.

Dallas Pryor eased into the lone room of the cabin

he called home. He'd been a long time riding, and he was dog tired. Ever since he'd taken that bitch Lupita, things hadn't gone right. He should have left her alone. She'd left some scratches on him and a bite that had barely begun to heal.

Fumbling for the lantern by the door, he grinned to himself. The girl had fight in her, he would hand her that. Damn, but maybe she'd been worth the trouble after all.

A match flared in the corner of the room, and he whirled around. He caught the smell of cigar smoke.

"That you, Mr. Hunter?"

"Are you expecting someone else?"

Dallas laughed nervously. Not like Earl Hunter to come calling at his place so late at night.

"You like a drink, Mr. Hunter?" he said. He turned and managed, in spite of shaking hands, to light the wick on the lantern, then reached for the bottle of whiskey beside it.

"Serve yourself, Dallas," Hunter said. "I take it they found Rafe Jericho."

Dallas took a long draw on the bottle of whiskey and leaned against the table behind him. The liquor felt good, gave him strength to answer.

"There were four of 'em looking. Including that girl. I kept close on their tracks, but they didn't know I was anywhere around. When they went toward the old nester place, I didn't worry." His voice took on a whining note. "Anyone would have been sure he was dead by then."

Hunter's voice was soft. "You should have killed him outright. Haven't I always told you not to do things by halves?"

"He was near dead when I left him. I liked the idea of letting him suffer, stalking me the way he did."

"Your problem, Dallas, is that your smart doesn't equal your mean. He's a witness against your killing the boy."

"He's not in much shape to do anything about it now."

"He will be. And there's that Ranger friend of his. It's only a matter of time before they come after you, Dallas. And bring all kinds of lawmen on the place. I've got to have a story for them."

Dallas took another swallow of whiskey. "I could take care of him now."

Hunter shook his head. "It's too late for that. You couldn't have killed all of them. And they'll be guarding him now." He puffed on the cigar. "And it wouldn't help. Sooner or later, they'll come snooping and I have to have answers."

Dallas stirred nervously. "What you getting at, Earl?"

"I'll move Cisco's body, hide it where it will never be found. Jericho will have the sheriff or that Ranger friend here before long. I'll have to say his story about you may be true."

"Like hell, you will," Pryor growled. "You ain't turning me over to no lawman."

"I have no intention of doing that, Dallas. I'll say you and Cisco are like a lot of rovers — you both just wandered off. One thing's for sure. I can't afford to have you around any more."

"You kicking me off the place?" Dallas said, his anger rising.

"Not exactly." Hunter sat straight in the chair. His

right hand moved. His gun blazed. The last sound Dallas Pryor heard was the explosion of the shot.

"Not exactly," Hunter repeated in the echoing noise, his cold eyes resting on Pryor's still body. "Too bad you must join Cisco while Rangers search for both of you."

Hunter puffed on the cigar. "It's just too damned bad, Dallas. You were the best man I had."

Chapter Fourteen

"All Rafe needs is lots of rest." Doc Crites stood in the midday sun outside the Arroyo Seco hacienda and patted Gabby's hands. "Bring him along slow on food. Best thing you can do for him is keep folks away."

"That shouldn't be difficult," Gabby said. "We're hardly on a major route."

"Don't be too sure. When Miguel Lozano came to get me, there were several folks in the waiting room. Word spread fast that Rafe's hurt. Never seen anything like it, the way everyone is concerned."

"They'll have to show it from a distance. If rest and solitude are what he needs, Doc, then that's exactly what he'll get. Anyone who thinks differently will have to answer to me."

Crites's intelligent gray eyes studied her. "I'd hate to cross you right now, Miss Deschamps," he said as he bid her good-bye. "That's for sure."

Gabby watched the doctor's buggy make its labored way up the incline leading to the main road, but her thoughts were on Rafe. Never before had she felt so protective about anyone or anything as she did about him.

During the long ride back to the hacienda, he'd talked incessantly, sometimes incoherently, about what had happened after he and Cisco left Lupita's hut. He slowed only at the description of digging Cisco's grave.

"It's due west behind the bunkhouse about two hundred yards," he said, watching Antonio as he talked. "I marked each step in my mind. Didn't want to forget."

"We will find it, Rafael," said Antonio, "and bring Cisco home."

Gabby's eyes blurred at the memory, but she brushed the tears away. In the past two days Rafe had been through more trouble than most men face in a lifetime; he would carry the loss of Cisco for a long time. No matter what he needed to bear that loss, she would see that he received it. Even Ben Hidalgo couldn't push her aside.

When they'd arrived back at the Seco, Ben had taken charge — she wasn't family, he'd let her know — but she couldn't trust him over the next few days to give Rafe the peace and quiet he needed, not irascible old Ben.

Gabby turned to reenter the hacienda but stopped at the sound of an approaching carriage. Here come the townspeople, she thought, before the dust has even settled from the doctor's visit.

She watched as the carriage made its way down to

the house, and was not surprised when she recognized its occupants.

"Judge Russell," she said in greeting, "and Emma. I should have known you would be out."

"Won't stay long," Emma said. "When I heard the judge was coming out, couldn't stay away, could I? Had to be sure how things were and"—her eyes twinkled—"dispense a little good advice on how to take care of Rafe. Doc's all right for some things, but if it's nursing the man is needing, leave that to a woman."

"Lord, Emma," Judge Russell said, stepping stiffly to the ground, "you keep that palaver up, we'll be here until midnight."

Emma's lips flattened, but she gave no reply as she accepted his hand to help her alight. It had been a long ride out, Gabby figured.

"Damned disgrace in this day and age," Russell said as they entered the house. "How's Rafe doing?"

"He needs rest," said Gabby.

"Just want to say hello."

"Doc Crites said he's not to be disturbed." Gabby softened her tone. "Why don't you talk to Ben? He's back in his office. If Rafe is awake when you're ready to leave, you can stop in for a short hello."

Reluctantly, the judge agreed. "I did work up a thirst on the ride out. Must have been all that listening."

When he was safely ensconced with Ben, Gabby and Emma moved quietly past Rafe's room and settled down with cups of coffee in the kitchen.

"Haven't heard much from you, Gabrielle, since you came out here," Emma said. "You're looking a little tired yourself, and I'm wondering if it's from more than last night. Things going all right?"

"They will be," Gabby retorted, "when Rafe's back on his feet and Dallas Pryor is six feet under the ground."

"Sheriff talked to Hunter this morning. Spread it all over town that he can't prove a thing on him."

"Rafe will testify against Pryor. That ought to flush out his boss," said Gabby.

"Don't be too sure. According to Hunter, Pryor was always a drifter. Said he pulled out sometime during the night. Even said Cisco most likely did the same thing, and Rafe's just trying to stir up trouble."

"Surely the sheriff doesn't believe that?"

"Course not, but prove it's not true."

"Rafe can. He knows where to find the grave."

Emma stirred her coffee. "I'm afraid not. That foreman of Rafe's took the sheriff out to the Perro early this morning. They found the ground torn up, but that could be laid to the heavy rains. There was no sign of any body."

Gabby's heart sank. "Are you sure, Emma?"

"The judge is real close to the sheriff. I let him talk once in a while on the ride out."

"This is going to hit Rafe hard."

"That's where a good nurse comes in. Keep him from finding out until he's able to do something about it."

"Antonio will figure out not to say anything just yet, not that it'll do any good. I imagine Judge Russell is in there telling Ben the news."

"Promised he wouldn't, but I can't swear what he'll do once he has a taste of whiskey under his belt.

Wouldn't hurt for you to talk to Ben after we're gone. Make sure he doesn't go telling Rafe everything he knows."

"Ben doesn't exactly welcome my advice, Emma. If I'm to take care of Rafe the way he needs, I'm liable to have trouble with the old man."

Emma reached for Gabby's hand. "You're right to protect Rafe, Gabrielle. He's a good man."

"I know that."

"A good man to spend the rest of your life with if Hunter doesn't succeed in killing him."

"For some girl."

"Why not you?"

Gabby held her head proudly. *Because he hasn't asked me, at least not since San Antonio. And even then his proposal had been more an assumption than anything else.*

"Emma," she said, pushing aside her thoughts, "the only thing I'm concerned about right now is getting Rafe well again. Next will come the apprehension of Cisco's killer. These are bad times around here, much too bad for me to be thinking about myself."

"When you do, Gabrielle, remember what I said. Don't let him get away. You'll regret it for the rest of your life. No matter what you came down here for, I'm thinking you found something else you want a whole lot more."

Gabby met her steady gaze. "That could be, Emma. But I've wanted a lot of things in my life that I didn't get. It could be I've just added to the list."

"Don't be a quitter, girl. Some things in this world are worth fighting for. Anybody who has a chance at Rafe Jericho would be a fool to let him go."

Emma's words stayed with her as she saw the

visitors on their way. Rafe had been resting quietly when Russell emerged from his visit with Ben, and the judge had agreed to return in a few days. Outside, Gabby had tried to ask him about the visit and what the two men had talked about, but all he would say was that Ben could be a reasonable man. If so, it was one side of him Gabby hadn't seen yet.

Making her way back to Rafe's side, Gabby stood quietly beside the bed and gazed down at him. She'd bathed and clothed him in warm flannel before Crites arrived, but his face was still covered with stubble and the half circles under his eyes looked darker than ever. She couldn't resist reaching out and touching his cheek. No matter what happened between them, she could rejoice that he was alive.

"Ah, *querida*," he said softly, his eyes still closed, "what kept you?"

"You're not supposed to be awake."

"I'm hungry."

"Any special requests?"

Rafe's eyes slowly opened, and under his slow appraisal she was glad she'd changed into a dress and combed the tangles from her hair.

His lips twitched. "Right now, Gabby, I'll have to settle for tortillas and beans." He rested a moment. "And a steak and . . . " His voice trailed off.

Taking time only to brush her lips against his cheek, she ordered him to rest until she returned. Fifteen minutes later, when she let herself back in, a tray in her hand, she was surprised to see him half sitting, struggling to adjust the pillow at his back.

"You're a stubborn man, Rafe Jericho," she admonished.

313

He lay back and managed a grin, his face wan against the white pillow. "Just a hungry one. Where's my steak?"

She sat beside him, the tray in her lap, and spooned up a gray, unidentifiable mass.

Rafe's eyes narrowed. "What did you do to the meat, run it through a grinder? There's nothing wrong with my teeth."

"Doc said you had a nasty crack on the head and there's always the danger of pneumonia. He didn't count on the strength of the bite you've got left."

"It's still something for you to keep in mind."

Gabby smiled down at him, forcing the cheerful look on her face. How pale he looked beneath the thick stubble of beard. Rafe might still be quick with a word, but she knew it cost him a great deal.

"Open wide," Gabby said, the spoon pressing against his lips. "This will make you feel better."

Rafe forced himself to swallow. "Did you taste this?"

"I know what it tastes like. It's just porridge."

Under protest, Rafe took two more spoonfuls, then rested his head deeper into the pillow. "Payment for the coal oil and sugar?" he asked.

Gabby set aside the tray and leaned closer to Rafe, her fingers stroking the thick hair on his forehead. "I searched your body for festering cuts, but all I could find were a few scratches. Nothing that I can put my hands to."

"Maybe," Rafe said, his voice barely above a whisper, "you overlooked one or two. It's all right with me—"

Gabby felt a pang of regret. "I'm not being a very good nurse, Rafe. You're supposed to be resting."

"That's hard to do"—he paused for a few deep breaths—"with you around. There were a few hours down in that well when I thought I would never see you again."

Gabby kept her voice light. "Don't you know you can't hide from me?"

Rafe reached up and, taking her hand, rested it against his heart. "Those are words I could have spoken," he said.

It was a tender moment, and Gabby could see that even in his exhaustion Rafe was prepared to say more. She forced herself to pull free. No sickbed declarations for her, she thought. If Rafe wanted to tell her a few things she would give the world to hear, she preferred him on his feet and clearheaded, not lying on his back and at her mercy. Only then would she know he was not confusing gratitude with love.

"There wasn't a chance," she said, "that anyone could have hurt me. I kept a firm grip on the bullwhip. You've seen me take out a row of tin cans with it. You know what a terror I can be."

The tenderness left his eyes, and Gabby's mind went to the young vaquero who had been her friend. She knew Rafe was sharing her thoughts. The laughing Cisco had been taken from them.

"I must talk to Jeff McGowan," he said suddenly.

"I already sent for him yesterday. He's in Dallas for at least a week. By the time he gets back, you should be on your feet."

"I don't want Pryor to enjoy one minute more of life than is necessary. At least send for the sheriff."

Gabby avoided his stare. "The sheriff is already out investigating. He'll be around later," she said, tucking the covers firmly around him, "when you're strong enough to talk to him."

Rafe's hands balled into fists and he struck the bed. "I'm not an invalid, damn it," he said.

"Of course you're not," Gabby said, moving to draw the draperies more tightly closed to the sun's rays. She turned to look down at Rafe. "I'll make you a deal. Rest for the afternoon so you'll be able to talk to the sheriff when he comes. And I'll cook you a real steak when you wake up."

"You drive a hard bargain," he said, but she noticed there was no real argument in his words.

Gabby brushed her lips against his. As she let herself out, closing the door carefully behind her, she was sharply aware of his uneven breathing. He had too much on his mind to rest the way he needed to. Doc said he needed to stay in bed a few days longer, but she wondered just how long it would be before Rafe was out seeking the revenge he had sworn. He'd not be willing to let the sheriff, or even Jeff, take care of Dallas Pryor.

Finding Lupita in the kitchen, she hugged her warmly and welcomed her back.

"I will be fine," Lupita said. "Antonio and you have helped much . . . and Senor Rafael."

"Could you help me see he's undisturbed . . . even by Ben?" asked Gabby.

"For Senor Rafael I would face *el Diablo* himself."

Gabby's second task came harder, but she knew what she must do. A sharp knock at Ben's door brought her no response, but she entered anyway and found him as usual behind his desk, upright and facing the door as though he'd been waiting for her.

316

"I bother you only because you are Rafe's grandfather. He's fine," she said briefly. "Or will be after a few days of rest. I'm sure you'll help me see that he gets it. He will be well but needs undisturbed sleep, particularly today. And that means keeping from him any unpleasant news that might upset him."

"You refer, perhaps, to the visit by Antonio and the sheriff to the Rancho Perro?"

"I see that Judge Russell talked more than he should have."

"Sometimes when Russell has a drink, he likes to talk. But I am not a fool. Through the years I have kept other news from Rafael that would only serve to disturb him. He will not learn from me anything that will slow his recovery."

The harsh lines of the old man's face softened. "Please allow me to thank you, senorita, for your part in the return of my grandson. Antonio tells me it was you who found him."

Gabby was almost moved by his gratitude. Almost. Too many ugly words had passed between them for her to believe it would last very long.

"It was Rafe who had the strength to cry out when he heard me," she said and turned to leave.

"One moment, senorita. I am not finished." The old man was smiling unpleasantly. "My talk with Judge Russell this afternoon concerned more than just the sheriff. Senorita Cordero." He spat out her name.

His kind words hadn't lasted until she could get out of the room, Gabby thought, but she held her ground. "It must be bad news for me," she said evenly. "With your grandson so ill only a few doors away, only that could make you look so pleased."

317

"My grandson will be riding the hills of the Arroyo Seco long after you have gone away."

Proudly, Gabby looked him in the eye. "Your grandson is a strong and brave man, Senor Hidalgo. But I am, perhaps, not so weak as you thought I was. I have not been driven away by hard work. And don't look so surprised. I know that was the only reason you allowed me to stay."

"I allowed you to stay," he said in a tone that would have withered a weaker adversary, "because I feared you held power over us. Now I find that is not true. Thanks to the visit by the good judge."

"My cause is as just as it ever was, senor."

"It is the dealings with the bank of which I speak."

"I have the papers in my room. Papers arranged by my lawyer that could give me title to the land if you do not make full payment in time. It is, however, a poor time to bring this up, with Rafe so recently near death. But it is you who do so, senor, not I."

"Spoken like a Cordero." His eyes glittered hatefully at her. "You are Maria's granddaughter, after all. And, like her, you make mistakes. We need only to make a small payment to keep title to our land. Judge Russell has informed me of this fact. There are legal terms that I do not understand, but this much I know. The papers give you little power to steal that which is ours."

Gabby almost laughed at the absurdity of his words. "Is this why he came out here? To tell you and Rafe? To help him in his recovery? I must tell you, senor, that I never had any intention of foreclosing."

Ben settled back in his chair, a look of triumph on his face. "The good judge did not need to speak to my grandson. Already Rafe knows your purchase is of little importance. He has known since the day of the fire when he consulted with the good judge. It was why he rode into town and was not here when the blaze began."

A picture of Rafe walking toward her at Emma Talbert's party flashed across her mind. At last she understood why he wanted to talk, why he had faced her with assurance instead of the fury she had expected. Before he was interrupted in the gazebo, Rafe hadn't been about to explode in anger or to try to bargain with her. Once more he'd been about to push aside her quest as insubstantial.

All Gabby could think of was the crushing disappointment that Rafe had kept the news from her so long, had let her believe those few pieces of paper from a San Antonio bank held power and made her his equal. He would never believe that she'd never planned to use them.

He'd let her fall more deeply in love with him and with the ranch, so much so that her very existence seemed tied up with him. All her dreams and hopes had found definition in his being. Rafe cared for her in his own way—she knew that—but it was not enough, had never been enough. She was wise to have veered from the moment of tenderness earlier in his room. He couldn't trust her and he couldn't put her above his land.

She felt Ben's cold eyes on her.

"Senor Hidalgo, you have hated me since the first day I visited you. I expected to be rebuffed, but I hardly expected the force of your ill will. But through your cruel reactions to Lupita's misfortunes, I learned something else. I am not alone in receiving your enmity. You feel little compassion for anyone else except Rafe. It matters not that you hate me. It doesn't separate me from the rest of the world. You haven't once mentioned the death of Cisco, a boy who grew to manhood working for you."

Gabby stopped. There was so much more she could have said, but there seemed little point in talking to a hate-filled, selfish old man who would never change. Whatever had happened in his life to make him so bitter would remain his secret; but she had to deal with the results.

Ben had lied at her grandfather's trial and was proud of it. The Corderos would forever pay for his crime against them.

Before he could work himself up into ordering her immediate removal from the Seco, Gabby let herself out and headed for her room to settle the turmoil in her mind. Rafe had let her believe a lie about the papers she held. And he'd invited her to remain on the ranch only to prove that she was a mere woman who could be driven by hatred of hard work into giving up her fight.

She stood indecisively in the hall thinking about the muddle her life had become. What had seemed to her a simple desire to regain the right to her father's inheritance and some part of a place she could call home had turned into a nightmare of deceit and thwarted love — all of it complicated by Earl Hunter's suddenly intensified war against Rafe.

Hurt and confused, she thought about leaving without so much as a good-bye. Perhaps somewhere, somehow she'd forget the tender Rafe she'd come to know lately and remember only his overbearance and deceit.

In leaving she would remove one threat against the land, but not the only one, not the one that also included a threat against Rafe's life. Hunter, too, wanted the Seco, and he would go to frightening extremes to get it.

After a few short weeks she realized that she'd grown contented just knowing the land was there. Even if she didn't own it, its mere *being* had given a continuity to her life that had been missing. But not if it fell into the hands of a scoundrel. Whatever happened between her and Rafe, Hunter must be stopped—and soon.

And that could be up to her. A plan was slowly forming in her mind.

Quickly Gabby changed into her gabardine riding clothes and boots. Rafe might know how to charm a woman and fight a fire, but he'd done a poor job of ridding himself of Hunter. The problem was he'd always approached him directly. That was just like a man, when a little guile could accomplish so much more. There was no reason *she* couldn't get evidence against Hunter, evidence that would stand up in court.

Gabby had no trouble saddling Tempest; armed only with her bullwhip, she urged the horse into a dead run on the road that would take her to the neighboring ranch. She must hurry if she were to return by the time Rafe roused and asked questions.

A fence line marked the boundary between the two ranches, but Gabby would have known she was on Hunter land even without the fence. The air seemed heavier, the ground dryer, the stretches of land bleaker. Reaching down, she patted the bullwhip—as though it was a guard against the Perro's desolation.

Even before she sighted the main house, she heard the barking of dogs. Tempest skittered nervously, but Gabby held the reins firmly, stroked the horse's neck, and talked to her the way Rafe had taught her. The mare's pace steadied.

It wasn't until Gabby dismounted in front of the house and tethered the mare that she faced one of the dogs. A snarling hound, fangs bared, rounded the corner of the house and bore down on her. Gabby reached for the whip and cracked it in the dust inches from the dog's snout. The startled animal yelped and backed up. Gabby let loose another crack of the whip, and the dog, with one last growl as if to salvage his reputation, slunk out of sight.

"Well done, Miss Deschamps."

Gabby turned to see Earl Hunter, a cigar clamped between his teeth, looking at her from the front porch. In his vested suit, he looked the picture of a gentleman rancher.

"You need to keep him penned," she said, coiling the whip and hanging it on the saddle in what she hoped came across as an act of cool deliberation.

Hunter removed the cigar and studied the long coil of ash before looking back at Gabby. "But my wife and I have so few visitors," he said, "and the boys do like their freedom."

The boys. Gabby shuddered. The particular "boy" who had accosted her would have liked nothing better than to sink his teeth into her throat.

"I'm afraid my wife is not here," Hunter said in the

same silky voice he'd used at their first meeting. "She's gone shopping in town."

"I didn't come to see Mrs. Hunter," Gabby said. "You and I have some business to discuss."

Hunter's eyes narrowed. At last she'd managed to break through his reserve.

"More questions about how I know about you? As I recall, that seemed to bother you greatly the other day."

Gabby shook her head. "If you really knew me, Mr. Hunter, you'd already have figured out why I'm here. I like a winner. And I figure in your war with Rafe, that's you."

"Don't take me for a fool."

"I could say the same. And a fool is exactly what I would be if I were trying some kind of trick."

Gabby held his gaze. She saw wariness in his eyes, and doubt. It was the doubt she played upon.

"Now we can stand out here and talk about how we're going to divide up the Seco, or we can go inside for a more civilized setting." Gabby smiled pleasantly. "It's up to you."

Again Hunter turned his attention to the cigar. She felt awkward and much too obvious. She thanked providence that Hunter didn't seem to notice.

"Where are my manners?" he said at last and opened the front door. "Please come in for a drink."

Hunter guided her through a surprisingly homey parlor—antimacassars on overstuffed chairs gathered around a hearth and a piano sat in one corner of the room. Their destination, Hunter's office, was equally comfortable with leather chairs, a broad oak desk, and lace curtains at the windows.

At his bidding, she settled into one of the chairs and accepted a glass of sherry. If she closed her eyes, she might imagine she was back at Miss Martha Emmett's School for Girls. Gabby sipped at the sherry and smiled. And waited for Hunter to speak. She didn't mention the sheriff's investigations and neither did he.

"I was in town this morning and heard about Rafe," he said. "How terrible to think he was found on my place. And how close he came to death."

"He wasn't very bright, was he, coming over like that with only the young Cisco?" Gabby took a deep swallow of sherry.

Hunter's eyebrows raised a fraction. "I don't know that this Cisco was here, but it's clear that Rafe was. You don't seem sorry that he was hurt."

"It really doesn't matter one way or the other. I just thought he could handle himself better. It's why I've been trying to ally myself with him."

"You surprise me, Miss Deschamps."

"I said you didn't know me as well as you thought. I learned early in life a girl has to take care of herself if she wants to be more than just a pawn."

"The same goes for men, too," he said, raising his glass in salute. Still she read caution in his eyes.

She pushed forward. "You might warn your man Pryor that Rafe plans to come after him as soon as he's on his feet."

"I wish him luck. Apparently Pryor pulled out sometime during the night. You know how it is with these cowboys. They're all rovers at heart."

Gabby would give a large slice of her bank account, dwindling though it was, to find out the truth about

Hunter's gunman. She was sure he hadn't just drifted off, leaving his stake in whatever enterprise Hunter had going.

He was a rapist and a murderer, and he'd tried to kill Rafe, all with at least the unspoken consent of her host. But Pryor had bungled the job. If he *were* gone, Hunter must have run him off.

"Miss Deschamps," Hunter said, pouring them each another glass of sherry, "you said something about our dividing the Seco. I didn't know it was ours to divide."

"It can be mine," she said, looking at him from under lowered lashes, trying to decide if he knew about the judge's injunction against her.

Hunter stared at her impassively, and she continued. "As you may have heard, I bought up the loan Rafe took out in San Antonio. It took most of my money, but it was worth it to know I could make him squirm."

Hunter nodded.

"You must be short of ready cash or you would have bought his paper before I did," she said.

"I am not without resources, Miss Deschamps. Let us just say you beat me to a wise investment." A look of calculation settled on his face. "What exactly do you want from me?" he asked.

"Well, Earl, you can start by calling me Gabrielle. Partners shouldn't be so formal, don't you agree?" She smiled beguilingly into his widened eyes, then stood and put her glass on Hunter's desk. Walking to the window, she whirled to face him. "I want Rafe and Ben Hidalgo ruined. And I want in on your smuggling deals."

Hunter's eyebrows climbed up his forehead. "I don't

know what you're talking about."

She dismissed his denial with a shrug. "I've seen the cut fence. What Rafe surmised makes sense. You're running things both ways across the river, and you'd like to run more if you could be sure the way was clear. Up until now you've been doing a lot of threatening, but the only action has been small-time—fence cutting and the slaughter of some stock."

"You have a strong imagination," he said.

"Call it anything you like. I've also got a good idea about what must have happened with Pryor. He's gone crazy, I figure, and you've had to do away with him. Which leaves you short-handed. That's where I come in. Men take one look at me and think I'm weak and stupid. That's their mistake."

Hunter poured another glass of sherry. "Perhaps," he said, "I should thank you for the warning."

"Not only that," Gabby continued, "while you may not have intended to do murder, you have an unfortunate penchant for hiring men with no such compunctions. And that has gotten Rafe after your hide. You need me to keep him occupied—the way I did in San Antonio before you came along and messed things up for me."

"I'm curious. Why don't you just call in his loan you claim to have purchased?"

"Because right now I find he can make the payments. It's up to you to see that he doesn't."

Gabby moved away from the window to lean across Hunter's desk. "Separately, Earl, you and I haven't managed to hurt Rafe enough to force him to sell. We team up with what we're already doing, and we've got him."

326

Hunter sat back in his chair. "Let me understand you—er, Gabrielle. You think I've been tearing up fences, and that rail spur going in? Killing prize stock? You want me to keep it up, in effect destroying Rafe's attempts to improve the Seco, and in return you'll become my partner in smuggling with an eye to ready cash."

"And eventually one half the Seco, don't forget," Gabby said. "I'll want a good portion of the profits and an agreement in writing. I'm not a fool, Earl," she said, keeping a bright, taunting smile pasted on her lips.

"I wonder just what you are, Gabrielle."

"You seemed very sure when you talked to Rafe back in San Antonio. I was using my charms to win him to my side. I'd still like to learn someday how you knew."

Gabby was surprised at how easy it was to lie, once she'd got the hang of it. The words came out without her even being aware of what she planned to say. She'd long ago quit worrying that he might hear the pounding of her heart.

Something about what she'd said seemed to convince him. She figured it was probably that naturalness of speech she'd affected. Gone was the mask of politeness behind which he'd hidden; in its place was a sharp-faced pragmatism that hinted he was ready to deal.

Hunter rose. "This has all been most illuminating, Gabrielle. It is possible we can work with each other," he said as he guided her into the hall. "It just so happens, I have a business acquaintance coming from Mexico tomorrow. You can talk to him then. If you can wait that long."

On the front porch she smiled beguilingly at him. "If I must," she said. "Once we are agreed as to terms, I can have my lawyer out here with the necessary papers in less than a day."

"Your lawyer?"

"Yes. Franklin Bernard."

"Ah, yes, I've met him once. He ought to do just fine."

Something about his words bothered Gabby, but she didn't take the time to think through what that something was. Things were rolling too swiftly her way for her to stop.

"I've waited most of my life for that land," Gabby said as she mounted Tempest, "and I'm tired of being done out of it, but a few more hours won't make any more difference, I suppose."

The return ride to the Seco hacienda was exhilarating. Hunter had taken the bait and he was even going to introduce her to one of his partners in crime. Perhaps, she thought, buoyed by her success, when Rafe was well enough he could join in her scheme. Gabby was convinced they could get enough evidence to hang the entire gang of smugglers.

And then, if he was of a mind to, they could turn their attention to the more delicate problems which lay between them. She didn't dwell too long on that part of her plans. For now, it was enough to know he would soon be safe from Earl Hunter.

It was almost dusk when she rode up to the Seco and decided providence was indeed smiling down on her. A buggy near the front of the house belonged to Franklin Bernard. He could tell her about rules of evidence they would need. Most important, she wanted to know what to put into a written business agreement between her and Hunter.

She found him just inside the door talking to a hesitant Lupita.

"Senorita Deschamps," Lupita said with a sigh of relief when she spied her, "I was just telling the gentleman that neither of the senors is seeing anyone. He didn't believe me when I told her you were not at home."

Gabby looked at the lawyer in surprise. Until Lupita had spoken, she'd forgotten how forward he had become during her last days in town, always questioning her and wanting to know her plans.

With a nod, she dismissed Lupita and turned to him. "Franklin, would you mind taking a walk with me toward the river? There's something I need to ask you."

"It's about time you consulted me, Gabrielle," he said.

Gabby ignored his officiousness and guided him around the house and down the path that led into the meadow. When they were out of sight and sound of the house, she got right to the point.

"Earl Hunter is to blame for Rafe's injuries."

Bernard stopped in his tracks. "How do you know this? You shouldn't go around bandying accusations in a careless manner."

"I could hardly hurt Earl's reputation, now could I?"

"But you're accusing him of criminal behavior."

"And I'd like to do so to Jeff McGowan when he gets back in town," she said impatiently. "The trouble is, I don't know exactly the proof I will need."

Gabby could almost hear the lawyer's mind chewing on her words.

"I rode over to Hunter's place this afternoon," she said, giving him more fodder, "and as much as got him to admit he keeps harassing the Seco to keep his smuggling activities going."

Bernard's eyes widened. "He told you this?"

"In so many words, yes."

"But nothing definite. Nothing in writing, I assume."

Gabby shook her head. "At first he was suspicious, but I hope to get him to sign an agreement."

"Then it's your word against his."

"I'm going back tomorrow to meet with one of the men he deals with in Mexico. We're to discuss the financial arrangements for dividing whatever stolen goods pass across the Seco."

"It would be best if you could get the agreement down on paper."

"That's certainly what I'm hoping to do. But if I can't, is my testimony enough?"

"It could be."

Getting a firm answer out of a lawyer was like trying to capture the wind. "I want to nail Hunter's hide to the jailhouse wall, Franklin," said Gabby. "What's the best thing that could happen tomorrow?"

Gabby could sense Bernard's hesitancy. He took a long time in replying. "Find out when he plans his next criminal activity and report it beforehand. Or better yet, go with him. The appropriate lawmen could be lying in wait."

"I can't hold off Rafe long. He'll be up and heading

for the Perro to avenge Cisco's death. He could make Hunter grow cautious."

Bernard nodded. "Your only solution, then, is to get that agreement in writing tomorrow."

Gabby sighed. "I hope I can, but Hunter is a slippery character. Right now it's to my advantage that he also wants the Seco. I guess I'll find out tomorrow just how much."

They walked in silence down the winding path, Gabby's mind wandering through the myriad problems facing her. They all revolved around Rafe and his ranch. For the first time in days she took time to look around at the ranch. The Seco smelled good to her. Overhead the first stars of evening were making their dim appearance, and at the edge of the horizon streaks of pink and gold marked the setting sun. The steady hum of cicadas provided a melodious background.

How peaceful it all seemed. Already across the landscape there were signs of green after the hard rains. Somehow the land always survived and prospered.

Without warning Gabby felt hands grip her waist, and she was pulled against Bernard's squat body. A moist mouth pressed against hers, and in her surprise she didn't push away. The lawyer's breath was cloyingly sweet and his lips full and soft. The unpleasant image of a grubworm came to her mind; repulsed, she shoved against Bernard's chest and pulled free of his hands.

"Franklin!" she said, staring at the heavily breathing lawyer in astonishment.

"Don't tell me you're surprised," Bernard said. "I've

been waiting to do that for a long time."

"You should have waited a lot longer! Whatever made you think I would welcome your attentions?"

A sly look passed over Bernard's broad face. "Now don't try to tell me you haven't been enjoying yourself out here. Rafe Jericho's not one to keep a woman that looks like you nearby and keep his hands off her."

"Whatever has happened between me and Rafe is certainly none of your business. And never would it lead to . . . to this!"

"Don't play coy with me, Gabrielle." Bernard's voice was a whine with a knife's edge.

"I'm not playing *anything* with you, Franklin."

Bernard's mouth twisted into a nasty sneer. "You'd better be careful how to brush me off."

"Are you threatening me?"

"I'm just saying you had best be careful."

Gabby looked at the lawyer as if seeing him for the first time. Men! Rafe Jericho was the most honest one she'd come across, and look at the sorry state of their affairs.

She turned to walk back up the hill. "I'd best be careful about a lot of things, Franklin. But so had you. Maybe I should speak in terms you understand. If you try anything like this again, I'll slap an assault charge on you so fast you'll have to drop all your other cases just to defend yourself."

Bernard held himself stiffly, his lawyer's facade back in place. "That will hardly be necessary, Miss Deschamps. I assure you I have . . . other things in mind than pursuing a liaison that is obviously distasteful to you."

Gabby didn't give a thought to what those other

things might be. Deep in her heart she hoped the plan would prove to Rafe the land meant more to her than just a legality — that she valued it for itself and would defend it even if winning against Hunter meant she lost her fight with Rafe and Ben.

Chapter Fifteen

Darkness heavy as a stone crushed against Rafe, shoving him deeper into the damp abyss at his back. If he didn't fight the weight, didn't push back . . . . But his arms were like the water waiting to enfold him.

"Rafe."

A silver voice came out of the void. An angel, sweet and gentle, called.

"Rafe!"

She was worried, this angel who called him away from a watery grave, but when he tried to call out to her for help, his voice came out a cry. Hands tugged at him, and with a rush he fell into whirling consciousness.

He lay still a minute, heart pounding, body bathed in sweat, as his mind raced to settle him in place and time. The firm hands that had been in his dream gripped his shoulders, and again came the gentle, insistent voice.

"Wake up, Rafe. It's me, Gabby."

Gradually the darkness that circled him subsided into quiet, cool stillness. He was in his bed; bending over him was Gabby, golden hair falling in tousled curls about her face, the white of her nightgown almost luminous in the dim light. She was the angel of his dream.

He reached up and pulled her into his arms. She was no insubstantial spirit of the night, but a flesh-and-blood woman whose warmth and sweet-smelling softness soothed him like a balm.

He held her long after the nightmare had faded from his mind. She pushed back to look down at him, her hair forming a curtain around them that shut out the world, and she brushed damp hair from his forehead.

Her fingers trembled as she touched him. How frightened she had been when he cried out, even knowing he must still be asleep. "You were having a nightmare," she said simply, as if by her words she could relegate the pulse-pounding experience to unimportance.

"I don't imagine it will be the last. I'll get over them."

"I thought you were calling for help," she said, apologetically, as though she had no right to enter his room.

He reached up to stroke her hair. "A clever ploy on my part, wouldn't you say, to get you in here?"

"And what, pray tell, do you plan to do about me?" she said, teasing away the tightness in her chest. "You slept right through the evening meal. I don't imagine even you can do much on three swallows of porridge in three days."

Rafe brushed his thumb against her lips. Gabby was only too right. Her presence filled him with the pleasurable unrest of desire, but he would make a poor showing as a lover if he tried to do anything about it. If only his body could function as well as his mind . . . . And yet there was great comfort to be had in simply holding her close.

"How long have I been out?"

"Let's see . . . about twelve hours." Gabby sat beside him on the bed. "It's after midnight."

"Madre de Dios!" He shifted his weight to his elbows, tugged at the covers, and dropped back against the bed.

Gabby straightened the quilt and patted his chest in a decidedly unromantic way. "Be careful. You'll be lightheaded from lying in bed so long."

"You're liable to lose one of those lovely hands, Gabby, if you continue to treat me like a child."

Now that sounds like the old Rafe. "You're definitely on the mend," she said, smiling. "Nothing like a little temper to give a man strength."

"You promised a steak. That ought to help, too."

"Doc says you're to take it easy on food."

"Did you get a look at Doc's middle? He hasn't seen his belt to buckle it in years. Ought to take a little of his own advice."

"I must admit, Rafe, there's nothing wrong with your middle."

"Querida, if you're supposed to help me rest, you're not doing a very good job."

Gabby pulled away from the bed. "Then I'll work on getting you stronger. But it's porridge or nothing."

"Ugh! I can wait." He looked at her long and hard

336

and forgot about food. "It's worth it when I'm waiting for the best."

She met his gaze unblinking. "I can't argue with you there, Rafe."

"You must have been in the hall when I cried out earlier. No way you could have heard me from your room."

"I couldn't sleep. Besides, I was keeping the water boiling in case you woke and were hungry. You'll never get your strength back unless you eat, but it has to be something light."

She stood in filtered moonlight, and Rafe was caught by the soft look in her eyes before she turned to leave for the kitchen, so caught that he didn't even complain about the proposed meal. While she was gone, thoughts tumbled through his mind, and he began cursing himself for the fool that he had been. It was as though his lightheadedness was making him see things more clearly.

The first time he'd seen Gabby, he knew right away she was special. In one short hour's time he'd been picturing her at the ranch with him.

What had gone wrong? Earl Hunter and his half-truths about her pursuits.

No, that was too easy. Rafe himself had gone wrong, had been too quick to doubt her purpose, too quick to accuse. And when she didn't rush to defend herself, he'd assumed there could be only one reason—she didn't want to admit the truth. She *was* after his land. She *was* using her feminine charms to soften him up. He'd been so sure he was right.

It hadn't occurred to him to consider how offended she might have been, waiting in a lonely hotel room for her first and only lover to return with more words of tenderness, only to be accosted by a self-righteous, angry fool.

He'd been too hurried all right, just the way he'd been too quick to hunt Dallas Pryor. He'd rushed off into the night with only a boy to back him up.

Too many others paid for his haste.

Gabby returned bearing a small tray with a steaming bowl and cup, a folded cloth beside them.

"We need to talk," he said.

There was a flat determination in his voice that hadn't been there when she left. Gabby concentrated on setting out the food on his bedside table. If she talked too long to Rafe, he would soon figure out that she was up to something. Somehow, some way he would manage, even from his sickbed, to keep her away from the Rancho Perro.

"Not yet," she said, stalling. "First we eat." She fluffed his pillow and put another to prop him up. He ate the sweetened porridge without complaint this time, then sipped at the cup of tea.

"Gabby," he said, setting the cup aside and patting the bed, "come here and lie beside me. No, not that way. You can stay on top of the covers. Matter of fact, it might be better if you do. I only want to talk. And to hold you."

It seemed so little to ask, she thought. Reluctantly, and at the same time eager to feel his arms around her, she did as she was bid. In the comfort of his embrace, she forgot that in a few short hours she must steal away to meet with his enemy.

"Querida," he whispered into her hair. "I need to tell you about San Antonio." He felt her stiffen. "Please

hear me out. I was wrong. Finding out who I was must have been as big a surprise to you as you were to me. Only I was the one who acted the fool."

Gabby pulled back and stared at him. "You don't have to do this, Rafe."

"Yes, I do. I've made too many mistakes lately to let them amount up any longer. It's time I started correcting a few."

"What made you change your mind?" Her voice was so low he could barely make out the words.

"Being with you. Watching you. Learning to —"

Her fingers touched his lips, stopping the words of declaration he wanted to say. Still so many differences stretched between them. She remembered the way he had deceived her about the loan, had let her believe she had power over him.

And now she was keeping from him her plans for the morning. She started guiltily at the thought.

"Not now, Rafe," she said. "I don't know what's on your mind, but it isn't anything that won't wait until you're able to stand."

His fingers stroked the sleeve of her nightgown. "Whatever happened to the girl who was willing to throw herself in my arms?"

"She's right here, Rafe. Only she's grown a great deal more cautious. I . . . I don't want you to think what you're saying is unimportant to me. It's just that we both have a great deal to say, and we need to be sure. No more quick decisions that we'll both regret."

"At least trust me in this. Slip under the covers and let me hold you for a while. In case I have trouble getting back to sleep, you can sing me a lullaby — or something." He grinned. "It'll be a kind of test as to

339

how strong I am. A weaker man would have that gown off of you in seconds, but I've got a will of iron. And I've been told that abstinence builds strength, too."

"Have you ever tried it?"

"I'm being honest with you, Gabby. I'd rather not answer that."

She hesitated for only a moment, then lifted the quilt and slid in next to him. Weakened by his ordeal, he was still stronger than anyone she had ever known. She would draw on that strength, let it seep into her and give her courage to face her morning's challenge. It was a long time before she was able to join him in sleep.

By the time Gabby was ready to keep her appointment the next morning with Earl Hunter, Rafe had at last gotten the steak he'd been asking for — although he'd eaten less than half, claiming the porridge of the night before had killed his taste for food. The man had a positive talent for holding on to an issue until he was sure everyone shared his view.

He'd tried to dress, but the effort had taken its toll and he'd ended up back in bed. "For one day," he'd growled, "that's all I give it."

Some of the saloon girls back in San Antonio ought to see him now, Gabby had thought as she looked down at him. Grouchy, bearded, hollow-eyed. His already lean face had taken on a few lines that hadn't been there before, and his mane of black hair was shaggy and wild. He'd never looked better, she decided, and she'd scratch the eyes out of any woman who came near.

Actually taking her leave came hard.

"You plan to go get the sheriff?" he asked when she walked into his room to say good-bye.

Gabby shifted nervously. She'd added one item of apparel to her riding clothes — a loose vest that was supposed to conceal the small buggy whip wrapped around her body. If Rafe missed it, with the close way he usually looked her over, then she had no doubt Hunter would, too.

She'd wanted to use Cisco's gift, but the size of the handle alone made it impractical. When she'd tried wearing it beneath her shirt, the whip looked like an extra breast. Now *that* Rafe would definitely have noticed.

"The sheriff?" Gabby smiled sweetly at him, glad that telling lies was coming more easily to her. "I promised I would."

Rafe's dark eyes looked up at her with a hint of suspicion. "I can't understand why he hasn't come calling. We could have headed out for the Perro long ago to hunt Pryor."

"You can't even get dressed. How are you going to handle a hostile gunman, or start out on a search for him?"

Rafe ignored her. "Where has Antonio been?"

Antonio had been staying away to keep from being questioned about his futile trip to the Rancho Perro with the sheriff, but she wasn't going to tell Rafe that. He'd told Gabby last night he wanted to wait one more day before telling Rafe about Cisco's missing grave and Dallas Pryor.

"Doc Crites said you're not to receive visitors.

341

Beside, Antonio's leg has been giving him some trouble," said Gabby. "Doc told him to stay off of it. And he"—the implication was clear—"plans to follow orders. You might consider doing the same."

Gabby let herself out of the bedroom just as a pillow hit the door. Excitement hummed beneath the surface of her calm exterior, an excitement that grew as she saddled Tempest and rode out once again. The air was clear and the sky a cerulean blue, all signs of the recent storms blown away by the cool October breezes from the north. She might be deceiving Rafe, but she hadn't a doubt she was doing the right thing.

When she rode up to the Perro ranch house, the dogs were nowhere to be seen. This time there was no cigar-chomping Hunter to greet her with his slippery smile. All was quiet, save the pounding of her heart. The hardest thing to do, she found as she walked onto the porch, was to keep from reaching for the whip.

Hunter was a long time responding to her knock, and she wondered if he were playing a game of nerves with her.

"Good morning, Miss Deschamps," he said. "You're earlier than I expected. Please come in."

Nothing suspicious in those words, she thought, and questioned why the nerves at the back of her neck tingled as she followed him toward the room where they'd talked yesterday. In his dark suit, he looked businesslike and ready to deal.

"Coffee?" he asked. They settled into chairs facing each other before the fireplace to the right of his large desk.

"This isn't a social call," she said, then cursed the tension that made her so snappish. It most certainly had social overtones, this getting together to discuss their future.

"I guess," she said more softly, "I just want to get on with our talk. Yesterday I said my waiting for the Seco had seemed a long time. It's easy to grow impatient when the end is near."

Hunter's eyes narrowed. "I couldn't agree more."

Gabby glanced around the room. "So where is the man you wanted me to meet?"

"He'll be here shortly." Then silence.

Gabby's fingers drummed against the arm of her chair. "I've been thinking, Earl," she said. His eyebrows raised slightly. "We need to be very specific about what each of us will get out of our arrangement. So there won't be any misunderstanding."

"How do you mean?"

The man sounded positively dense. "I mean we should spell out in writing what you expect from me and what I expect from you," she said. "Land rights. Percentages of profit. That kind of thing."

"In writing, you say?" Although as far as Gabby could tell he was immaculately clad, he brushed invisible lint from his sleeve. She noticed for the first time how stubby his hands were. "I agree you should know exactly what you have coming," he added.

He reached inside his coat, and she watched in fascinated horror as he pulled from his belt a huge Colt and aimed it toward her. "You can come in now," he said in the direction of the closed door behind him.

The Mexican, of course, Gabby thought. Was this some kind of game the men were playing to intimidate her? If that was the case, it was working. She had never been so terrified in her life.

343

The surprises weren't over. Gabby looked toward the door and watched as Franklin Bernard entered the room, a look of smug triumph on his face.

"Franklin!"

The lawyer was full of surprises, she thought, remembering his unexpected and unwanted assault of the evening before. For one wild moment she thought he'd come to represent her in her dealings with the outlaws, but there was no Mexican with him. Panic rose in her, and she dug her nails painfully into her hands to keep from losing control.

"What is the meaning of this?" She looked from Bernard back to Hunter. "I can hardly do business with a man who pulls such surprises."

Hunter's smile didn't reach his eyes. "Understandable, Gabrielle. I feel exactly the same way." His eyes flicked to Bernard, who had come to stand beside Gabby's chair. "Fool, I told you to bring some rope."

The lawyer made a hasty exit.

"You seem to have him well trained," said Gabby.

"I pay him enough."

Gabby caught her breath. "He was the one back in San Antonio. The one who told you why I had come back to town."

"Too smart too late, Gabrielle," said Hunter. "Franklin Bernard has been in my employ for some time now. Strictly sub rosa, of course. He's not smart enough to gather information for me if it's known he's on my side."

He settled back in his chair. "Not that he hasn't earned his money. You didn't think he was making a social call last night, did you? Ah, I can see you did. You must learn to question motives, Gabrielle. He

344

went under my express orders to learn Rafe's condition—and his plans, in case you weren't being completely honest." He gestured with the gun. "As, of course, you weren't."

Gabby sat stunned. The memory of her conversation last night with the lawyer dimmed the last ray of hope that she might still bluff her way out of the room. She had revealed all to Bernard. And, thanks to her misplaced confidence that she could take care of herself, no one outside the Perro knew where she was.

Bernard's return was less dramatic than had been his initial entrance, and she barely gave him a glance.

"So what are you going to do now? There will be a hundred men coming down on this place if I'm not back at the Seco by afternoon."

"Nice try, Gabrielle. But you've been too protective of your lover to let him know where you are. And he'd never have allowed you to undertake such a foolish mission." With his free hand Hunter reached for a cigar on his desk. "As for anybody else, we can simply deny you were here; or that you stayed. I promise all traces of you will be removed."

"The same way you did with Dallas Pryor?"

Hunter struck a match on the sole of his boot and lit the cigar, his eyes never leaving Gabby. "It was too bad about Pryor, but you must admit there is a certain justice in having him share a grave with his victim. I rather regret not being able to let Rafe know."

"You have a strange sense of right and wrong." Gabby's mind raced. "And does your wife approve of all of this?"

345

For the first time since she'd come into the room, Hunter appeared ruffled. "Sarah is none of your concern. And don't count on her for help. Unfortunately, she was called away this morning to visit a sick relative. No doubt, when she learns the summons was false, she'll return. By then you'll be gone."

"At least tell me what you plan. I'd rather know." Gabby refused to grovel, but was unable to keep her eyes off the gun Hunter had pulled. The bore on it looked the size of a cannon, and his finger seemed to be whitening as he put pressure on the trigger.

Hunter moved the Colt slightly sideways to point to the left of her. "You'll know in time. I'm not going to kill you, if that's what you fear. Unless you give me no choice. No, Gabrielle, I have something entirely different in mind. In fact, if you would only adopt the right attitude, something similar to your mother's perhaps, you might not find the experience altogether unpleasant."

Unmindful of the weapon trained on her, Gabby rose out of the chair and went for Hunter's face with her fingernails. One hand easily seized her wrists, and he raked her cheek with the gun sight, leaving a red welt on her skin. She was helpless to fight him as he twisted her arm behind her. Gabby was enraged to see his cigar still clamped between his teeth.

Hunter held her in a cruel grip, with her arm raised painfully behind her. Suddenly he twisted around and gave a shove that sent her stumbling into Bernard.

"Tie her up," Hunter barked. "Enough of this talk."

Gabby found herself jerked by the shoulders and shoved against the wall. The Franklin Bernard who was staring at her was not the obsequious lawyer she'd thought he was. His eyes bored into her with a look of lust. He held power over her, and he planned to use it however he chose.

Rough hands gripped her, but when he tried to press his wet lips against hers she was ready and this time her fingernails connected. They raked across his flaccid face, leaving a bloody trail on one cheek.

"*Bastardo,*" she hissed.

Behind Bernard, Hunter laughed derisively. "Tie her up, Franklin, the way I told you to in the first place, and take her around to the shed in back. If you can manage it."

Even while she was being yanked about, Gabby noticed Hunter didn't leave until he was certain her hands were securely tied in back of her. He strolled over and ran a blunt finger down her cheek and throat, stopping at the deep vee of her shirt. Gabby held her breath lest he should move lower and discover the whip.

"You were curious about the smuggling, Gabrielle. It is another bit of ironic justice that you should become a part of it. I imagine once Rafe learns what we've done to you, he'll be a little more willing to deal."

The full import of how foolish she'd been struck Gabby, and she couldn't keep the horror from her eyes. That she was in danger was bad enough, but Hunter knew what he was talking about. Rafe would come after her.

All he'd said the night before when they lay together flooded over her. He would come into danger as much for her as for the Seco.

Bernard dug one hand into her upper arm and pulled her down a hall toward the back of the house and out into the backyard. He shoved her inside a small shed, where she stumbled over a paint can and fell against the far wall. With her hands behind her, she couldn't avoid sprawling awkwardly on knees and chin. Behind her Bernard laughed before coming forward to heave her upright.

In the light from the open door they glared at each other. "At least untie the rope," she said. "I can hardly do you harm now."

"I think not," he said and, fingering the huge bolt on the door, he started to back out.

"No!" she cried and flung herself forward. "Don't leave me like this. I'm terrified of the dark."

Bernard's hand went to his injured face. "That's hardly likely to make me do what you want."

Gabby made herself lean weakly against him. In her fright it wasn't hard to do.

"Please. I promise not to try anything." She could almost hear him thinking. She sighed, and without the least effort on her part tears began to roll down her cheeks. Her sob was barely audible in the stillness.

When his hand squeezed her breast, she jerked away.

"That's what I thought," he said in a razor-sharp sneer. Backing out, he banged shut the door to the shed and she heard the bolt slam into place.

She quickly shrugged off the urge to huddle in a corner and give vent to howls of frustration. The darkness held no special fear for her; it was the meanness of Hunter and that no-good lawyer that struck terror in her heart. Knowing she must not remain in their power, she had no time for tears.

First she had to remove the rope. That Franklin Bernard had never tied anyone before was obvious. She'd remembered the lessons Rafe had taught her about keeping the rope snug around a calf's legs; otherwise he would pull free. When Bernard had tied her, she was careful to keep a little slack between her wrists, not enough to be obvious, but a sufficient amount, she hoped, to give her maneuverability.

Even so, freeing herself wasn't easy. She had no idea how long her efforts took, but by putting painful force into stretching the slack in the rope, she worked her bloodied wrists free. Hastily she tossed the rope aside and sat with her back to the wall by the door to wait. In one hand she gripped the small buggy whip that she hoped would bring her salvation.

Imprisoned as she was in darkness, only narrow slips of light floating in from the few cracks in the walls, she studied the interior of her prison but spotted nothing to use for an additional weapon and certainly no way to escape. A wide shelf ran along the periphery some five feet off the ground, but when she tested it she couldn't so much as loosen one nail.

She got up to rattle the door. Its frame was set in concrete and the door itself was heavy and solidly made of oak slabs.

She kicked the empty paint bucket, but decided it was too lightweight to be of any use in her defense. She sat back down in what she judged would be the darkest corner whenever the door was opened once again. It was impossible to judge how much time went by. An hour? Two? It could have been close to dusk

349

for all she knew. She spent much of the time remembering the steak Rafe had left on his plate — and feeling foolish that she should be hungry when her life was in danger.

Her head was nodding when she heard the sound of footsteps approaching the shed. Convulsively she tightened her fist, but the whip was no longer in her grasp. Forcing calmness, she began surreptitiously to grope for her only weapon.

The door was flung wide to reveal Franklin Bernard, his hand shading his eyes as he peered into the dark interior of the shed, his squat figure blocking her path to freedom.

"I've been thinking," he said, "that maybe you need some manners taught."

Searching frantically for the whip, Gabby rose to sit on her heels.

"I hear you breathing. By the time I'm through, you'll be breathing a lot harder than you are now. Try anything like scratching me again, and you may not be breathing at all."

Gabby let him talk, held her breath, kept her hands moving until she found what she'd been seeking. By the time Bernard had closed the door behind him and come looking for her, she had the fallen whip in her hand and was waiting. She had a major advantage. He was used to the sunlight, but she'd kept her eyes away from the brightness streaming in the door. She could see him moving about in the darkness.

She didn't wait long to attack. The crack of the whip split the silence. Just as she'd intended, the leather tip slashed across Bernard's face. With a scream, he backed up, protecting himself with both hands, and she lashed out again, this time striking him across the knuckles.

He cried out, tried to lunge for her, but turned in anguish as the whip landed again and again. Cornered, he turned his back to her in a futile attempt to protect himself. For a brief, mad time Gabby continued her assault, stopping when she saw him drop to the ground.

She flung herself at the door and hurtled outside. Blinded by the bright light, she shaded her eyes and stared wildly about. She was about twenty yards behind the house at the edge of some kind of garden. The barn was visible on the far side of the house. Tempest must be there, and she set out on a run.

When she was less than halfway to her destination, three snarling hounds came racing around the corner of the house, stopping her in her tracks. She raised her whip to strike them, but even over the menacing growls she heard the click of a gun.

"Down, boys." The order was fierce, and the dogs immediately obeyed. Gabby looked past them to the dark-suited figure of Earl Hunter.

"Going for a ride?" he asked, smiling.

There was no arguing with either the dogs or the gun. "I guess not," she said.

"You're a smart woman, Gabrielle. I can imagine how you got free. Bernard again, no doubt. He's been brooding ever since you attacked him this morning."

"Defended myself, you mean."

"Whatever. I suggest you turn around and walk back. And, of course, drop the whip. I can only speculate where you had it concealed. Remind me not to underestimate you again."

Gabby flung the whip into the midst of the dogs and turned to see the lawyer staggering out of the shed, his coat and shirt shredded and stained with blood. She shuddered at the violence within her that could cause such injury. But she also knew she would do it again.

As she neared him, Bernard gave her a wide berth.

"I hope all of Mexico makes use of her," he sneered.

Behind Gabby, Hunter growled in anger. "Get inside and try to clean up. Then head for town. I don't want any sign of you when Rafe comes calling."

Bernard dabbed at his face with a torn sleeve. "What about my money?"

"I'll see that you get it. You've earned it," he said, stepping beside Gabby, "even if you can't put a decent knot in a rope." The dogs were close on his heels.

Gabby made no protest when he gestured toward the shed. Head high, she walked inside.

Hunter stood in the doorway. "I want no repeat performance, Gabrielle. No escape. To ensure your imprisonment, I think you need an extra guard."

Without looking down, he snapped his fingers at one of the hounds and patted him on the head. "Watch!" The command was enough. The dog took a position at the door of the shed, a growl building deep in his throat. Gabby had no choice but to hurry past him into the darkness of her musty prison.

"I suggest you remain inside," Hunter said. "Unfortunately, you'll have to stay there for some time. Senor Ramirez will be along shortly, but he won't be leaving again until he has the protection of dark."

The door slammed shut, and for the second time she listened to the metallic sound of the bolt sliding into place. Somehow it seemed far worse the second time. This time she knew with certainty that there was no escape.

How she managed to sleep, she couldn't imagine, but sometime late in the day she drifted off to blessed unconsciousness. She was slow to awaken when at last the door was opened. The first thing she saw as she blinked into a lantern's light was the hound still at his post. Stiffly she pulled herself to her feet, not even curious as to who had come for her.

When she tried to walk, her knees buckled. A hand came out to assist her, but she pulled herself upright and walked on her own power into the dark of night.

"My compliments, Gabrielle," Hunter said. "You haven't had hysterics once."

"I—" She had to cough to find her voice. "I haven't found it necessary to."

"A point well taken. I have a meal waiting for you inside, as well as your guide on the trip south. Juan Ramirez knows the way well and has assured me it is not difficult. Certainly not for a horsewoman as fine as you."

No doubt he'd been watching her ride up to the house. To his other crimes, Gabby added sarcasm.

Inside, there was still no sign of Sarah Hunter, and Gabby figured the smartest thing she could do now was keep herself strong—or work back toward it. She accepted the plate of beans and hard fried meat that was thrust her way. Tasteless it might be—Hunter had obviously dismissed all the household help and prepared the meal himself—but she wouldn't have enjoyed it regardless of quality. Only the red wine went down easily.

She looked sideways at him at the end of the table. "Don't you have any workers around here?"

"There are plenty in case I need help. I simply chose to keep them away during your brief visit. What a man doesn't know, he can't be forced into revealing."

Halfway through the meal they were joined by the man Gabby had come to meet, Juan Ramirez. She quickly took in his slender frame, well-tailored suit, and trimmed moustache and hair. A dandy, she thought, and immediately began trying to figure out how to use that fact.

Then she looked into his eyes. Black beads, she thought at first, reflecting only the light, telling her nothing about the man. They stared down at her in concentrated study. She shuddered. Ramirez seemed less human than even Earl Hunter.

He moved smoothly to her side and reached out to touch her hair. She pulled away.

"Senor de Leon will be pleased with the offer of such a one. We must, of course, bathe and perfume her, but after the journey." His eyes slid to Hunter. "You have done well."

"Just watch her," Hunter said. "She just looks frail and innocent. She has more tricks in her than . . . than I do."

Ramirez turned his gaze back to her. "Women usually have. It is part of their charm. Only"— beneath the pencil moustache his lip twitched—"this one would be wise to take care. If she tries to get away and I find it necessary to harm her, she becomes damaged goods. And, of course, no use to me. Senor de Leon prefers a lady. One without scars."

"I assume, Senor Ramirez, that means you will kill

me." Gabby held his cold stare.

"Nothing so kind. I will simply find . . . other places where a woman as beautiful as you will be welcome. With men who are not quite so refined as Senor de Leon."

Gabby reached for her glass of wine. *Refined.* She found it hard to imagine the word suiting a man who would buy a *Yanqui* to serve as his concubine. What Ramirez probably meant was that if this de Leon did leave any marks on her body when he used her, he would be careful that when she was dressed they didn't show.

Chapter Sixteen

"Halt, senorita."

From behind Gabby came the voice of Juan Ramirez in the uncompromising tone he'd used during their long trek into Mexico, and just as she'd done every time before, she responded without protest, tightening the reins against the drooping neck of her roan. Tempest came to a weary stop.

There were some things, Gabby figured, she was better off not challenging — and the Mexican's short-bladed knife, worn tucked inside his boot, was at the top of the list. The stiletto could fly through the air like a bullet with unerring accuracy — she'd found that out when she reached for the pot of boiling coffee their first night on the trail, prepared to fling it in her captor's face.

One sleeve of her coat had been pinned to the yellow dirt, and she'd been tied up after that, hands in front of her on horseback. At night she was forced to lie on the hard ground, hands behind her back and attached to her ankles.

Ramirez urged his horse beside hers. "Behold the valley of El Brazo," he said, gesturing grandly in a wide sweep of one hand. "The Arm. It is said to reach from one mountain range to another in an effort to get to Monterrey."

Gabby looked down the steep, cactus-studded slope to the small settlement, which lay bathed in a soft afternoon sun. Across the narrow, mountain-walled valley, thatch-roofed huts grew like mushrooms, each linked together by a silver-ribbon stream. If she hadn't been three days in the saddle and bone-tired, she might almost have appreciated the view.

Almost. Somewhere in that pastoral scene was a man named Porfirio de Leon who would be given the chance—for a goodly fee—to make her his whore. Ramirez assured her she must pray that he did, for her other choices were far less benign.

That this village with no trains and no modern conveniences was their destination came as a disappointment.

"We're not to go to Monterrey?" she asked.

Ramirez nodded toward the far end of the valley. "It is another day's journey. Surely you are tired, senorita, and would wish that Senor de Leon is in his home in the mountains." He grinned nastily. "Although the senor may give you little chance to rest."

Gabby didn't answer but lifted bound hands to wipe sweat from her forehead. Used to the cool travel across the mountains of northern Mexico, she felt the heat rise from the verdant valley. In the middle of October autumn had not yet come to El Brazo.

"Let us proceed, senorita," he said, and once more

she began the journey out of the mountains, this time with a lightening of her heart. At least now, she thought as she flexed her bound wrists, there was a chance she might escape. Besides, friend of Ramirez or not, any change in company would be welcome after three days alone with her thin-faced warden.

On their journey the laughter and high, shrill voices of the Indito mountain inhabitants had sometimes echoed across their path, but other than rare glimpses of them, she'd had no other company.

They hadn't gone more than a dozen yards when Ramirez gestured to a wagon trail cut into the side of the hill to the right. Wordlessly she followed. The pathway was lined with yucca, and agave, the century plant said to blossom once every hundred years, rose like sentinels to guard their destination.

Silently they rode through a gate, its arched top centered with a massive letter *L* scrolled in iron. The house was wedged into the mountainside in tiers, how many she couldn't determine, but most of the walls not protected by land were composed of windows with enough glass, Gabby thought, to replace half the windows in Laredo. No thatch-roofed hut for Senor de Leon.

As they dismounted, she looked around for a sign of guards, but the only person in view was a young Mexican who came from the side of the house and took their horses. Ramirez gripped her firmly by the arm, one long-fingered hand reaching for his boot. He pulled out the knife and slit the rope that had rubbed against her wrists, then led her inside the house.

Even as Gabby stretched the kinks from her tired body, her mind worked furiously. What did she know about this de Leon? How might she use her knowledge? He was rich and powerful, of course, and Ramirez said he would want a lady. That most certainly would let her out right now, with her hair a tangled mass beneath her straw hat and her face no doubt streaked with dirt. Worst of all, after three days on horseback without benefit of fresh clothing, she smelled very much like a stable.

A broad-hipped woman came into the large tiled entry and guided them to a wide room filled with dark, massive furniture and, like the entryway, with many windows, their brocade draperies pulled open to let in the afternoon sun. Standing beside the unlit fireplace, a brandy snifter in his hand, was a man no taller than she, but broad and solidly built. His waist-length black coat was elaborately trimmed with silver threads. His brown face, with its aquiline nose and sharply defined bones, was lined by the passage of years — she estimated his age to be around fifty — but his straight black hair was without gray and grew back at the temples.

As expert eyes flicked over her, Gabby could sense control pass from Ramirez to the man she assumed to be de Leon. He seemed to see through her crumpled clothing and knew exactly what was his to buy.

"I give you greetings, Juan," de Leon said in Spanish, his eyes never leaving Gabby. "You are most welcome in my home."

Ramirez bent at the waist in an obsequious bow. "Senor de Leon, the pleasure is mine, for I bring you a treasure for your consideration. She comes from Senor Hunter."

"Has he grown tired of such a one and seeks to sell her now?"

Ramirez coughed nervously. "Senor Hunter considers her as the other goods he sends you. Somewhat soiled from the long journey, it is true, but I assure you, senor, that she will be well worth the price that—"

A flick of de Leon's eyes stopped Ramirez.

"There is no need to apologize." To Gabby he said, "Come closer, senorita. I would look at you without the light to your back. Ah, that is better." His perusal stopped at her wrists. "Was it necessary to bind you, senorita? This speaks"—his thin mouth twitched—"of spirit. Of fire."

Not, Gabby thought, of the fact she had been forced to the journey, but she refused to speak, instead directing her stony stare into the cold ashes behind him.

"I like a woman with spirit." De Leon slowly circled her. "This time Hunter has done well. I feel certain we can reach an agreement as to her purchase."

He pulled a cord that hung beside the fireplace. The woman who had been in the hall made an immediate appearance.

"Senora Sanchez, my housekeeper," de Leon said. "Please see that the senorita is taken care of."

Fat fingers gripped Gabby's arms and she found herself propelled toward the door. She jerked free and whirled to face de Leon.

"You will make a mistake to deal with Senor

Ramirez over me," she said.

From Ramirez came a low growl, but de Leon silenced him with a snap of his fingers. "And why is this so, senorita?" he asked.

"Because I am not what you want." She held out her hands, palms up. "Are these the mark of a lady? Of course not. They are callused, and the nails are split and torn."

"In time," he said, the twitch again at his lips, "they can be made soft again. How slender they are, and the fingers are long and supple. They can be the instrument of much pleasure for a man."

Gabby dropped her arms, her hands forming fists at her side, her breast seething with anger.

"There is more. I am not an innocent girl for you to despoil, a virgin. I have known a man." She eyed him contemptuously. "After him, anyone else would only be a cause to make me laugh."

De Leon's eyes widened appreciatively. "I think, senorita," he said, "that if I placed you in one of my bordellos in Monterrey, the laughter would soon stop."

Gabby squeezed her hands tightly. She would not quail before such an evil one. If only she could spit in his face, but her mouth had gone dry.

"And I think," she said contemptuously, "I would welcome the honest man who comes seeking relief rather than submit to you."

"You speak of one man, senorita, but there would come a time when you would be asked to . . . provide 'relief' as you say for more than one."

"Senor, you cannot keep me against my will. It is madness. You cannot always watch me. Somehow I will get away. And I will be seeking vengeance on you. Is it not better to let me go now?"

He waved his hand impatiently at Senora Sanchez. "Take her away and do as I bid."

This time she was pulled from the room and through one of the doors that led from the entryway into the interior of the labyrinthine house. So much for trying to use what she knew of de Leon. Apparently he cared little whether she was a virgin—or was even soft and well-groomed. And, Gabby realized, her threats had meant little. He trusted the isolation to keep her prisoner.

A winding staircase emptied onto the narrow hallway of the floor above. In the center of the sumptuous room into which she was taken was a canopied bed as large as the Seco corral. Scarlet covers draped to the floor, and covering a large portion of the ceiling was a gilt-edged mirror.

At one side of the room was a copper tub sunken into the floor. Beside it a sullen-eyed senorita, her full red lips pouting, poured from a bucket of steaming water. Round eyes flashed resentfully at Gabby.

"Josita, see that this one is made clean for our *padron*," ordered Senora Sanchez.

Gabby retreated to the far side of the bed, but the stern-faced housekeeper advanced with implacable purpose. Rather than have her clothes stripped from her body by someone else, Gabby did it herself. The senora eyed her impersonally, then exited, leaving her prisoner to the younger girl's care.

Lowering her stiff body into the hot water, Gabby determined that she would enjoy at least her bath.

Perfumed soap that smelled of lilacs felt luxuriously soothing against her skin, and she used it to clean her hair and body until all trace of the trail was washed away.

Just as Gabby leaned back and was prepared to give in to her exhaustion, Josita shook her rudely to wakefulness.

"Porfirio" — she said his name with impudent familiarity — "comes to inspect what he has purchased."

Gabby came out of the water in an instant and reached for a towel. She barely had time to wrap it around her body before the door opened and de Leon stepped inside the room.

With a snap of his fingers, he dismissed Josita, then turned dark, appreciative eyes on Gabby.

Damp hair clung to her face and neck, and rivulets of water ran down her bare legs to pool on the tile floor at her feet. Clutching at the inadequate towel that brushed the tops of her thighs, she met de Leon's stare.

He nodded curtly but Gabby stood unmoving. He strode over and jerked the towel from her hands, tossing it aside as he stepped back for his inspection. His eyes lingered longest on her breasts and, at last, on the triangle of fair hair between her thighs. Gabby felt herself growing pink with shame, and she began to sidle toward a solid-backed, carved Spanish chair.

She willed herself to think of other things — of Tempest and whether she had been properly seen to, of Rafe and the way he had looked at her before she left.

No, not of Rafe. Not in this room with this man so

close by. Better not to think at all.

De Leon waved his hand at her. "Hide for now. I have seen enough. You are, senorita," he said in a low voice, "not a woman who colors her hair, but one who is naturally fair. Such women are highly prized."

Gabby forced herself to speak. "Then you have decided to keep me."

"Earl Hunter has sent me fine stock before, both women and horses, and promises me much more. But never such a one as you. Such arms. Such legs to wrap around a man."

Gabby gripped the chair back and fought rising panic. "Did Ramirez tell you I will never be contented until I have made my escape?" Her eyes blazed with pride. "Did he tell you I would never willingly submit to you?"

De Leon airily waved aside her words. "All this is of little importance. He tells me that no one other than Senor Hunter knows of your presence in El Brazo. It is not a village on any map, Gabrielle." He extended her name in a long, soft trill. "And Ramirez is too careful a man to leave a trace of your journey."

"You can't keep me here against my will."

De Leon's eyes lightened dangerously. "So you have said. They are brave words. It is foolish to challenge me. And yet it excites my blood. Senor Ramirez drives a hard bargain for a woman who does not have the prize of her innocence, but perhaps you offer that which is far more valuable." He moved closer until she could smell the sickly sweet lotion that he wore. It was almost like a woman's perfume.

"Yes," he said silkily. "I have decided to keep you.

364

You will provide much pleasure for me and for my friends." One hand reached out and stroked her breast. Gabby stepped free of his touch.

De Leon scowled. "I would break you of that habit, fair one," he said, "if I but had the time. Unfortunately, it is necessary for me to take care of business at my home."

Almost forgetting the precariousness of her situation, Gabby looked at him in surprise. "You don't live here?"

"Some of the time, yes. But the family of Porfirio de Leon is an honored one in Monterrey."

"You have a wife?"

"And six little ones." He sounded proud.

Gabby laughed contemptuously. "What a fine husband and father you are."

"I feed them when others about are starving. You will not find the Senora de Leon crying in complaint. But enough of them. You shiver with the cold." He strode toward the door and threw it open. "Josita!"

The girl appeared in the room almost instantly. "Yes, Don Porfirio," she said, her thick-lashed eyes flashing boldly.

"Bring the senorita something to protect her body from the cool air."

De Leon's face hardened. "Take care, Gabrielle. The women of this house can be cruel. I will of course leave orders that you are to be treated as the lady you claim you are not. But if you cross them, I cannot guarantee they will do as I bid."

He turned abruptly and took his leave without a backward glance, leaving Gabby with the resentful young woman.

"Take heed of what the senor says," Josita hissed. She pointed to a large armoire. "Here are clothes that once were mine to wear. May they burn against your skin."

Gabby grabbed up the towel and wrapped it once more around her body. Her eyes stole around the room and rested briefly on the wall of windows that looked out onto the distant valley below.

"It is a long drop, senorita," Josita said softly. "I can only pray that you try to escape."

And you can bet your last peso I most certainly will, Gabby thought as Josita let herself out of the room, locking the door after her.

Gabby immediately set herself to looking for traveling clothes. The massive wardrobe yielded a storehouse of frills and feathers, but not one thing suitable for scaling a wall—if such was to be her lot. Gabby wanted to be prepared for anything. The soiled gabardine riding garb had been left in a heap beside the sunken tub, and without a thought she quickly dressed. Somehow, with her body redolent of lilacs, the clothes smelled all the more of Tempest and of three days on the trail. But there were far worse things than smelling bad.

She spent the remaining hours of daylight studying the terrain outside the room. A formidable sight it was, with only two views—the sharp slope of the mountain at each side of the house and a vertical drop to the pathway where she had turned Tempest over to the stable boy.

Straight down were the open windows of the room

366

below, probably the one where she had first met de Leon, but the knowledge did her little good, for outside those lower windows were clusters of sharp-spined cactus plants more daunting than a row of armed sentries. If she could somehow manage to lower herself to the ground, she'd find herself in a bed perhaps as uncomfortable in its own way as the one her captor planned.

Unless. . . .

A key sounded in the lock, and Gabby pushed aside her thoughts to lunge for the scarlet covers of the bed, pulling them up around her neck just as Josita made her appearance, tray in hand. With little ceremony and less graciousness, the girl dropped the tray on a table beside the bed.

"Eat," was her lone communication before exiting. Again the door was locked.

Gabby was able to force down half the food before giving up to nervous anticipation. She pushed the tray aside.

Sitting in the gathering gloom, she fingered the satin bedcovers. In her mind was a vision of the waiting cactus spines. In frustration she pulled at the slippery cloth. She paused, then tugged again. With grim purpose she took one edge of the top cover and tried with all her might to tear it, and was grateful when she failed. The satin should be strong enough to support her hanging weight.

She leaped to her feet and pulled the covers after her, thanking de Leon for his dissolute ways, without which he might not have had such a large bed and with it acres of satin material.

She tied two bedsheets together and with difficulty added the heavy fringed coverlet, using neat square knots. She jerked tight the last one around the sturdy bedpost next to the window, then paused to caress its satiny contours.

The last square knots she'd tied had been under the patient tutelage of Rafe, and she allowed herself a brief memory of him. The images of him crowded in. She thought of him as she'd seen him on the wild stallion, his muscled legs gripping the horse, one arm raised, his body a thing of graceful beauty as it went about its work.

She saw his brown eyes flashing in anger, in pride of a job well done; Rafe, sooty but triumphant after the fire. And one more: Rafe by the pump in the yard drenching himself in water and moonlight, preparing himself for a night that belonged only to them.

Such memories were an inspiration to hurry back to Texas, and she gave one more tug on her knots. She decided they would hold. The sun had set behind the mountains, giving her the darkness she needed to hide her drop down the side of the white-walled house.

Searching the room in vain for a pair of gloves, she gave thanks for her callused palms. She took a deep breath, then threw the makeshift rope from the window, praying it came near enough to the ground. She swung her legs through the window and took a deep breath before winding the slippery material around her arms and edging her behind off the window sill. Turning to brace her feet on the wall, she scraped a knee and cursed softly. Somehow the imagining of her escape had gone faster and far more safely than the reality.

She forced herself to remember the way de Leon had studied her with open admiration and the way he had fondled her. The memory was enough to overcome any timidity, and she slowly climbed down the side of the building until her booted feet were close to the window below.

Ignoring her aching shoulders, she clung to the satin rope and cautiously inched lower, lower, until she felt one boot touch the bottom of the window frame. Her skirt caught in the spines of a cactus leaf; balancing on the ledge, she pulled it free.

She peered into the open window and was jubilant to see that the room was empty, although a fire had been lit and she feared someone would return soon. Even though she was suspended in the dark in a highly unusual place, all it would take was one glance at the window for someone to see her. Quickly putting the last part of her plan into action, she escaped the prickly guard of cactus by slipping inside the room. Much as she would have preferred hiding her unorthodox ladder, she could see no way to do it and she quickly abandoned the idea.

Sidling around the edge of the room, she stopped at the door and listened. From somewhere in the recesses of the house, she heard the women talking and then the clatter of dishes. With a prayer that her luck would hold, she let herself into the entryway and, emboldened by its quiet emptiness, made a dash for the front door.

The night was cold and overcast—a blessing and a

curse as she headed in the direction she figured led toward the stables. She would stand little chance of escape without Tempest. No doubt the stables, wherever they were in the strange configuration of the place, would house a stableboy or two, and she'd better be prepared to sneak around them somehow.

The pathway ran in front of the house, and she slipped along the edge of light that spilled from the windows. Passing the main building, she stumbled over a boulder and landed painfully on her hands and knees. To her ears the fall sounded like the crash of an oak. She held her awkward position, listening for the scurrying footsteps of her captors. The night settled in around her, and she heard only the hum of cicadas and the hoot of an owl from somewhere on the mountainside.

Gabby pushed aside her fears. Time was her enemy, too. Hurrying away from that house, she concentrated on the dark, squat outbuilding that loomed at the end of the narrow trail. As she opened the wide doors, she listened for a rasp or squeak that would reveal her presence.

All was quiet, save for the restless movement of the animals in their stalls. Gabby's good luck ran out when she found Tempest. The mare whinnied in recognition. From his perch in the loft, a stableboy raised the alarm.

Gabby waited for thundering footsteps, gunshots, the excited voices of a dozen men answering the boy's cries. Instead, the burly figure of one guard came crashing through the barn doors. With his rifle pointed at her head, he was enough.

The stable boy hurried down the ladder, lantern held high. Gabby stared helplessly into the guard's unflinching eyes. Behind him she saw the familiar faces of Josita and the housekeeper.

Josita stepped into the light, and Gabby could read triumph in her wide-set eyes. "Bring her to the house," the girl said scornfully.

Bile rose in Gabby's throat; it had the taste of defeat.

Gabby spent the next week sleeping on a bare mattress in a room locked tighter than the vault to a bank. She had a lot of time to think where she had gone wrong. Heading out into the unknown mountains on foot would have led to certain capture—or worse. Rafe's instructions had not included wilderness survival.

And her downfall in the village would have been even surer. Leading Gabby to her new prison, Josita had let her know the lay of the land. The village existed primarily to receive goods that de Leon would move out to other parts of Mexico and to Texas. Gabby had no trouble figuring out that no import or export tariffs were ever paid as part of the transit.

She rarely saw either Josita or the housekeeper and never the men. The routine never varied. Each morning she was given a fresh pitcher of water for bathing, and three times a day a tray of food was set inside the door and removed an hour later. Gabby was left to pace the room and curse her fate. The irony of her situation was not lost upon her. She was being kept to play courtesan for a wealthy married man and his friends.

When the routine abruptly changed one evening, she knew de Leon had returned. She was returned to the large bedroom from which she had escaped and shown that on the mountainside a vaquero with a huge bandolier across his chest stood guard. Buckets of hot water were brought by Josita and the house-keeper, and Gabby was ordered to bathe. She had no sooner lowered herself into the water when de Leon strode into the room.

His eyes warmed at the sight of her hair pinned carelessly atop her head, her defiant stare, and her breasts curving into the suds of lilac soap. "You are more lovely than I remember, Gabrielle, and it is your good fortune that I forgive your foolish attempt to escape. You will serve me well. For a while. When I have had my fill, you will be taken to work in Monterrey. But until such a time —"

Gabby bit her lip to keep from responding. She would kill herself rather than submit to his plans for her.

"I see you defy me still. I have a way to curb that spirit of yours. Not to kill it, of course. That would be a shame."

He started to leave, then paused. "Tonight is a special one, senorita. I have brought with me from Monterrey a man who offers much in the way of business. In return, I wish to reward him with some-thing special."

De Leon's lips twisted into an ugly smile. "The senor has a special taste for the . . . unusual. He likes

372

to tame the spirit of a woman who is less than willing. You are, of course, such a one."

Gabby's heart turned to stone and she shivered. "Never will I give in!"

"Ah, I am pleased, Gabrielle, that in my absence you have not forgotten how to speak. Even though, I am told, you forgot my words of warning about trying to escape. I think, perhaps, you will be receiving no more than you deserve."

"And I repeat, senor, that the man you have brought will have to kill me before I will be tamed."

De Leon's lips twitched. "I would be sorry, Gabrielle, to lose such an investment as you. My friend has a mad look about his eyes. I think perhaps if you were to suffer death at his hands, it would not be the first time for him. He has even suggested the use of a whip. Of course I told him to bring anything he chooses."

He turned to Josita. "Prepare her," he said and left, closing the door behind him.

Ordering Gabby from the tub, Josita thrust out the clothes she was expected to wear — a sheer black wrapper and underneath it silken hose held in place by a red satin garter belt. And nothing else.

Gabby forced herself to don the ridiculous garb while Josita spread satin sheets once more on the wide bed. When the young woman left, she sat on the edge of the bed and waited for the arrival of the brute de Leon had brought for her to entertain. Her fingers played against the cool satin. At least she had the sheets back again, but she had not the vaguest idea how they could be put to use. As a hangman's noose for her visitor was the best idea she could come up with.

So he was bringing a whip, was he? Now there lay definite possibilities. He'd have no idea what an expert she was. She strolled to the window and looked out at the setting sun. The sound of a window breaking might easily be taken below as one of the brute's more violent aberrations.

The door opened and Gabby whirled around to face her fate. When the man walked into the room, she forced herself to look at him, and she gasped. Staring at her from a distance of twenty feet away, the bullwhip Cisco had given her gripped in his hand, was Rafe.

Chapter Seventeen

Rafe came to a halt close to the scarlet-sheeted bed. "Senorita Deschamps," he said with a slight bow, the bullwhip brushing against his thighs, "I am happy to make your acquaintance. And, naturally, I look forward to the time we will spend together."

Gabby was scarcely aware of his words. *Rafe.* Her mind sang his name, even as her eyes flicked down his long frame, took in the elaborately embroidered suit as black as his hair and as smooth-fitting as skin. The shock of recognition gave way to a physical need that raced through her. He loomed before her like the masterful lover she knew him to be. Somehow in the vast wilderness of northern Mexico, he had found her.

"Senorita." Rafe's lips twisted into an insinuating smile. "Don Porfirio spoke truly. I have often traveled far in search of such as you to tame."

Gabby ignored the sharp edge to his words. He spoke for enemy ears, not hers. Her eyes devoured him. If there were signs of his recent weakness—a tightness in his glance, a gauntness to his cheeks, a pale cast beneath his tawny skin — they were signs that only she could read. She was well aware of how foolish she was being and of how unexpected and inappropriate was her response to his presence. Yet, tremulous with relief and joy, she felt an overwhelming urge to rush into his arms.

The dark, warning look in his eyes stopped her. She was left stunned that in the space of a few seconds she could need him so completely, and fearful that she might actually have given vent to her needs. Summoning her pride and will, she brushed the feelings aside.

Rafe read each thought in the liquid pools of blue that were her eyes. He longed to show his own relief that she apparently had not been harmed. De Leon had indicated he was offering up his golden prize without having first tasted its sweetness, but Rafe had been unable to believe him. The don was hardly an honorable man. And who could resist the beauty looking at him with wide, wonderful eyes? Even in her whore's dress with her dark nipples seductively visible through the folds of the transparent wrapper and the triangle of hair outlined by the thin straps that held her stockings, she looked defiantly majestic.

Anger and terror that she should have placed herself in such danger had sent him hurrying across the border to bring her safely back to Texas. He'd come prepared to interject himself into whatever situation faced him and to slip out undetected with Gabby under his arms — quite literally, if necessary. And here he was moved by her as much as he'd been the first time they met. No, much more than that. Then he had only speculated about the woman she could be.

Now he knew she was everything that he had imagined, and more.

"Senorita," he said, barely able to keep his emotions in check, "Don Porfirio does not lie. You have much to offer a man."

There was a little too much warmth in his voice for Gabby to believe he spoke only to the unseen de Leon. He shared her brief flare of desire. She would need time to explain why she'd gone to see Hunter without him—and how she'd gotten herself trapped. And then would come a long time of consolation as they gave in to their needs.

But first they must escape. Gabby forced herself back into her role of defiant captive. "Never," she hissed, "will I submit."

"Never?" His voice was a challenge. "I think there you are wrong." For one brief, tantalizing moment a glimmer lit his eyes.

Gabby dropped her gaze. If he kept looking at her like that, she would find it impossible to avoid leaning against him and telling him how glad she was he had come.

By the time she looked up, the curtain of coldness was back in his eyes.

Gabby looked toward the open door to de Leon's pleasure dome and saw a shadow cross the threshold. She flung her head back proudly. "Be very careful how you use me, senor. You will pay for your passion."

"These are words to warm my heart." He raised the whip. "There can be pleasure in pain, as I will soon demonstrate." He turned at the sound of footsteps, in the process putting himself between Gabby and anyone who might walk into the room. "Ah, Don Porfirio, you are a man of your word. The senorita does indeed promise fiery delights."

"You will find, Rafael, that I am always a man of my word. In my own way. If I promise goods, whether bars of silver or a woman, I will deliver. And I expect the same."

"Do not doubt me, Don Porfirio. You will receive everything I have promised. You deliver such a treasure to me as this Gabrielle, you should receive fair payment. I think we are men who were meant to deal with one another."

"The treasure is yours, Rafael, but it will also be mine, you understand." De Leon cast dark eyes on the whip and then toward the ceiling. Gabby's eyes followed his gaze, and for the first time she noted that the designs around the overhead mirror were really slots through which an onlooker might view the proceedings below.

She started backing away from the men, but a sharp glance from Rafe stopped her.

"And," de Leon went on, "you must not leave her scarred where she will not be desirable in Monterrey."

"I know what I am about," said Rafe. "The marks will be few and will soon heal. I, too, am a man of my word. Watch, if you will. It makes no difference to our original arrangements. The senorita will not be damaged unreasonably. And you will collect from many once she is tamed."

Gabby knew she should have been terrified for Rafe's safety, as well as for her own, but the longer he stayed bartering with their mutual enemy, the stronger became a curious kind of nervous gaiety and confidence that had overcome her. Rafe would have come with a plan.

"I ask an indulgence of you, Don Porfirio," said Rafe.

"Of course, Rafael."

"I find myself quite wearied by our journey from Monterrey and would like refreshment before undertaking what might prove to be a rather strenuous activity."

Gabby listened in admiration at Rafe's ability to dissemble. Ever since he had come into the room sending her messages with his eyes, he'd sounded alternately menacing and foppish. Right now he reminded her of the young men who'd called at Miss Martha Emmett's.

But only by the tone of his voice. The strenuous activity he was referring to was far more than just a chaste kiss stolen in the shadows beside the school, involving as it did satin sheets and a whip. And de Leon, polite host that he had now become for another man, was equally polite in his agreement to brandy and a light repast.

"Perhaps Senorita Deschamps would join us," Rafe said.

Gabby took her cue. "Perhaps in a more appropriate dress," she said. To her great relief de Leon bowed.

"As you wish . . . for now," he said.

Rafe turned to follow his host. "Do not spend an overlong time. You will not be dressed for long." His cold tone of voice belied the warm glow in his chocolate eyes.

As soon as the door shut upon them, Gabby threw herself into searching the contents of the wardrobe for a costume that would give her protection should she and Rafe have to ride cross-country. For a minute she wondered if perhaps an ostrich hadn't at one time molted inside the wardrobe—if ostriches did, indeed, molt.

She settled on a forest green silk dress with long sleeves and a belled skirt that dragged the floor and hid her riding boots. She topped the dress with a thin but brightly colored and fringed shawl that would serve to hide the low cut of the neckline. As she walked through the unlocked door of the room, she felt a little like a gaudily plumed bird let free of its cage. Sliding her hand down the banister of the wide stairway, she descended on tiptoe.

Of immediate concern was the indelicate clomp of her booted feet on the tiled floor, which forced her to take mincing, small steps. When she entered the room where she'd first met de Leon, she lowered the shawl to display the curve of her breasts. Leers from Rafe and de Leon told her neither would ever notice her boots.

Rafe rose to his feet, and de Leon followed suit. They all seemed to be playing a game, as though she were a lady coming down to dine. As though one of them wasn't supposed to take her upstairs shortly and beat her until she gave in to his sexual desires. As though the other didn't plan to watch.

"Gentlemen," she said in greeting, allowing Rafe to waft her to a chair beside his and away from that occupied by de Leon. She sat at the edge of the seat, her booted feet primly placed together beneath the folds of green silk.

The men returned to their brandy—an expensive French import, Gabby noted, remembering Erin had once called it special stock for special customers at her Hidden Nugget Saloon. De Leon's brandy was smuggled goods, Gabby figured. She accepted a glass from Rafe, wrinkled her nose at the burning sensation caused by the tiniest of sips, and settled in to listen for clues in Rafe's words as to exactly what he planned.

"Your home is unique, Don Porfirio," he said. "It must offer great protection."

"Such is the truth, Rafael. There is need for few guards, but if such a need arises I need only to sound a bell that echoes across the valley. A man in my business finds such a retreat of great benefit."

What, Gabby wondered, did de Leon think was Rafe's business? And, for that matter, what name was Rafe going by? Surely not Jericho. De Leon obviously considered Rafe a citizen of Mexico who offered access to some goods—perhaps the silver bars he had mentioned. Had Rafe set himself up as a source of the precious metal?

And, come to think of it, how had Rafe managed to work himself into the smuggler's confidence so quickly, enough so that he would bring him to his love den hideaway? Rafe Jericho did, indeed, display a variety of surprising and useful talents. The list of questions she planned to put to him as soon as they were free kept growing.

The housekeeper slipped into the room and set down a tray of cold meats and bread. Now much at home, Rafe helped himself. Again Gabby followed suit, wondering if she shouldn't be trying to hide some of the meat for the flight back to Texas. If that was what Rafe had in mind. For all she knew, he might well be taking her into Monterrey for their reservations on the Laredo train.

She talked little, choosing instead to watch closely and simper at each man when it seemed necessary. Rafe took it upon himself to tell Senora Sanchez that she would no longer be needed and could retire for the night.

The brandy flowed freely between him and de Leon, but Rafe no longer offered her a drink, concentrating instead on filling de Leon's glass and pouring little into his own. Nevertheless his voice grew loud and his words slurred. She thought it an obvious ploy, but then Rafe seemed to know what he was about; De Leon never refused a drink, and at each one Rafe and Gabby cast sly, knowing looks at each other. De Leon would not be in shape to accompany them upstairs and look through his peephole above the scarlet-sheeted bed.

Time passed slowly, but at last Rafe stood and stretched his long body. "The hour grows late, and I have much that awaits me, Don Porfirio," he said. Gabby rose, and their host began struggling to get out of his chair. Each one watched him narrowly. Finally he fell back in his chair, murmuring to himself.

"There is no need for you to rise," Rafe said. "I know the way. And, I think, the senorita will be most willing to please me in everything that I demand."

"It is so," de Leon said.

Rafe indicated the door, and Gabby began the long walk in front of him. His hand touched her waist, and with a squeeze, he guided her away from the stairs. Behind them they could hear de Leon pour himself another drink. The housekeeper was nowhere in sight. Could their escape really be this easy?

Drawing Gabby back beside him, Rafe grasped the outside door handle and eased it open. Instead of welcome darkness and solitude, he found himself face to face with another visitor, his hand raised to signal his late arrival with a knock.

"Rafe Jericho!" The man exploded with the name. His narrow eyes darted from Rafe to Gabby. "Senor de Leon," he shouted, at the same time reaching for his boot.

"It's Ramirez. He has a knife!" Gabby screamed, flinging herself against him.

The unexpectedness of Gabby's movement sent her and Ramirez sprawling to the ground. Strong hands lifted her into the air and thrust her aside just as Ramirez came up with the knife, its long, slender blade glinting in the moonlight. He scrambled to his feet. Rafe pulled his own knife from the recesses of his sleeve and ran down the walkway after him. Another talent, Gabby thought in amazement as the blade clicked into view.

"I think I will kill you," Ramirez said, assuming a fighting crouch, the knife at shoulder level.

Rafe matched his stance, and the two men circled each other, first one and then the other lashing out to keep their distance steady. Gabby fought down her rising panic. Someone would be coming along to back up Ramirez, and she knew who that would most likely be.

Trusting Rafe to handle Ramirez, she headed for the house. De Leon wasn't so far gone that he shouldn't have heard Ramirez's cry. Any second she expected him to raise the alarm. Seizing the whip from off the entryway table where she'd seen it on her descent of the stairs, she ran toward the main room. She entered just as de Leon was pulling a pistol from the center drawer of his desk.

He looked up in amazement, swaying on his feet, his hands fumbling with the gun. With a cry of triumph, she raised the bullwhip and lashed out. The tip wrapped around de Leon's gun hand, and the pistol clattered to the floor. With his free hand de Leon grabbed for the whip, but Gabby pulled it out of his grasp and again sent it lashing out to land with stinging accuracy against his face. A thin, red line of blood spurted as if by magic across his cheek. A low growl came chillingly to Gabby's ear as he stumbled around the desk and came for her.

Gabby bought precious time with a few slashes of the whip, but de Leon was no Franklin Bernard who could be intimidated forever with such a maneuver. Her next movements were instinctive. De Leon was a snake. And snakes were afraid of fire.

Pulling off her shawl, she flung one end of it into the fireplace. The fringe burst into flames, and she dragged the garment back onto the floor. De Leon went for the fire, his second major mistake of the day. Trusting Rafe had been the first. Gabby jerked the shawl out of his grasp and, running across the room, threw it against the draperies at one end of the tall windows.

Flames crackled up the heavy brocade, just as Josita and the housekeeper ran into the room. De Leon rushed toward the windows, too occupied with the danger of fire to give them notice. Gabby was more confident with the whip where the women were concerned, and she forced them against the wall with a few loud cracks. Grabbing up the brandy, she sent the bottle crashing against the hearth. More flames issued forth, and this time, shoving mightily with a booted foot, she added to the conflagration the chair in which de Leon had been sitting.

A quick glance over her shoulder told her de Leon was losing his battle with the burning brocade. Flames licked toward the ceiling, and she hurried past the frightened women toward the front door. She'd given them enough to do without bothering to chase after her.

Outside, Rafe was having his own troubles. Whoever this Ramirez was, he knew his way with a knife and had managed to slash across Rafe's left sleeve and into his arm. The cut was shallow, but it served as warning that Rafe might have met his match. He could give little attention to wondering where Gabby had gone—and why she hadn't returned.

The rustle of silk in the doorway behind Rafe gave him the advantage he needed. In the fraction of a second it took for his opponent to react to the sound, Rafe kicked savagely at the Mexican's knee, sending him buckling to the ground. Before Ramirez could regain his footing, Rafe came at him, swinging the blade in an arc, slashing across his chest through the layers of cloth, laying open the skin to the bone.

Ramirez pulled himself upright, looked down incredulously at his red-soaked clothes, and pitched forward, impaling himself on Rafe's upturned knife. He was dead by the time he hit the ground.

It took a powerful yank to free the knife, and Rafe folded it once more up his sleeve. He turned to find Gabby staring in silent horror at the body sprawled across the walkway. He noticed with satisfaction the whip in her hand. Most obviously Gabby had learned her lessons well, for there was no armed and dangerous Porfirio de Leon charging up behind her.

Instead, he saw over her shoulder a red glow through the open door. For the first time he inhaled the acrid smoke that was rapidly filling the air.

"Let's get out of here," he said, grabbing her arm.

"Lead on," she said.

With a grunt of satisfaction, he pulled her after him across the front of the house in the direction of the stables. As they hurried in front of the windows where the fire was blazing in full force, Gabby decided that in its proper place fire could be a beautiful sight.

On the floor inside the stables Gabby was surprised to see the bound and gagged figures of the stableboy and the burly guard who had captured her a week ago.

Rafe grinned at her surprise. "I insisted on rubbing down my own horse," he said. "The don went on inside."

With the first signs of smoke drifting into the darkened barn, the horses whinnied nervously. Gabby had no trouble finding Tempest. Precious seconds were spent locating the bridle and saddle, and in her nervousness she found herself fumbling around in a way she hadn't done since early in her riding career.

Masterful hands took over, and within minutes, they rode past the burning house, Rafe mounted on a fresh stallion he had selected from among the fine choices in de Leon's stable. Strapped to his thigh was a pistol that had been with his saddle. Already they could hear the sound of horses fast approaching from

386

the village.

They turned left up the path that led into the mountains, the same path Gabby had ridden down a week ago. Only this time she rode with a man she trusted. This time her hands were free.

Overhead a bright moon sent its muted rays to light their way, and Rafe rode with such assurance that Gabby could only assume he knew where he was heading. She followed, silently concentrating on keeping to the trail.

Sometime later, just as the moon was fading from view, they came to a mountain stream, and Rafe pulled up.

"We'll stay here for the night."

Rafe sprang down and lifted Gabby from the saddle. Able to take care of herself, she willingly gave into his ministrations. Their eyes met for a moment, and their hands, as he set her on her feet. A brief smile lit his face, then he turned and pulled out two bedrolls from behind his saddle. "Brought 'em with me from Monterrey," he said. "Roll them out over there," he said, gesturing well off the path, "while I take care of the horses."

Gabby was in awe of his control of the situation and of his preparedness. When he returned, she half expected him to be carrying a tray with tea and biscuits. Or, considering the tenacious set of his mind, a bowl of porridge prepared especially for her.

What she got was a canteen of fresh mountain water. It tasted like champagne.

Gabby didn't know what she expected next, but it certainly wasn't for Rafe to drop like a dead weight onto the nearest blanket.

"Are you all right?" she said anxiously.

"Try to get some sleep, Gabby," he said gently.

"What about your cut?" she asked, remembering the slash across his left sleeve.

"It's not serious. I washed it in the stream."

"But—"

"Tomorrow. We'll have to get an early start. They'll be after us once the fire is taken care of."

She would have argued further, but she remembered the tightness of his face and the pale cast to his skin when he had first come into her room this evening. He wasn't as tough as he would have her believe, and she was soon greeted by the sound of even breathing which forestalled anything she might have said.

Gabby tugged her blanket closer to his and huddled against his back, pulling the warmth of his body into hers. Her arms stole around him, and within minutes she joined him in sleep.

It was not yet daylight when she heard him rustling about saddling the horses. Cursing her inappropriate dress, she struggled out of the blanket and then immediately dove back into its protective warmth. As high in the mountains as they were, the air must be close to freezing. Gabby quickly decided she wasn't as tough as she wished.

Another canteen of water was offered her, this time accompanied by berries that Rafe had collected close to the stream. Downing breakfast quickly, she headed out to take care of her morning ablutions. When she returned, her hair was plaited into two long braids and the hem of her dress was pulled up between her legs and tucked into her waistband to form a rough imitation of the divided skirt she'd been forced to leave behind.

Rafe needed only one look at her bare shoulders and half-exposed breasts to shrug out of his coat and hand it to her.

"You'll be cold," she said.

Ignoring her protest, he rested the coat on her shoulders, and Gabby covered his hands with her own. She studied the lean lines of his curiously gentle eyes. "I knew I'd see you again, Rafe, but I thought you would be angry."

Rafe grinned. "I won't disappoint you, Gabby. Once I get you back to Texas, you've got a lot of explaining to do."

"I was only trying to protect you from Hunter."

Rafe pressed his fingers against his lips. "Later. Either the fire is out or the place burned to the ground," he said, looking back toward El Brazo. "In any case, someone will be coming along. You're not out of danger yet."

"For what it's worth, Rafe, de Leon never really touched me. He was gone most of the time. Besides," she said, smiling, "I figure with that riddled ceiling, all he really wanted to do was watch. I guess that was why he brought you along."

Rafe slowly winked. "*Querida*, we could have given him quite a show."

Gabby's heart caught in her throat, and she fought the urge to caress him. Later, he had said. He'd been referring to his postponed anger. Gabby was thinking of something else.

"Shouldn't we be moving on?" she said.

Rafe grinned. "Only you could make me forget de

Leon and his men."

"And there's still Hunter, remember. We've got a great deal to take care of, Rafe."

With a brisk nod, he led out. All day they rode fast, stopping occasionally for water and what they could forage to eat. Rafe seemed to know the country, and she figured he must have ridden often into Mexico. They kept to the narrow trail, staying away from the Indito settlements and an infrequent mountain village. There would be no one to tell their pursuers which way they had come, or when.

As Gabby rode, the questions mounted in her mind. Chief among them was how Rafe had known where to find her. And he'd never really told her why he'd come. She especially wanted to hear what he had to say about that.

On his larger horse, Rafe was always slightly above her as he led her through the wilderness. He seemed bigger than he actually was. He was bareheaded, and his dark, tousled hair curled down to the gleaming white collar of his tucked evening shirt. The shirt stretched tautly across his shoulders. She memorized each movement of his muscles as his arms went about their business of guiding the horse. She imagined them rippling under her hands. She hoped never again to see Rafe's rangy body still and injured. His body spoke only of life.

During the times they walked the horses to rest them, he often turned to her and then she could look at the tanned throat rising from the vee of his shirt. Later seemed a long time away.

The second night passed much as the first, both of them too tired to talk much but lying in comfort together. It wasn't until early the next morning that they noticed signs of pursuit. The ground had leveled out and in the distance to the south they saw a cloud of dust. Gradually they could make out riders marking good time now that they weren't impeded by mountain trails. How many neither could say.

Slowly the pursuers narrowed the distance between them. At times they disappeared into an arroyo, only to rise a little closer still riding hard.

The first break for Gabby and Rafe came as they discovered a shallow, rocky stream. On the opposite bank was a small herd of cattle grazing at the water's edge.

Rafe fingered the Colt in its holster. "We'll ride into the water, then you head downstream," he said. "I'll be right along." He rode on across straight into the midst of the herd. A little prodding set the animals in motion, destroying any tracks that might have shown whether or not he and Gabby actually crossed the stream.

Rafe quickly caught up with Gabby, and they rode two hours as fast as the water would allow them. Finally he picked a rocky bank on the south side of the stream for their route onto dry land. De Leon and his men would assume they were headed north and would search that shore for their point of exit.

Exploring a thick copse a half mile away, they came upon an abandoned barn set in the midst of some tumbledown sheds.

"We'll hole up here for a while," Rafe said. "Until we're sure it's safe to venture out."

Gabby gave him no argument. Any minute she expected de Leon to come thundering up behind them, his guns blazing.

The barn was musty and one wall leaned precariously inward, but it had two advantages that made it seem a palace: hay for the horses and refuge from searching eyes. Rafe motioned for Gabby to position herself in the doorway as lookout while he took care of their mounts.

Using the Mexican jacket as a pillow, Gabby collapsed against the splintered frame of the door and tried to concentrate on the route that led back to the stream, but her eyes kept drifting to Rafe moving about in the semi-darkness. Her heart warmed at the sight. No matter how precarious their situation, she would rather be with Rafe than anywhere else on the face of the earth.

When at last he dropped down beside her in the shadows, she could hold back her questions no more.

"How *did* you find me, Rafe?"

"You can thank Sarah Hunter for that."

"Sarah!" The answer seemed incomprehensible to her.

"Hunter did a little bragging to her. He finally went too far."

"But why would she want to save me?" Gabby knew the answer as soon as she spoke and added softly, "She did it for you. Because you wanted to know."

"She did it because she couldn't stand the knowing. Sarah is a good woman who got caught in a situation she couldn't handle. Hunter did a good job of fooling her father."

"Did Sarah know about Porfirio de Leon?"

"She'd heard stories about him. Primarily through some man named Juan Ramirez who worked for both de Leon and Hunter. I gather he's the one who tried to stop us."

Gabby remembered Ramirez falling on the knife. Twice Rafe had been forced to kill to protect her. She kept her gaze steady on the stretch of land outside the barn. "He must have seen you back in Texas sometime and recognized you as soon as you opened the door."

"If he'd been more in control, he'd be alive now. I wouldn't have recognized him from Benito Juarez," Rafe said.

Gabby reached out and touched his hand. "You did what you had to do, Rafe. I . . . I always seem to get you into situations where you have to—"

Rafe sat still and quiet, and she pulled back her hand. "De Leon said he met you in Monterrey. How did you get down there so fast?"

For the first time since they'd come into the barn, Rafe's expression lightened. "As a matter of fact, I caught the train out of Laredo."

"The train!" she said in a fervent whisper, thinking of her long, uncomfortable ride.

"I was almost rested by the time I got there and approached de Leon."

"He certainly accepted you quickly, to bring you out to El Brazo."

"Sarah again. We owe her a lot of thanks for watching and listening to what was going on around her. And for deciding to act. She gave me a few names to drop. De Leon was ready to believe I had access to a huge supply of silver and wanted his help in setting up a smuggling route into the States. Greed will do crazy things to a man, even a wily rascal like

393

him. He couldn't even decide whether to keep you for himself or use you as an investment."

In the rear of the barn, the horses began to stir, and Rafe jumped to his feet. Gabby followed him.

"Could be someone's coming," he said. "Take care of Tempest."

Breathlessly Gabby nodded and imitated Rafe, holding the roan's nose to prevent any sound that might betray their hiding place. Cracks in the old wall allowed them to look outside. No one appeared, but still they waited long, worried minutes.

Gradually Gabby became aware of Rafe standing beside her in the narrow stall. She felt his breath on her cheek.

"Do you think anyone will come along?" she asked, unable to look up at him.

"I doubt it. This is a wide country. We could be anywhere."

Gabby breathed a sigh of relief. "Then I guess we'll be starting out again."

"Better wait until morning. Just to be safe."

Gabby nodded. "It'll be warmer sleeping in here." Her hands rubbed against the cold silk sleeves of her dress. "I sure wish I had something else to wear. I feel guilty always keeping your coat."

"You never seem to have the right clothes for the predicaments you find yourself in."

She raised her head defiantly. "Don't tell me you're going to mention the range fire again."

"It seems I don't have to. You did it for me."

Gabby gave Tempest a pat and strode back toward the barn door where it was light. She heard Rafe behind her and she stopped, still in the shadows, waiting for him to slip his arms around her, to caress her, to tell her how glad he was that she was all right.

When he didn't, she turned around and was startled to see him staring at her from out of the dark.

"Gabby," he said huskily.

It was there in his eyes, all the longing she herself had been feeling since she'd first seen him back at de Leon's. With a low cry, she flung herself into his arms.

Chapter Eighteen

Gabby slipped easily into Rafe's arms, and they clung to one another, his fingers massaging the nape of her neck, the gentle curve of her back and waist. Even knowing she had come to no harm, he wanted to hold her, to touch her and make sure she was all right. As if his touch could forever erase for both of them the memory of her nightmare in Mexico. As if his touch could at once and for all time make her his.

Slender and strong, fragile and invincible, Gabby was everything to him. He held her tightly. How frightened he had been and how angry when she'd disappeared, but nothing matched the emotions tearing through him now.

"I thought you were lost to me," he whispered into her hair. His lips kissed their way to her mouth, a gentle touch that gradually deepened.

Gabby trembled against the power and wonder that was Rafe. Everything that she had done since the range fire had been for him, and she'd succeeded only in placing him in jeopardy. Somehow he had neutralized her foolish mistakes and had rescued her. In a world that could hold such peril as she had faced and the equally insidious desolation of loneliness, he was her *refuge primitif*. The miracle was that he could still want her as much as she wanted him.

The past days of torment gave way to the exhilaration of the moment. Their lips parted, and Rafe pressed soft kisses against her eyes, the corners of her mouth, the hollow at her throat. When he pulled away, she felt dizzy and lost and reached out to rest both hands against his chest.

He kissed the tips of her fingers, the palms of each hand, then drew her onto the thick pile of straw in one of the darkened stalls. Taking her into his arms, he gazed into her face, then removed an endearing piece of straw caught in a wisp of curl that had worked loose from her braids. Slowly he unplaited her hair, running his fingers through the long, golden strands before reaching to the closure at the back of her dress. With maddening slowness he worked at the buttons. His fingers burned against her skin as he moved slowly down her back.

Strange, Gabby thought, how he could touch one part of her body and her whole being responded. Her breasts ached for the feel of his hands and lips, hot blood coursed through her veins.

She kept her gaze on his face as he worked. Neither seemed to breathe. Black hair fell carelessly across his forehead, and his strong, lean face was shadowed by the beginnings of a beard. She ran fingers down his cheeks, thrilling to the rough texture of him. She longed to feel that roughness brushed against her soft, exposed skin. He leaned closer to reach the last of the buttons, then bent his head for one long kiss before leaning back to gaze at her once more.

Gabby thrilled that each time of lovemaking with Rafe was more exciting than the last. When he looked at her, his eyes were dark and searing. They were the color of desire.

Rafe saw his passion mirrored in the depths of her incredible blue eyes. He forced himself to move slowly, pulling the green silk from her shoulders to expose the fullness of both dark-tipped breasts. She turned slightly, and her head fell back against his arm. He smoothed the masses of loosened blond hair, kissed her creamy neck. He stroked each breast until Gabby felt a throbbing need invade her, beginning at the tips where his hands delivered such exquisite torture and coursing downward.

With sure movements he continued his gentle assault with his hands, slipping the dress from her body, caressing her smooth, ivory skin. When she was naked before him, he stretched out beside her and nestled her against him.

"The hay, Gabby. Is it too rough against your skin?"

She brushed her face against his and rejoiced in its firm masculinity. "Better than satin, Rafe," she whispered softly into his ear. "Better than the finest down."

An image of a scarlet bed flashed across his mind, of a mirrored ceiling with apertures bored into its intricate design. Had she remained with de Leon she would have found shame on the satin sheets, and pain from the cruel man who would have been her master. Forgetting gentleness, forgetting all tender concern, Rafe claimed her lips in a demanding kiss, his plundering tongue probing the dark recesses of her mouth. Only Gabby could erase the nightmare of his almost losing her.

Gabby responded with the same urgent need. Her hands ran frantic strokes across his chest, cradled his face, played through the thick hair curling at the edge of his collar, and at last pressed against the taut muscles of his back to hold him tight against her naked breasts.

Rafe leaned back only far enough to unfasten his shirt and pull it aside to feel the fullness of her breasts against his own naked body. His hands burned a trail down her spine, cupped her buttocks, and settled her firmly against his pulsating manhood. She rubbed against the material of his trousers and her undulating hips drove him to the brink of madness.

"Now, Rafe, now," Gabby whispered breathlessly, pulling at his waistband. His fingers brushed against hers as he took over the task of unfastening his clothes. She dropped her hand inside the opening of his pants and held him for one ecstatic moment. His own hand pressed against hers, but she needed no lesson to know how to please him. Pleasing—and teasing—Rafe came high on her growing list of delights.

Rafe felt himself losing control, and with a strength

of will that he almost regretted, he pulled her hand away. He stood to strip his body of its unwanted clothes, then lay beside her, his hands and lips touching, caressing, inflaming Gabby to a fervor that matched his own.

When he bent his head to her breasts, Gabby found the roughness of his beard as thrilling as she'd known it would be. His tongue played an erotic tune on her body as his fingers moved lower, stirred the soft triangle of hair between her thighs, burned against her skin.

With a naturalness born of love, she opened herself up to his loving caresses, trembled at the intimacy, and at last shuddered under the relentless touch of his hand.

Rafe shifted his body to lie beside her, kissing and stroking her until he was sure she was ready for him, then moved between her thighs. He entered in a slow, extended movement. The gentleness lasted for only one sweet moment as desire curled through them both, driving them to frenzied thrusts that both gave and demanded satisfaction. Made savage by their passion, they existed only for the moment. Whatever peril awaited them outside their roughly built paradise ceased to exist.

Rapture enfolded them, held them in its powerful grip that for one electrifying moment seemed extended to the edge of time, then slowly released them to an awareness of time and place.

Gradually the world intruded. In a nearby stall the horses shifted. Light from the lone window of the barn drifted overhead, pale and indecisive as if it hated to intrude. Dust motes danced in its muted beam.

Still they clung to one another, as if in doing so they could ward off unwelcome sights and sounds. Much as she wanted to prolong the peace and oneness that their union had brought, Gabby found herself unable to remain still and silent.

"Rafe," she whispered.

"Yes, *querida?*" He held his breath, waiting for words of love.

"I'm afraid, with my mind on other things a little while ago, I spoke too hastily."

He pulled back and looked down at her, concern in his eyes. Gabby was upset about something. Had he displeased her? Even as the thought occurred to him, he brushed it aside. If there were one thing he knew, it was that she had enjoyed as much as he their stolen moments in the barn.

"What's wrong, Gabby?" he asked.

She scratched at her arm. "The straw. I guess when you come right down to it, satin sheets do have their advantage. In the proper setting."

Rafe threw back his head and laughed, then planted a short, firm kiss on her lips. "Of all the things you could have said, *querida,* that was the one I least expected."

Reluctantly he let go of Gabby and unwound his long, lithe body to stand beside her. He reached down and, taking her hand in his, pulled her to her feet. "Think you can stand to wear the dress for a few more

401

hours?"

Gabby shook free of the hay that clung to her hair, which fell in long, golden curls against her shoulders and her breasts still swollen from Rafe's touch. "If you can stand to look at it."

Rafe stroked her face. "Of that you should have no doubt. We must talk when we arrive back at the Seco."

"Talk. Of course we must." She kept her voice steady.

"First I will see you safe. And then. . . ." A look of rigid determination shadowed his face. "Then Earl Hunter will pay for what he has done. To Cisco and to you. I believed his lies in San Antonio, Gabby. About your knowing who I was. I was wrong to believe him."

Gabby caught her breath. She reached up and touched his hand, which lay gently against her cheek.

"And I was wrong not to defend myself, Rafe. I let you believe the worst because I was hurt. I wanted only. . . ." She paused. Somehow she could not tell him she had only been after a home. It would sound as though she were asking him to provide that home, to take her in and to keep her. Such an idea must come from him.

Rafe's eyes held hers for a long moment, and she tried to read what was on his mind. Never had he reiterated words of love and marriage, not after Hunter had spread his poison. Whatever feelings of commitment Rafe had harbored then had not returned. For a while love had flared in his heart; when

402

it died, only physical desire had burned in its place.

Gabby knew beyond all doubt what he wanted to talk about. She looked away to hide the pain in her eyes. Rafe enjoyed her presence, even thrilled to their mating, and he was in no hurry to let her go. But she was a Cordero, the daughter of a courtesan. He would keep her, all right, but what he had in mind was far different from the offer of a home. He would not want her as the mother of his children.

In the stillness she worried that he could read her thoughts, and she spoke in a rush. "There's one other thing I'd like to clear up, Rafe. The loan. I never intended to take over the Seco. Not, of course"—her voice softened—"that I ever could have."

"You know about my visit to Judge Russell? How?"

Gabby dropped her gaze to the hollow of his throat. "When the judge came to see about you, he had a few drinks with Ben."

Rafe sighed in exasperation. "No need to say more. I meant to tell you myself about the injunction Russell proposed, but word of the fire got in the way."

"Your grandfather was happy to make up for the omission."

Rafe pressed his lips against her forehead. "Ben and I have a great deal to make up for, Gabby."

She caught her breath. There it was again, this hint of gratitude instead of love. She freed herself of his embrace and, grabbing up her clothes, moved out of the stall to get dressed. Rafe watched her carefully. Something had upset her. Was it the thought of staying with him? Of being his wife? Surely she could read the love in his eyes. Surely she knew how he felt.

As soon as they were free of the dangers that might still surround them, as soon as Earl Hunter was taken care of, he would make his declaration and force her to answer. There was only one word he would accept. A simple yes.

The evening passed slowly, and Rafe grabbed a few needed hours of sleep while Gabby kept watch at the window. They traded places, Gabby swearing she would be unable to close her eyes. The next thing she knew Rafe was shaking her awake.

"It will soon be dawn," he whispered. "The river is not far. If we leave now, we can be back at the hacienda by noon."

Gabby scrambled to her feet, and they saddled the horses in the dark. Soon they were on their way, retracing their steps back to the stream. Rafe's coat felt good against her bare skin in the cool morning air.

"Is this wise, Rafe, going back this way?"

"We will not go all the way back to the original path. There is another that will take us to the Rio Grande near the Seco crossing."

Gabby forgot her weariness. The Seco meant food and a hot bath and clean clothes. That it also might mean something painful she refused to consider. She had told herself she must take each moment as it came, rejoice in Rafe's presence, be satisfied with whatever comforts she could receive, no matter how transitory. By the time the sun was nearing its apex she had convinced herself she would be all right.

As they rode down the steep incline that led to the crossing, Rafe looked across the Rio Grande to Texas and to the Arroyo Seco.

"Home. Looks good, doesn't it, Gabby?"

She couldn't have put it better herself. The sandy banks along the river, the stubby trees that clung tenaciously to the hard, rocky soil beyond, the dense brush and sharp-spined cactus that covered the broken land were grander and more glorious than the stateliest of landscapes anywhere in the world.

The river was down, and the crossing was made without incident. They directed their horses away from the water and along the path that wound into the thickening undergrowth. Rafe, leading the way, halted. A warning tingle worked at his neck. His hand rested against the Colt strapped to his thigh.

"Something's wrong," he said, his eyes darting warily around them.

"What do you think it is?"

"I don't know. But something, or someone, is watching. I can feel it."

Gabby followed his gaze. The noon sun cast a bright light on the land and glinted against the silver embroidery of the coat that she wore. The only movement she was able to detect was a rustle of leaves from the slight breeze and the slow circling of a hawk overhead. All seemed peaceful.

Tempest shook her head nervously and whinnied. Gabby leaned forward to stroke the roan's neck and quiet her with soothing words at the same instant a shot rang out. The movement saved her life. A bullet

405

splintered the bark of a tree behind her on a level where her head had been.

She kept leaning and dropped, landing heavily on the ground and scrambling behind a small rock outcropping on the edge of the copse. Rafe jumped down beside her, gun in hand, as the two horses took off in fright back down the winding trail.

"You all right?"

She managed a weak smile. "I'm too tough to take out that easily."

Relief flooded his face. "You look damned vulnerable to me." He crouched beside her in the brush at the edge of the path and glanced in the direction of the shot. It had come from somewhere west of the trail, probably a small stand of scrub oak.

"Whoever is out there won't know for sure whether he got you." He holstered his pistol. "It won't reach whoever has a rifle," he said.

"Want to speculate who the someone was?"

Rafe snorted in disgust. "No need. What I can't figure out is why Hunter went for you." He looked at the coat she wore and muttered a curse. "The *bastardo* could have taken you for me."

Another shot rang out and hit the dirt near their feet. Rafe jerked her deeper into the brush behind the rock. Wherever the rifle fire was coming from, it was doing a damned good job of keeping them pinned down.

"Maybe Hunter's out here to meet someone, another contact besides Ramirez," said Gabby.

"More likely Sarah talked to someone else besides

406

me. McGowan or the sheriff. She said she was going to. I figure he's trying to scuttle to safety in Mexico and saw us coming up the trail."

He motioned for Gabby to give him the coat, then hung it on a forked stick and raised it. Immediately, a shot sounded, and a hole bloomed among the rows of silver braid on the shoulder of the coat.

Gabby shuddered, remembering how close a similar shot had come only minutes before. "Why is he attacking us? Couldn't he have ridden out until we passed? We'd never have known he was there, and he'd have gotten clean away."

"Hunter is *loco*," said Rafe. "One of those derelicts of the war who'd rather keep on hurting others than earn an honest living. And he's been playing cat and mouse with me ever since he rode into town."

"Because of Sarah?" asked Gabby.

Rafe shrugged. "Maybe. With a man as mean as Hunter, it's hard to believe he cares for anybody." Sitting on his haunches, Rafe peered around, and Gabby feared what he might try.

She lay prone in the dirt and gripped his forearm. "What can we do?" she asked.

"I don't know. Yet. We can't go to the river and swim away. He's covering the crossing. I guess we wait until dark and try to work our way out. If he gives us that long. Our best hope is that he doesn't realize we're without rifles."

Carefully Rafe stole to the edge of the brush and raised the coat. The gun spoke, sending another bullet into the material, this one lower and just over

407

Rafe's head. He came crawling back. "Still in the same place, but he'll plan something soon."

A gun cracked again, and Rafe's face brightened. "Another one heard from." He raised his head cautiously and parted some brush to gaze to the west. Another shot sounded. "That was Hunter firing another direction. Now's our chance."

He pulled aside thorny branches and gestures for Gabby to work herself deeper into the bush. "Protect your face," he said as he lowered the branches across her huddled figure. The green silk of her gown amongst the thick leaves served as a natural disguise. "He'll have to look hard to see you in there. And don't come out until I tell you to. While he's distracted, I'm going to try to join up with that second gun."

The harsh edge to his voice brooked no disagreement. Much as Gabby wanted to go with him, much as she feared what would happen, she figured now was not the time to give him trouble. She'd already done enough of that.

Rafe headed out in a wide circle to come up behind Hunter or meet with the second gunman. He took his time to keep from disturbing so much as a leaf that would call attention to his progress should Hunter have time to look that way. The second rifle was keeping up a fairly steady barrage.

Finally abandoning caution, Rafe barreled through brush and headed straight for the sound of the gun battle. Pistol drawn, he crashed onto the trail no three feet behind the crouched figure of a man. He aimed a kick at the rifle Hunter was about to fire, and the weapon went flying into the underbrush.

Still on one knee, Hunter whirled to face Rafe and looked into the barrel of the Colt. His hand edged toward a holstered pistol, then stopped. Rafe could smell the fear rising in him.

"Who else is out here, Earl?" Rafe said. "I'd like to thank him."

From somewhere down the trail came a muttered curse about getting out of the line of fire. Rafe grinned. Jeff McGowan.

Rafe kept his eyes on Hunter. "Drop your gun belt, Hunter."

Hunter's lips twitched. The hate in his eyes was enough to daunt most men. Rafe held his ground.

"Damn you, Jericho."

"Drop the gun belt," Rafe repeated.

Hunter pulled himself to his feet. Rafe's eyes never wavered. Hunter shrugged as if in defeat, then went for his pistol. Rafe lashed out with his left fist, crashing it against Hunter's face.

It landed with a satisfying thud, and blood spurted from his nose. Hunter answered with a swift right which landed with ineffectual imprecision against Rafe's shoulder. Rafe holstered the Colt and let fly with a right and then a left. Hunter dropped beside the trail and lay still.

Rafe reached toward the inert body to retrieve Hunter's guns. He stared for a long minute at the bloodied face close to his boots. As he rubbed the scraped knuckles of his right hand, a satisfied smile stole onto his face.

The tall, broad frame of the Ranger came lumbering down the trail toward him.

"I almost had him, Rafe," Jeff drawled as he came up beside him.

Rafe dropped the Colt back into its holster and handed him Hunter's pistol. "I'm glad you didn't. There was a lot of pleasure in knocking the bastard out."

"You know, Rafe," Jeff said, nodding in appreciation, "you just might make a Texas Ranger yet." He bent and snapped cuffs on Hunter's wrists but left him lying in the dirt. "You alone?" he asked, concern showing on his face. "I heard you went looking for Miss Deschamps. I didn't figure you to come riding back without her."

For answer, Rafe turned and whistled. "Come on out, Gabby. It's okay," he called through cupped hands.

"Now that's what I expected," Jeff said with a grin. "There you were on a vacation down in Mexico with your woman while I was watching this scum, watching him get ready to run. Sorry I let him get too far ahead."

The men talked softly over the prostrate body of Hunter, who was beginning to moan.

"More social talk, gentlemen?" Gabby's gently sarcastic voice came from behind Rafe. "Every time you two gather at a body lying on the ground you seem to be renewing an old friendship."

Rafe turned warm, inquiring eyes to Gabby as she came to a halt between the two men. One sleeve of

410

her dress was torn, her hair was matted into a tangled disarray, and her face was streaked with dirt. She looked magnificent.

"You might say that," Rafe said. "Only this time Jeff did more than just act as a witness. And this time I was able to get you out of the line of fire."

"I stayed hidden all right when the fireworks were exploding." Her voice tightened. "It was the silence that got me." She eyed Hunter, who had worked himself up to a sitting position. His face was darkened by a scowl.

Gabby wanted to throw herself against Rafe and break out into a girlish flood of tears. What she did was take his hand in her trembling own.

McGowan reached down to haul Hunter to his feet. Hunter's normally impeccable suit was covered in Seco dirt, one eye was swollen closed, and his lip split open. But he seemed to notice none of it as he stared sullenly at Rafe.

"Hunter," Rafe said, "you're a fool. You could have had what most men only dream of. A good woman. A good life. You lost it all."

Hunter spat at Rafe's feet. "I only hope, Jericho, you didn't find *your* woman too soon."

Jeff jerked back on Hunter's arms. He winced in pain.

"Keep your mouth shut," the Ranger growled. "I'd just as soon take you back to town unconscious. I'm not even too particular about whether you're breathing or not. Your wife filled us in on a lot of things that you'll be wanting to explain. You and that two-

411

bit lawyer Bernard. Now, let's cut the palaver. Rafe, can you round up the mounts?"

Rafe returned shortly and handed Gabby Tempest's reins. "We'll ride on in to the hacienda and you can rest. If you're not needing me, I'd like to go into town and make sure Hunter's behind bars. And I'll want to give a statement about de Leon and a few of his Texas business partners beside Ramirez and Hunter. We wouldn't want them to get away."

Gabby slowly nodded, knowing that when Rafe returned he would want to have the talk he'd mentioned back in Mexico. She grew heartsick contemplating where that talk might lead, and she pushed all thought of it from her mind.

They stopped at the hacienda only long enough for the men to grab a bite to eat thrust at them by a smiling Lupita, and for Rafe to assure Ben he was all right. Gabby stood in the doorway and watched him ride away on a fresh mount. He'd asked if she needed him. Foolish man. It would take until the end of time for her to tell him how much.

Chapter Nineteen

When Gabby turned and entered the house, she had nothing more in mind than a long soak in the copper tub that stayed in her room. Lupita had already assured her she would have it filled with warm water.

Having neither the strength nor the inclination for a confrontation with Ben, she walked quietly past the room where he spent much of each day. She had barely cleared it when the door flung open and the old man stepped into the hallway.

"Senorita Cordero," he said to her back. "Please come in. It is time we talked about you and your family."

Gabby grimaced. He'd brought up the one issue that might tempt her into that hated sanctum of his. She turned, brushing a wayward tangle of curls from her forehead. "I don't suppose you could wait until after I've rested."

"I cannot," he said, his eyes cold and grim.

At least, Gabby rationalized as she followed him into the room, she wouldn't be weakened by a few minutes of rest and a clean body. She tugged at the torn sleeve of her dress and smoothed the wrinkled skirt. As tired and disheveled as she was, she was ready to take on a bear.

As was his usual habit, Ben settled himself behind the safety of his desk. Also as usual, the curtains were drawn to the sunlight and the air was warm and stale. Gabby looked around her. A mausoleum—that's what this place was—in which Ben had buried himself alive.

She stood stiffly across the desk from him. "What about my family, Ben? What do you have to say after all this time that can't wait an hour or two?"

"Nothing that concerns my grandson can wait. And you'd know that if you cared anything about him. But then you're a Cordero. You don't care about anything but yourself."

Alarm caused Gabby to start. "What's wrong with Rafe? Has something happened while he was in Mexico? Something that involves the Corderos?"

"It's been happening. I've watched you weave your evil spell over my grandson, so much that he risked his life by going after you. I prayed to the blessed saints for his return alone. But you are back and I see the way he looks at you. He wants you the way men want women. But don't be fooled into thinking it is more than that."

Gabby lifted her head proudly. "This is what you wanted to tell me? It is something better left to your

414

grandson."

"There are things my grandson does not know. Bad blood flows in your veins. The blood of your grandmother Maria."

"You speak ugly words, old man. Give me facts."

"I speak words that bring pain, but they also speak of the truth." Ben leaned back in his chair, a faraway look in his watery old eyes. The pain was there, all right, in that shadowed gaze, but it was not the pain of anger that Gabby had seen so often. It was the pain of loss.

"It has been more than fifty years since she came to this land from Spain," said Ben. "Maria." Her name was a whisper. "A young girl promised in wedlock. Her hair was like the raven's wing, and there was sunlight in her eyes. And her smile. Ah, that smile could warm the coldest heart."

Gabby watched in amazement as the memories softened the old man's face. Without a word she settled in a chair and waited.

His voice turned sharper. "Carlos and I had grown from childhood together. We rode together. Alas, we were too much alike. We loved the same woman. But she was promised to him." His thoughts came out of the past and focused on Gabby. "Like you, senorita, she played the games of love. She taunted me and caught my heart. All the while she knew she would wed Carlos."

Here was the Ben she knew well, and Gabby could not still her protest. "What makes you think I am like her, Ben? I never knew her. I never even knew this story until now."

Silently Ben reached into a lower drawer of the desk

415

and pulled out a small box. He lifted the lid and Gabby could see something resting on the red velvet lining. Gold glinted in the lamplight. Shaky hands lifted the object from its resting place. Gabby could see it was a picture of some kind. Ben stared long and hard at the miniature before handing it over to her.

The painting was of a young woman in fine array, her dark hair twisted in a mass of curls atop her head. She knew immediately it was her grandmother Maria. The artist had captured the sunlight in her black eyes, the smile that could warm the coldest heart. Gabby recognized the craftsmanship that could accomplish such a feat, but it was not that which made her gasp. Except for the dark eyes and dark hair, she might have been holding a painting of herself.

She stared in rapt attention at the face. Here was what she had sought in coming to the border, a link with her past, a glimpse into the dark unknown of her ancestry. Could a woman who could smile with such innocent, infectious pleasure be filled with deceit? Gabby knew only that she returned to Spain after the death of her son Roberto, refusing even to correspond with his widow Colette.

She looked at Ben. "Tell me more about her."

Again came the gentle look on the old man's face, and he nodded slowly. The enmity that had stood between them seemed to fade.

"Maria was filled with a love of life that brought much happiness to this land. Our families worked hard to survive. She made us smile again."

"The French have a saying. *Joie de vivre.*" She stared at the painting. "I understand."

"She had been raised a wild young thing in her

416

homeland. She could ride like the wind. You must understand this was most unusual for a girl of her careful upbringing. The three of us were seldom apart."

Ben poured two glasses of brandy and offered one to Gabby. She accepted, unwilling to break the spell of the moment, but left it untouched. Gently she placed the miniature on the desk.

"But sometimes," Ben said, "Carlos would drink too much. Sometimes they would quarrel, and Maria and I would find ourselves alone. We were young. Hot blood flowed in our veins. We fell in love." His hand gripped the crystal brandy glass. "At least such was true for one of us. Maria played the games with me. She married a Cordero."

Ben fell into silence. At last Gabby spoke. "Was she not promised to him? Had the marriage not been arranged?"

"You speak as she did. She came to tell me she had made her choice. Carlos followed and witnessed the kiss of good-bye that she gave me. He misunderstood. Ugly words were passed between us. I called her the whore that she was to sell herself to him, and Carlos defended her. It was I, he said, who was without honor."

Gabby tried to picture the scene. Maria had been a young woman in love with the dashing young buck that Ben must have been, but she was also a young woman who was bound in honor to marry his best friend. Ben would have seen only his own side.

And what of her grandfather Carlos, who found his betrothed at the Hidalgo ranch? He had little understood that she had gone there to say good-bye. The mysterious feud that the lawyer Oscar Cantu had mentioned back in San Antonio was not so mysterious after all.

"This is why you lied in court and swore my grandfather had paid allegiance to Mexico during the war with Texas."

"He took my woman. Through the years my anger grew. I would have his land."

Gabby shook her head at the strange and bitter thinking that could lead to such perfidy.

"And what of the death of Carlos? What can you tell me of that?"

"He was a madman after the trial. Justice did no sit well with him. He came with a gun."

"And you shot him."

"It was an act of self-defense. By this time I had child of my own. Consuelo. The woman I had chose for my own wife was weak and died in giving birth to her. The child became my life."

"And you no longer loved Maria?"

Ben finished the brandy and poured himself an other glass. "This is a question that should not be asked. Maria witnessed the shooting and knew I was innocent of murder. She took her son Roberto to San Antonio, and I never saw her again. I heard that she returned to Spain and there met a peaceful death." He drank deeply of the brandy. It was awhile before he spoke.

"When Rafael was born to Consuelo and the fore man Sam Jericho, I knew my life still had meaning The line would go on."

In the stillness Gabby put the pieces of the past together, of Ben and Maria in love, of Maria's sen

418

of honor which led to Ben's betrayal in court, and at last of the love that Ben still carried for the young Spanish girl of the painting. It was a love that had turned him bitter. He had spoken of her death. No wonder, Gabby thought, he had attacked her when she first approached him and asked for a portion of her birthright. When he had looked at her, he must have seen only Maria and all of the bitterness came flooding back.

And now his greatest fear might possibly come true. His grandson might wed a Cordero; the heirs of his enemy might once again inherit the land.

How wrong he was. Gabby saw with painful clarity what would inevitably happen if she remained. Rafe wanted her, as Ben had said, in the way a man wants a woman, but he had not spoken of permanency. Her own sense of honor and the memory of her mother's sacrifice would not let her settle for anything less than being Rafe's wife.

Such was impossible. For a marriage to take place he must choose between her and his grandfather. This she could not ask him to do. Never could she mean to him everything that she wanted to mean. He was her life, but she could receive only a portion of his love.

With a dignity born of determination, she stood and placed the untouched brandy on the desk beside the painting.

"Have no fear, senor," she said. "I will not stay. And I give up all claim to your land. I see now that it can never be my home, and that is all I ever really wanted." She ignored his look of pleased surprise. "Do not, however, think I am a fool. I have invested in the Teco and I want a return. The loan must be repaid and with interest. My lawyer in San Antonio will be in touch with you as to the time and method of payment."

She didn't wait for Ben's inevitable agreement. He had won. She hurried from the room, closing the door behind her. In the sanctity of her own quarters, after she had thanked Lupita for the waiting bath, she let the tears flow. Hot, bitter tears for what would never be. How tough she had tried to be, and tough she would be again, but not now when the grief of her resolution was upon her.

She dropped to the floor beside the copper tub and gave in to that grief. When at last the tears stopped when at last she was able to thrust the image of Rafe from her mind, she gave thought to what she must do. Since coming to Texas she had acted impulsively on far too many occasions. Her leavetaking must be done with far greater care.

Somehow she must get to San Antonio, maybe even stay there until after Erin's baby was born. Then she would go back east, most likely. She'd made friends there. She still had a little money, and there would be the income from the Seco loan. She might not live royally, but at least she would live.

But first to get to San Antonio. And she knew just who to ask for help. After a long bath in which she worked through the details of her plan, she dressed in a simple cotton skirt and blouse, glad to discard the tattered finery she'd taken from Porfirio de Leon, and went in search of Lupita.

Over a much-needed meal she told the girl what she wanted—a horse and wagon loaded with her luggage, hidden and waiting behind the barn shortly before dawn. And no word to anyone, not even Antonio, that she was leaving. Rafe would be coming in later. Lupita was to tell him Gabby, exhausted from the past few days, had fallen into a deep sleep. He could see her in the morning. Wide-eyed and obviously upset, the girl reluctantly agreed.

Sometime during the evening, as she lay huddled beneath the covers of her bed feigning the sleep that would not come, she heard Rafe enter and whisper her name. With great force of will she kept her breathing steady, her eyes closed. She would have given almost anything for one last glimpse at him, one last kiss — she would have given anything, that is, but her chance to leave. She knew too well that if she called out to him, all her firm resolve would be melted in his embrace.

When at last he closed the door and she heard his departing footsteps, she stared into the empty air and told herself she was doing what was right.

For once in her life, Gabby thought as she settled against the uncomfortable seat of the early morning Great Northern train bound for San Antonio, everything was going according to plan. She'd taken her leave of the Arroyo Seco shortly before dawn, her only good-byes given to Lupita and Tempest. Quiet was settled over the ranch, and she gave as little thought as she could manage to the man she was leaving behind.

The horse and wagon were hitched at the train station, waiting for someone from the Seco to fetch them. Sometime at mid-morning Lupita was to let slip where they were. Long after the train was under way. Long after Gabby was gone.

She'd given some thought to stopping by Emma Talbert's, but there was no way she could subject herself to one of the woman's lectures about what she was giving up. As if she didn't realize it. The nightmare of her difficulties with Earl Hunter and his partners in crime paled beside the speculation of what life would be like without Rafe.

Enough. Every time his name passed through her mind, her vision blurred and she found herself drifting into thoughts of what might have been. That was no way to go through life. She might as well start trying to forget him here and now.

She probably should have left behind the golden cross that she wore beneath her traveling dress. It could only serve to bring bitter memories of a brief happy time in her life. But strong as she was, that was one thing she simply could not do.

Reaching down into the portmanteau at her feet she pulled out the knitting that she had abandoned long ago at Emma's. The ride to San Antonio would take all day. She would get that red shawl yet.

Despite her concentration, progress proved to be as slow as the train, which stopped at every settlement and crossing to pick up freight and occasional passengers. She wasn't even suspicious when the train pulled to a halt in the middle of a deserted stretch of flatland. She glanced around the half-filled car, wondering who might have been hitching a ride in such desolate area.

She didn't have to wait long to find out. The door at the far end of the car opened, and her eyes locked onto a very determined looking Rafe striding down the narrow aisle toward her.

Joy welled in her heart, but she quickly doused it. She mustn't fall into the trap of listening to him, or even of looking at him too closely. She would patiently explain that things just wouldn't work out between them. For once he would have to listen and to understand. So everyone in the car would get an earful. At least it would break the monotony of the long trip.

She should have known he wouldn't give her the chance to speak. Ungentle hands tossed the knitting aside and lifted her from the seat. She found herself being carried in a most unladylike way down the aisle, slung over his shoulder like a sack of grain.

She pummeled Rafe's back. "Put me down!" she ordered. He continued his pace, and she craned her neck to see the passengers staring open-mouthed at the sight of her abduction. Following them down the aisle was the florid-faced conductor.

"It's all right, folks," she heard him say. "Nothing to get upset about. Lady just caught the wrong train."

Caught in Rafe's merciless grip, Gabby ceased struggling and listened in disbelief as the procession entered the vestibule.

"Thanks, Tom," Rafe said, tossing him a coin and dropping lightly to the ground as the train began its fitful start. He didn't put her down until they were well away from the railroad tracks in the shade of a lone oak tree where he had tethered his horse. She watched in dismay as the train gathered speed on its journey north once more.

"My luggage!" she cried. "My purse. Everything's

still on board."

"The conductor will hold all of it in San Antonio until they can be sent for," Rafe said matter-of-factly.

Gabby's eyes flashed angrily. "You mean until I can collect them myself. Although how I'm to manage that, I do not know. There aren't any more trains likely to come along."

"It wouldn't make any difference if there were."

She stared at him incredulously. "Rafe, I got on that train because it was the right thing to do. It wasn't a decision I came to quickly. And it wasn't a decision I intend to forget." Unable to take in his dark, intent stare any longer, she dropped her eyes. "You're only postponing the inevitable."

"I could say the same to you."

He stared at the small, feathered hat tilted at an absurd angle in the midst of her golden hair, at the thick lashes resting against her cheeks, at the slender hands clenched in determination. How easy it would be to pull her into his arms and kiss her into submission. But then she would never know for sure the real reason he wanted her to come back.

"There's nothing inevitable," she said softly, "about my going back. I can't."

"Why? Because of Ben? Or because you don't love me?"

She raised her head in indignation. "That's not fair. You throw questions at me that are not easy to answer."

"Seems to me they are. Ben either drove you away or he didn't. You either love me or you don't."

"You see things as being very simple, Rafe. That's rarely the case."

"Now there you're wrong. I've spent most of the time since we met trying to complicate things. Trying to figure out what you're after, whether or not you lied. And most of all, what you want from me. If I'd followed my instincts from the beginning, we'd both be a hell of a lot better off. I knew what kind of a man Hunter was, and yet I let him mess up the one thing that means more than life itself to me."

"What's that, Rafe?" Her voice was little more than a whisper.

"My feelings for you. And yours for me. That's what I told Ben this morning when I found you'd gone. He finally told me about his trouble with the Corderos. I'd guessed some of it already, but as he talked I realized the truth behind what had made him live such a miserable life. He'd lost the woman he loved. I don't intend that to happen to me."

Gabby's heart caught in her throat. "Ben won't change. And I won't come between you."

"You're a little late saying that, Gabby. You already have. Ben knows it, if you don't."

"He'll never accept me."

"There you're wrong. He cares enough for me and for the ranch to sacrifice even his bitterness. Without you, the Seco is nothing more than a pile of dirt and cactus. With you, it becomes home. I thought I was tied to the place already, but I learned to see it through your eyes. Everything was wonderful to you, a new experience to be enjoyed, a lesson to be learned. I want our children to feel that same way about it."

Our children. A rush of warmth coursed through her, and with it came the beginnings of hope. "You make it sound so easy," she managed.

"It won't be. There are times you'll have to fight Ben, times the old bitterness will come back. But you're tough. And, for what it's worth to you, you'll have the strength of my love."

Rafe watched an indefinable emotion play on her face. Behind him the horse snorted, as if in impatience. Rafe was beginning to feel much the same way.

"It seems to me you have two choices, Gabby. You can either mount up with me and head back for the Seco. Or you can start walking to San Antonio."

Gabby's lips twitched, and she fought against a smile. "You really know how to sweet-talk a girl, don't you?"

He shrugged. "As you've pointed out before, I don't get many complaints." He turned to reach for the reins.

Gabby watched him in surprise. He really meant to ride away unless she declared herself.

"Rafe!" she cried out. "A snake!" He spun back in time to catch her in his arms. She clung tightly to him, her face buried in the crook of his shoulder.

"Where?" he asked, glancing around at the tufts of grass growing beneath the oak, ready to draw the Colt strapped to his thigh.

Gabby lifted her head. Her breath was warm on his cheek. "Must have been the breeze," she said, a twinkle in her eyes. "I could have sworn I heard something. Or maybe it was just my heart telling me to say yes."

Rafe's eyes warmed, and his lips hovered a scant inch from hers. "Does your heart tell you anything else, *querida?*"

"It tells me that loving you the way I do, I'd be a fool to leave. If you still want me after all the trouble I've caused. And of course I'm not dressed right for the ride back. Something you're sure—"

Rafe stopped her with a long and satisfying kiss.

FIERY ROMANCE
From Zebra Books

SATIN SECRET (2116, $3.95)
by Emma Merritt

After young Marta Carolina had been attacked by pirates, shipwrecked, and beset by Indians, she was convinced the New World brought nothing but tragedy . . . until William Dare rescued her. The rugged American made her feel warm, protected, secure—and hungry for a fulfillment she could not name!

CAPTIVE SURRENDER (1986, $3.95)
by Michalann Perry

Gentle Fawn should have been celebrating her newfound joy as a bride, but when both her husband and father were killed in battle, the young Indian maiden vowed revenge. She charged into the fray—yet once she caught sight of the piercing blue gaze of her enemy, she knew that she could never kill him. The handsome white man stirred a longing deep within her soul . . . and a passion she'd never experienced before.

PASSION'S JOY (2205, $3.95)
by Jennifer Horsman

Dressed as a young boy, stunning Joy Claret refused to think what would happen were she to get caught at what she was really doing: leading slaves to liberty on the Underground Railroad. Then the roughly masculine Ram Barrington stood in her path and the blue-eyed girl couldn't help but panic. Before she could fight him, she was locked in an embrace that could end only with her surrender to PASSION'S JOY.

TEXAS TRIUMPH (2009, $3.95)
by Victoria Thompson

Nothing is more important to the determined Rachel McKinsey than the Circle M—and if it meant marrying her foreman to scare off rustlers, she would do it. Yet the gorgeous rancher felt a secret thrill that the towering Cole Elliot was to be her man—and despite her plan that they be business partners, all she truly desired was a glorious consummation of their vows.

PASSION'S PARADISE (1618, $3.75)
by Sonya T. Pelton

When she is kidnapped by the cruel, captivating Captain Ty, fair-haired Angel Sherwood fears not for her life, but for her honor! Yet she can't help but be warmed by his manly touch, and secretly longs for PASSION'S PARADISE.

Available wherever paperbacks are sold, or order direct from the publisher. Send cover price plus 50¢ per copy for mailing and handling to Zebra Books, Dept. 2291, 475 Park Avenue South, New York, N.Y. 10016. Residents of New York, New Jersey and Pennsylvania must include sales tax. DO NOT SEND CASH.